BEYOND
THE LOOKING GLASS

From *A New Child's Play*,
illustrated by E.V.B. (Eleaner Boyle).

BEYOND THE LOOKING GLASS

Extraordinary Works
of
FANTASY AND FAIRY TALE

Editor:
Johnathan Cott

Introductions:
Johnathan Cott
and
Leslie Fiedler

STONEHILL

Book design by David Dalton

CONTENTS

NOVELS, STORIES AND POEMS

ACKNOWLEDGEMENTS

I would like to thank the Ingram Merrill Foundation for the grant which enabled me to complete *Beyond the Looking Glass*. And this anthology would not have been possible without the help of the following persons: Justin Schiller and Raymond Wapner, who aided me in obtaining many of the books and illustrations reproduced here, who furthered my appreciation and knowledge of children's literature, and whose enormous and beautiful collection of early children's books is one of the quiet wonders of New York City; Mrs. Ruth Blaine, who lent several books of Victorian illustrations and Mrs. Vera Ries, who made available from her private collection a copy of Maggie Browne's *Wanted—A King*; Ned Arnold, Ann Druyan, Robin Magowan, and Susan Stern, who encouraged me to do the book; Jeremy Cott and Linda Healey, who read and criticized the introduction; Dee and Jeffrey Steinberg, Paulette Nenner and Pat French who literally "made it real"; and David Dalton, whose "special pleading" for this anthology revealed itself in the care and perspicacity with which he designed it—and whose words, in a letter, distilled for me the meaning of *Beyond the Looking Glass*:

"It prickled me awake again to all the wonders, mysteries, and codes embedded in all tales of the impossible and supernatural, and how elemental the Victorians were, how intact that cord was that tied them to savage celtic tradition, almost like an underground railway transporting treasures from the incredible depths of the past to the very door of the crystal palace. A curious contract seems to have existed between what was possibly the most repressed society ever and the imagined innocence and irridescence of pre-history. Perhaps a secret kindom deep within only flowers in eras when it is most needed, a cosmic equilibrium of forces.

"The testimony of Alexander Carmichael; the tears of Kenneth Grahame that become the damp imp-infested air we breathe; the Well of Childhood; communications with stars, frogs, and trees; a luminous alphabet; 'the infanta's bundle'; the angelic child; the fate of Robert Kirk; the infinite planes of being like Magritte's Summer Steps, ascending and descending from the demonic to the sublime—and interchangeable; Pentacostal Magic; Tolkien's beautiful image of the Crucifixion as the Eucatastrophe of the planes; Pigwiggin's cowslip assignation; the bee as a divine emblem; Lewis Carroll's transformation of concrete into a fairy promise; post-Darwinian tents. . ."

Jonathan Cott

INTRODUCTION

By

Leslie Fiedler

We sometimes forget that Victorian fairy tales, whatever their remotest origins, belong in our culture not to the folk tradition but to popular literature. They do not come to us orally and anonymously, but in print and associated with the names of writers. And yet, in some sense, they exist, too, in the public domain—being in this respect more like other Victorian Pop, such as *The Adventures of Sherlock Holmes* or *Dracula* than Henry James' *The Ambassadors* or *The Scarlet Letter*.

That they are fairy tales has nothing to do with the presence or absense of "fairies," for there are no fairies in either *Red Riding Hood* or *The Three Bears,* while *A Midsummer Night's Dream* is full of them. Yet it is the former not the latter which we label "fairy tales"—a rather misleading name. In the Victorian period and especially in the *Kunstmärchen,* (the kind of artistically ambitious nursery story collected here) fairies were everywhere; but in the longer tradition of the *genre* they are clearly optional. What are inaccurately called "fairy tales" are the first form of "children's literature," which is also, perhaps, the first form of popular literature. But what *is* popular literature?

It is, first of all, a kind of literature which came into existence only after the invention of printing had further atomized an already divided audience. "Literacy" and the exclusivism of Christianity had, even before the days of the printing press, led to the classification of song and story into three distinct categories: Scripture, High Literature and Folk Literature. It is a classification which represents priorities imposed by the time-consuming process of manuscript transmission. Yet it persisted through the Gutenberg era into our own post-Gutenberg times, at least vestigially; and we must therefore understand it, if we are to understand our own responses to literature.

Scripture is distinguished from other forms of writing not only because of its extra-literary sanction, but because it is thought of as a whole body of work given once and for all—not to be tampered with or added to, merely faithfully copied, then explicated and taught. For the latter purpose, some argued that it might be translated into the vulgar languages, while others demurred; but all agreed it was best transmitted in the original Holy Languages: Hebrew, Aramaic and Greek— along with the transnational language of the Roman Empire, Latin.

High Literature, on the other hand, is regarded as never complete; since it is a growing body produced by men of genius, who achieve a kind of immortality by producing it. And it is to be judged by the critics, who measure all new efforts against their Greek and Latin prototypes. Once critically accepted, such works become demi-canonical; never sacred like the Scriptures, but the kind of secondary guides to leading "the good life," appropriately taught to younger students, since they delight as well as instruct.

Folk Literature, finally, belonged neither to Church nor School, and its authors were allowed to fade from memory long before their works, which were themselves considered unworthy of manuscript preservation. Unrecorded, they went also uncriticized—being merely dismissed in general. To make more specific distinctions in so ephemeral a realm, to speak, for instance, of better or worse folk tales or work songs, would have seemed palpably absurd. And yet finally such "inconsiderable trash" did get recorded, because with the invention of moveable type, the era of mass production begins; and in that world, whatever is possible tends to become actual. More specifically, the printing industry demanded more and more literature to keep its machines running, its technicians employed, its entrepreneurs—including, after a while, authors themselves—prosperous.

In the Age of Gutenberg, High Literature began, therefore, to assimilate its neighbors on either side: moving first into the area occupied by the folk tale and folk ballad; then into the territory occupied by Scripture itself. The first thrust led to collecting, editing and adapting certain folk forms, then to counterfeiting or imitating them for publication, thus creating a new category: Popular Literature. The second led to approaching the Christian Bible as just one more collection of poems and stories, to be judged as other books are judged. And after the "Death of God," in fact, Scripture tended to become confused with the demi-canonical Great Books, and the whole thought of as a kind of ever-expanding new New Testament of the humanist faith, destined to replace Christianity. The moment of apogee of this Culture Religion is the Victorian Period, when (as the stories of George MacDonald in this collection testify) the fairy tale, itself, began to acquire a "pop" scriptural status.

The fairy tale entered the world of literature towards the end of the seventeenth century apologetically, proffering itself as one more pastoral entertainment for courtiers, and pretending to be work not of the respected academician who sponsored it, but of his child and/or the Old Nurse of that child. Her voice had presumably droned on at the hearth for centuries, attended to but unrecorded, until in 1697 (when he himself had reached almost three-score and ten), Charles Perrault committed it to print so that it could be heard in the *salons* of his own time, and, after the collapse of the *ancien regime,* could return via the bookstores to the nurseries of the post-Gutenberg world.

Neither the courtly ladies nor the academicians, however, understood the true nature of the Mother Goose Tale, which Perrault had intuitively grasped, and the engraver, had made manifest in the image in the book's frontispiece of the Old Crone telling, not reading, a story to a young child. Both are unlettered, both unlearned; but the one possesses a kind of wisdom which the other lacks and transmits it behind the backs, or at least in the absence of, the middle generation of the three-generations of family. Father and mother we assume are off making love in these gallant times; but grandmother and grandchild stand on either side of sexual maturity.

Overt sex tends to be symbolized by violent assault, acts of terror committed by Ogres and Witches and Wolves, palpable disguises for Father and Mother as the incestuous enemies of True Love. But parents are, in any event, the common enemy of grandparents and grandchild; perhaps especially in the case of the youngest child, the unlucky third son or daughter, who in fairy tales suffers the tyranny of older siblings as well as that of his parents.

Sometimes the fairy tale seems especially virulent towards mothers, as if it represented the point of view of the paternal grandmother, to whom her son's wife seems necessarily a supplanter, a "Step-Mother." Certainly there is a frequent tendency, as in "Cinderella," to portray the father as less the villian than the victim of the Bad Witch he marries; but there are in fairy tales truly Bad Fathers as well, sometimes disguised as supernatural monsters; occasionally, as in Boiteau's "Donkey Skin" candidly presented as lusting after their own daughters.

Often the archetypal teller of the tale seems separated from the family situation she describes by class as well as generation. And, indeed, if she were a peasant Nanny rather than a blood grandmother, she must have remained forever a stranger to everyone in the household but the children, quite like the black Uncle Remuses of the American nineteenth century. No wonder such old women appear in their own tales as creatures from another world, disguised as withered beggars and uncanny hags; or, shifting genders in response to the sexual ambiguity of old age, tottering wizards and ancient dwarfs. Primitively they are portrayed, too, as talking domestic animals or trees, or, in the guise preferred by Perrault, fairy-godmothers: the story-teller turned *dea ex machina*.

We must not be misled by the Christian overtones of that potent figure. The compromise with the established Church which it represents is more nominal than real; for the implicit values as well as the explicit mythology of the fairy tale remain outside Christianity, as the many theologians who condemned the form seem to have realized. However popular the Christian faith may have been in its beginnings, by the seventeenth century it had been essentially preempted by the literate, the learned, the beneficiaries of patriarchal power. It may have been even at that point chiefly old women who filled its churches and lit the candles at its shrines; but when they dreamed aloud to the listening children before the fire, it was another faith: a faith long banned and almost forgotten, except in the feared witch-craft revivals (one of which had peaked just before the time of Perrault), and in the apparently harmless Tales of Mother Goose. In them, the Holy Trinity does not normally appear, nor the Blessed Virgin, nor angels, nor demons, nor the innumerable Saints of the Church; only, when supernatural machinery is demanded, Kobolds and Gnomes, and, most notably, "Fairies," *fata, fees,*[1] surviving though degraded deities of an Old Relition not only "pagan" but matriarchal as well.

By the close of the seventeenth century, the *conscious minds* of Western Europeans may have been so thoroughly Christianized that the sole threat to the cultural hegemony of the Church seemed to come not from the past but the future, in the form of that "New Philosophy" which was calling "all in doubt,"

---

[1]For a discussion of the nature of these elusive creatures, the reader should consult Jonathan Cott's illuminating "Notes on Fairy Faith and the Idea of Childhood" which follows.

i.e., modern science. But in the fantasies of the grandmothers we remanded to the hearthside, that past had not died; and these fantasies live on in the unconscious of us all.

In the fairy tale, bliss and misery are not equated with Christian Salvation and Damnation, Hell and Heaven—but with Getting Married and Being Eaten. And the former at least seems to have replaced forever in the popular imagination its Christian alternative. To live "happily ever after" has come to mean for all of us, not as it would for, say, St. Augustine, to choose Holy Chastity for the sake of one's beloved, but to beget children, who will in turn be joined forever, etc., etc. This is the pagan dream of natural immortality, not of individuals but of humanity: the passage from generation to generation by a death and rebirth like those of other animals and plants—with whom in such a state of non-alienation we could obviously converse.

It is easy enough to understand the meaning of "Getting Married," but the significance of "Being Eaten" is less obvious. Yet cannibalism is an obsessive theme in the fairy tale, and we cannot understand the form without solving the mystery. Some scholars have argued that it represents simply a vestigial memory of a time when human beings did in fact eat each other both ritually and in combat; or perhaps rather the vestiges of an attempt to exorcize that primordial hunger and the guilt it occasions—rather like the Christian Mass, which substitutes Bread and Wine for flesh and blood. Such historical explanations seem especially unsatisfactory, however, in a time like our own when cannibalism, especially in the form of vampirism, has become again a compulsive theme of popular literature, indeed a central feature of mass culture in general.

It is today possible, for instance, for a small child to buy in his local store a confection called "Vampire's Blood," with which, before swallowing it down, he can smear his own neck in a properly sanguinary way. Meanwhile, his mother may be ordering from *Ramparts* a post-card appropriate for sending to her feminist friends, since it portrays a girl's head smugly looking down at a male skeleton over the caption, "He asked me to eat him and I did." And his older brother and sister could well be watching the twin bill, *I'll Drink Your Blood* and *I'll Eat Your Skin*. If either of them happens to mention the first film in their Freshman Class on "Horror Classics" next day, their professor might be moved to tell them that it is based on the Manson Case; and that Charles Manson in turn had been influenced in his lifestyle by Robert Heinlein's *A Stranger in a Strange Land*, which defends not only communal sex but cannibalism, and probably took its title from the touching self apology spoken by the vampire hero-villain of Stoker's eternal bestseller, *Dracula*.

Such stories normally treat not the eating of noble enemies by their conquerors (as practised, for instance, by American Indians), or of the hero-father by his rival sons (as analyzed by Freud in *Token and Taboo*), but the very reverse of the latter: the eating of children by parent-surrogates, which is to say, the inhibition of the future by re-incorporation of what has already been separated from its past by the pangs of birth. One metaphorical name for this is "incest," one "cannibalism." In the world of myth, they become finally a single terror.

Perhaps the first archetypal projection of that terror is the story of Kronos eating his children, while a quite recent one is that favorite movie of the student "underground," *The Night of the Living Dead,* in which the old eat the young in order to grow no older, in order not to die. But this is the underlying fable of *Dracula* as well; and in that book it is made clear that incest-cannibalism is forever in vain; since the aging suckers of young blood do not themselves become immortal, merely "un-dead." What they can do is purely negative, namely, destroy the only immortality which Old Wives can imagine: *the Eternal Return of courtship, marriage, childbirth. . .courtship, marriage, childbirth. . . .*

In a way, fairy tales constitute a kind of charm against whatever disrupts that process; or rather, perhaps, a sort of conduct book for boys and girls about to assume their roles in that endless round. The girl's role, Mother Goose defines as essentially passive. Her obligation is to wait, only dreaming, which is to say wishing her Happy Ending, on the dusty hearth or in the enchanted wood, until at last her deliverer arrives. To be sure, it helps if she is good—soft-spoken, submissive, pure of heart—but finally she must get lucky as well, being a kind of needle in the haystack that some young man, who has proven himself in action, must find. And he, too, needs luck, or as it is called in the tales themselves, "magic," good magic.

Sometimes, as in "Puss in Boots," luck is enough to insure success, even without virtue: the omnipotent wish which cues our dreams. But more often, the young man must be able to perceive, beneath rags or the foul skin of a beast, the true beauty of a princess; or, alternatively, to break through the tangle of forest around her, or scale the glass hill on which she sits in loneliness. He must, in short, be able to penetrate the disguises imposed by a jealous mother, pass the ordeals contrived by an incestuous father; and finally broach the barrier of her own shyness and the awkwardness of adolescence to rouse her with a kiss.

But nothing can help the girl whose luck turns bad, who turns out to be Red Riding Hood rather than Cinderella. Sometimes the Beast she meets in the wood is not a prince in disguise, but a real, an ultimate Beast; and sometimes she finds cannibalistic lust in the bed of love, the Wolf in the form of Grandmother herself. "Cinderella" and "Red Riding Hood" live forever in our deep imagination, embodying as they do the polar possibilities of the fairy world: a day dream which stays in control, a nightmare which plunges into horror.

In Grimm's Fairy Tales, we find a version of "Red Riding Hood" in which Grandma and the girl are not swallowed down forever, as in Perrault, but are saved by the intervention of a Woodcutter, who chops the wolf open and provides them an instant resurrection. In this form, however, the tale seems even bleaker, even more clearly, as Erich Fromm has argued, a female fantasy in which male sexuality is portrayed as cruel and destructive, whether it is baffled (the rapist castrated), or triumphant (the rapist satisfied and unapprehended).

The fairy tale assumes, in defiance of Christian orthodoxy, that sex is neither evil nor a punishment for sin, but essentially benign: a fulfillment and a benediction, eternally recreating the unchanging Happy Family, in which the bride and groom are transformed by their bliss into a King and Queen.

Meanwhile, fantasy was growing even more embattled: pressed on the one side by the novel, which had from the middle of the eighteenth century become the reigning literary form; and on the other by Science, which asserted ever more strongly its claim to being the sole arbiter of "reality." Invented for the printing press with no oral or manuscript pre-history, the modern novel is the first unequivocally popular form of literature; and beside it the fairy tale seems sometimes only proto-pop. Certainly from the first, the new genre took a stand against the fantastic, turning its back on older times and claiming the present for its subject. Eventually a compromise was to be worked out in the kind of fairy-novel whose characters moved back and forth in time, like MacDonald's *Phantastes,* for instance, or C. S. Lewis's Narnia books; but first the Old Wives Tales had to come to terms with Science, and the pioneers in this area were also Germans, Jacob and Wilhelm Grimm, who published their *Household Tales* between 1812 and 1815. Earlier they had faithfully transcribed these tales as they heard them from unlettered storytellers; and they continued to sift them with "scientific" rigor, in quest of what was truly native and authentic. They may have been more naive about such matters than they suspected, and they may even have manipulated their material more than their posture of being editors rather than authors suggests. But they worked devotedly, motivated by patriotic impulses as well as a dedication to Science; since to them, the familiar tales they collected seemed the fragments of an ancient Teutonic mythology.

Earlier German scholars had searched for the common "Aryan" source of all Indo-European story, and had speculated on the possibility of a single point of origin, perhaps in India. But, for the Grimms, comparative myth-study served to demonstrate the uniqueness, and helped to protect the purity of the *Volk* heritage from "foreign" corruption. It is no accident, then, that their efforts sowed the seeds not only of a scientific folk-lore but also of the mythicized German nationalism which was to pass via Richard Wagner to Adolf Hitler. Hitler himself seems to have realized this, too, for during his regime Perrault's "Tales of My Mother Goose" were banned in Germany, while the Grimms' collection achieved almost scriptural status.

It was presumably the "immorality" of Perrault which offended the Nazi leader, especially in such a story as "Puss in Boots," with its glorification of a kind of cunning that must have seemed to him disturbingly "Jewish"; but maybe the fact of his being French was enough to condemn Perrault in Hitler's eyes. Appropriately enough, just after the war against Hitlerism, certain American liberals sought to drive the Grimm's fairy tales out of the nursery, presumably because of their "violence" and "sadism"; but maybe their Germanness would have been enough.

Even in the full tide of Victorianism, England did not forget, at the moment of the Winter Solstice at least, the "wassel bowl": symbol of a past whose mythology was priapic as well as bacchic. Perhaps it was precisely this persistent awareness of the demonic and erotic substrata of the fairy tale which made its survival in the nineteenth century so difficult.

As early as 1823, Edgar Taylor remarked that "Popular fictions and traditions are somewhat out of fashion. . ." And by the middle of the century, the first attempt to revive them seems to have petered out, perhaps because no major talent had appeared in the field, at least in England. To be sure, Hans Christian

Andersen had published his tales between 1835 and 1844, and both his melancholy and his moralizing appealed strongly to the contemporary English. At home however, the highest achievement was represented, perhaps, by Ruskin's *King of the Golden River,* the sole story out of the earlier period included in this volume. But though Ruskin was quite as moralistic as his Danish opposite number and as obsessed by a fear of sexuality, his tale never achieved the truly popular status of "The Ugly Duckling" or "The Little Match Girl" or even "The Little Mermaid."

The age itself was aware of the fact, and debated the question of whether the disappearance of the popular tale was finally good or bad; some arguing that the genre was so closely linked historically to Satanism and Witchcraft that it deserved to die, others responding that to let the "marvelous" die meant losing a source of strength for all literature. The earlier stages of the debate are recorded in Dickens' magazine, *Household Words,* which appeared in the mid-fifties; but the final word was spoken by Andrew Lang, who presides over the second fairy tale revival of the seventies and eighties. Indeed, that revival was almost his single-handed creation.

His name has been largely forgotten and his children's anthologies tend to be thought of these days as anonymous. Yet Lang has left behind an extraordinary number of books and articles dealing with all the subjects that concerned men in his time, from cricket and golf to occultism, from classic epic to folk-lore. All his life long he remained a free-lance writer, however, an unattached amateur who took on such academic authorities on popular literature of his time as Max Müller and James Frazier with especial fervor. Unlike some of his professorial opponents, however, he was not merely an editor and theorizer but a translator (of "Cupid and Psyche" and Grimm, as well as of Homer), as well as a poet who versified passages in other men's popular novels, and himself the author of at least one pop novel, *The Heart's Desire.*

More than any other influential critic of the time, Lang resisted his age's tendency to separate élitist art from popular "entertainment," to drive a wedge between the minority and mass audience. In the controversy between Henry James and Robert Louis Stevenson over whether such a division was desirable in the field of fiction, he supported the anti-"art" stand of the latter—rejecting the notion of a literary *avant-garde* which was just then being imported from the Continent; and preferring to the *symbolistes* and naturalists alike such a writer as Mark Twain, who he praised not despite the fact but precisely because he was "vulgar."

He seems even to have sensed dimly that if the fairy tale was to be redeemed from preciosity and triviality, on the one hand, and didacticism and moralizing, on the other, it must associate itself with other aspects of mass culture, in which the *merveilleux* tended more and more to be ghetto-ized as Victoria's reign wore on: not just the "thriller" and American boys' books, but Pop occultism and Nursery "non-sense" as well. Unfortunately he was too genteel or timid to identify with the underground workers in the ultimate cultural ghetto of that era, the pornographers; though they had links with the shabbie denizens of the world of the occult, spiritualist mediums and telapathists whom he did, like Conan Doyle a little later, defend.

Frances and the Leaping Fairy
Photograph Number Three from the Cottingley Photographs: Photograph taken from *Fairies*—actual photographs taken in Yorkshire as verified and described by Edward L. Gardner. Reprinted by permission of The Theosophical Publishing House, Ltd.

Frances and the Fairies

Photograph Number One from the Cottingley Photographs: Photograph taken in Yorkshire as verified and described by Edward L. Gardner. Reprinted by permission of The Theosophical Publishing House, Ltd.

If on the one side, Victorian occultism was bounded by the esoteric Christianity of George MacDonald, on the other, it bordered on the pornotopiam neverland of those whom Stephen Marcus has called "the other Victorians." (Edward Sellon, for instance, who in 1865 issued his flagrantly pornographic autobiography, *The Ups and Downs of Life.*) Moreover, there was even in Lang's time, perhaps, already a link between the study of folk-lore and sexually oriented occultism.

If Lang suspected this, he gives no evidence of it. Nor does he seem to have been aware of the crypto-sexuality of almost all children's literature in Victorian times: the way in which the genteel Cult of the Child merged into pathological pedophelia from Ruskin, who could not abide females after they had sprouted pubic hair, to Lewis Carroll, eternally trying to cajole his friends into letting him photograph their small daughters nude. In the juvenile novels of Dickens as well, especially *The Old Curiosity Shop,* the same endemic kink appears; for Quilp, the grotesque luster after not-quite-pubescent girls, is in one sense—as Dickens himself confessed—a portrait of the artist.

Surely one of the oddest events in the history of human dealings with fairies is the case of the Cottingley photographs, taken in 1917 by a ten-year-old girl and her thirteen-year-old cousin in a "wooden glen" near the home of the latter. It is all well and good for a recent writer on the subject, like K. M. Briggs, to declare those pictures "aesthetically" unconvincing, precisely because they conform to the ikon inherited by the Edwardians from the generation before. But the plates on which the demure and diminutive creatures seem to hover in the air in filmy pantomime garb have been examined and re-examined by experts who assure us that there is no evidence of tampering or even double exposure.

To be sure the Cottingley girl and her friend were just the age at which occult forces seem to work through young girls for their own ambiguous ends: the age of the adolescent hysterics who cued the Salem Witchcraft trials, or those attentive sisters, who in that strange summer of 1865 evoked in Lewis Carroll the darkest and dirtiest and most delightful of all Victorian children's books. But, in any case, why should the mischievous wielders of a power older than science not assume whatever shape is expected of them—even before the cameras of a generation earnestly resolved to "believe in fairies."

I have before me as I write, a picture postcard sent to me just the other day from Disneyland, which shows Tinker Belle still as gauzy-winged as ever, but with the face of a spoiled little girl set on the body of a mini-foldout from a men's magazine. It is a version which would surely have distressed Andrew Lang, or for that matter, George MacDonald; and it must seem to many even now as naive and vulgar as the *Tales* of Perrault once seemed to the estimable Boileau. But this constitutes, after all, a Happy Ending to our story: the last puckish joke of the *real* fairies, who presided at the birth of the popular arts, and will not die as long as these arts survive.

Leslie Fiedler
State University at Buffalo
January 1973

NOTES ON FAIRY FAITH
AND THE IDEA OF CHILDHOOD

By

Jonathan Cott

1

Childhood is the well of being . . . The well is an archetype, one of the gravest images of the human soul. That black and distant water can mark a childhood. It has reflected an astonished face. Its mirror is not that of the fountain. A narcissus can take no pleasure there. Already in his image living beneath the earth, the child does not recognize himself. A mist is on the water; plants which are too green frame the mirror. A cold blast breathes in the depths. The face which comes back in this night of the earth is a face from another world. Now, if a memory of such reflections comes into a memory, isn't it the memory of a before-world?
　　　　　　　　　　　　—Gaston Bachelard: *The Poetics of Reverie*

In the distance things appear small to us, and as we draw back, they seem to fade away. We tend to look slightingly on the exiguous and the tiny—like wanton boys at flies, like the Brobdingnags at Gulliver. But, as Swift demonstrates, being a giant or a midget is merely a function of a specifically perceived relationship: spatial and temporal changes demarcate new contexts. In *The Golden Age,* Kenneth Grahame writes of the child's view of the "Olympians" who "talked over our heads during meals"; but the writer, now an old man, will soon disappear, too, like the crying, disappointed little boy he describes: "One dissolution of a minute into his original elements of air and water, of tears and outcry—so much insulted nature claimed."

Conversely, the meaning of stories like David and Goliath, Ulysses and Polyphemus, Tom Thumb, and Jack and the Beanstalk suggests the power, or the *mana*, inherent in the diminutive—the little holding the big on a leash, as the painter Jean Arp once wrote. (It is during the wee hours when our most immense dreams come to us.) And our sense of loss concerning the idea of our own distant childhoods parallels our obliviousness to the fact that the child archetype—often imagined as a hermaphrodite—is a symbol of potential wholeness which suggests the reconciliation of past and future, male and female, light and dark (see "The Day Boy and the Night Girl")—as well as of the small and the large: "Not to be confined by the greatest, yet to be contained within the smallest, is divine." In this sense, the idea of childhood reminds us of Pascal's conception of God—whose center is everywhere and circumference nowhere—as well as of the description of the Hindu *atman*—"smaller than small and bigger than big...the size of a thumb...encompassing the earth on every side...ruling over the ten-finger space."

In his beautiful book, *The Poetics of Reverie*, Gaston Bachelard speaks of the "zodiac of memory," within which is lodged that "reverie toward childhood" which returns us to the source of Reverie—a kind of nostalgia of nostalgia in which our former being imagines itself alive again. Bachelard's concern with the origins of memory centers on what he calls the "nucleus of childhood"—an immobile, immutable, but ever-present childhood, whose great once-upon-a-time is precisely the world of the first time. "Childhood remains within us a principle of deep life," Bachelard writes, "of life always in harmony with the possibilities of new beginnings. Everything that begins in us with the distinctness of a beginning is a madness of life. The great archetype of life beginning brings to every beginning the psychic energy which Jung has recognized in every archetype."

If we see childhood as our goal, we might begin to understand that activities which we once considered symptomatic of neurotic retroversion are in fact simply signs of an attempt to arrive at the heart of divine consciousness. In this light we can perceive the aim of George Herbert's great poem "Prayer (I)" which, through meditation, turns back time, decreating the "six-daies world," erasing the separations between earth and heaven, water and land, and man and his childhood garden:

> Prayer the Churches banquet, Angels age,
> Gods breath in man returning to his birth,
> The soul in paraphrase, heart in pilgrimage,
> The Christian plummet sounding heav'n and earth;
> Engine against th' Almightie, sinners towre,
> Reversed thunder, Christ-side-piercing spear,
> The six-daies world transposing in an houre,
> A kinde of tune, which all things heare and fear;
> Softnesse, and peace, and joy, and love, and blisse,
> Exalted Manna, gladnesse of the best,
> Heaven in ordinarie, man well drest,
> The milkie way, the bird of Paradise,
> Church-bels beyond the starres heard, the souls bloud,
> The land of spices; something understood.

Gulliver with the Lilliputians
From a 19th century French children's edition of *Gulliver's Travels*, illustration by Jean Geoffroy.

2

From infancy I came to boyhood, or rather it came to me, taking the place of infancy. Yet infancy did not go: for where was it to go to? Simply it was no longer there. For now I was not an infant, without speech, but a boy, speaking.

—Saint Augustine: *The Confessions*

When Dido asks Aeneas to tell her of the Trojan War, he says: *"Infandum, regina"* (Unspeakable, queen). The mystery of *infancy* (derived from *infantia—* inability to speak), as of language, is impossible to articulate. But we can say that the history of the embryo, recapitulated in the evolution of the species, mirrors the development of the child's ability to speak and read.

Speculating on the origins of writing, Claude Lévi-Strauss has suggested that literacy is a form of enslavement, concomitant with the Fall, resulting in a discourse which rushes by, as Roland Barthes says, like "a metaphor without brakes." In his essay *"Abecedarium culturae:* structuralism, absence, writing," the critic Edward Said elaborates:

> *Before writing, man had lived at a zero point, which is described elsewhere by Lévi-Strauss as an original state preceding the neolithic age; life at the zero point was ruled over by a central 'floating signifier', a kind of spiritual etymon, whose ubiquity and perfect consistency allowed it the power to act as a pure semantic value. This, in Lévi-Strauss's judgment, corresponds to Marcel Mauss's notion of mana, an almost magical value that permits primitive, preliterate societies to make a whole range of universal distinctions between force and action, between abstract and concrete, and between quality and state. (The parallels between preliteralism and Eden before the Fall are fascinating indeed.) One beautifully functional key, mana, therefore unlocks every signifier because it is the Origin of all signifiers.*

The state of childhood represents such a "zero point"—ruled over both by the infant's undifferentiated consciousness and by the child's spontaneous animistic feelings towards the world. As we observe over and over again in fairy tales, children speak openly to the stars, frogs, and trees. And it is ironic that the phrase meant to keep children in their place—"Children should be seen and not heard"—literally expresses the silent origins of speech itself while perhaps revealing the adult's repressed desire to return to that state in which the word was the Word. In this image, children themselves become the bearers of words which emerge as if for the first time, from silence. (A stutterer, in fact, might be seen as someone giving a difficult birth to words.)

The birth of every child augurs the hope for the renewal of innocent and honest speech (as in "The Emperor's New Clothes"). But as the child grows up, language becomes a defence, and autism is perceived of as a threat not so much to the child as to the family and the species (vividly presented in Mrs. Clifford's "Wooden Tony," a frightening story of depersonalization included in this collection). Language is the link of human relationships, and before they are anything else, fairy stories are the original family romances.

3

The infant who was too fragile as yet to take part in the life of adults simply
"did not count": this is the expression used by Molière, who bears witness to
the survival in the seventeenth century of a very old attitude of mind. Argan
in Le Malade Imaginaire has two daughters, one of marriageable age and little
Louison who is just beginning to talk and walk. It is generally known that he
is threatening to put his elder daughter in a convent to stop her philandering.
His brother asks him: "How is it, Brother, that rich as you are and having only
one daughter, for I don't count the little one, you can talk of putting her in a
convent?" The little one did not count because she could disappear.
                                        —Phillipe Ariès: *Centuries of Childhood*

Not until the seventeenth century did the idea of childhood enter popular consciousness. "All mine die in infancy," Montaigne wrote. And children who survived infancy in the Middle Ages were considered to be regular members of the community; in medieval painting, they appear as part of the scene, portrayed simply as adults on a reduced scale. The word "child" designated a familial relationship or defined a dependent role (even today servants, menials, and oppressed persons are called "boy" (*garçon*), "girl," etc. no matter how old they are) but the word was never used in reference to age. This absence of definition in medieval times extended to all social activities: games, crafts, arms. "There is not a single collective picture of the times," Ariès writes, "in which children are not to be found, nestling singly or in pairs in the *trousse* hung round women's necks, or urinating in a corner, or playing their part in a traditional festival, or as apprentices in a workshop, or as pages serving a knight." And as part of this communal life, both children and adults listened to the tales of scops, bards, gleemen, minstrels. Around community fires the old taught the young, and the latter became the repository for and the preservers of supernatural and magical lore.

Not until the development of the idea of childish "innocence" and the need to safeguard it against sinful behavior were stringent rules applied to children's social and sexual lives. The diary of Heroard, Henry IV's physician, records amazing details of the young Louis XIII's infancy. When the child was not yet one year old, "he laughed uproariously when his nanny waggled his cock with her fingers." When he was one year old "he made everybody kiss his cock." At three, "he and Madame, his sister, were undressed and they were placed naked in bed with the King, where they kissed and twittered and gave great amusement to the King. The King asked him: 'Son, where is the Infanta's bundle?' He showed it to him, saying: 'There is no bone in it, Papa.' Then, as it was slightly distended, he added: 'There is now, there is sometimes'."

While The Rite of Circumcision was the most important public religious ceremony for children in the Middle Ages, The First Communion assumed that role several centuries later. The new morality for children was developed and encouraged by the Jesuits, the Brothers of Christian Doctrine, Port-Royal

Illustration by Arthur Hughes from Christina Rossetti's *Sing-Song*: A Nursery Rhyme Book.

Illustration by Winifred Smith from *Children's Singing Games*.

educators, and by seventeenth-century moralists, lawyers, and pedagogues. The rise and diffusion of schooling—the organizing of colleges and *pedagogicas*—led to the development of an idea of childhood that insisted on the fostering of "character" and "reason."

Finally, the rise of the middle class, with its ideal of the self-contained family unit, enforced on children their own space, beds, morality, nurses and tutors, uniforms, games, reading matter, and special diet. Here is John Locke on a child's proper digestive education: "For breakfast and supper, milk, milk-pottage, water-gruel, flummery, and twenty other things, that we are wont to make in England, are very fit for children: only, in all these let care be taken, that they be plain, and without much mixture, and very sparingly seasoned with sugar, or rather none at all: especially all spice, and other things, that may heat the blood, are carefully to be avoided."

Infants were coddled and fussed over (much to the chagrin of Montaigne who wrote: "I cannot abide that passion for caressing new-born children, which have neither mental activities nor recognizable bodily shape by which to make themselves lovable, and I have never willingly suffered them to be fed in my presence"), but along with this attitude we find an exigent moral solicitude, exemplified by Locke's "carefully to be avoided" approach. However, his generally humane, solicitous writings about children's education exhibit a radical departure from the Puritan's vision of children as "Brands of Hell." Still, Locke was writing about children who lived in a private and separate world, their behavior sanctioned by adults they rarely saw.

Yet even today, there are some "primitive" and communal societies that display an unbroken continuum of life's activities. The long-living Abkhasians, for example—a people who live between the Black Sea and the Caucasus Mountains—propose no separate "facts of life" for children and adults. As Sula Benet points out in *Abkhasia: The Long Living People of the Caucasus*, the Abkhasians all participate in the same games, the same work, and have the same socially perceived needs. The great-grandparents are, appropriately, the story-tellers to the children. And it is with a longing for a return to the heterogeneous, undifferentiated communal life of medieval times that Ariès concludes *Centuries of Childhood:*

> The old society concentrated the maximum number of ways of life into the minimum of space and accepted, if it did not impose, the bizarre juxtaposition of the most widely different classes. The new society, on the contrary, provided each way of life with a confined space in which it was understood that the dominant features should be respected, and that each person had to resemble a conventional model, an ideal type, and never depart from it under pain of excommunication. The concept of the family, the concept of class, and perhaps elsewhere the concept of race, appear as manifestations of the same intolerance towards variety, the same insistence on uniformity.

4

During all these centuries the Celt has kept in his heart some affinity with the mighty beings ruling in the Unseen, once so evident to the heroic races who preceded him. His legends and faery tales have connected his soul with the inner lives of air and water and earth, and they in turn have kept his heart sweet with hidden influence.

—A. E.

Ariès has pointed out that only three distinct "types" of children appear by themselves in medieval painting—the angel, the Infant Jesus (wrapped in swaddling-clothes), and the naked child. He writes:

> *It was the allegory of death and the soul which was to introduce into the world of forms the picture of childish nudity. Already in the pre-Byzantine iconography of the fifth century . . . the bodies of the dead were reduced in scale. Corpses were smaller than living bodies. In the Iliad, in the Ambrosian Library the dead in the battle scenes are half the size of the living. In French medieval art the soul was depicted as a little child who was naked and usually sexless. The Last Judgments lead the souls of the righteous to Abraham's bosom in this form. The dying man breathes the child out through his mouth in a symbolic representation of the soul's departure.*

This identification of the soul with the child occurs frequently in many parts of the world. In the Hindu tradition the soul is often described as smaller than a mustard seed. A central Australian tribe believes that the spirit—no larger than a grain of sand—enters the womb through the navel where it develops into a baby. On Greek vases the human soul is often depicted as a pygmy issuing from the body through the mouth. And William Blake illustrated the progress of the soul from birth to death in *The Gates of Paradise,* picturing the embryonic soul of man as a cocoon—a baby asleep in its chrysalis.

The identification of child and soul reveals again the symbolic importance of the diminutive, for the emblem most easily conceived of to express the invisible is that of a tiny human being. And closely connected with the idea of the soul is that of the "angel." G. van der Leew writes: "We still speak of the angel who protects children, but we seldom realize that it is not an angel sent by God that guards the little one, but the power which the child itself has emitted. The beautiful saying of Jesus: 'Take heed that ye despise not one of these little ones; for I say unto you, That in heaven their angels do always behold the face of my Father which is in heaven,' indicates the correct interpretation."

When angels lose their soul-character and separate themselves from their bearers, they become demons. But in ancient Persia they were also thought of as energies sent forth by Ahura Mazda, symbolizing his qualities—the Good Thought, Immortality, Divine Dominion, etc. To the Jews, according to St. Paul, angels were mediators of the law. And to the Christians they were messengers of God, whom their task was to praise through all eternity. But, as van der Leew writes:

It is scarcely to be doubted that all these angelic powers were origi-
nally independent revelations of the one Power, and only attached
themselves to a single divine figure later as his ambassadors. In the
case of Persia this is very clear: Asha is the world order, in the guise
of a power, which we have already considered. For the angels are
older than the gods ... Exactly as man experiences himself dually,
once as himself—and in this way he can imagine nothing and repre-
sent nothing to himself—and a second time as a wraith-soul-angel, so
he experiences God in the same dual way, first as a Power and a Will
that can neither be imagined nor represented, and again as a presence
with definite form. The belief in angels, therefore, is equally momen-
tous for the idea of revelation and for the type of the concept of
God.

In testimony given in 1871 to Alexander Carmichael, Roderick Macneill gave his explanation of the origin of fairies:

> *The Proud Angel fomented a rebellion among the angels of heaven,*
> *where he had been a leading light. He declared that he would go and*
> *found a kingdom for himself. When going out at the door of heaven*
> *the Proud Angel brought prickly lightning and biting lightning out of*
> *the doorstep with his heels. Many angels followed him—so many that*
> *at last the Son called out, "Father! Father! the city is being*
> *emptied!" whereupon the Father ordered that the gates of heaven*
> *and the gates of hell should be closed. This was instantly done. And*
> *those who were in were in, and those who were out were out; while*
> *the hosts who had left heaven and had not reached hell flew into the*
> *holes of the earth, like the stormy petrels. These are the Fairy Folk.*
> *(Quoted by Evans-Wentz in The Fairy Faith in Celtic Countries)*

Associated with this idea is the notion—until recently common in Cornwall—that the *Pobel Vean* (small people) are not disembodied spirits, but the living souls and bodies of the old pagans who, having refused Christianity, are condemned to decrease in size until they vanish.

Commenting on the lexicographer's definition of fairies—"supernatural beings of diminutive size, in popular belief supposed to possess magical powers and to have great influence for good or evil over the affairs of man"—J. R. R. Tolkien in his essay "On Fairy Stories" remarks: "*Supernatural* is a dangerous and difficult word in any of its senses, looser or stricter. But to fairies it can hardly be applied, unless *super* is taken merely as a superlative prefix. For it is man who is, in contrast to fairies, supernatural (and often of diminutive stature); whereas they are natural, far more natural than he. Such is their doom."

And in his extraordinary *The Fairy Faith in Celtic Countries (1911)*, Evans-Wentz writes: "If fairies actually exist as invisible beings or intelligences, and our investigations lead us to the tentative hypothesis that they do, they are natural and not supernatural, for nothing which exists can be supernatural." Where saints were likely to have visions of angels and demons, Evans-Wentz'

What is Man?
"The Sun's Light when he unfolds it
Depends on the Organ that beholds it"

"At length for hatching ripe he breaks the shell"

Aged Ignorance
"Perceptive Organs closed their Objects close"

"I found him beneath a tree"

William Blake
Emblems from *The Gates of Paradise*
1793 edition (subtitled "For Children").

"I want! I want!"

informants from Scotland, Ireland, Wales, Cornwall, and Brittany, who were interviewed at the turn of the century, report innumerable viewings of and encounters with fairies of all types—banshees, pixies, knockers, gnomes, trolls, corrigans, brownies, dwarfs, piskeys, kelpies, boggarts, manes, etc.

Evans-Wentz visited the district of Aberfoyle in Scotland where in 1692 a minister named Robert Kirk (the author of *The Secret Commonwealth of Elves, Fauns, and Fairies*—1691) who, while studying the "good people's ways," was taken by them. In a dream Kirk appeared to his cousin, stating he was the fairies' prisoner and asking the cousin to throw a dagger over his head when he manifested himself at a forthcoming christening. So astonished was the cousin to see Kirk, however, that he did nothing, and the minister was never seen again.

In *The Anatomy of Puck*, Katherine Briggs has reprinted a seventeenth century traveler's account of a fairy market he saw in Somerset (see Christina Rossetti's *Goblin Market*). The traveler reported that the fairies buffeted him, kicking him about the legs, and he found himself lame afterwards. Even in 1960, moreover, Ruth Tongue recorded a similar story—called a *memorat:* a personal account of an experience with the supernatural—as told by a farmer's daughter in the Quantock Hills, also in Somerset (see *Folktales of England,* edited by K. M. Briggs and R. L. Tongue).

There are at least four theories that have been presented to account for the nature and origin of fairy faith: the Mythological Theory suggests that fairies are the diminished figures of old pagan Aryan divinities. "Those elements," wrote Wilhelm Grimm, "which we meet in all the tales are like the fragments of a shattered stone, scattered on the ground amid the flowers and grass: only the most piercing eyes can discover them. Their meaning has long been lost, but it can still be felt and that is what gives the tale its value." And for the Grimms, just as mythical characters personified natural phenomena, so fairy tales reflected a cosmic and meteorological drama. Thus Sleeping Beauty is the Winter sleep awakened by Spring, and Little Red Riding Hood's hood is the red glow of dawn devoured by the Wolf of the Night—spring overcome by winter.

The Pygmy theory posits the idea that fairy faith grew out of a folk memory of a prehistoric Mongolian race which inhabited the British Isles and parts of Europe and which died out after the Celtic nations drove them into the mountains and forests. (An interesting corollary of this theory suggests that the Iron Age Celts, having driven the population of pre-Celtic stone and bronze age inhabitants underground, were visited by the "malicious" beings who had formed a kind of guerrilla fairy liberation front. And even today in the Shetland Islands, flint arrowheads are called "elf shot" or "Fairy arrows.") The Druid theory also supposes a similar folk memory, this time of the Druids and their magical practices. And the Naturalistic theory identifies fairies as a product of man's attempts to explain natural phenomena. Thus we find frightening water-kelpies in the rough mountainous regions of the Scotch Highlands and the gentle "good people" in the pleasant dells of Connemara. (The climax of Mary de Morgan's story "Through the Fire" describes the embracing of a fairy prince and princess as a vision of rain blowing through a window into the flames of a cottage fire.)

Scholars have pretty well discredited the Pygmy and Druid theories, especially the former, since they point out that the appearance of giants in the fairy tradition rejects this idea, as does the fact that while there were never any pygmies in North America, fairies have their true believers there as well. About the Naturalistic theory—which may today strike us as the most appealing—Evans-Wentz remarks: "There must have been in the minds of prehistoric men, as there is now in the minds of modern men, a germ idea of a fairy for environment to act upon and shape. Without an object to act upon, environment can accomplish nothing . . . The Naturalistic Theory examines only the environment and its effects, and forgets altogether the germ idea of a fairy to be acted upon."

His own psychological theory postulates the fairy faith as belonging to a world-wide doctrine of souls, part of the universal animistic spirit that has manifested itself to the Australian Arunta tribe as Alcheringa (the spirit race inhabiting an invisible world), a "race" that seems similar to the Irish *Sidhe*, the Persian *jinns* and *afreets*, the Roumanian *Iele*, the Siamese *Thevadas*, and even the Greek *sylphs* and *nereids*.

One of Evans-Wentz's percipients distinguishes five classes of fairies:

> *(1) There are Gnomes, who are earth-spirits, and who seem to be a sorrowful face. I once saw some of them distinctly on the side of Ben Bulbin. They had rather round heads and dark thick-set bodies, and in stature were about two and one-half feet. (2) The Leprechauns are different, being full of mischief, though they, too, are small . . . (3) A third class are the Little People, who, unlike the Gnomes and Leprechauns, are quite good-looking; and they are very small. (4) The Good People are tall beautiful beings, as tall as ourselves, to judge by those I saw at the rath in Rosses Point. They direct the magnetic currents of the earth. (5) The Gods are really the Tuatha De Dannann (Sidhe), and they are much taller than our race . . . (Recorded on October 16, 1910).*

Evans-Wentz observes that the highest pantheon of Irish fairy deities corresponds to the Greek, Egyptian, and Hindu pantheon of gods. (The nineteenth century folklorist S. O. Addy, incidentally, saw a correlation between Robin Hood's merry men and the Norse pantheon.) And he also comments that the most famous of all Welsh heroes, Arthur, equally with Cuchulainn, "can safely be considered both as a god apart from the human plane of existence, and thus like the Tuatha De Danann or Fairy-Folk, and also like a great national hero and king (such as Mongan was) incarnated in a physical body. The taking of Arthur to Avalon by his life-guardian, the Lady of the Lake, and by his own sister, and by two other fairy women who live in that Otherworld of Sacred Apple-Groves, is sufficient in itself, we believe, to prove him of a descent more divine than that of ordinary men." Evans-Wentz considers Arthur a reincarnated sun divinity. And he associates Carnac in Brittany with Egypt's Karnak, Ireland's New Grange with the Great Pyramid, and the Celtic Otherworld with the Elysian Fields. For him, the Celtic Silver Branch, like the Golden Bough, are both signs of the symbolic bond between *that* and *this* world.

Evans-Wentz concludes: "Fairyland exists as a supernormal state of consciousness into which men and women may enter temporarily in dreams, trances, or in various ecstatic conditions; or for an indefinite period at death . . . Fairies exist, because in all essentials they appear to be the same as the intelligent forces now recognized by psychical researchers, be they thus collective units of consciousness like what William James has called 'soul-stuff,' or more individual units, like veridical apparitions." And we are reminded of Jung's comment about the wind of the Pentecostal miracle: "The souls or spirits of the dead are identical with the psychic activity of the living; they merely continue it . . . The concentration and tension of psychic forces have something about them that always looks like magic."

What are we to make of all of this? Surely we might begin to feel that the relationship between humans and the spirit or fairy worlds derives from the fortuitous contact of two interdimensional planes. And even the most "literary" fairy stories themselves attest to the residue of magical and alchemical beliefs, for the stories appropriate the beings, aspects, and rites of the fairy faith itself: changelings, talismans, possession trances, exorcisms, food taboos and food sacrifices, spells, and all types of metamorphoses.

But meanwhile the fairies themselves—the People of Peace, the Good Folk, the Silent Moving Ones—unable to exist in an increasingly incredulous, covetous, and materialistic world, were observed by travelers riding down to the sea where they began their voyage across the Western oceans to Tir na nOg—the Land of the Ever Young.

5

So long as the evil spirit is caught in the upper world, the princess cannot get
down to earth either, and the hero remains lost in paradise.
— Carl Jung: *"The Phenomenology of the Spirit in Fairytales"*

The preceding discussion concerning the magical and animistic elements of fairy faith presents an almost forgotten mode of belief, one which the prevailing psychological criticism of fairy tales has avoided mentioning, simply discarded, or else has treated as remnants of unconscious materials or as "concealing memories," significant only inasmuch as they reveal or support certain psychological suppositions. And something should be said in passing about this kind of interpretation of both fairy tales and children's literature in general.

"When we look back at this unashamed period of childhood," Sigmund Freud once wrote, "it seems to us a Paradise; and Paradise itself is no more than a group phantasy of the childhood of the individual." Freud characteristically would never have accepted the possibility that the childhood of the individual itself was a reflection of Paradise—in the sense that Wordsworth understood it in his *Ode on Immortality:* "trailing clouds of glory do we come."

Just as birth is but a sleep and a forgetting, so the "adult" consciousness finds it difficult to remember its childhood past, an occurrence attributed by Freud to the repression of infantile sexuality. But Ernest Schachtel, in his essay "On Memory and Childhood Amnesia," suggests rather that the formation of memory schemata which "socialize" and conventionalize our remembrances are unsuitable vehicles either to receive or reproduce intense childhood experiences. And Schachtel also shows that this conventionalizing process operates in the realm of dream amnesia as well.

Hesiod, Schachtel reminds us, once wrote that Lethe (Forgetting) is the daughter of Eris (Strife)—the strife which Schachtel sees as a result of the "conflict between nature and society and the conflict in society, the conflict between society and man and the conflict within man." But, as Schachtel concludes,

> *Memory cannot be entirely extinguished in man . . . It is in those*
> *memories of experience which transcend the conventional memory*
> *schemata that every new insight and every true work of art have*
> *their origin and that the hope of progress, of a widening of the scope*
> *of human endeavor and human life, is founded.*

However, few psychologists ever point to the therapeutic effects that can result from the telling of "mythic" stories and fairy tales. Jung has mentioned, for example, that in ancient Egypt, when a man was bitten by a snake, a priest-physician was called in; taking a manuscript from the temple library, he would begin to recite the story of Rā and his mother Isis to the sick man, in this way raising the personal ailment into a "generally valid situation" and thereby mobilizing the patient's unconscious forces in such a way as to affect his nervous system.

And Susan Sontag in her essay "Trip to Hanoi" has described the North Vietnamese's extraordinary treatment of the thousands of prostitutes who were rounded up after the liberation of Hanoi from the French in 1954:

> They were put in charge of the Women's Union, which set up reha-
> bilitation centers for them in the countryside, where they first
> passed months being elaborately pampered. Fairy tales were read to
> them; they were taught children's games and sent out to play.
> "That," Phan explained, "was to restore their innocence and give
> them faith again in man. You see, they had seen such a terrible side
> of human nature. The only way for them to forget that was to
> become little children again."

It is not surprising that psychoanalysts and psychologists have turned to dreams and fairy stories (which represent "the childhood of art") in order to explore the hidden-away sources of our early experiences. Freud himself points out that in some people "a recollection of their favorite fairy tales takes the place of memories of their own childhood: they have made the fairy tales into screen-memories." And he subtly analyses fairy tale motifs and situations as they occur in his patients' dreams.

It is also interesting to mention that psychoanalysts and psychologists tend to interpret fairy stories and children's literature along the lines of their conceptual biases and with the methodological techniques of their particular dream-work analyses. Freud's interpretation of "The Emperor's New Clothes" as a study of repressed exhibitionism, Fromm's discussion of "Little Red Riding Hood" as an elaboration of a young girl's experience of puberty, and Jung's extraordinary explication of "The Princess in the Tree" in which he reflects on the tale's characters (prince, princess, three- and four-legged magic horses) as representations of rapidly transforming psychic processes are all revealing examples of the powers of psychological criticism.

Now, many fairy tales are, of course, simply wisdom or teaching stories—often depicting initiation rites—and psychological criticism in these cases often misses the point. An analysis, however, of a story like "Beauty and the Beast" that examines the complex nature of the father-daughter relationship (with the Beast appearing as an aspect of the double father figure) can often deepen an understanding of a work. The main problem of psychological criticism as it is applied to fairy tales and children's literature lies in the unsubtle and perverse use of symbolic reductionism. And it is in this regard that the Freudian critics are most culpable.

In his thorough and informative study of the fiction of George MacDonald entitled *The Golden Key*, for example, Robert Lee Wolff discusses the story "The Golden Key," included in this collection:

> The little boy, like his father long ago, finds his phallus as a child,
> but does not know where to find the lock to which it belongs. This
> he must do by himself and without help. The mossy bed on which
> he sleeps, the moss on the stone on which he reads as he grows older,
> and which gives him his name when it eventually grows on him, is
> surely the pubic hair of maturity.

Illustration by Archie MacGregor from *Katawampus*.

While Wolff at least has the good sense to mention that we must read this story "at other levels"—suggesting that the key may also stand for "poetic imagination, for warmth and kindness, for religious faith, for love"—the Freudian critic Martin Grotjahn humorlessly and irreducibly interprets Alice in *Alice in Wonderland* as a phallus. Carroll's masterpiece is rich enough to sustain scores of interpretations (see Robert Phillips' *Aspects of Alice*, an anthology which includes forty different readings, including Grotjahn's, of the work). But Grotjahn's "method," which has its origin and "inspiration" in Otto Fenichel's symbolic equation "Girl-Phallus" (via Freud's own dream interpretation of the "child" as phallus), reflects not only an ultimately ludicrous interpretative approach but also reflects and supports a rigidified attitude which owes its allegiance to the "tyranny of genital sexuality," an attitude which itself is open to psychological examination. Consider, for example, Grotjahn's explanation of the appeal of *Ferdinand the Bull* (the famous story of the bull who liked to sit under the cork tree smelling flowers instead of fighting in the ring) to an adult reader:

> *Adults like to read this book to children, telling them in this way*
> *that Ferdinand enjoys everlasting love, peace, and happiness so long*
> *as he behaves like a nice little calf who does not grow up. In this case*
> *the book is used as a clear-cut castration threat, like most famous*
> *books for children.*

If, in children's literature, every key, little girl, tree trunk, or magic wand is seen to represent a phallus (although Geza Roheim makes a good case for the wand), then almost every phallus must represent something else. For though the landscape of fairy tales is filled with luminous and mysterious objects, it is the atmosphere in which these objects are perceived that colors and defines them. And it is finally the landscape itself which is charged with an energy and affect that corresponds to the unrepressed bodily feelings of Freud's polymorphously perverse child.

It is this landscape of the body that Coleridge described in *Kubla Khan* or that Proust was constantly returning to when he felt the uneven pavement at his feet; it is the landscape of the fairy tale—the fields and forests, the worlds beneath the woods and seas, inside the bedroom screen, or on the other side of the mirror. "The magic wand," Ortega y Gasset once wrote, "is endowed with the gift of transforming the universe in a landscape populated by desired things. In fact," he concludes, "the real magic wand is the child's own mind."

6

. . . Although now long estranged,
Man is not wholly lost nor wholly changed.
Dis-graced he may be, yet is not de-throned,
and keeps the rags of lordship once he owned;
Man, Sub-creator, the refracted Light
through whom is splintered from a single White
to many hues, and endlessly combined
in living shapes that move from mind to mind.
Through all the crannies of the world we filled
with Elves and Goblins, though we dared to build
Gods and their houses out of dark and light,
and sowed the seed of dragons—'twas our right
(Used or misused). That right has not decayed:
we make still by the law in which we're made.

—J. R. R. Tolkien

Marc Soriano has made the acute connection between the "art of childhood" and the "childhood of art." And we can still hear in fairy tales what Walter Benjamin calls "the voice of the anonymous storyteller who was prior to all literature." In his essay "The Storyteller," Benjamin writes that the art of storytelling—which he sees embodied in the "resident tiller of the soil" (the person who stays at home) and the trading seaman (the person who takes a trip)—has reached its end because "the epic side of truth, wisdom, is dying out." Benjamin sees in the rise of the short story and the novel (in which Georg Lukas saw "the form of transcendental homelessness") an "essential dependence on the book" written by the solitary individual who, himself uncounseled, can no longer counsel others. The modern emphasis on the importance of disseminating "information" which lives only for and at the moment; the inability of most persons to take the time to give themselves over to repeated listenings of stories—"boredom is the dream bird that hatches the egg of experience"—as Benjamin writes; the inability of modern man to work at what cannot be abbreviated; and the decline of the ideas of eternity and death—all of these, to Benjamin, seemed to be concomitant signs reflecting the diminished sense of the possibility of the communicability of experience to which the storyteller once bore witness. But the fairy tale to Benjamin is truly "the first tutor of children because it was once the first tutor of mankind. The first true storyteller is, and will continue to be, the teller of fairy tales . . . He is the man who could let the wick of his life be consumed completely by the gentle flame of his story."

For Tolkien, an understanding of a fairy story does not depend on any definition or historical account of elf or fairy, but rather "upon the nature of Faerie: the Perilous Realm itself, and the air that blows in that country . . . Faerie itself may perhaps most nearly be translated by Magic—but it is magic of a peculiar mood and power, at the furthest pole from the vulgar devices of the laborious, scientific, magician. There is one proviso: if there is any satire present in the tale, one thing must not be made fun of, the magic itself." ("On Fairy Stories")

The fairy story must satisfy certain primordial human desires: one of which is "to survey the depths of space and time"; the other, "to hold communion with other living beings." By this definition, Drayton's *Nymphidia*—in which the Knight Pigwiggen "rides on a frisky earwig and sends his love, Queen Mab, a bracelet of emmets' eyes, making an assignation in a cowslip-flower"—is less a fairy story than *Morte d'Arthur*. (Evans-Wentz would certainly agree.) What Tolkien seems to desire is a "living, realized, sub-creative art . . . But if a waking writer tells you that his tale is only a thing imagined in his sleep, he cheats deliberately the primal desire at the heart of Faerie: the realization, independent of the conceiving mind, of imagined wonder."

Fairy stories must offer: Fantasy, Recovery, Escape, and Consolation. And finally we understand that for Tolkien the search for the Perilous Realm—and the need to immerse oneself in a world of imagined wonder—is nothing but a belief in, and hope for, salvation. It is the Gospels themselves which contain a "fairy story, or a story of a larger kind which embraces all the essence of fairy stories." And he concludes:

> But this story has entered History and the primary world; the desire and aspiration of sub-creation has been raised to the fulfillment of Creation. The Birth of Christ is the eucatastrophe of Man's history. The Resurrection is the eucatastrophe of the story of the Incarnation. This story begins and ends in joy. It has pre-eminently the "inner consistency of reality." There is no tale ever told that men would rather find was true, and none which so many sceptical men have accepted as true on its own merits. For the Art of it has the supremely convincing tone of Primary Art, that is, of Creation. To reject it leads either to sadness or to wrath . . . The Christian joy, the Gloria, is of the same kind; but it is pre-eminently (infinitely, if our capacity were not finite) high and joyous. But this story is supreme; and it is true. Art has been verified. God is the Lord, of angels, and of men—and of elves. Legend and History have met and fused.

7

Tolkien's attempt to draw from the "ideal" fairy story a correspondence with the Christian idea of redemption and also to see in it a "gleam of *evangelium* in the real world" suggests an affinity with C. S. Lewis' religiously allegorical Narnia books, as well as with the fairy tale novels and stories of the greatest visionary writer of children's literature, George MacDonald. But it was in fact the early English ecclesiastics who, when they couldn't transform a pagan goddess like Bridget into St. Bridget or when they couldn't appropriate a pagan custom like the dedication of a wishing well to nymphs and replace these creatures with saints, tried to suppress the belief in fairy spirits. Although Hobbes in *Leviathan* identified the fairy realm with the Kingdom of Darkness—which he considered to be the ecclesiastical dominion itself—Chaucer's Wife of Bath claims that it was the friars who drove the fairies away: "For ther as wont to walken was an elf/Ther walketh now the limitour himself." Her own Canterbury tale describes a fairy circle of dancing sprites, and in it also appears the old, wizened, often spiteful fairy godmother figure—a figure which derives from the pre-Christian embodiment of the Fate (the French *fée* is derived from the Latin *fata*).

The influence of Christianity was certainly a factor in the denigration not only of fairies (which the Church associated with black magic) but also of fairy stories; unrepressable as they were, they were superciliously allocated to "the children," who hopefully would soon outgrow them. But it is important to remember that literary fairy stories were originally intended for adults. Perrault attributed the authorship of his *Tales of Mother Goose*—first published in France in 1698—to his son, Pierre Darmancour. Although Perrault pretended that the stories were written by a young person for children, these tales were in fact intended for readings at upper class Parisian salons. As Ariès has written: "At the end of a century of rationality the 'chimaeras' could no longer 'return' without an alibi, and *the child furnished that alibi.*"

This alibi reveals the fact that by the seventeenth century, children had become the recipients of a body of lore that was now considered by "adult" standards to be nugatory and even unacceptable. In England as well, Aesop's fables (first translated from the French by Caxton in 1484), *Reynard the Fox*, *Gesta Romanorum* (the early fourteenth century collection of historical, mythical, and spiritual tales and fables from which Shakespeare received the basic themes of *The Merchant of Venice*), the Bestiaries, ballads, the Arthurian romances, and stories like that of Bevis of Southampton (which Shakespeare refers to in *King Lear*)—all of these examples of popular literature of ancient and medieval origin now took their specific place as the literature of upper and middle class children as it was passed down orally by peasant nurses and servants. The practical magic of the smiths; the remembrance of seed, horse, and plough magic; the witchcraft controversy which promulgated and dredged up all kinds of superstitious ideas (Robert Graves points out that, in its Latin sense, superstition simply refers to the left-overs from early magical tradition)—all contributed to an on-going promulgation of the supernatural lore of the countryside and village. (See George Ewart Evans' marvelous *The Pattern Under the Plough*.)

Belief in fairy lore continued to have the longest life. Mrs. Page in *The Merry Wives of Windsor* talks of the "urchins, ouphes [elves] and fairies, green and white." And Shakespeare's Ariel, Queen Mab—"the fairies' midwife"—and fairy pantheon in *A Midsummer's Night Dream* obviously reveal how much fairy lore the playwright absorbed as a child in Warwickshire. Oberon, whose House Spenser reports in the *Faerie Queene*, is descended from Prometheus has been identified with the *Niebelungelied* dwarf king Albrich who, in turn, was transformed into the French Auberich-Auberon; and he has even been traced back to the Hindu pantheon. In Ovid's *Metamorphoses*, Oberon's wife Titania is another name for Diana; and in Mark Lemon's *Tinykin's Transformations* she appears as a half-motherly, half-erotic goddess.

There is no space here to elaborate the various explanatory theories meant to account for the origins of fairy tales—invention, inheritance, and diffusion among them—but there are certain specifically English fairy figures of whom Robin Goodfellow is the most famous. Known as Puck and associated with the devil (*poucke*), he is also Lob lie-by-the-Fire, the Lubber Fiend in Milton's "L'Allegro," and the Puck of Kipling's Pook Hill. T. F. Dyer even reports the claim that Cwm Pucca (Puck Valley in Wales) is the original setting of *A Midsummer's Night Dream*.

Chaucer, Nashe, Shakespeare, Drayton, Herrick, and Fletcher were all acquainted with fairies and, since they probably didn't take them as seriously as Evans-Wentz' informants, used them for their own purposes. (See K. Briggs' *The Anatomy of Puck*—an examination of fairy beliefs among Shakespeare's contempories and successors.) But they kept fairy lore alive. And after them, the "faith" was preserved by the English chapmen—traveling salesmen who peddled news-sheets, ballads, and broadsides throughout the country. In the seventeenth century the true "chapbook" appeared, and stories of Jack the Giant Killer, Guy of Warwick, Dick Whittington, Tom Thumb, Robin Hood, Cock Robin, Dr. Faustus, and Francis Drake were read by adults as well as by many children—as we can observe from Sir Richard Steele's account of his godson's reading habits:

> I perceived him a very great historian in Aesop's Fables: but he
> frankly declared to me his mind, "that he did not delight in that
> learning, because he did not believe they were true"; for which
> reason I found he had very much turned his studies for about a
> twelve-month past, into the lives and adventures of Don Bellianis of
> Greece, Guy of Warwick, the Seven Champions . . . . He . . . could
> find fault with the passionate temper in Bevis, and loved Saint
> George for being the champion of England; and by this means had
> his thoughts insensibly mounded into the notions of discretion,
> virtue, and honour . . . . "The little girl, Betty," the mother told me,
> "deals chiefly in fairies and sprights."

Woodcut from an 18th century Chapbook of *Robinson Crusoe*.

Woodcut from an 18th century Chapbook entitled *The True Tale of Robin Hood..*

Notice the sexual "moulding" of reading habits: adventures for the boy, fairies for the girl.

All together, the chapbooks provided what Harvey Darton calls "a universal library, which was at the same time a sub-history of English literature ... The chapbook from 1700 to 1840 or thereabouts, contained all the popular literature of four centuries in a reduced and degenerate form: most of it in a form rudely adapted for use by children and poorly educated country folk" (quoted from *Children's Books in England*, 1932; rev. 1958—still the wittiest, most informative, and most interesting book on the history of this literature).

By the end of the eighteenth century, fairy lore was being driven underground. While William Blake was creating the greatest poems ever written for "children of all ages," his more famous contemporary Mrs. Trimmer was about to found a magazine called *The Guardian of Education,* in whose pages she reviewed books, answered correspondents, and generally passed *ex cathedra* judgments. She banished Cinderella from the children's library after one of her readers wrote to her stating that the story "paints some of the worst passions that can enter into the human breast, and of which little children should, if possible, be totally ignorant; such as envy, jealousy, a dislike to mothers-in-law and half-sisters, vanity, a love of dress, etc., etc." *Robinson Crusoe* (which was in fact the *only* book Rousseau approved of for children) was also forbidden because it might lead to "an early taste for a rambling life, and a desire of adventures." Mother Goose's tales were "only fit to fill the heads of children with confused notions of wonderful and supernatural events, brought about by the agency of imaginary beings." In her *Essay on Christian Education,* Mrs. Trimmer summed it up: "Formerly children's reading, whether for instruction or amusement, was confined to a very small number of volumes; of late years they have multiplied to an astonishing and alarming degree, and much mischief lies hid in them."

This kind of thinking is in part a result of the inheritance of the Puritan attitude towards children a century earlier. One of the most amazing Puritan children's books from that period by James Janeway has the explicit title: *A Token for Children: being an Exact Account of the Conversion, Holy and Exemplary Lives, and Joyful Deaths of several young Children. To which is now added, Prayers and Graces, fitted for the use of Little Children.* One of several woodblocks shows three little children whipping a top (a grave sin), while another presents a child contemplating a corpse. The text, as the title might suggest, recounts the deaths of little martyrs who realized that they were "by Nature, Children of Wrath." And Janeway warned the parents: "Are the Souls of your Children of no Value? . . . They are not too little to die, they are not too little to go to Hell, they are not too little to serve their great Master, too little to go to Heaven."

John Bunyan's *The Pilgrim's Progress* was quickly adopted by children as one of the classics of their library, but Bunyan also wrote a book specifically for them, *Divine Emblems,* one of which is entitled "Upon the Bee":

> *The Bee goes out, and Honey home doth bring;*
> *And some who seek that Honey find a Sting.*
> *Now would'st thou have the Honey, and be free*
> *From stinging, in the first place kill the Bee.*

Upon which Harvey Darton comments: "Herrick, Milton, Dr. Watts all found lessons or metaphors in the bee. But Bunyan alone conceived of the insect as immoral." (Not only did he find it immoral, but he advised the death penalty.)

This vituperative attitude, which still infects most of our righteous political attitudes today, was mollified by Locke, Rousseau, and their followers. In spite of the basically didactic and minatory attitude of most children's book writers in the eighteenth and early nineteenth century, authors like Maria Edgeworth, Thomas Day, Isaac Watts, William Roscoe and later Catherine Sinclair began to create works about and for real children. But the Puritan spirit continued to live on in unlikely places. Twenty years after he illustrated the first English edition of Grimm's *Popular Stories* (1823-6), George Cruikshank, who had now become a violent teetotaller and obsessive moralist, made an about face and rewrote the tales as temperance tracts. In the "new" version, when Cinderella is about to be married, "all the wine, beer, and spirits in the place were collected together, and piled upon the top of a rocky mound in the vicinity of the palace, and made a great bonfire of on the night of the wedding." Even Mrs. Trimmer might have felt too nervous to make an appearance.

8

Our childhood would then be the Lethe where we had drunk in order not to dissolve in the former and future All, to have a suitably limited personality. We are placed in a sort of labyrinth; we do not find the thread which would show us the way out and, doubtless, it is essential that we do not find it. That is why we attach the thread of History to the place where the thread of our (personal) memories breaks, and when our own existence escapes us, we live in that of our ancestors."

—K. P. Moritz, quoted in Bachelard's *The Poetics of Reverie*

In the first part of the eighteenth century, Perrault's Mother Goose Tales were translated into English. About the same time, stories by the Countess D' Aulnoy ("The White Cat" and "Goldylocks") arrived. And the first English translation of the *Arabian Nights* appeared in 1704-17 (although these tales had already burrowed their way into Aesop, *Gesta Romanorum,* and Chaucer's "The Squire's Tale").

In 1818 Benjamin Tabart collected and revised stories of Perrault, "Beauty and the Beast" (which came from the eighteenth century French fairy tale encyclopedia *Le Cabinet des Fées),* Aladdin, Tom Thumb, and many others. But it was the English translation of Grimms' *German Popular Tales* (1823-6) that heralded the "literary" acceptance of fairy stories. *Struwelpeter* followed a couple of years later, Robert Southey's first published version of "The Three Bears" became popular in the 1830's, Hans Christian Andersen's stories were translated in 1846, scores of "folktale" collections appeared, the Rev. F. E. Paget published *The Hope of the Katzekopfs* (1845—one of the first important fairy tale novels—and John Ruskin, in a preface to an 1868 edition of *German Popular Stories,* wrote that a child

> should not need to choose between right and wrong. It should not be capable of wrong. It should not conceive of wrong . . . Obedient, as bark to helm, not by sudden strain or effort, but in the freedom of its bright course of constant life . . . gentle, through daily entreatings of gentleness, and honourable trusts, and pretty prides of child-fellow-ship in offices of good . . . self-commanding, not in sick treatment of mean appetites and covetous thoughts, but in vital joy of unluxuri-ous life, and contentment in narrow possession, wisely esteemed . . ,Children so trained have no need of moral fairy tales.

"His voice was thunderous in those days," Harvey Darton writes. About Ruskin. "Thus, nearly five centuries after the Wife of Bath had complained of the fairies' outlawry, the first Slade Professor of Fine Art at Oxford removed the ban."

From the 1840's-1890's, Victorian England witnessed undoubtedly the greatest flowering of writing for children in the history of literature. This statement is hardly an exaggeration. Within this fifty year period appeared: Charles Kingsley's *The Water-Babies,* the *Alice* books and *Sylvie and Bruno,* Lear's "nonsense" poetry, Thackeray's *The Rose and the Ring,* George MacDonald's *At the Back of* the *North Wind* and *The Princess and Curdie,* Charles Dickens' *A Holiday Romance,* Andrew Lang's *Prince Prigio* and *Prince Ricardo,* the novels of Mrs. Ewing, Mrs. Molesworth, and Jean Ingelow—as well as the works collected in this anthology. Children's magazines proliferated: *Aunt Judy's Magazine* (edited by Mrs. Gatty, the mother of Mrs. Ewing), *Chatterbox, Good Words for the Young, The Charm, Little Folks,* etc. A number of extraordinary fairy tale collections began to appear—the most famous being Joseph Jacobs' *English Fairy Tales* (1890) and *Celtic Fairy Tales* (1893) and, still popular today, Andrew Lang's twelve *Blue-to-Lilac* volumes, the first of which—*The Blue Fairy Book*—was published in 1889. Finally, the period produced the still unequalled illustrations of artists like George Cruikshank, Richard Doyle, John Tenniel, Walter Crane, Eleanor Boyle (E. V. B.), Randolph Caldecott, Kate Greenaway, and the sensational Laurence Housman—the undeservedly neglected illustrator brother of A. E. Housman. (His own fairy stories are the height of preciosity, but his illustrations for Rossetti's *Goblin Market*—included in this collection—as well as his illustrations for many other works, are stunning.)

No one reason can fully explain this munificent productiveness. Writing fairy tales for children had become an acceptable literary activity. Not only had Thackeray, Ruskin, Dickens, and Christina Rossetti done so, but Victorian children's book writers were generally less involved than "adult" literary writers in the contemporary debates concerning "moral aesthetics" engaged in by Tennyson, Ruskin, Arnold, Buchanan, and Pater. In some way the Victorian writers for children had transcended the age-old debate concerning the purposes of "literature" (instruction vs. delight) as well as the equivalent moral tract vs. fairy story argument regarding children's literature. Certainly very few children's "authorities" would have conceived of making the following comments which appeared in the utilitarian *Westminster Review:* "Literature is a seducer; we had almost said a harlot. She may do to trifle with; but woe be to the state whose statesmen write verses, and whose lawyers read more in Tom Moore than in Bracton." Children's literature of this period almost always had a moral or religious basis, but it was often just this conflict between morality and invention (or morality and eroticism in Christina Rossetti's *Goblin Market*) that created some of this era's greatest works.

There is no one social explanation that can account for the wealth of writing for children that occurred specifically in England rather than on the continent. Certainly the English differentiation between *infant* and *child* suggests a more subtle appreciation of the special state and aura of childhood than is communicated by the all-embracing French *l'enfant.* It is tempting to turn back to the idea suggested in Michel Foucault's *Madness and Civilization* that "in the classical period, the melancholy of the English was easily explained by the influence of a maritime climate, cold, humidity, the instability of the weather; all those fine droplets of water that penetrated the channels and fibers of the human body and made it lose its firmness, predisposed it to madness." The famous eccentricities associated with Lewis Carrol, Edward Lear, and others might attest to some connection between writing for children and madness: Foucault interestingly suggests that the nineteenth century's judgment of someone considered "mad" relegated to that person the status of childhood.

The real reason for the greatness of Victorian children's literature is that, for the first time, men and women could explore their senses of childhood without apologizing for their wishing to do so or having to use alibis—as Perrault felt he had to. It is my claim, however, that, like the *Alice* books, the works collected in this anthology are enjoyed and understood best by "adults," for the recovery of childhood—exemplified in these writings—has retrieved for English literature the telluric and animistic wisdom which the mainstream of Victorian culture tried to demean—the kind of "wisdom" which is one of the most natural and basic elements of Latin American writing, *e.g.,* Estrada, Asturias, Marquez, Paz, and Neruda; or of a writer like I. B. Singer who, in his American-Yiddish "fictions"—rooted as they are in the ecstatic folk culture of Hasidism—continually display the magical and demonic as the most basic and operative facts of existence. And while it is true that the fairy tale genre at the end of the Victorian period degenerated into the sentimental ladies'-art-school/bleeding poppy bouquet of the "aesthetic" eighties, the golden era of Victorian children's literature rediscovered and adapted the fairy lore which "official" cultural attitudes found impossible to repress: it in fact insists on reappearing in the "adult" fantasy novels by William Morris, Lord Dunsany, and E. R. Eddison; in writers like A. E., W. B. Yeats, James Stephens, and Herbert Read *(The Green Child)*; and also in rock music in the songs of Donovan *(A Gift from a Flower to a Garden),* Tyrannosaurus Rex *(My People were Fair, Prophets, Seers and Sages),* and especially Pink Floyd *(The Piper at the Gates of Dawn)* and the Incredible String Band. It is interesting to realize that it was post-war middle-class English "children" who, in their music and culture, rediscovered the importance of "fairy faith." Imagining themselves as "Children of Los," they reawakened the creatures of Oz and the Piper at the Gates of Dawn, as their memories turned back to Stonehenge and Glastonbury.

It was in large measure the accomplishments of Victorian children's writing that had earlier enabled Kenneth Grahame to write a novel about misogynist English gentlemen in Oxfordshire and have it come out as *The Wind in the Willows . . .* while in the United States L. Frank Baum would produce *The Wizard of Oz*—still America's greatest fairy story—which is nothing but a kind of quasi-Sufi tale concerning a tin woodman wanting a heart, a scarecrow desiring brains, a lion wishing for courage, and a young girl hoping to find her home. It is, of course, exactly these things that the characters all contain within themselves as they reveal them to each other in the course of the book. And in *The Fellowship of the Rings,* Tolkien, like an archeologist of fairy lore, attempted singlehandedly to define and explore the hidden terrain of man's lost awarenesses of the secret kingdom, while at the same time he imagined the possibilities of a "mended" world in which consciousness would become both as large and as small as a grain of sand.

Lewis Carroll reports having misjudged a sign which, at a distance, seemed to read: *Romancement,* but which, closer up, said: *Roman cement.* One of the many paradoxes about the Victorian period is that while the "typical," idealized middle class family allowed children their own world—defined by a "prudent" moral code and upbringing—the judicial system, which had once placed juvenile offenders within a separate court system, now subjected the working-class child to prison and the workhouse. Teenagers were hanged for petty crimes in the 1850's. And Pitt's comment to industrialists who were asking for a reduction of the minimum wage was: "Take the children."

Steven Marcus has demonstrated that the world of Victorian pornography was the "mirror-image" of the prevailing high-toned standard of prudery. But, as Gertrude Himmelfarb points out, the various forms of Victorian "unbelief"—Utilitarianism, Positivism, Darwinism, Aesthetic Humanism, and Rationalism—actually intensified the moral zeal. "It was not morality," she writes, "that required the security of religion; it was the unbeliever who required that security—required it not for the sake of morality but for the sake of belief itself. And lacking the security of belief, he compensated, or overcompensated, for its lack by making the most of the morality he had."

The relationship of this morality to the "idea" of children shows signs of confusion and diverse intentions in the writing for and about them. It was as possible to encounter passive and oppressed heroes like Oliver Twist and Mrs. Clifford's Wooden Tony as it was to come across the active spiritual child initiates of George MacDonald's stories: e.g., "The Golden Key" and "The Day Boy and the Night Girl." In between these extremes, many writers attempted to use the "child" as a way to mediate the conflicting claims of evolutionary change and ethical improvement, of environment and technology, of Mr. Podsnap and Mr. Gradgrind. To this end, the depiction of children became the link between two seemingly irreconcilable beliefs. And the "child," having become a crucible for the ideal of Goodness, found itself being offered as an emblem of wholeness.

The "child," however, was not only a "solution"; it also reflected the etiology of wavering social certainties. Chambers and Lyell's Uniformitarian thesis, which questioned the theological idea of a Creation at a specific moment of time, raised the problem of origins; and, as mentioned previously, the child archetype specifically implies a connection with the mysteries of the Beginning. Darwin's *Voyage of the Beagle,* moreover, suggested a similar ontological anxiety. As Jan Gordon has interestingly observed: "The menagerie that moves through *Alice's Adventures in Wonderland* clearly exists in a post-Darwinian tent, and new species can be called into existence merely by a mutation in the child's imagination or as a function of her size. They are the products of an anthropomorphic intelligence." And the question of sexual-social and of spiritual identy is constantly tested in children's books of this period—Maggie Browne's *Wanted—A King* is an example of the first concern and George MacDonald's stories, of the latter. The search for one's true past, of course, occurs throughout Victorian literature—one immediately thinks of Pip, Little Joe, and Dorothea Brooke. And whereas a writer like Mary de Morgan emphasized the heartbreaking nostalgic feelings for the "lost home" (see "The Wanderings of Arasmon"), George MacDonald took the mythologeme of the "orphan" child and identified it—as was done in the Gnostic *Hymn of the Pearl*—with the soul.

It is impossible to overlook the importance of the evangelical tradition in Victorian children's literature. While many writers like Mrs. Ewing and Mrs. Molesworth seem by temperament to have subscribed to the "rights of property and the duties of labour" school, and though they often identified redemption with *class* redemption—as did most Victorian "adult" novels—their insistence on the internal personal experience of a selfless spiritual reality finally aligns them

Mrs. George MacDonald, four children and Lewis Carroll, 1862.

more with Pusey, Keble, and John Mason Neale—if not with the Wesleys and William Law and later Christian Socialists like Charles Kingsley, J. M. Ludlow, and F. D. Maurice (who founded the Working Men's College and who, incidentally, was an important influence on George MacDonald).

Most of the works in this anthology are colored in some way by this evangelical tradition which emphasized regeneration and conversion—a kind of *Selbsttötung* (rendered by Michael Hamburger as "egocide" or "unselfing"), and in this sense these works share similar concerns with Victorian novels like *Great Expectations, The Ordeal of Richard Feverel, Romola,* as well as with the personal dramas of Mill and Newman. Behind the fairy possession of *Tinykin's Transformations,* the political satire of *Petsetilla's Posy,* or the social education of *Children of the Castle* lies the possibility of *kairos*—the time of grace. It is the time of fairy stories—once-upon-a-time—when the eternal present reveals itself to us once again.

Jonathan Cott
New York City
January 1973

THE KING
OF
THE GOLDEN RIVER
OR
THE BLACK BROTHERS

BY

JOHN RUSKIN

ILLUSTRATED
BY
RICHARD DOYLE

John Ruskin wrote *The King of the Golden River* in 1841 at the request of his twelve-year-old distant Scottish cousin, Euphemia (Effie) Chalmers Gray, whom he married in 1848. This ill-fated marriage was annulled six years later, and Effie went on to marry John Everett Millais. Ruskin's archetypal fairy story about little Gluck and his two selfish brothers Hans and Schwartz, as well as the magnificent King of the Golden River, himself, displays "true Alpine feeling" so characteristic of the world of Grimm's tales. Illustrated with the now-famous drawings of Richard Doyle, Ruskin's fairy story was first published in 1851, ten years after its creation.

Parenthetically, it is interesting to note that, although *The King of the Golden River* was Ruskin's only "original" contribution to children's literature, it was his Introduction to the 1868 edition of Grimm's Tales that first gained, for these tales, their wide acceptance.

THE KING of the

GOLDEN RIVER

OR THE

BLACK   BROTHERS

A LEGEND
OF
STIRIA

THE KING
OF
THE GOLDEN RIVER
OR
THE BLACK BROTHERS

CHAPTER I

a secluded and mountainous part of Stiria there was, in old time, a valley of the most surprising and luxuriant fertility. It was surrounded, on all sides, by steep and rocky mountains, rising into peaks, which were always covered with snow, and from which a number of torrents descended in constant cataracts. One of these fell westward, over the face of a crag so high, that, when the sun had set to everything else, and all below was darkness, his beams still shone full upon this waterfall, so that it looked like a shower of gold. It was, therefore, called by the people of the neighbourhood, the Golden River. It was strange that none of these streams fell into the valley itself. They all descended on the other side of the

5

mountains, and wound away through broad plains and by populous cities. But the clouds were drawn so constantly to the snowy hills, and rested so softly in the circular hollow, that in time of drought and heat, when all the country round was burnt up, there was still rain in the little valley; and its crops were so heavy, and its hay so high, and its apples so red, and its grapes so blue, and its wine so rich, and its honey so sweet, that it was a marvel to everyone who beheld it, and was commonly called the Treasure Valley.

The whole of this little valley belonged to three brothers, called Schwartz, Hans, and Gluck. Schwartz and Hans, the two elder brothers, were very ugly men, with over-hanging eyebrows and small dull eyes, which were always half shut, so that you couldn't see into *them*, and always fancied they saw very far into *you*. They lived by farming the Treasure Valley, and very good farmers they were. They killed everything that did not pay for its eating. They shot the blackbirds, because they pecked the fruit; and killed the hedgehogs, lest they should suck the cows; they poisoned the crickets for eating the crumbs in the kitchen; and smothered the cicadas, which used to sing all summer in the lime trees. They worked their servants without any wages, till they would not work any more, and then quarrelled with them, and turned them out of doors without paying them. It would have been very odd, if with such a farm, and such a system of farming, they hadn't got very rich; and very rich they *did* get. They generally contrived to keep their corn by them till it was very dear, and then sell it for twice its value; they had heaps of gold lying about on their floors, yet it was never known that they had given so much as a penny or a crust in charity; they never went to mass; grumbled perpetually at paying tithes; and were, in a word, of so cruel and grinding a temper, as to receive from all those with whom they had any dealings, the nick-name of the "Black Brothers."

The youngest brother, Gluck, was as completely opposed, in both appearance and character, to his seniors as could possibly be imagined or desired. He was not above twelve years old, fair, blue-eyed, and kind in temper to every living thing. He did not, of course, agree particularly well with his brothers, or rather, they did not agree with *him*. He was usually appointed to the honourable office of turnspit, when there was anything to roast, which was not often; for, to do the brothers justice, they were hardly less sparing upon themselves than upon other people.

At other times he used to clean the shoes, floors, and sometimes the plates, occasionally getting what was left on them, by way of encouragement, and a wholesome quantity of dry blows, by way of education.

Things went on in this manner for a long time. At last came a very wet summer, and everything went wrong in the country around. The hay had hardly been got in, when the haystacks were floated bodily down to the sea by an inundation; the vines were cut to pieces with the hail; the corn was all killed by a black blight; only in the Treasure Valley, as usual, all was safe. As it had rain when there was rain nowhere else, so it had sun when there was sun nowhere else. Everybody came to buy corn at the farm, and went away pouring maledictions on the Black Brothers. They asked what they liked, and got it, except from the poor people, who could only beg, and several of whom were starved at their very door, without the slightest regard or notice.

It was drawing towards winter, and very cold weather, when one day the two elder brothers had gone out, with their usual warning to little Gluck, who was left to mind the roast, that he was to let nobody in, and give nothing out. Gluck sat down quite close to the fire, for it was raining very hard, and the kitchen walls were by no means dry or comfortable looking. He turned and turned, and the roast got nice and brown. "What a pity," thought Gluck, "my brothers never ask anybody to dinner. I'm sure, when they've got such a nice piece of mutton as this, and nobody else has got so much as a piece of dry bread, it would do their hearts good to have somebody to eat it with them."

Just as he spoke, there came a double knock at the house door, yet heavy and dull, as though the knocker had been tied up—more like a puff than a knock.

"It must be the wind," said Gluck; "nobody else would venture to knock double knocks at our door."

No; it wasn't the wind: there it came again very hard, and what was particularly astounding, the knocker seemed to be in a hurry, and not to be in the least afraid of the consequences. Gluck went to the window, opened it, and put his head out to see who it was.

It was the most extraordinary looking little gentleman he had ever seen in his life. He had a very large nose, slightly brass-coloured; his cheeks were very round, and very red, and might have warranted a

7

supposition that he had been blowing a refractory fire for the last eight-and-forty hours; his eyes twinkled merrily through long silky eye-lashes, his moustaches curled twice round like a corkscrew on each side of his mouth, and his hair, of a curious mixed pepper-and-salt colour, descended far over his shoulders. He was about four-feet-six in height, and wore a conical pointed cap of nearly the same altitude, decorated with a black feather some three feet long. His doublet was prolonged behind into something resembling a violent exaggeration of what is now termed a "swallow tail," but was much obscured by the swelling folds of an enormous black, glossy-looking cloak, which must have been very much too long in calm weather, as the wind, whistling round the old house, carried it clear out from the wearer's shoulders to about four times his own length.

Gluck was so perfectly paralyzed by the singular appearance of his visitor, that he remained fixed without uttering a word, until the old gentleman, having performed another, and a more energetic concerto on the knocker, turned round to look after his fly-away cloak. In so doing he caught sight of Gluck's little yellow head jammed in the window, with its mouth and eyes very wide open indeed.

"Hollo!" said the little gentleman, "that's not the way to answer the door: I'm wet, let me in."

To do the little gentleman justice, he *was* wet. His feather hung down between his legs like a beaten puppy's tail, dripping like an umbrella; and from the ends of his moustaches the water was running into his waistcoat pockets, and out again like a mill stream.

"I beg pardon, sir," said Gluck, "I'm very sorry, but I really can't."

"Can't what?" said the old gentleman.

"I can't let you in, sir,—I can't indeed; my brothers would beat me to death, sir, if I thought of such a thing. What do you want, sir?"

"Want?" said the old gentleman, petulantly. "I want fire, and shelter; and there's your great fire there blazing, crackling, and dancing on the walls, with nobody to feel it. Let me in, I say; I only want to warm myself."

Gluck had had his head, by this time, so long out of the window, that he began to feel it was really unpleasantly cold, and when he turned, and saw the beautiful fire rustling and roaring, and throwing long bright

9

tongues up the chimney, as if it were licking its chops at the savoury smell of the leg of mutton, his heart melted within him that it should be burning away for nothing. "He does look *very* wet," said little Gluck; "I'll just let him in for a quarter of an hour." Round he went to the door, and opened it; and as the little gentleman walked in, there came a gust of wind through the house, that made the old chimneys totter.

"That's a good boy," said the little gentleman. "Never mind your brothers. I'll talk to them."

"Pray, sir, don't do any such thing," said Gluck. "I can't let you stay till they come; they'd be the death of me."

"Dear me," said the old gentleman, "I'm very sorry to hear that. How long may I stay?"

"Only till the mutton's done, sir," replied Gluck, "and it's very brown."

Then the old gentleman walked into the kitchen, and sat himself down on the hob, with the top of his cap accommodated up the chimney, for it was a great deal too high for the roof.

"You'll soon dry there, sir," said Gluck, and sat down again to turn

10

the mutton. But the old gentleman did *not* dry there, but went on drip, drip, dripping among the cinders, and the fire fizzed, and sputtered, and began to look very black, and uncomfortable: never was such a cloak; every fold in it ran like a gutter.

"I beg pardon, sir," said Gluck at length, after watching the water spreading in long, quicksilverlike streams over the floor for a quarter of an hour; "mayn't I take your cloak?"

"No, thank you," said the old gentleman.

"Your cap, sir?"

"I am all right, thank you," said the old gentleman rather gruffly.

"But,—sir,—I'm very sorry," said Gluck, hesitatingly; "but—really, sir,—you're—putting the fire out."

"It'll take longer to do the mutton, then," replied his visitor drily.

Gluck was very much puzzled by the behaviour of his guest; it was such a strange mixture of coolness and humility. He turned away at the string meditatively for another five minutes.

"That mutton looks very nice," said the old gentleman at length. "Can't you give me a little bit?"

"Impossible, sir," said Gluck.

"I'm very hungry," continued the old gentleman: "I've had nothing to eat yesterday, nor to-day. They surely couldn't miss a bit from the knuckle!"

He spoke in so very melancholy a tone, that it quite melted Gluck's heart. "They promised me one slice to-day, sir," said he; "I can give you that, but not a bit more."

"That's a good boy," said the old gentleman again.

Then Gluck warmed a plate, and sharpened a knife. "I don't care if I do get beaten for it," thought he. Just as he had cut a large slice out of the mutton, there came a tremendous rap at the door. The old gentleman jumped off the hob, as if it had suddenly become inconveniently warm. Gluck fitted the slice into the mutton again, with desperate efforts at exactitude, and ran to open the door.

"What did you keep us waiting in the rain for?" said Schwartz, as he walked in, throwing his umbrella in Gluck's face. "Ay! what for, indeed, you little vagabond?" said Hans, administering an educational box on the ear, as he followed his brother into the kitchen.

11

"Bless my soul!" said Schwartz when he opened the door.

"Amen," said the little gentleman, who had taken his cap off, and was standing in the middle of the kitchen, bowing with the utmost possible velocity.

"Who's that?" said Schwartz, catching up a rolling-pin, and turning to Gluck with a fierce frown.

"I don't know, indeed, brother," said Gluck in great terror.

"How did he get in?" roared Schwartz.

"My dear brother," said Gluck, deprecatingly, "he was so *very* wet!"

The rolling-pin was descending on Gluck's head; but, at the instant, the old gentleman interposed his conical cap, on which it crashed with a shock that shook the water out of it all over the room. What was very odd, the rolling-pin no sooner touched the cap, than it flew out of Schwartz's hand, spinning like a straw in a high wind, and fell into the corner at the further end of the room.

"Who are you, sir?" demanded Schwartz, turning upon him.

"What's your business?" snarled Hans.

"I'm a poor old man, sir," the little gentleman began very modestly, "and I saw your fire through the window, and begged shelter for a quarter of an hour."

"Have the goodness to walk out again, then," said Schwartz. "We've quite enough water in our kitchen, without making it a drying-house."

"It is a cold day to turn an old man out in, sir; look at **my** grey hairs." They hung down to his shoulders, as I told you before.

"Ay!" said Hans, "there are enough of them to keep you warm. Walk!"

"I'm very, very hungry, sir; couldn't you spare me a bit of bread before I go?"

"Bread, indeed!" said Schwartz; "do you suppose we've nothing to do with our bread but to give it to such red-nosed fellows as you?"

"Why don't you sell your feather?" said Hans, sneeringly. "Out with you!"

"A little bit," said the old gentleman.

"Be off!" said Schwartz.

"Pray, gentlemen——"

"Off, and be hanged!" cried Hans, seizing him by the collar. But he

12

had no sooner touched the old gentleman's collar, than away he went after the rolling-pin, spinning round and round, till he fell into the corner on the top of it. Then Schwartz was very angry, and ran at the old gentleman to turn him out; but he also had hardly touched him, when away he went after Hans and the rolling-pin, and hit his head against the wall as he tumbled into the corner. And so there they lay, all three.

Then the old gentleman spun himself round with velocity in the opposite direction; continued to spin until his long cloak was all wound neatly about him; clapped his cap on his head, very much on one side (for it could not stand upright without going through the ceiling), gave an additional twist to his corkscrew moustaches, and replied with perfect coolness: "Gentlemen, I wish you a very good morning. At twelve o'clock to-night I'll call again; after such a refusal of hospitality as I have just experienced, you will not be surprised if that visit is the last I ever pay you."

"If ever I catch you here again," muttered Schwartz, coming, half frightened, out of the corner—but, before he could finish his sentence, the old gentleman had shut the house door behind him with a great bang: and there drove past the window, at the same instant, a wreath of

13

ragged cloud, that whirled and rolled away down the valley in all manner of shapes; turning over and over in the air, and melting away at last in a gush of rain.

"A very pretty business, indeed, Mr. Gluck!" said Schwartz. "Dish the mutton, sir. If ever I catch you at such a trick again—bless me, why, the mutton's been cut!"

"You promised me one slice, brother, you know," said Gluck.

"Oh! and you were cutting it hot, I suppose, and going to catch all the gravy. It'll be long before I promise you such a thing again. Leave the room, sir; and have the kindness to wait in the coal-cellar till I call you."

Gluck left the room melancholy enough. The brothers ate as much mutton as they could, locked the rest in the cupboard, and proceeded to get very drunk after dinner.

Such a night as it was! Howling wind, and rushing rain, without intermission. The brothers had just sense enough left to put up all the shutters, and double bar the door, before they went to bed. They usually slept in the same room. As the clock struck twelve, they were both awakened by a tremendous crash. Their door burst open with a violence that shook the house from top to bottom.

"What's that?" cried Schwartz, starting up in his bed.

"Only I," said the little gentleman.

The two brothers sat up on their bolster, and stared into the darkness. The room was full of water, and by a misty moonbeam, which found its way through a hole in the shutter, they could see in the midst of it an enormous foam globe, spinning round, and bobbing up and down like a cork, on which, as on a most luxurious cushion, reclined the little old gentleman, cap and all. There was plenty of room for it now, for the roof was off.

"Sorry to incommode you," said their visitor, ironically. "I'm afraid your beds are dampish; perhaps you had better go to your brother's room: I've left the ceiling on, there."

They required no second admonition, but rushed into Gluck's room, wet through, and in an agony of terror.

"You'll find my card on the kitchen table," the old gentleman called after them. "Remember, the *last* visit."

"Pray Heaven it may!" said Schwartz, shuddering. And the foam globe disappeared.

Dawn came at last, and the two brothers looked out of Gluck's little window in the morning. The Treasure Valley was one mass of ruin and desolation. The inundation had swept away trees, crops, and cattle, and left in their stead a waste of red sand and grey mud. The two brothers crept shivering and horror-struck into the kitchen. The water had gutted the whole first floor; corn, money, almost every movable thing had been swept away, and there was left only a small white card on the kitchen table. On it, in large, breezy, long-legged letters, were engraved the words:—

15

OUTH-WEST WIND, Esquire, was as good as his word. After the momentous visit above related, he entered the Treasure Valley no more; and, what was worse, he had so much influence with his relations, the Wet Winds in general, and used it so effectually, that they all adopted a similar line of conduct. So no rain fell in the valley from one year's end to another. Though everything remained green and flourishing in the plains below, the inheritance of the Three Brothers was a desert. What had once been the richest soil in the kingdom, became a shifting heap of red sand; and the brothers, unable longer to contend with the adverse skies, abandoned their valueless patrimony in despair, to seek some means of gaining a livelihood among the cities and people of the plains. All their money was gone, and they had nothing left but some curious old-fashioned pieces of gold plate, the last remnants of their ill-gotten wealth.

"Suppose we turn goldsmiths?" said Schwartz to Hans, as they entered the large city. "It is a good knave's trade; we can put a great deal of copper into the gold, without any one's finding it out."

The thought was agreed to be a very good one; they hired a furnace, and turned goldsmiths. But two slight circumstances affected their trade: the first, that people did not approve of the coppered gold; the second, that the two elder brothers, whenever they had sold anything, used to leave little Gluck to mind the furnace, and go and drink out the money in the ale-house next door. So they melted all their gold, without making money enough to buy more, and were at last reduced to one large

16

drinking mug, which an uncle of his had given to little Gluck, and which he was very fond of, and would not have parted with for the world; though he never drank anything out of it but milk and water. The mug was a very odd mug to look at. The handle was formed of two wreaths of flowing golden hair, so finely spun that it looked more like silk than metal, and these wreaths descended into, and mixed with, a beard and whiskers of the same exquisite workmanship, which surrounded and decorated a very fierce little face of the reddest gold imaginable, right in the front of the mug, with a pair of eyes in it which seemed to command its whole circumference. It was impossible to drink out of the mug without being subjected to an intense gaze out of the side of these eyes; and Schwartz positively averred, that once, after emptying it, full of Rhenish, seventeen times, he had seen them wink! When it came to the mug's turn to be made into spoons, it half broke poor little Gluck's heart; but the brothers only laughed at him, tossed the mug into the melting-pot, and staggered out to the ale-house: leaving him, as usual, to pour the gold into bars, when it was all ready.

When they were gone, Gluck took a farewell look at his old friend in the melting-pot. The flowing hair was all gone; nothing remained but the red nose, and the sparkling eyes, which looked more malicious than ever.

"And no wonder," thought Gluck, "after being treated in that way." He sauntered disconsolately to the window, and sat himself down to catch the fresh evening air, and escape the hot breath of the furnace. Now this window commanded a direct view of the range of mountains, which, as I told you before, overhung the Treasure Valley, and more especially of the peak from which fell the Golden River. It was just at the close of the day, and when Gluck sat down at the window, he saw the rocks of the mountain tops, all crimson, and purple with the sunset; and there were bright tongues of fiery cloud burning and quivering about them; and the river, brighter than all, fell, in a waving column of pure gold, from precipice to precipice, with the double arch of a broad purple rainbow stretched across it, flushing and fading alternately in the wreaths of spray.

"Ah!" said Gluck aloud, after he had looked at it for a while, "if that river were really all gold, what a nice thing it would be."

"No it wouldn't, Gluck," said a clear metallic voice, close at his ear.

"Bless me! what's that?" exclaimed Gluck, jumping up. There was nobody there. He looked round the room, and under the table, and a great many times behind him, but there was certainly nobody there, and he sat down again at the window. This time he didn't speak, but he couldn't help thinking again that it would be very convenient if the river were really all gold.

"Not at all, my boy," said the same voice, louder than before.

"Bless me!" said Gluck again, "what *is* that?" He looked again into all the corners and cupboards, and then began turning round, and round, as fast as he could in the middle of the room, thinking there was somebody behind him, when the same voice struck again on his ear. It was singing now very merrily, "Lala-lira-la;" no words, only a soft running effervescent melody, something like that of a kettle on the boil. Gluck looked out of the window. No, it was certainly in the house. Upstairs, and downstairs. No, it was certainly in that very room, coming in quicker time, and clearer notes, every moment. "Lala-lira-la." All at once it struck Gluck that it sounded louder near the furnace. He ran to the opening, and looked in: yes, he saw right, it seemed to be coming, not only out of the furnace, but out of the pot. He uncovered it, and ran back in a great fright, for the pot was certainly singing! He stood in the

18

farthest corner of the room, with his hands up, and his mouth open, for a minute or two, when the singing stopped, and the voice became clear, and pronunciative.

"Hollo!" said the voice.

Gluck made no answer.

"Hollo! Gluck, my boy," said the pot again.

Gluck summoned all his energies, walked straight up to the crucible, drew it out of the furnace, and looked in. The gold was all melted, and its surface as smooth and polished as a river; but instead of reflecting little Gluck's head, as he looked in, he saw meeting his glance from beneath the gold the red nose and sharp eyes of his old friend of the mug, a thousand times redder and sharper than ever he had seen them in his life.

"Come, Gluck, my boy," said the voice out of the pot again, "I'm all right; pour me out."

But Gluck was too much astonished to do anything of the kind.

"Pour me out, I say," said the voice rather gruffly.

Still Gluck couldn't move.

"*Will* you pour me out?" said the voice passionately, "I'm too hot."

By a violent effort, Gluck recovered the use of his limbs, took hold of the crucible, and sloped it so as to pour out the gold. But instead of a liquid stream, there came out, first, a pair of pretty little yellow legs, then some coat tails, then a pair of arms stuck a-kimbo, and, finally, the well-known head of his friend the mug; all which articles, uniting as they rolled out, stood up energetically on the floor, in the shape of a little golden dwarf, about a foot and a half high.

"That's right!" said the dwarf, stretching out first his legs, and then his arms, and then shaking his head up and down, and as far round as it would go, for five minutes, without stopping; apparently with the view of ascertaining if he were quite correctly put together, while Gluck stood contemplating him in speechless amazement. He was dressed in a slashed

19

doublet of spun gold, so fine in its texture, that the prismatic colours gleamed over it, as if on a surface of mother of pearl; and, over this brilliant doublet, his hair and beard fell full halfway to the ground, in waving curls, so exquisitely delicate, that Gluck could hardly tell where they ended; they seemed to melt into air. The features of the face, however, were by no means finished with the same delicacy; they were rather coarse, slightly inclining to coppery in complexion, and indicative, in expression, of a very pertinacious and intractable disposition in their small proprietor. When the dwarf had finished his self-examination, he turned his small sharp eyes full on Gluck, and stared at him deliberately for a minute or two. "No, it wouldn't, Gluck, my boy," said the little man.

20

This was certainly rather an abrupt and unconnected mode of commencing conversation. It might indeed be supposed to refer to the course of Gluck's thoughts, which had first produced the dwarf's observations out of the pot; but whatever it referred to, Gluck had no inclination to dispute the dictum.

"Wouldn't it, sir?" said Gluck, very mildly and submissively indeed.

"No," said the dwarf, conclusively. "No, it wouldn't." And with that, the dwarf pulled his cap hard over his brows, and took two turns, of three feet long, up and down the room, lifting his legs up very high, and setting them down very hard. This pause gave time for Gluck to collect his thoughts a little, and, seeing no great reason to view his diminutive visitor with dread, and feeling his curiosity overcome his amazement, he ventured on a question of peculiar delicacy.

"Pray, sir," said Gluck, rather hesitatingly, "were you my mug?"

On which the little man turned sharp round, walked straight up to Gluck, and drew himself up to his full height. "I," said the little man, "am the King of the Golden River." Whereupon he turned about again, and took two more turns, some six feet long, in order to allow time for the consternation which this announcement produced in his auditor to evaporate. After which, he again walked up to Gluck and stood still, as if expecting some comment on his communication.

Gluck determined to say something at all events.

"I hope your Majesty is very well," said Gluck.

"Listen!" said the little man, deigning no reply to this polite inquiry. "I am the King of what you mortals call the Golden River. The shape you saw me in was owing to the malice of a stronger king, from whose enchantments you have this instant freed me. What I have seen of you, and your conduct to your wicked brothers, renders me willing to serve you; therefore, attend to what I tell you. Whoever shall climb to the top of that mountain from which you see the Golden River issue, and shall cast into the stream at its source three drops of holy water, for him, and for him only, the river shall turn to gold. But no one failing in his first, can succeed in a second attempt; and if anyone shall cast unholy water into the river, it will overwhelm him, and he will become a black stone." So saying, the King of the Golden River turned away and deliberately walked into the centre of the hottest flame of the furnace. His figure

21

became red, white, transparent, dazzling,—a blaze of intense light—rose, trembled, and disappeared. The King of the Golden River had evaporated.

"Oh!" cried poor Gluck, running to look up the chimney after him; "oh dear, dear, dear me! My mug! my mug! my mug!"

CHAPTER III

HE King of the Golden River had hardly made the extraordinary exit related in the last chapter, before Hans and Schwartz came roaring into the house, very savagely drunk. The discovery of the total loss of their last piece of plate had the effect of sobering them just enough to enable them to stand over Gluck, beating him very steadily for a quarter of an hour; at the expiration of which period they dropped into a couple of chairs, and requested to know what he had got to say for himself. Gluck told them his story, of which, of course, they did not believe a word. They beat him again, till their arms were tired, and staggered to bed. In the morning, however, the steadiness with which he adhered to his story obtained him some degree of credence; the immediate consequence of which was, that the two brothers, after wrangling a long time on the knotty question, which of them should try his fortune first, drew their swords and began fighting. The noise of the fray alarmed the neighbours, who, finding they could not pacify the combatants, sent for the constable.

Hans, on hearing this, contrived to escape, and hid himself; but Schwartz was taken before the magistrate, fined for breaking the peace, and, having drunk out his last penny the evening before, was thrown into prison till he should pay.

When Hans heard this, he was much delighted, and determined to set out immediately for the Golden River. How to get the holy water was the question. He went to the priest, but the priest could not give any holy water to so abandoned a character. So Hans went to vespers in the

23

evening for the first time in his life, and, under pretence of crossing himself, stole a cupful, and returned home in triumph.

Next morning he got up before the sun rose, put the holy water into a strong flask, and two bottles of wine and some meat in a basket, slung them over his back, took his alpine staff in his hand, and set off for the mountains.

On his way out of the town he had to pass the prison, and as he looked in at the windows, whom should he see but Schwartz himself peeping out of the bars, and looking very disconsolate.

"Good morning, brother," said Hans; "have you any message for the King of the Golden River?"

Schwartz gnashed his teeth with rage, and shook the bars with all his strength; but Hans only laughed at him, and advising him to make himself comfortable till he came back again, shouldered his basket, shook the bottle of holy water in Schwartz's face till it frothed again, and marched off in the highest spirits in the world.

It was, indeed, a morning that might have made any one happy, even with no Golden River to seek for. Level lines of dewy mist lay stretched along the valley, out of which rose the massy mountains—their lower cliffs in pale grey shadow, hardly distinguishable from the floating vapour, but gradually ascending till they caught the sunlight, which ran in sharp touches of ruddy colour along the angular crags, and pierced, in long level rays, through their fringes of spear-like pine. Far above, shot up red splintered masses of castellated rock, jagged and shivered into

24

myriads of fantastic forms, with here and there a streak of sunlit snow, traced down their chasms like a line of forked lightning; and, far beyond, and far above all these, fainter than the morning cloud, but purer and changeless, slept, in the blue sky, the utmost peaks of the eternal snow.

The Golden River, which sprang from one of the lower and snowless elevations, was now nearly in shadow; all but the uppermost jets of spray, which rose like slow smoke above the undulating line of the cataract, and floated away in feeble wreaths upon the morning wind.

On this object, and on this alone, Hans' eyes and thoughts were fixed; forgetting the distance he had to traverse, he set off at an imprudent rate of walking, which greatly exhausted him before he had scaled the first range of the green and low hills. He was, moreover, surprised, on surmounting them, to find that a large glacier, of whose existence, notwithstanding his previous knowledge of the mountains, he had been absolutely ignorant, lay between him and the source of the Golden River. He entered on it with the boldness of a practised mountaineer; yet he thought he had never traversed so strange or so dangerous a glacier in his life. The ice was excessively slippery, and out of all its chasms came wild sounds of gushing water; not monotonous or low, but changeful and loud, rising occasionally into drifting passages of wild melody, then breaking off into short melancholy tones, or sudden shrieks, resembling those of human voices in distress or pain. The ice was broken into thousands of confused shapes, but none, Hans thought, like the ordinary forms of splintered ice. There seemed a curious *expression* about all their

25

outlines—a perpetual resemblance to living features, distorted and scorn-ful. Myriads of deceitful shadows, and lurid lights, played and floated about and through the pale blue pinnacles, dazzling and confusing the sight of the traveller; while his ears grew dull and his head giddy with the constant gush and roar of the concealed waters. These painful circum-stances increased upon him as he advanced; the ice crashed and yawned into fresh chasms at his feet, tottering spires nodded around him, and fell thundering across his path; and though he had repeatedly faced these dangers on the most terrific glaciers, and in the wildest weather, it was with a new and oppressive feeling of panic terror that he leaped the last chasm, and flung himself, exhausted and shuddering, on the firm turf of the mountain.

He had been compelled to abandon his basket of food, which became a perilous incumbrance on the glacier, and had now no means of refreshing himself but by breaking off and eating some of the pieces of ice. This, however, relieved his thirst; an hour's repose recruited his hardy frame, and with the indomitable spirit of avarice, he resumed his laborious journey.

His way now lay straight up a ridge of bare red rocks, without a blade of grass to ease the foot, or a projecting angle to afford an inch of shade from the south sun. It was past noon, and the rays beat intensely upon the steep path, while the whole atmosphere was motionless, and pene-trated with heat. Intense thirst was soon added to the bodily fatigue with which Hans was now afflicted; glance after glance he cast on the flask of water which hung at his belt. "Three drops are enough," at last thought he; "I may, at least, cool my lips with it."

He opened the flask, and was raising it to his lips, when his eye fell on an object lying on the rock beside him; he thought it moved. It was a small dog, apparently in the last agony of death from thirst. Its tongue was out, its jaws dry, its limbs extended lifelessly, and a swarm of black ants were crawling about its lips and throat. Its eye moved to the bottle which Hans held in his hand. He raised it, drank, spurned the animal with his foot, and passed on. And he did not know how it was, but he thought that a strange shadow had suddenly come across the blue sky.

The path became steeper and more rugged every moment; and the high hill air, instead of refreshing him, seemed to throw his blood into a

26

fever. The noise of the hill cataracts sounded like mockery in his ears; they were all distant, and his thirst increased every moment. Another hour passed, and he again looked down to the flask at his side; it was half empty; but there was much more than three drops in it. He stopped to open it, and again, as he did so, something moved in the path above him. It was a fair child, stretched nearly lifeless on the rock, its breast heaving with thirst, its eyes closed, and its lips parched and burning. Hans eyed it deliberately, drank, and passed on. And a dark grey cloud came over the sun, and long, snake-like shadows crept up along the mountain sides. Hans struggled on. The sun was sinking, but its descent seemed to bring

27

no coolness; the leaden weight of the dead air pressed upon his brow and heart, but the goal was near. He saw the cataract of the Golden River springing from the hill-side, scarcely five hundred feet above him. He paused for a moment to breathe, and sprang on to complete his task.

At this instant a faint cry fell on his ear. He turned, and saw a grey-haired old man extended on the rocks. His eyes were sunk, his features deadly pale, and gathered into an expression of despair. "Water!" he stretched his arms to Hans, and cried feebly, "Water! I am dying."

"I have none," replied Hans; "thou hast had thy share of life." He strode over the prostrate body, and darted on. And a flash of blue lightning rose out of the East, shaped like a sword; it shook thrice over the whole heaven, and left it dark with one heavy, impenetrable shade. The sun was setting; it plunged towards the horizon like a red-hot ball.

The roar of the Golden River rose on Hans' ear. He stood at the brink of the chasm through which it ran. Its waves were filled with the red glory of the sunset: they shook their crests like tongues of fire, and flashes of bloody light gleamed along their foam. Their sound came mightier and mightier on his senses; his brain grew giddy with the prolonged thunder. Shuddering he drew the flask from his girdle, and hurled it into the centre of the torrent. As he did so, an icy chill shot through his limbs: he staggered, shrieked, and fell. The waters closed over his cry. And the moaning of the river rose wildly into the night, as it gushed over **The Black Stone.**

CHAPTER IV

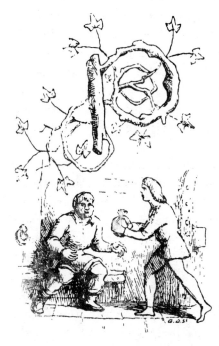

OOR little Gluck waited very anxiously alone in the house for Hans' return. Finding he did not come back, he was terribly frightened, and went and told Schwartz in the prison all that had happened. Then Schwartz was very much pleased, and said that Hans must certainly have been turned into a black stone, and he should have all the gold to himself. But Gluck was very sorry, and cried all night. When he got up in the morning there was no bread in the house, nor any money; so Gluck went and hired himself to another goldsmith, and he worked so hard, and so neatly, and so long every day, that he soon got money enough together to pay his brother's fine, and he went and gave it all to Schwartz, and Schwartz got out of prison. Then Schwartz was quite pleased, and said he should have some of the gold of the river. But Gluck only begged he would go and see what had become of Hans.

Now when Schwartz had heard that Hans had stolen the holy water, he thought to himself that such a proceeding might not be considered altogether correct by the King of the Golden River, and determined to manage matters better. So he took some more of Gluck's money, and went to a bad priest, who gave him some holy water very readily for it. Then Schwartz was sure it was all quite right. So Schwartz got up early in the morning before the sun rose, and took some bread and wine in a basket, and put his holy water in a flask, and set off for the mountains. Like his brother, he was much surprised at the sight of the glacier, and had great difficulty in crossing it, even after leaving his basket behind him. The day was cloudless, but not bright: there was a heavy purple haze hanging over the sky, and the hills looked lowering and gloomy.

30

And as Schwartz climbed the steep rock path, the thirst came upon him, as it had upon his brother, until he lifted his flask to his lips to drink. Then he saw the fair child lying near him on the rocks, and it cried to him, and moaned for water.

"Water indeed," said Schwartz; "I haven't half enough for myself," and passed on. And as he went he thought the sunbeams grew more dim, and he saw a low bank of black cloud rising out of the West; and, when he had climbed for another hour the thirst overcame him again, and he would have drunk. Then he saw the old man lying before him on the path, and heard him cry out for water. "Water, indeed," said Schwartz, "I haven't half enough for myself," and on he went.

Then again the light seemed to fade from before his eyes, and he looked up, and, behold, a mist, of the colour of blood, had come over the sun; and the bank of black cloud had risen very high, and its edges were tossing and tumbling like the waves of the angry sea. And they cast long shadows, which flickered over Schwartz's path.

Then Schwartz climbed for another hour, and again his thirst returned; and as he lifted his flask to his lips, he thought he saw his brother Hans lying exhausted on the path before him, and, as he gazed, the figure stretched its arms to him, and cried for water. "Ha, ha," laughed Schwartz, "are you there? remember the prison bars, my boy. Water, indeed! do you suppose I carried it all the way up here for *you!*" And he strode over the figure; yet, as he passed, he thought he saw a strange expression of mockery about its lips. And, when he had gone a few yards farther, he looked back; but the figure was not there.

And a sudden horror came over Schwartz, he knew not why; but the thirst for gold prevailed over his fear, and he rushed on. And the bank of black cloud rose to the zenith, and out of it came bursts of spiry lightning, and waves of darkness seemed to heave and float between their flashes over the whole heavens. And the sky where the sun was setting was all level, and like a lake of blood; and a strong wind came out of that sky, tearing its crimson clouds into fragments, and scattering them far into the darkness. And when Schwartz stood by the brink of the Golden River, its waves were black, like thunder clouds, but their foam was like fire; and the roar of the waters below, and the thunder above, met, as he cast the flask into the stream. And, as he did so, the lightning glared into

31

his eyes, and the earth gave way beneath him, and the waters closed over his cry. And the moaning of the river rose wildly into the night, as it gushed over the **Two Black Stones**.

CHAPTER V

HEN Gluck found that Schwartz did not come back he was very sorry, and did not know what to do. He had no money, and was obliged to go and hire himself again to the goldsmith, who worked him very hard, and gave him very little money, So, after a month or two, Gluck grew tired, and made up his mind to go and try his fortune with the Golden River. "The little king looked very kind," thought he. "I don't think he will turn me into a black stone." So he went to the priest, and the priest gave him some holy water as soon as he asked for it. Then Gluck took some bread in his basket, and the bottle of water, and set off very early for the mountains.

If the glacier had occasioned a great deal of fatigue to his brothers, it was twenty times worse for him, who was neither so strong nor so practised on the mountains. He had several very bad falls, lost his basket and bread, and was very much frightened at the strange noises under the ice. He lay a long time to rest on the grass, after he had got over, and began to climb the hill just in the hottest part of the day. When he had climbed for an hour, he got dreadfully thirsty, and was going to drink like his brothers, when he saw an old man coming down the path above him, looking very feeble, and leaning on a staff. "My son," said the old man, "I am faint with thirst, give me some of that water." Then Gluck looked at him, and when he saw that he was pale and weary, he gave him the water; "Only pray don't drink it all," said Gluck. But the old man drank a great deal, and gave him back the bottle two-thirds empty. Then he bade him good speed, and Gluck went on again merrily. And the path became easier to his feet, and two or three blades of grass appeared upon it, and some grasshoppers began singing on the bank beside it; and Gluck thought he had never heard such merry singing.

Then he went on for another hour, and the thirst increased on him so
that he thought he should be forced to drink. But, as he raised the flask,
he saw a little child lying panting by the roadside, and it cried out
piteously for water. Then Gluck struggled with himself, and determined
to bear the thirst a little longer; and he put the bottle to the child's lips,
and it drank it all but a few drops. Then it smiled on him, and got up,
and ran down the hill; and Gluck looked after it, till it became as small as
a little star, and then turned and began climbing again. And then there
were all kinds of sweet flowers growing on the rocks, bright green moss,
with pale pink starry flowers, and soft belled gentians, more blue than
the sky at its deepest, and pure white transparent lilies. And crimson and
purple butterflies darted hither and thither, and the sky sent down such
pure light, that Gluck had never felt so happy in his life.

Yet, when he had climbed for another hour, his thirst became intoler
able again; and, when looked at his bottle, he saw that there were only
five or six drops left in it, and he could not venture to drink. And, as he
was hanging the flask to his belt again, he saw a little dog lying on the
rocks, gasping for breath—just as Hans had seen it on the day of his
ascent. And Gluck stopped and looked at it, and then at the Golden
River, not five hundred yards above him; and he thought of the dwarf's

words, "that no one could succeed, except in his first attempt"; and he tried to pass the dog, but it whined piteously, and Gluck stopped again. "Poor beastie," said Gluck, "it'll be dead when I come down again, if I don't help it." Then he looked closer and closer at it, and its eye turned on him so mournfully, that he could not stand it. "Confound the King and his gold too," said Gluck; and he opened the flask, and poured all the water into the dog's mouth.

The dog sprang up and stood on its hind legs. Its tail disappeared, its ears became long, longer, silky, golden; its nose became very red, its eyes became very twinkling; in three seconds the dog was gone, and before Gluck stood his old acquaintance, the King of the Golden River.

"Thank you," said the monarch; "but don't be frightened, it's all right"; for Gluck showed manifest symptoms of consternation at this unlooked-for reply to his last observation. "Why didn't you come before," continued the dwarf, "instead of sending me those rascally brothers of yours, for me to have the trouble of turning into stones? Very hard stones they make too."

"Oh dear me!" said Gluck, "have you really been so cruel?"

"Cruel!" said the dwarf, "they poured unholy water into my stream: do you suppose I'm going to allow that?"

"Why," said Gluck, "I am sure, sir—your majesty, I mean—they got the water out of the church font."

"Very probably," replied the dwarf; "but," and his countenance grew stern as he spoke, "the water which has been refused to the cry of the weary and dying, is unholy, though it had been blessed by every saint in heaven; and the water which is found in the vessel of mercy is holy, though it had been defiled with corpses."

So saying, the dwarf stooped and plucked a lily that grew at his feet. On its white leaves there hung three drops of clear dew. And the dwarf shook them into the flask which Gluck held in his hand. "Cast these into the river," he said, "and descend on the other side of the mountains into the Treasure Valley. And so good speed."

As he spoke, the figure of the dwarf became indistinct. The playing colours of his robe formed themselves into a prismatic mist of dewy light; he stood for an instant veiled with them as with the belt of a broad rainbow. The colours grew faint, the mist rose into the air; the monarch had evaporated.

And Gluck climbed to the brink of the Golden River, and its waves were as clear as crystal, and as brilliant as the sun. And, when he cast the three drops of dew into the stream, there opened where they fell a small circular whirlpool, into which the waters descended with a musical noise.

Gluck stood watching it for some time, very much disappointed, because not only the river was not turned into gold, but its waters seemed much diminished in quantity. Yet he obeyed his friend the dwarf, and descended the other side of the mountains towards the Treasure Valley; and, as he went, he thought he heard the noise of water working its way under the ground. And, when he came in sight of the Treasure Valley, behold, a river, like the Golden River, was springing from a new cleft of the rocks above it, and was flowing in innumerable streams among the dry heaps of red sand.

And as Gluck gazed, fresh grass sprang beside the new streams, and creeping plants grew, and climbed among the moistening soil. Young flowers opened suddenly along the river sides, as stars leap out when twilight is deepening, and thickets of myrtle, and tendrils of vine, cast lengthening shadows over the valley as they grew. And thus the Treasure Valley became a garden again, and the inheritance, which had been lost by cruelty, was regained by love.

And Gluck went, and dwelt in the valley, and the poor were never driven from his door: so that his barns became full of corn, and his house of treasure. And, for him, the river had, according to the dwarf's promise, become a River of Gold.

And, to this day, the inhabitants of the valley point out the place where the three drops of holy dew were cast into the stream, and trace the course of the Golden River under the ground, until it emerges in the Treasure Valley. And at the top of the cataract of the Golden River, are still to be seen two **Black Stones**, round which the waters howl mournfully every day at sunset; and these stones are still called by the people of the valley **The Black Brothers**.

PETSETILLA'S POSY

BY
TOM HOOD

ILLUSTRATED
BY
F. BARNARD

Tom Hood, the English humorist and editor of *Fun*—the comic newspaper founded in 1861—was the son of the famous English poet Thomas Hood, author of "The Bridge of Sighs" and the long comic poem *Miss Kilmansegg and Her Precious Leg,* which was later adopted as a "children's" book.

Petsetilla's Posy was published in 1870, with illustrations by F. Barnard. Obviously influenced by Thackeray's *The Rose and the Ring,* this extraordinary political satire seems even stronger today than when it was published, and its humor and inventiveness are reminiscent of both Smollett and Sterne.

PETSETILLA'S POSY

THE BIRTH OF THE PRINCESS.

"May it please your Majesty," said the First Caudle-cup-in-Waiting, making her obeisance to King Bungo, who was smoking his cigar in the library after dinner, "May it please your Majesty, her most gracious Highness your Royal Consort has just presented you with a little girl."

"Dash my buttons!" said the monarch, with touching solemnity; a remark which was immediately entered in the State archives by the Secretary, who was seated at the top of the library ladder reading a large folio.

Immediately there was a great ringing of bells of all sorts, shapes, sizes, and descriptions, throughout the kingdom of Aphania. The steeples rocked again with the peals that were clashed out of them.

You see, the birth of the Princess was the signal for an unlimited number of appointments and promotions. For King Bungo and Queen Belinda had hitherto been childless; and trade, commerce, and Court had suffered in consequence. Now, however, every baker dreamed of a royal permission to write up, "Manufacturer of Tops and Bottoms to Her Infantile Highness;" and so on through all the trades, from the possible "Hairdresser-in-Chief to Her Serene Baldness the Baby," to the probable "Maker of Perambulators in Ordinary to the Juvenile Members of the Royal Family."

In the palace the excitement was yet greater, for there was no end of posts to be given away. There were Gold Papboat-in-Waiting, and Bottle-bearer-in-Chief, and Lord High Coral and Rubber-of-the-Royal-Gums, and First Lady Bib, and Second Lady Bib, and First Rocking Lady of the Bedchamber, and so on. Even the domestics were on the look-out. The pages, indeed, were at dreadful strife as to which of them ought to be the Princess's Husher-in-Chief. The duties of the office, though onerous, were of a distinguished and confidential character, consisting as they did of saying "Kitchee-kitchee!" whenever the royal infant was restless and desired amusement.

Perhaps the only person not entirely delighted at the birth of the Princess was King Bungo himself, who had fixed his hopes on a male heir to the crown. However, he was well enough pleased at the notion of having a child at all, and immediately gave his mind to the ordering of ceremonies and celebrations to do honour to the event.

His first object was to fix a day for the christening of the baby. As he was meditating on the best way of arranging the banquet for that occasion, he was interrupted by the entrance of the Royal Remembrancer.

"Your Majesty will permit me, I trust, to call to your august memory the fact that this is the Eighty-first of Blowsy."

You must know, my good readers, that in Aphania they had only four months in the year. They were called Growsy, Rosy, Blowsy, and Snowsy, and corresponded with our four seasons, Spring, Summer, Autumn, and Winter. The first-named three months counted ninety-one days each, while Snowsy boasted ninety-two and a quarter—an arrangement by which Leap-year, always a chronological anomaly, was very cleverly avoided.

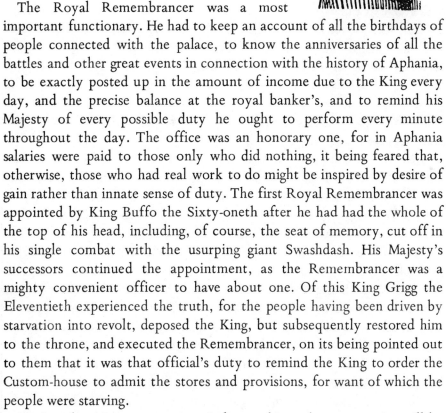

The Royal Remembrancer was a most important functionary. He had to keep an account of all the birthdays of people connected with the palace, to know the anniversaries of all the battles and other great events in connection with the history of Aphania, to be exactly posted up in the amount of income due to the King every day, and the precise balance at the royal banker's, and to remind his Majesty of every possible duty he ought to perform every minute throughout the day. The office was an honorary one, for in Aphania salaries were paid to those only who did nothing, it being feared that, otherwise, those who had real work to do might be inspired by desire of gain rather than innate sense of duty. The first Royal Remembrancer was appointed by King Buffo the Sixty-oneth after he had had the whole of the top of his head, including, of course, the seat of memory, cut off in his single combat with the usurping giant Swashdash. His Majesty's successors continued the appointment, as the Remembrancer was a mighty convenient officer to have about one. Of this King Grigg the Eleventieth experienced the truth, for the people having been driven by starvation into revolt, deposed the King, but subsequently restored him to the throne, and executed the Remembrancer, on its being pointed out to them that it was that official's duty to remind the King to order the Custom-house to admit the stores and provisions, for want of which the people were starving.

During the reign—or, more strictly speaking, the regency (as will be

45

hereafter explained)—of Bungo the First the situation of Royal Remembrancer had been a little arduous. Bungo was an irascible monarch, and when his memory—in the shape of the Remembrancer—jogged him to the performance of an irksome duty, he had the opportunity, which few of us have, though most of us would like it, of kicking his memory. The plaster, by numerous indentations on its surface, proved how often he had kicked that useful but unpleasant official up to the ceiling. But the State archives gave even stronger evidence of the fact. In those archives the Royal Secretary had to take down minutes of all the sayings and doings of the reigning monarch of Aphania; and when that potentate died, his successor had to learn the archives by heart, and had to pass a strict examination on them before the Civil Service Commissioners before he was allowed to ascend the throne.

Now, the Secretary of King Bungo had found the necessity of entering the kicking of the Royal Remembrancer so frequent, that when he got a new diary, he had printed after the date of each day, "His gracious Majesty was pleased to kick the Honourable the Royal Remembrancer ... times," and filled up the blank with a figure, which he found a mighty saving of time. It only remains to be stated that King Bungo's successor would have—calculating the amount by an average of five years—to remember a sum running to seven figures at least: rather hard would it prove to him if the Civil Service Commissioners elected to be strict on this particular point; as they were likely to be, the object of the

examination being to see how far the new King had seen his predecessor's faults, in order that he might avoid them.

However to return to our story.

"Your Majesty," repeated the Remembrancer, "will, I trust, permit
me to recall the fact that this is the Eighty-first of Blowsy."

His Majesty glanced at the calendar on the library mantelpiece, and
nodded rather sulkily.

"To-morrow, therefore, your Majesty, will be the Eighty-second of
that month, the day on which the Court pays its annual visit to the crypt
and the statue of his lamented Highness King Rumti the Hundred and
Ninetieth."

"Well, then, you must put a paragraph in the 'Royal Gazette,' that in
consequence of an event of paramount interest in the Royal Family, the
usual ceremony will be put off for a time, and that when the day is fixed
for its celebration, an announcement will be made."

The Royal Remembrancer bowed and withdrew, and King Bungo was
soon deep in the preparation of the list of distinguished guests to be
invited to the christening of the Princess.

KING RUMTI'S STATUE

I shall devote this chapter to an explanation of the Remembrancer's reference to the statue of King Rumti.

King Rumti was one of the most popular monarchs Aphania had known. He divided his time into two equal portions, devoting one-half to labours for the welfare of his people, and the other to study. He was at once the most benevolent and the most learned of men. He had founded no less than seventy alms-houses and a hundred hospitals, and had enriched the literature of his country by some two thousand valuable volumes.

You must know that Aphania was a peculiarly literary country. In all that regarded *belles lettres* its institutions were admirable. There was a special statute-book for literary offences, and a Court of Letters, pre-

sided over by six judges, who received immense salaries as a compensa-
tion for their necessary abstention from literature. They administered
justice promptly and impartially. Any person found guilty of borrowing
from the works of other writers, whether of Aphania or elsewhere, were
sent to the treadmill for three years. Adaptations from the French were
contraband, and violations of syntax were visited with capital punishment without benefit of clergy. Any one presumptuous enough to pen
such a sentence as, for example–"These laws of grammar, originally
promulgated by Lindley Murray, *and which* have been sanctioned by
general usage"–would have been immediately executed. To ensure
purity of style, all adjectives were kept at the National Library, and no
writer was allowed to use more than a certain number per diem without
a special licence from three at least of the Judges of Letters. In spite of
this stringency, numbers of books were published yearly, and most of
them were works of worth. With regard to publishing the regulations of
Aphania were peculiar. The publisher was allowed to repay himself for
every volume sold, at a certain rate on the cost of paper, type, and
binding, varying from one to five per cent, according to the style in
which he brought it out. As he ought to be, if anything, a better judge
than other people of the value of the books offered him, it was decreed
that he justly suffered the entire loss of publication if the book was
worthless. The writers, on the other hand, received everything (except
this percentage) which the books realized, it being laid down that the
success of the work depended entirely on what they added to the paper,
type, and binding common to all books. In case of failure they were held
acquitted by the cost of lost time and damaged reputation.

King Rumti had devoted so much of his time to study that he was still
a bachelor. He had been affianced in his cradle to one of the seventeen
daughters of the Archduke Koscybusco, of the neighbouring state of
Nexdorea, but had never been able to find time to select from the
family.

The Archduchy of Nexdorea supplied most of the neighbouring countries with queens, and had done so for many generations. All the female
children of the archdukes were turned out wild into an old palace and
park belonging to the ruling family. There they were allowed to grow up
without being taught their own language even. On reaching a marriage-

able age, they were duly catalogued, and a description of their beauties was sent to all surrounding and single potentates. As soon as one of them was selected for marriage by one of these princes she was transferred to the Royal Nursery Palace, where masters and governesses duly qualified speedily taught her the language of her future country, and the accomplishments and manners in vogue there.

The Ministers of King Rumti had ever been most anxious that he should make his matrimonial selection from the Archduke's daughters. One day when they were especially solicitous, and he was very anxious for a little quiet for study, he consented to marry the princess whose description he opened upon first in the Nexdorea Almanack, which contained the only authorized catalogue of the princesses. The book opened at page 116—chiefly because a young page had placed at that particular spot a fine specimen of the *Bedullus niger* or blackbeetle, which he had caught on the palace stairs. Without glancing at the letterpress, he passed the almanack to his First Lord Puller-of-the Purse-strings. That nobleman rose with dignity, and addressing the assembled Ministers, said in an impressive voice, "His Majesty will now oblige. Page one hundred and sixteen in the book. The Princess Ninni-Asterafina!"

Unhappily she was the eldest of the seventeen. Her age was thirty-two, and her looks unprepossessing. His Majesty's Ministers were cast down. But King Rumti, in the innocence of his heart, having first signed the official form for a proposal of marriage and immediate affiancing, dismissed his Council and gave himself up to his studies.

The fact was, that in the "Philosophical Transactions" published by the Royal Aphanian Society for the Promulgation of Apparent Absurdities, he had fallen in with a problem to investigate which he had devoted all his powers. The question propounded in the treatise was, to be plain, "How many caudal prolongations of the vaccine vertebrae would it require to describe a right line from the nearest point of the lunar periphery to a given point in the Earth's superficies?"

The Ministers quitted their King, and at once dispatched a special courier to Nexdorea to convey to the Archduke his Majesty's decision, gracious proposal, and act of betrothment.

Rumti plunged into his problem. "Taking," said he, for he thought aloud, like all great men in books, "the average bovine complement of caudal vertebrae to be twenty-six, and it being granted that each vertebral section varies in size in every instance; then there is no reason in logic to disprove the assertion that, supposing each such vertebral bone to be a twenty-sixth of the whole distance from this planet to its satellite, consequently it requires only twenty-six vertebrae, or, to put it briefly, one cow's tail, to reach"——

"Will your Majesty kindly give a poor woman a trifle of bread for three starving children?" said a plaintive voice outside the study window.

"Confound you, no! Go away!" bellowed his Majesty. He had already relieved seventeen beggars that morning.

A report like a cracker followed. The poor woman disappeared, and in her place stood a fairy, with tears in her beautiful eyes.

51

"Eh! what?" said the King, looking up. "I beg your pardon—you see—well!"

But the fairy only wrung her hands.

"What's the matter?" said Rumti.

"Oh, dear! oh, dear! how unlucky!" said the fairy; "I shall have to give you some dreadful punishment, and I don't want to do so. I know you were busy and didn't mean it; but it's out of my power to do anything—it's out of my jurisdiction. Nothing remains for me but to pass upon you the sentence imposed by the outraged laws of Fairyland. And I know you've been relieving no end of beggars, and that you didn't mean it—and oh, dear! what *shall* I do?"

And these two good-hearted creatures mingled their tears for a time in silence.

"I can't help it, really," said the fairy, after a pause; "but you know it's contempt of the Fairy Court, and the sentence is awful, and without the option of a fine."

"What is it?" asked Rumti in a perturbed voice. "You know I was hard at a very difficult calculation, and I'm very charitable—I am indeed."

"Yes, I know all that," said the fairy, weeping; "but the sentence of the Court is that you are to be changed into a stone statue, and remain in that shape until touched by an honest hand."

"You'll give me a little time to make a few arrangements?" said Rumti, nervously.

"All I can do is to order the transformation to begin from the toes up. So write away for dear life."

"Oh, only just a line to ask brother Bungo, the Regent during my temporary suspension of power, to get an honest man to touch me—that's all. It won't take a minute; and as soon as he sees it he'll have me

52

touched, and it will be all right again—and I shall be able to finish my paper in time for publication in the next 'Transactions.' "

Rumti seemed quite cheerful, and wrote his note with great spirits. But the fairy was not quite so hilarious: she shook her head at the mention of his speedy release.

As our readers will learn presently, the fairy had some reason to shake her head. The editor of the "Philosophical Transactions of the

Royal Society for the Promulgation of Apparent Absurdities" waited until the last moment for King Rumti's promised contribution; but the copy was not forthcoming, and, on the eve of going to press, he had to supply its place by inserting a paper by the President of the Statistical Institution "On the Nature and Properties of the *Faba coerulea*, or Blue Bean, with a Critical Commentary on its relations to the Mystical Number, Five."

When his Majesty had completed his note, he signed, sealed, and directed it. Then becoming aware that his transformation had begun and that his legs were changed into stone pedestals, he composed—or rather posed—himself to endure his doom with dignity. He submitted to the fate of being made a statue with more resignation and equanimity than would be likely to be displayed by any Englishman of note, if he knew how he was likely to look when "done in stone" after death.

A few hours afterwards King Rumti's Ministers, desiring an audience with him, entered, and found him turned to stone. Before him lay a note addressed to his brother Prince Bungo. They took it to that distinguished personage, and learnt that it contained his late Majesty's orders that Prince Bungo should be Regent during his (Rumti's) indisposition, and that the Regent should, in order to restore him (Rumti) to life and power, have the stone figure touched by some honest gentleman of his retinue.

On reading this epistle, Prince Bungo smiled, and then nodded three

53

times. At once assuming the second best crown (the Sunday one was changed into stone with Rumti), he proceeded in state to the study, and taking his seat on the royal dais, which was close to the dictionaries, he ordered the Court to pass before him in review, each individual laying his hand on the stone effigy of Rumti as he went by it.

When all present, from the Chancellor and Archbishop down to the Assistant Under-Warmingpan, had gone through this ceremony without restoring the stony monarch to life, King Bungo addressed his people—read them his brother's letter—stated that evidently that beloved monarch had forgotten to mention some other formula necessary for the reversal of the spell—and decreed that on that day, the Eighty-second of Blowsy, in every year, the Court should assemble and go through the ceremony of touching King Rumti's effigy, in hopes of restoring him to his mourning country and afflicted family. At this point his Majesty turned aside, it was believed with the intention of wiping away a pious tear. Something, at all events, affected his left eyelid!

At first there was some desire expressed by the common people of Aphania to see and touch the figure of their beloved King; but Bungo's Prime Minister addressed them, and explained that the lamented Rumti had expressly desired that "some honest gentleman of King Bungo's retinue" should break the spell, and that it would be a gross violation of their beloved monarch's last command to allow the charm to be reversed in any other way.

After a time the stone figure was found to be rather inconvenient as a piece of furniture in the library, so it was removed by the ten Lords-in-Waiting, in a crimson velvet sedan chair, and deposited in a crypt below the palace. The King kept the key of the crypt, which he visited once a year, according to his first arrangement, accompanied by his Court, and the ceremony of touching the effigy was gone through with due solemnity.

But still the whole Court, from the Chancellor and Archbishop down to the Assistant Under-Warmingpan, and even the Deputy-Assistant Under-Warmingpan, touched the figure without producing any change.

It was, indeed, stated in the principal literary review of Aphania, which was a very satirical journal, that the figure was observed to wink on one occasion when touched by Wangi, the Royal Fool. But it happened on that particular occasion that the Royal Cook complained to his Majesty that Wangi, in passing through the kitchen *en route* for the crypt, had stolen two black puddings, and this turning out to be true on the turning out of the accused's pockets, Wangi was whipped for dishonesty. What these cynical writers wanted to imply was that the Fool was the only man likely to be honest—in other words, that honesty is folly. Whereas it has been approved again and again that it is dishonesty that is folly, and that to be an honest man one has need to be wise indeed.

THE PRINCESS'S CHRISTENING.

By the time the christening feast was prepared, poor King Bungo was heartily tired of his paternal duties. You see, it was no joke to be the father of a princess and issue the invitations for her christening in those days. It is bad enough to give a party nowadays and forget to ask somebody who thinks he or she has a right to be a guest; but in those times, when every sixth person you met dealt in magic, and your next-door neighbour probably was a wizard, and your third cousin very possibly a fairy, the results of giving offence were awful.

It was a very common occurrence at that period, if we may trust contemporaneous history and the chronicles of Fairyland, to have some spiteful sorceress tumble down the chimney at a christening, abuse papa and mamma, frighten the sponsors into fits, and bounce away out of window in a car drawn by frogs, leaving some shocking spell behind her as a gift for the blessed babe, instead of a silver knife, fork, spoon, and mug.

King Bungo was too deeply read in the unhappy experiences of neighbouring potentates to commit any oversight of this sort. He had the whole kingdom of Aphania roofed in with tent-cloth, thus converting it into one gigantic banqueting-hall, and he inserted in the papers an announcement that everybody was invited to the feast, with a little note—"Friends will kindly accept this intimation," so that nobody could say he was not asked.

To be sure this was rather an expensive way of doing things, to dine people by provinces, and supply beef by acres and wine in real rivers. The First Lord Puller-of-the-Pursestrings ventured to hint as much to his Majesty, but was speedily reminded that his master was one of the first financiers of his day.

"My dear Duke," said the King, "charge this dinner at two pounds a head in the shape of a tax, and the outlay will recuperate itself, with a fair margin for profit."

Of course there was considerable difficulty in managing a breakfast of this territorial extent. Even with the aid of all the telegraph companies it would be impossible to get through the single toast of the Princess's health, for instance, in less than two days. At this rate it was computed that the dinner would be got through in one month—of course I mean an Aphanian month of ninety-one days.

The programme laid down for the day's (or rather month's) proceedings stated that immediately after the breakfast the royal infant would be borne to the cathedral, where the Archbishop would at once proceed to christen her in the presence of the whole nation—or at least so much of it as could get within sight even by the aid of the most powerful telescopes. The demand for such glasses was enormous. The papers teemed with advertisements of the wonderful properties of various lorgnettes.

THE CHRISTENING TELESCOPE will show the time by a Geneva watch twenty miles, a tandem whip at fifty, Jupiter's moons, the Royal Infant, &c.

THE BABY BINOCULAR.—The best, cheapest, and most powerful ever produced! Fits vest pocket, and arranged for use in Cathedral.

THE ROYAL INFANT.—The hair has positively been observed growing on the head of Her Infantile Royal Highness, by aid of Smouch's Binocular, at a distance of twenty miles and upwards.

Still, his Majesty protested, serious as such a gigantic undertaking as this banquet was, it was better to do it than to run any risk of offending some cantankerous sorceress or evil-disposed old maiden fairy. "Look at the King of Drowsihed!" said he, speaking of a neighbouring monarch. "His daughter was the victim of an oversight of this description. Some old crone took offence at not being invited, and doomed the child, if she touched a spindle before twenty, to fall asleep till some prince rescued her. Well, of course she *did* touch a spindle, and fell asleep according to the charm, and dozed away for a hundred years or so. To be sure at last the Prince *did* come, and she was brought to life again, and so was her father with all his Court. But look at the result! Did you ever see people

58

so awfully behind the age? Why, his Majesty won't trust himself in a train *now,* and he's been awake twenty years; and as for his Ministers, if their obstinate opposition to all progress does not drive the nation (which has not been asleep) into rebellion some of these days, my name is not Bungo!''

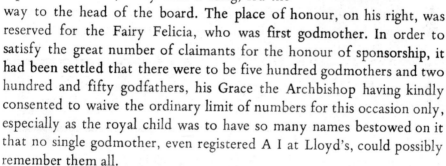

And really I think there was some force in his Majesty's remarks.

At length the day arrived for this most important pageant. King Bungo, looking a little pale and agitated, but in other respects, as the reporters declared, every inch a King, led the way to the head of the board. The place of honour, on his right, was reserved for the Fairy Felicia, who was first godmother. In order to satisfy the great number of claimants for the honour of sponsorship, it had been settled that there were to be five hundred godmothers and two hundred and fifty godfathers, his Grace the Archbishop having kindly consented to waive the ordinary limit of numbers for this occasion only, especially as the royal child was to have so many names bestowed on it that no single godmother, even registered A I at Lloyd's, could possibly remember them all.

It was customary to bestow a host of names upon children at their christenings at that period: of course, with the exception of one or two, they were afterwards dropped. In this case the baby's principal name was to be Petsetilla—and a very pretty name too, to my thinking, though his Majesty's First Lord Librarian, who was passionately given to geography, thought that Popocatapetl would have sounded very much prettier.

The place of honour on the Sovereign's right hand was, as I said, reserved for Fairy Felicia, an amiable and very powerful fay. King Bungo was leading her to her seat with ineffable joy, and with the inward satisfaction of seeing everything was going right, when he saw a sight that froze his blood with fear.

THE PLACE OF HONOUR WAS ALREADY TAKEN!

A most objectionable old sorceress, who was better known than respected throughout the country by the name of Aunt Sarah, had appropriated Felicia's seat.

She was a malignant but mighty sorceress; and when he thought of the necessity of asking her to vacate her chair for Felicia, poor King Bungo felt a stream of cold water running down his back.

Aunt Sarah was a person of repulsive appearance; and if her features were the reverse of attractive, her manners were simply loathsome. Her face was a smeary black, her lips were of the tint of vermilion, her eyes were odd, and her hair was like tow. She wore a dirty white nightcap with a wide flapping border, innocent of starch, had a dirty and ragged shawl pinned across her shoulders, and, worst of all, carried a pipe in her mouth!

"Here's a pretty go!" gasped his Majesty, all his accustomed eloquence and courtliness of diction deserting him in an instant.

"Never mind," said Felicia; "I shall be just as happy anywhere else: I'll sit on the other side of you. Don't run the risk of offending the old cat on my account."

The King darted a glance of gratitude at the good-tempered fairy, and led her to the seat on his left. Then he turned round and gave a sickly attempt at a smile of joy and welcome to Aunt Sarah.

"Well, Majesty," said that sprightly person, "here we are!" and then launched out into a flow of conversation so rapid and confusing that Bungo lost his head altogether, and took pounded sugar and marmalade with his salmi of pheasant.

However, he recovered himself in time, and the festivities proceeded. At last, just before the time to form the procession to church, Aunt Sarah bent over to the King, with a hideous smile, and said, "I am much flattered by your proposing to name the child Sarah."

"But, your Excellency," said Bungo, "we have no such intention—in fact—er——"

"Oh, yes, you *do* intend to name her Sarah," repeated the sorceress, with deep meaning.

The poor King's jaw fell on the frill of his shirt. He was confounded. All his plans for evading difficulties had failed utterly. He could only croak and wag his head.

"Come, out with it!" said Sarah sharply: "Yes or no?"

His Majesty did not know what to say or do. At last an escape suggested itself. He said he could not take upon himself to alter the Queen's arrangements.

"Here, you!" said Sarah, addressing the First Lady Back-comb of the Chamber, "go and ask her if the baby is not to be christened Sarah at once. Go!" And she stamped with her foot violently on the floor.

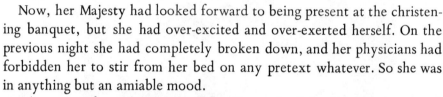

The First Lady Back-comb of the Chamber went and did as she was desired.

Now, her Majesty had looked forward to being present at the christening banquet, but she had over-excited and over-exerted herself. On the previous night she had completely broken down, and her physicians had forbidden her to stir from her bed on any pretext whatever. So she was in anything but an amiable mood.

When, therefore, the First Lady Back-comb of the Chamber came and told her of the presence and conduct of Aunt Sarah, and laid before her that ill-conditioned person's demand to have the royal babe christened after her, her Blessed Majesty said flatly, "No!"

When Aunt Sarah received the Queen's answer she turned nearly white with rage. She stamped and jumped with fury. She threw the stump of her pipe into the silver tureen of real turtle. She tore her cap-border into ribbons. Having somewhat relieved herself by these means, she grew sufficiently composed to address the King, who sat quaking in his chair without venturing to open his mouth.

"Harkee here, you wretched dummy of a King—you doll set up in a real King's place! I'll punish you for your pride and stuck-up notions! You won't give your child the simple and unaffected name of Sally! But I'll be revenged! Your daughter shall marry a beggar—there!"

With these words she waved her stick in the air, and a huge shandry-dan, drawn by daddy-longlegs spiders, made its appearance. Taking her place in the body of the vehicle, she shook her fist at the assembled company, took a fresh pipe out of her driving-box, and was commencing

to smoke it when her nimble steeds dragged her from the sight of the assemblage.

This little event threw a deep gloom over the company. His Majesty wept copiously into his plate, and as a point of etiquette his **guests** were compelled to follow his example.

The fact of his Majesty's weeping, and the cause which led to it, were promptly telegraphed to the guests at the foot of the table, who were so many miles off that even with the best telescopes they could not make out what was going on. The news spread over the whole country in the course of the day, and a general briny dilution of the soup was the result.

It will be observed by the careful reader that the soup was the last course at the banquet. This was the invariable custom at the royal table. It had been ruled by the Lord Chamberlain that a king ought not to eat

his dinner like any ordinary person, so the monarchs of Aphania always
began with the sweets and game, and finished with the soup. It was only
on great State occasions like the present that the general public was
permitted to imitate royalty, and eat its dinner wrong-side foremost.

However, to resume our theme. The malediction of the wicked sorceress brimmed the King's cup of misery, and his grief was shared by his
guests. But the Fairy Felicia was not dismayed at the spite of Old Sarah.

"Cheer up!" said she to King Bungo. "She might have done something
more terrible than that. If your daughter *does* marry a beggar, he will
cease to be one the moment he becomes your son-in-law. At any rate, if I
cannot remove the bane, I can administer an antidote."

As she said this she took from her waist, where it was fixed beside her
pocket-handkerchief, a large bouquet of pansies, the finest that you ever
saw. Approaching the cradle of the tiny Princess, she laid them on the
little thing's breast, saying,

"I give you heart's-ease, little one! while you have that you will be
content and happy, whether you wed an emperor or a beggar."

A ringing shout welcomed the enunciation of this pleasing sentiment.
The feeling of gloom disappeared, and the rest of the ceremony went off
with the greatest *éclât*.

KING BUNGO'S MEASURES

The day after the christening his Majesty rose late, but lost no time in calling together his Ministers, and consulting with them how he might best take measures for the safety of his august offspring. He was, as might have been expected, far from well this morning. His royal digestion was so generally out of sorts that he never was particularly well the day after a feast. On this occasion he took a frugal breakfast, a herring and a mug of small beer, having dispatched which repast, he put on his best coat, threw his dressing-gown over the back of the throne, and hastened to the Council-chamber. There he found all his Ministers assembled, and at once opened the proceedings by ordering the Clerk of the Council to read the report of the christening ceremony from the "Gazette."

This preliminary over, his Majesty called on his Cabinet to advise him how he should provide against the contingency of the Crown Princess becoming the bride of a beggar. The Ministers were immediately supplied with wet towels to stimulate their mental faculties and enable them to think more freely. The Pages of the Council-chamber, specially appointed for the duty, brought round the damp huckaback in silver pails. The Minister who dried the greatest number of towels in the session was rewarded with a real quill toothpick, at the annual ministerial dinner, in recognition of the activity of brain he thus displayed. In accordance with the customs of the Royal Assembly of Aphania, Bungo called upon the First Noodle of State in Council for his opinion.

Now, the First Noodle of State in Council was a most important dignitary. He was his Majesty's Chief Adviser, and was chosen from the Popular Talkhouse, which was a representative assembly looking after the laws and the taxes. The member who talked most nonsense and did least real work in that assembly was raised to his Majesty's Privy Council as First Noodle of State, and held that office for life, or until he began to talk sense, which disqualified him for the post. This office was first established by King Rumti's grandfather, Cagofango, surnamed The Easygoing, who said that the First Noodle was calculated to save him a deal of trouble, for that when once he knew what the First Noodle thought, he knew the opinion of that great majority of his subjects—the Nincompoops.

The First Noodle always commenced the discussion of any subject brought before the Council, and in any case on which the Council was divided he gave a casting vote, and whichever side he gave his vote for lost the division. You may well imagine, therefore, that he was greatly courted by his brother Ministers, who strove in every way to ingratiate themselves with him, and so win him over to the side—of their opponents.

The First Noodle in office at the time of this most veracious history was one Volliplas, who had earned the post by a silly habit of singing in the Popular Talkhouse, and on account of his constant asseveration that Boguey was at the bottom of everything. He had been in office twelve years, and it was very evident that he was not destined to break the rule that had ever held good—"Once a First Noodle always a First Noodle." No First Noodle (although as a rule First Noodles lived to a very great

65

age) had ever lost office on account of becoming disqualified by a sudden access of common sense.

This distinguished functionary, when called upon to propose measures to guard against the possibility of the Princess marrying a beggar, shook his head gravely, and was lost in thought for some time. At length he rose and expressed his opinion. He said he thought this was a design of Boguey's, and was going into a long tirade on the subject, when Bungo stopped him and brought him back to the point. He then said he saw two ways out of the difficulty: one was to pass a law declaring that no man might adopt the profession of a beggar unless he was married; and the other was to wed the Princess at once to the wealthiest single peer of the realm, and throw him into prison until she was of marriageable age, and a neighbouring prince had been chosen for her husband, when the nobleman's head might be cut off, and every obstacle removed.

This latter proposition was, of course, opposed by all the wealthy noblemen in the Council. As regards the former, it was upset by Duke Tunsend, who observed that beggary was not a profession that is sought, but a calamity that befalls a man. He was for hanging all vagrants out of hand.

Bungo, who was not a cruel monarch, would not listen to this, nor was he more inclined to adopt the suggestion of the Colonial Secretary, who was for exporting beggars, and exchanging them for tea, sugar, and foreign produce.

The Lord Chancellor at length proposed a measure which was generally approved, and in the end carried. It was, that a tax should be levied to build almshouses for all poor people who were too old or too ill to work, and that officers should be appointed in every town and village, who should be bound, on penalty of losing their heads, to find employment and wages for the able-bodied poor on works of public utility. As all members of the royal Cabinet were exempt from taxes, there was no opposition to the scheme, and "An Act for the Better Regulation of

Mendicity" was at once made and passed. And that Act directed that all persons who were found after the date of its promulgation begging contumaciously and in disregard of the royal mandate should be then and there executed by the common hangman without the option of a fine. In the matter of this last section the First Noodle proposed to add, in order

to insure vigilance, that one-half of the penalty should go to the informer.

His Majesty, before dismissing the Council, begged of them to advise him in an affair which was not of public importance, like the suppression of beggars, but was of the deepest personal interest to him. His daughter had received a nosegay from the Fairy Felicia, who promised her happiness as long as she preserved her gift. What was best to be done to preserve it?

The First Noodle rose and said, that "although this was not an official assembly, he would take the liberty of opening the proceedings and making the first motion—the more, because he felt that the proposal he was going to make was so admirable a one that he felt sure it would at once disqualify him for the high office which it had been his honour and delight to hold so long."

At this there was a slight commotion among the Ministers, and all gave ear in breathless silence.

"What were the facts of the case before them?" asked his Noodleship. "The Fairy Felicia had presented the royal babe with a bunch of flowers. While the royal babe kept those flowers she would retain complete happiness; if she lost them, happiness would depart. Now, taking into consideration the existence of Boguey, he thought it not improbable that the flowers would be lost. What he proposed, therefore, was that, in order to prevent any possibility of the Princess's losing the posy, his Majesty should have it burnt at once."

The Council gave one sigh of relief, and the motion was ordered to be

brought forward again "to-morrow"—which was the official term for "never," because to-morrow never comes. Duke Bingi suggested that his Majesty would do well to consult the Most Honourable Guild of Gold-smiths and Jewellers, who would contrive some safe but ornamental depository for the treasure. And his Majesty saw the propriety of the suggestion, and thanked his Grace. Whereupon the Council was dissolved, and the Ministers went away to luncheon.

The Most Honourable Guild of Goldsmiths and Jewellers were promptly summoned to the palace, and Bungo explained to them that a fairy had presented the baby Princess with a bunch of flowers, which would insure her contentment and happiness so long as she preserved it. He desired them, therefore, to devise some very costly and beautiful casket wherein the posy might be enshrined, and which the Princess might be able constantly to wear.

The Most Honourable Guild of Goldsmiths and Jewellers at once laid their heads together, and the result of the combination of blocks was that they agreed to send in designs for the casket by the end of the week for the King's approval.

Accordingly, at the appointed time the competing designs were submitted, and a splendid assortment they formed. The King was quite at a loss how to decide, for it had always been a tacitly acknowledged rule of the competitions that the Royal Jeweller should carry off the prize; but in this instance his design (perhaps because he made sure of success) was not at all a good one. Now, his Majesty Bungo had never murmured about the rule when the competitions related to services of plate for public purposes or decorations for publics *fêtes*; but in this case his private and personal interests were touched, so he very naturally hesitated to act according to the old precedent.

He determined, like a brave man, to ask his wife's advice, and then, if her opinion were the same as his, he could lay the blame of this departure from precedent on her shoulders.

Her Majesty at once pronounced in favour of a small casket, or rather large locket, shaped like a heart. It was to be made of the purest gold, inlaid with huge diamonds. On one side of it was to be the Princess's monogram, each letter being formed of a distinct gem of a corresponding initial; for example, "P" for Petsetilla was to be of pearls. This insured a pleasing variety, because, though the babe would be known as Princess Petsetilla, she bore also a hundred family names as well, which were always conferred on the crown Princess of Aphania.

On the other side of the casket, which was encrusted with fine rubies, there was to be a representation in jewels of the fairy's gift, with the legend in diamonds, "PETSETILLA'S POSY."

It should have been mentioned that while the Honourable Guild of Goldsmiths and Jewellers were to compete for the design, they were to combine to execute it, in order that the best work might be insured. The

selected design was to receive a premium equal to two thousand eight hundred pounds nineteen shillings and elevenpence three farthings, as nearly as can be given in English money, the Aphanian currency being a very complex decimal coinage, which it would take too long to explain.

The jeweller whose design was selected was one Rusko Pobochinki—and he took the prize like a man. But the artist who drew it for him—Clemmo by name—only received about five shillings for his work, and was a poor man with a large family to support. However, to Pobochinki's credit be it recorded that he generously presented the struggling draughtsman with a share of the premium—the odd three farthings, in fact.

It may be noted that the excellence of the design was confirmed by the decision of the Noodle-in-Chief. That distinguished functionary, when it was submitted to him, at once assumed the airs of a connoisseur. Placing the drawing against a chair, he retired to a convenient distance, and, standing on his head, inspected it gravely for several minutes. He then rose, and, standing on one leg, regarded it for a quarter of an hour through a long roll of blue paper. Next he carefully rubbed the back of the drawing against his organ of benevolence, and finally pronounced that "the technicalities were badly scumbled, the middle distance was out of keeping, and the *chiaroscuro* was *impasto;* in short, the design was bad." This was at once pronounced a conclusive triumph for Pobochinki.

His Majesty ordered the Most Honourable Guild of Jewellers and Goldsmiths to proceed forthwith to execute his commission with the greatest dispatch. He gave them ten days to complete the locket, and declared that on every day that they kept him waiting beyond that time he would behead a master craftsman. The result was that, although one or two workmen perished from over-heat and over-work, not a hair of the head of a master craftsman came into peril, for the casket was delivered at the back door of the palace two hours before the expiration of the ten days.

The casket was a masterpiece, and charmed their serene Majesties beyond everything. In fact, everybody was delighted except the Royal Jeweller, who did not approve of any one but himself gaining a competition. He took the liberty to explain this to King Bungo when next his Majesty called to have his royal watch regulated.

"Well, you see," said the King, leaning over the counter and speaking in a low voice, "I thought some of that service of plate you made for the Corporation was not eighteen carat; and though I did not care to make a disturbance about such a trifle, why—eh?"

And the abashed jeweller hung down his head.

"Not a bad shot!" said King Bungo, as he left the shop. And, truth to tell, it was but a random shot, for the King had never looked at the Corporation plate at all. He wanted an excuse, and that was the first that came into his head. But the Royal Jeweller was conscious that some of the minor articles were not of the best gold. The salt-spoons lay heavy on his conscience, so he held his tongue and hung down his head.

PETSETILLA'S YOUTH, AND BUNGO'S BOTHERS

I have told you that the Aphanian nation was given to literature. As a consequence it had always encouraged a vast number of beggars. I do not mean that it encouraged a quantity of needy authors, for the laws of the country were wise ones, and protected the interests of its writers. But you cannot make books without paper, and in Aphania—at least in those times—you could not make paper without rags. The rulers of Aphania, therefore, had most judiciously shown favour to the mendicant who was an importer of rags from other countries, where he was looked on with less favour. The new Act for Repressing Mendicancy accordingly caused a considerable stir throughout the kingdom, and was not regarded with entire satisfaction by the tax-paying community.

But another class suffered beside the tax-paying class. The manufacture of paper, being one of the largest trades in Aphania, had created another industry—the rag-collecting trade. This was in reality one of the largest and most important interests in all Aphania.

There were immense numbers of people engaged in it, from the highest to the lowest. For while the capitalist sold rags by the ton to the paper-maker, he had to collect it from the marine-store dealer by the hundredweight, and the marine-store dealer bought it by the pound from the rag-collector.

The rag-collectors were but poor people, though they were better paid than English agricultural labourers. They had laborious and unpleasant work to perform. Like the *chiffoniers* or rag-collectors of Paris, they had to grope in the mud of the kennel for the rags, and, like them, they had to work at night; for it was found, very early in the existence of Aphania as a literary nation, that it was impossible to allow the rag-gatherers to bring their calling into collision with the street traffic during the day.

Now, when the new Act for the Suppression of Beggars came into force, though it did away with the old class of mendicants, it almost produced a new one. The rag-gatherers were nearly made beggars, owing to the loss of a large source of material. The people of Aphania began to murmur, and to hold meetings, and to clamour for a repeal of the law. They didn't care much about the beggars, they honestly admitted; but what with the loss of the rag supply and the increase of taxes, they were too hard pressed, and they called on King Bungo to do something to ameliorate their condition.

King Bungo was a very crafty monarch, and he met his people—so he told them—half-way. He assured them that the additional taxation and the decrease of mendicancy were State necessities. It was impossible to repeal the Act which enforced them, but he would do what he could to lessen the burdens they inflicted. He promulgated a sumptuary law by which he compelled all his courtiers and every citizen who signed himself "Esquire" to have a new suit of clothes every month, and throw the old ones into the street. This, his Majesty observed, would give a new impetus to an important industry, and the improved condition and larger profits of that industry would make themselves felt through every grade, and would go far to compensate for the extra taxation by extra prosperity.

His Majesty moreover passed a bill for the further representation of his people. By this statute he allowed them to send a representative of their own choosing to the royal Cabinet Council, such representative to be styled "The Under-Noodle of State in Council."

The people of Aphania were satisfied with these concessions and promises, and his Majesty beheld, with great satisfaction, peace and contentment reigning throughout his kingdom.

In the meantime the little Princess Petsetilla grew up. A more amiable child never was met with. Her kindness of heart and her happy disposition, her patience and her consideration for the feelings of others, made her the idol of the palace.

She always wore about her neck the massive gold chain to which was attached the magnificent locket containing the fairy's gift. This was one of the first objects of which she learnt the meaning. She cut her teeth on it as a baby. She learnt her alphabet from it as a child—at least all the letters of the alphabet contained in the device upon it. And now when she was a young girl of seventeen she still remembered what had been constantly dinned into her ears—that that locket was the thing on which all her good fortune depended. Her nurses taught her this lesson at the very dawn of her understanding. "There, my dear," they would say, "as long as you keep that locket you are all safe!" or "That locket will guard you against all the ills of life if you only take care never to part with it."

Now, this was all very well in its way, but it never occurred to them to tell the child that the virtue lay not in the locket, but in the little withered bunch of pansies inside it. I think it very likely they really had come to forget what was inside it—or indeed that it contained anything. But what came of all this? Why, that little Petsetilla was taught from infancy that it was the locket that was the charm—that as long as the gold and the jewels were hers she was safe. So no wonder she thought more highly of the gold and jewels than they deserved.

Furthermore, she heard at times, when people praised her and said what a sweet duck of a child she was, that "Oh! of course she is: it's because she wears that locket she's so good!" So she began to think that only those people were good who wore gold and jewels.

But the sweet disposition with which Fairy Felicia's gift endowed her shielded her from the ill effects of this teaching. She was not haughty or

74

unkind to people even who did not wear gold and jewels, but she used to be sorry for them, because she feared they were not good, and sometimes she wanted to give away her bracelets and rings to poor people because she thought that would make them good.

She was a very beautiful girl now. Her hair was of the most lovely golden hue, and her eyes were quite blue like forget-me-nots. She had a skin as white as milk, and her cheeks were delicate rose. Her lips were like two cherries, and her teeth seemed like a string of pearls. In fact, she was exactly as beautiful as all the princesses in all the fairy tales always are.

Her portrait, according to the usual custom of romantic lands and times, was sent round to all the neighbouring Courts. But whether it was that photography had done scant justice to her charms—and indeed a fair person never looks well in a *carte*—or the neighbouring princes did not feel assured of the throne of Aphania while there was a chance of King Rumti's being restored to animation, it is impossible to say, but it is very certain that nobody sought her hand in marriage. His Majesty was greatly distressed at this lack of suitors. He was most anxious to see his daughter well married, for the words of that vindictive old Aunt Sarah were constantly ringing in his ears.

A DECLARATION OF WAR, AND BATTLE ROYAL

To make matters more unpleasant for Bungo, his people about this time began again to show signs of discontent.

The Under-Noodle of State in Council was found to do little to promote the interests of the people. This is hardly to be wondered at, since in the royal Council he had not even as much weight as the First Noodle. It had turned out, too, that the sumptuary law was of little service to the rag interest. The clothes thrown away each month were in such good condition they could not be manufactured except at a great outlay, and instead of going to the paper-mill, they were caught up by ready-made clothesmen, who did a large export trade in them. The only people who gained anything were the tailors. They made so much money that they clubbed their wealth together, in companies of nine, to purchase a peerage—peerages were sold in Aphania, though they cost immense sums of money—and they used to take it in turns to wear it for a year at a time.

The tailors, I say, profited by the sumptuary law, but all other trades suffered. For wealthy people even when they were compelled by law to spend so much money on clothes, found it necessary to reduce their expenses in every other respect. So there was a very general discontent throughout all Aphania, and public meetings were called again, and popular orators made violent speeches, and the Ministers could not advise his Majesty what to do, so that he was for once very nearly driven to take the advice of the First Noodle of State, and cut off everybody's head. But he was saved by the Under-Noodle's objecting that if he did so he would have no subjects left, and as a man can't be a king if he has no subjects, he would have ceased to be a king. So after all, even the Noodles couldn't help his Majesty, and he was at his wits' ends.

You may be certain that the disturbances in Aphania were sure to get into the papers, and their importance was rather exaggerated than diminished. By this means, the news of them came to the ears of the Archduke of Nexdorea, who was no friend to Bungo. The Archduke determined to take advantage of Bungo's misfortunes; but it so turned out—as it often happens—that this enemy was the best friend his Majesty had.

The Archduke of Nexdorea was the intended brother-in-law of King Rumti. His father, the Duke Koscybusco, had died in a fit of apoplexy, produced by the sumptuous wedding banquet of his seventeenth and youngest daughter. Of all the seventeen daughters but one remained unmarried, the Princess Ninni-Asterafina. Of course, as she was betrothed to King Rumti, and he was not dead, though he could scarcely be described as alive, she was not marketable. The new Duke had therefore to maintain his spinster sister, and he didn't like it, and as a consequence felt a grudge against all Aphania in general and King Bungo in particular. He was a man of an impetuous and vindictive temperament, was the new Archduke. His name was Fizpopoff, and he was married, but his wife had presented him with boys only. Now, as the fortunes of the reigning family of Nexdorea had been chiefly made by their large families of daughters, for whom they made good marriages, the Archduke was not

too pleased at his Archduchess's obstinate predilection for male offspring. On the birth of the tenth boy he had expostulated with her vehemently. It was even reported that he had resorted to argument in the form of a horse-whip. But he failed to convince her. It was a great trial for him, poor man! for the Duchy of Nexdorea was but a small place—it was nearly all swallowed up by the royal park where the Princesses were allowed to run. It did well enough as a nursery-ground—a sort of forcing-bed for royal marriages, but it was a poor place to have twenty Princes to provide for.

But a bright idea occurred to the Archduke one day. He must enlarge his kingdom by conquests. If the Duchess went on as obstinately as she began, he would soon have quite an army in his own family. Yes! he determined to invade some neighbouring territory. He had everything to gain and nothing to lose. He was allied by the marriages of his sisters to a great many potentates, who would protect him if the worst came to the worst, and if his invasion ended in the conquest of his own duchy by the enemy. In fact, his first great difficulty was to find out somebody to invade who was not a relation. While he pondered over this, Aphania occurred to his mind, but it was so very large a country he had not the courage to invade it. Now, however, when he learnt that it was racked by internal dissensions, his scheme did not appear so impossible of execution.

His Grace was seated at the breakfast-table, reading his paper, when the idea of invading Aphania flashed across his mind.

The Princess Ninni-Asterafina was making the breakfast, for the Arch-duchess was upstairs, having just presented her lord with the twentieth boy.

Alas! the Princess Ninni-Asterafina was sadly changed for the worse. She was the oldest and plainest of the Princesses when King Rumti chose her for a bride, and though the portrait of her in the Nexdorea Almanack was a most flattering one, it is doubtful whether, had he looked at it, he would not have telegraphed after his messenger to stop the proposal; but, as we know, he was changed into stone before he had time to work out the problem about the cow's tail, and long before he could have had a chance of consulting the portraits in the only authorized official catalogue of the marriageable Nexdorean Princesses.

Princess Ninni-Asterafina was terribly altered. Her nose was longer and sharper, her eyes were more like boiled gooseberries, and her cheeks were hollower and yellower than when she was first taken up from the park to the palace, to be trained in the language and customs of Aphania.

She had conceived a violent affection for King Rumti, although she had never set eyes on him or his portrait; but she had been dimly conscious that, when he demanded her hand, several of her younger sisters had been promoted to matrimony over her head, and she began to think she was doomed to celibacy. She was very grateful, therefore, to the monarch who chose her, and when she heard of his sad metamorphosis she fainted away, and had a violent fit of hysterics, and altogether behaved in a most sentimental and affectionate manner.

She was still brought up to be Queen of Aphania, although Rumti had not been restored to life, and she became attached to the country which was practically her native country, for of the land in which she was born she knew nothing, and therefore could care nothing for it, thanks to that admirable provision of a park for the rearing of wild princesses.

When she had finished her education, as Rumti was still metamorphosed, she was transferred from the training-palace to the archducal residence. Her father Koscybusco was still living when first she came, and after his death of course her brother could not in decency turn her out; but he made it remarkably uncomfortable for her. If she had been his wife he could not have treated her worse. In fact, he behaved towards his wife and his sister with the sternest and strictest impartiality. If he threw his right boot at the head of one, he always threw the left at the head of the other, to maintain the balance of power. Of course, on those

79

interesting occasions when the Archduchess was confined to her room upstairs, the Princess Ninni-Asterafina got both boots, and therefore she was twice as miserable as she was when her sister-in-law shared her troubles.

On this particular morning the Archduke had been less ferocious than usual. He only threw his slippers at her, because his boots had not yet been brought upstairs. His flinging the toast-rack at her because his third cup of coffee was rather cold was so slight an attention it could hardly be considered anything. When, however, he roared aloud for his boots, openly declaring that he wanted them in order that he might at once set out to seize on Aphania, the Princess gave a little shriek.

"What, invade Aphania, Fizpopoff! No such thing!"

"No such thing, indeed! How dare you interfere, Miss?" bellowed his

80

Grace, snatching up a plate of buttered toast and launching it at his sister's head. The Princess, who had had some practice, dodged the missile adroitly.

"You can't invade my kingdom—you shan't!—it's mine!"

"Yours? Pshaw! Why, don't you know that some kind fairy changed old Rumti into a stone figure in order to save him from the misery of marrying *you*, you old fright?" And the Archduke emphasized the "you" by discharging the sugar-basin at his sister.

"Monster!" screamed the lady, rising defiantly above the hailstorm of sugar-nobs; "monster! you know that is untrue, and that he may be restored at any moment to wed me, and then I will be avenged!"

"Humph!" said the Duke, "if he was fool enough to propose to marry you then, he would certainly know better than to think of it now, when you're as old and as ugly as his great-grandmother!"

"I'll appeal to the husbands of my sisters!" said the Princess, with dignity.

This was an unpleasant threat. Out of sixteen brothers-in-law he might well expect to meet with some who would oppose his unprincipled scheme of aggrandisement. The Archduke scowled, and stretched out his hand for the poker, which seemed the only logic left him to close the argument. But all of a sudden the gloomy expression changed for one of pleasure: he burst into a loud guffaw.

"Look here, you old cat! Am I not the most affectionate brother in the world? I am going to invade Aphania because I consider that you are its rightful Sovereign. There, what do you say to that?"

"I don't believe a word of it," said his sister, frankly.

"I don't care whether you do or not—other people will."

"But you can't conquer Aphania! They would beat you disgracefully, as you deserve."

"No, they won't, because they are in a state of open rebellion almost, being discontented with their present ruler, and my offer to place the wife of their beloved Rumti on the throne would insure my success."

"Then I'll have my ever-lamented Rumti restored to life if you do," said the lady, spitefully.

81

"No, you won't! for first of all I shall break the old image up to mend the roads with, and have another made like it, and then all the honest men in the world may touch it till their fingers are sore!"

And I regret to say that his Serene Highness the Archduke was so delighted with this idea that he put his hands on his knees, like Clown in the pantomime, and waggled his head, and said, "YAH!"

Now, if there was one thing more than another which exasperated the generally amiable Princess Ninni-Asterafina, it was her brother's performance of the pantomimic feat just recorded, and his utterance of that irritating monosyllable "Yah." She could not bear it, so without more ado she threw the coffee-pot at him. He retaliated with the kettle, and a battle royal ensued. The noise became so loud that it reached the kitchen where the archducal footmen were. Those gallant fellows knew what the uproar meant.

"There's their r'y'l 'Ighnesses hat it agin. Let's go and clear hup."

Whereupon they went up in a body, and at once removed everything from the room. The Archduke and the Princess having then no missiles left to throw, left off throwing, and peace was restored.

"Send me the Chief Secretary," said the Archduke to the head footman. "Tell him to bring pens, ink, and paper—and, here—stop!—tell him I shall want some 'declaration of war' forms—he can get them at the nearest stationer's. And," his Serene Highness added after a pause, "Tomkins, you'd better order a new breakfast service."

REMSKY IN RAPTURES

There dwelt in Aphania at this time a rag-gatherer whose name was Raggatti, and who had an only son called Remsky, apprenticed to a market gardener whose garden was without the city gates.

The market gardener was employed to supply peas to the palace for the royal pigeons, and the youthful Remsky was entrusted with the task of conveying the peas every week to the Lord High Pigeoner.

You must not for a moment suppose that there were any royal pigeons. No such things! There had been once upon a time, but so long ago that the very pigeon-cotes had tumbled into decay and gone the way of all firewood. In the reign of Gorgius, who was a great gourmand, and in fact died of a surfeit produced by an over-feast of larks' tongues stewed in truffles, the whole of Aphania was overrun, or I should perhaps say, overflown, with pigeons. That dainty monarch considered that pigeons were made only to lie with their feet sticking out through pie-crust—and he adored pigeon pie. So he kept a multitude of pigeons, and appointed a Lord Pigeoner to look after them. In order to restrain the birds from injuring the crops of his subjects, the King commanded the Lord Pigeoner to supply them with fifty bushels of peas daily, to be thrown down in the palace courtyard. After the death of Gorgius, his son and successor having become rather bored with pigeon pie, which he had had every day for dinner since he was a boy, allowed the birds to be killed and eaten by his subjects. The Lord High Pigeoner, however, was a man of great influence, so the young King did not dare to interfere with his perquisites and dignity. So the Lord Pigeoner continued—long after the last pigeon had made its acquaintance with pie-crust—to order in the fifty bushels of peas daily. For the market gardener who supplied the peas for which the Privy Purse paid, supplied the Lord Pigeoner with fruit and vegetables all the year round *gratis*. Of course his lordship did not care to relinquish this profit, and so the peas were sent in every day.

It was the etiquette of the Court of Aphania—as, I have read, it is also of every other Court—never to notice anything. Wherefore the peas were allowed to accumulate—to the no small inconvenience of those about the Court—and nobody said a word about them, till the King, one morning going out to cross the courtyard, was nearly knocked down by a rush of peas directly he opened his private door. The new monarch was young and inexperienced, so, without calling his Ministers together, he ordered the peas to be instantly removed. He was obeyed. But before long he found that he had been guilty of a crime against the constitution.

The Lord Chamberlain explained to his youthful Majesty that his interference with the peas precedent was dangerous and most unconstitu-

85

tional—that monarchs had lost their crowns, and heads too sometimes, for less. But he proposed a way out of the difficulty. Of course the Lord High Pigeoner must still order in the peas, and the peas must still be delivered in the courtyard as heretofore; but his Sacred Majesty might appoint a Lord Comptroller of the Peas, who would have those vegetables conveyed from the courtyard to a convenient and capacious warehouse in which they could be stored, to be dispensed gratuitously to the poor in the form of pea-soup.

Young Remsky, as I have said, brought the peas to the Royal Palace every day. It was hardly possible that he should perform this daily duty very long without catching sight of the Princess. It was *quite* impossible that he should see her without falling in love with her.

Remsky was a very handsome lad. He was tall and well proportioned. His long hair fell in dark ringlets on his shoulders, and his eyes were piercing black. A downy moustache shaded his upper lip, and his complexion was of an olive colour.

One morning when this goodly youth was superintending the usual uncarting of the peas for the figurative royal pigeons, he happened to cast a glance up to one of the galleries which ran round the courtyard, and he beheld one of the loveliest visions that he had—I won't say ever *seen*—but ever dreamt of!

A beautiful girl, with long golden tresses, and the most exquisite complexion, clad in a simple white robe, edged with what fashion-books would call a *ruching* of pale blue ribbon, was passing along the gallery. She was petting a lovely little green paroquet which she carried on her finger, and the silvery tones of her voice as she spoke to it, enlarged to hopeless dimensions the hole which her bright eyes made in the susceptible heart of the young market gardener.

It was the Princess Petsetilla.

How intensely poor Remsky wished he was that green paroquet! *He* couldn't have pecked at her lovely finger, as the ungrateful bird did after the fashion of its unamiable species. *He* wouldn't have called himself "pretty Polly" in the presence of such unrivalled beauty, as the pert creature did, after the manner of such conceited birds.

What would he not have given to exchange his monotonous task of providing peas for imaginary pigeons, for the delightful duty of feeding the green paroquet which he so envied! That was a duty, by the way, which three pages were appointed to perform. They were young noble-men, of course, varying in age from eight to thirteen, and they liked to play at leap-frog and hop-scotch better than to feed the Princess's bird; so the "Pages of the Paroquet" had an easy time of it, like many other officers about the Court, and Princess Petsetilla, as she did not wish to see her pet starved, had to feed it herself, and a pretty penny it cost her out of her moderate weekly allowance to keep it in finger-biscuits, for the dainty little wretch would eat nothing else.

From that fatal morning poor Remsky could think of nothing but the beautiful Princess—for he soon learnt that the lovely being who had made so deep an impression on his heart was the Crown Princess.

He became quite an altered young man. He grew pensive and studious. He lost all his interest in horticultural pursuits, and gave his mind up to growing capital "P's" in mustard and cress all over his master's garden, until that exemplary nurseryman, feeling sure that the popular taste for cress and mustard was not extensive enough to make this lavish sowing remunerative, put a stop to it.

The only resource the poor lad had was to fling himself with greater ardour than ever into the cultivation of peas for the royal pigeons. He solaced himself with the knowledge—a knowledge which he owed to his zealous attention to his lessons at school—that "P" stood for Petsetilla as well as for Pigeons and Peas.

The attention which he bestowed upon the peas was not at first very pleasing to his employer, who thought that quite inferior peas would answer admirably to feed imaginary pigeons or make soup for poor people. But his apprentice grew such remarkable peas that people noticed them; and, as soon as they learnt that they were grown to supply the royal pigeons, they offered the gardener large sums of money per peck for them. Because, you see, there were plenty of persons who felt in a sort of way that they were dining with Royalty, if they could only have a dish of the royal peas.

Of course, when he went home at night, poor Remsky could grow capital "P's" in mustard and cress as much as he liked, and he did so in every available spot. Now, as you can grow mustard and cress in a saucer, on a basket, and on a bit of flannel or a nightcap, you will easily guess

what a large field the young market gardener had for the horticultural expression of his passion. His father and mother were devotedly fond of him, and rather than interfere with his pursuits, put up with a great deal of inconvenience. But when his mustard-and-cress mania had been carried so far that they all three had to eat off one plate, and take tea off one saucer, and Raggatti's last nightcap was engaged in rearing a promising crop of green stuff, it was necessary for the parents of the misguided boy to question him as to the meaning of his eccentric gardening.

His mother, unfortunately, had not been to school; and she described his efforts at vegetable caligraphy as "growing soup-ladles in mustard and cress." His father, however, was well educated, and deciphered his green efforts. They pressed him closely for an explanation, and he loved them too well to withhold it.

"I am," he said, "merely a poor gardener's-boy, and I can only express my feelings in the language and in the manner to which I have been accustomed all my life. If I were a poet, I would sing the name of the lady I love in such exquisite verse, that all the world would stand still to listen. If I were a painter, I would depict her with such noble skill, that everybody should lose their hearts to the canvas, as I had lost mine to the reality. If I were a mariner, I would sail the world round till I discovered some new Paradise in the sea, which I might name after her. If I were a soldier, I would carry her favour in my helmet through all opposition and over every obstacle and compel all whom I conquered to confess her the Queen of Beauty. If I were any of these, I would do what each might and should do. But I am only a poor gardener's-boy, and so all I can do is to grow the initial of her beloved name in mustard and cress!"

"You're in love, then?" said his mother.

"And her name begins with a P," said his father.

"I can't bear the name of Polly," said the mother.

"Peggy is worse, I think," said the father.

"Patty isn't nice!" said she.

"Nor Prue, either, for that matter!" said he.

"But isn't Petsetilla a beautiful name?" cried the unhappy Remsky, forgetting what a confession he was making.

The two old people were struck dumb for a time.

"Princess Petsetilla!" they both gasped out at last.

And then Raggatti began to shake his head, and went on shaking it for just three quarters of an hour and four minutes, while the mother covered her head with her apron, and sobbed audibly.

When they had quite exhausted their grief, Remsky told them how and where he had first seen the Princess, and confessed that he was deeply, madly, desperately in love with her; but his was a happy disposition, he said, and a contented mind. He loved her, but his love did not make him miserable. He would go on loving patiently and sincerely, and he felt, somehow, that some day he might have a chance of proving his devotion. If not, he should die satisfied with the knowledge that he had loved the loveliest of princesses.

Whereupon, as there was nothing better to be done, they went to bed.

HOW THE POSY CHANGED HANDS

I began the last chapter by telling you that Raggatti, the rag-collector, and his son, lived in Aphania, near one of the city gates; but I had so

90

much to say about Remsky, and the way in which it came about that he
fell in love with Petsetilla, that I was not able to give you much
information about Raggatti.

Raggatti was the most industrious of all the rag-gatherers of Aphania.
He was the earliest astir in the evening, and the last to turn in of a
morning, and he went over his ground so carefully, that the man who
happened to go rag-gathering in his wake didn't get much for his trouble.
He had a well-earned character for honesty, too. Of course, the rag-
gatherers were constantly picking up articles of value that had been
dropped in the streets. Now, by strict letter of the law, as laid down by
an Act passed in the reign of Cagofango, all articles so found became the
property of the finder; "for," said the learned legists who drew up that
statute, "if the previous owner had valued the article, he would have
taken pains not to lose it." But, as very often happens, public opinion in
Aphania did not coincide with the ruling of the statute; and all honest
people restored "treasure trove" to its rightful owner. Nevertheless, the
less scrupulous folk could lawfully appropriate what they found; and, as
a rule, the rag-gatherers were not scrupulous, except as far as the rigid
observance of this one particular statute was concerned. But Raggatti
had never been known to avail himself of the law. He always took pains
to find the owner of anything he picked up, and made it a point of
honour to take no reward for his honesty, though at times he wanted
money sorely enough.

There were members of the rag-gathering profession who formed a
society which they called "The Honesty League." They pledged themselves always to restore all treasure trove, and never to take, keep, or
hold anything that did not belong to them. Those members who had
never been found out in a breach of this pledge were crowned with
wreaths of roses, and the society used to march in procession at times,
wearing these crowns and garlands, and blowing trumpets in their own
honour.

Raggatti would not join this society, or accept a wreath of roses, for
he said that to be honest was only one among a dozen equally important
duties, which every good citizen should perform. He did not see, he said,
why he should be crowned for being honest, any more than for being
sober; that if a man was to be crowned for doing one duty, he ought to

91

be crowned for doing each of the others; and that if that were so, the longest-headed man in all Aphania would not have enough cranium to accommodate the wreaths.

This gave great offence to the Honesty League, and as Raggatti often received presents from people who admired his character, the members of the society endeavoured to pass a law which should make the receiving of presents a punishable offence. They argued that because people took what was given to them, they became liable to take what was not given to them; that, in short, the mere fact of taking was likely to tempt them to the crime of stealing. As, however, the only person they could prevail upon to bring this measure before his Majesty's Ministers was the First Noodle of State, the bill never became law.

Raggatti, being a very humble-minded creature, went on his way quietly, never supposing that a lot of clever people were trying to crush him by Act of Parliament. He worked hard, late and early, and was grateful to all who aided him, not less grateful to those who only gave him a kind word. He continued to get his daily food, pay his rent, and, what was more, sent his boy to a good school, and then apprenticed him to the royal market gardener. If he had been an Englishman, instead of an Aphanian, he would probably, when he was sixty years of age, have received a pair of new corduroys and twenty shillings from an appreciative country gentry, but as he was only an Aphanian, he did not get even that. But he had the satisfaction of a clear conscience, a good appetite, and the knowledge that his son might do better than his father had done, if he was only equally ready to make the most of his opportunities.

I don't fancy Raggatti thought that Remsky had made the best of his opportunities when he discovered that the youth had fallen over head and ears in love with the Crown Princess. But he felt that the lad could not help it, and he pitied him; for, you see, Raggatti, like most good men, had fallen desperately in love with his wife before he married her (not that I mean he didn't continue to love her after they were married), and so he could feel for his son and appreciate the love he bore for the Princess Petsetilla.

Very early one morning he was hard at work turning over a heap of dust close underneath the palace walls. It was just daybreak, and the golden sunlight was streaming up the sky, filling all the air with a gleaming haze of glory, in which the larks would have been lost but for their songs. For there were larks in Aphania, because, by the great charter of Aphania, out of every ten acres included within the city wall, two were bound to be left in a wild uncultivated state of heath, as play-ground and lungs for the neighbourhood.

The Princess Petsetilla thought the song of a lark one of the sweetest things you could hear; and she always rose early to listen to it. And it so happened that on this particular morning she opened her window, and looked out just as old Raggatti was below.

The rag-gatherer heard the sound of the opening casement and looked up. It was the first time he had ever seen the Princess, for he was not one to run after State processions, having business of his own to attend to. He knew from the description Remsky had given him that this must be Petsetilla, and he felt that his son had shown remarkable taste in fixing his affections on so lovely a being.

So there stood Raggatti looking up at Petsetilla, and there stood Petsetilla looking up at the larks. And there was one very big and very melodious lark soaring just over the palace—so big and so melodious that I think it must have been, as was afterwards reported, the Fairy Felicia in disguise. Petsetilla listened to it and watched it with the greatest delight, and in order to see it better as it soared still higher towards heaven she leant far out of the window. In doing so, without noticing it, she pressed the spring of the locket she wore round her neck against the window-sill. The locket opened—and a withered bunch of heart's-ease fell out of it and dropped into the street.

The little dry, insignificant-looking bunch of pansies fell at Raggatti's feet. He knew nothing of their history, and supposed they were only some dead flowers the Princess was throwing away.

"I'll take them home to Remsky," said he. "They will be a relic for the poor boy to keep. They have stood upon the Princess's table, and no doubt while they were fresh and bright she loved and admired them, and so he will value them thought they are withered."

As for Petsetilla, she did not see the locket open and did not notice the fall of the posy. I very much doubt, if she had seen it fall, whether she would have thought anything about it. For, you see, she was told that the locket was the charm—that her happiness and welfare depended

93

on that gold and jewelled ornament, and she had never heard a word about its contents.

But somehow, just as Raggatti picked up the posy, Petsetilla felt that the morning was rather chilly. She gave a little shiver, and thought to herself how silly it was to get up at that early hour just to hear a little bird chirp. Her tirewoman was sound asleep, for the Princess never used to wake her to dress her at such an early hour. But she felt this morning that it was very lazy of her attendant to sleep on so soundly. She shut the window down with a bang, and suddenly determined to undress and get into bed again. But she could not get to sleep at all. She was restless and unsettled, and tossed and tumbled, and never closed an eye until nearly nine o'clock, so that she had just got into a nice doze when her tirewoman brought her her early cup of tea. But Petsetilla didn't want the tea and didn't like being disturbed, and so for the first time in her life she spoke crossly to the poor girl. And then when she had done it she was angry with herself, so she vented her dissatisfaction by finding fault with the tea, and at last turned over in a pet and tried to go to sleep again. But she didn't get her nap until she cried herself to sleep over the thought that she was very naughty and fretful.

But she never guessed the real cause of the change, and as for the locket, that had snapped-to again, so that she would have no reason to suspect its contents were gone even had she known that it had ever had anything inside it.

Raggatti had not had a very profitable night's work, but as soon as he picked up the posy he turned his steps homeward.

"I've been very lucky," said he to himself, "very lucky indeed, for besides the rags I've gathered—and I might not have found any at all!—I've seen the Princess, and I've got a keepsake for Remsky."

So he hurried homeward singing cheerily all the way, and so happy and contented that he quite forgot he had had nothing to eat all night until he saw the breakfast that his good wife had prepared for him. And then he sat down and ate with a relish, and never seemed to know that the bacon was a little rancid and that there were too many horse-beans in the coffee.

He had not sat down many minutes before Remsky made his appearance. Raggatti would not tell his son about the posy till the lad had finished his breakfast, for fear pleasure should spoil his appetite. But when Remsky was just ready to go, the old man told him of his morning's adventure, and at last produced the little withered bunch of flowers.

Remsky seized the poor posy and kissed it reverently. Then he folded it up in a clean kerchief, and buttoned it up beneath his jerkin over his heart. And after that, as it was time for him to go to his work, he took leave of his parents and hastened away to the garden.

"Poor boy!" said Raggatti, "I'm glad I was able to bring it to him—though, to be sure, I wasted some time about it. I haven't collected half as many rags as I ought to have done—I've not done a good night's work. But, my dear," said he, turning suddenly to his wife, "what's the matter with the bacon? I didn't notice it till this minute, but it tastes very odd! what can it be?—it isn't the coffee, is it? That doesn't seem as good as it should be."

You see, Raggatti had parted with the posy now, and that made a difference in him.

And what alteration did it make in Remsky? why, none at all! He was happy and contented already, and all the fairy posies in the world couldn't improve his disposition in that respect.

But as Felicia's gift was thus entirely lost on the gardener's boy, I can't help thinking what a pity it was that Petsetilla didn't get it back at once, for she was fretful and peevish now, and all her attendants suffered for it, and suffered the more because they had never known her to be anything but good and kind and considerate before.

95

"Lawk bless us!" said one of the waiting-women to another as they stood behind the Princess's chair while her hair was being done, during which operation the Gold Brush-and-Comb in Waiting caught it rather severely, "lawk bless us! any one would think she'd lost the fairy locket, only you can see it's there round her neck!"

"What is all that noise?" asked the Princess presently.

"If you please, your Highness, it's the peas being brought in for the pigeons," said the First Lady in Waiting.

Now, the Princess had seen the peas brought in often and often, but it seemed to her there had never been so much fuss and noise about it, so she looked out to see how it was that it annoyed her so.

She saw Remsky superintending the unloading of the carts.

"Dear me! what a handsome young man!" said she; "it's a pity he's not good and happy and contented, which he is not, for he has no gold or jewels about him—not so much as a stud or sleeve-link!"

And Remsky, looking up, said to himself, "Fairest of princesses, what bliss it is only to look upon you! I am too blest to have the privilege of being so near you."

And then he went back to the garden and sowed a very large letter P in mustard and cress.

WAR DECLARED

There was some consternation, I can tell you, in Aphania when the
Envoy of his Serene Mightiness Fizpopoff, Archduke of Nexdorea, rode

97

into the market-place; for it was evident from his wearing his helmet wrong side foremost that he was bound on a warlike mission. The Archduke's herald, by name Bramantip, was a person of commanding appearance. He rode on a splendid black charger, and bore a huge silver clarion. His tabard was splendidly broidered, and a long white ostrich plume adorned his helm. The arms of Nexdorea were blazoned on the herald's tabard and on the banner attached to his clarion. The arms of Nexdorea, I ought to tell you, were, according to the Heralds' College, "gules, on a bend, or, a goose and six gooselets waddlant in their pride, proper; crest, a blue-nose baboon snorant, proper, in an arm-chair, argent; supporters, two hen's eggs proper, cracked, sable:—Motto, "Poached or Pickled."* These armorial bearings, as you may suppose, looked very noble when embroidered in gold, silver, and bright silks.

Bramantip reined up his charger in the centre of the market-place, and blew a single blast on his silver clarion. Thereupon, Disamis and Dimaris, the heralds of King Bungo, who had been duly informed by post of the proposed visit of Bramantip, took up their place on the steps of the town hall, and dispatched their pages, Baroko and Bokardo, to ask the stranger's mission, and conduct him to the Royal Heralds.

The pages led Bramantip to the town hall, each holding one of his gilded reins. When he had saluted the Royal Heralds by dropping the mouth-piece of his clarion towards the ground three times, he placed it to his lips and blew a challenge.

Disamis and Dimaris answered with a blast on their gold bugles, and then the parley began in the prescribed form.

"How many horses has your master got?" asked Disamis.

"Three," replied Bramantip, in a defiant tone.

"What colour are they?" asked Dimaris.

"Crimson, yellow ochre, and ultramarine!" responded the herald.

"Then turn round three times and state what your master's instructions have been," was the answer.

Then Bramantip doffed his helmet, and, resting his reversed clarion on his knee, made the following proclamation in a loud voice:—"Know all

---

*The chief produce of Nexdorea consisted of hens' eggs, which were exported to all the surrounding countries. Hence the allusions to poultry in the arms.

men by these presents"—here he tossed a handful of silver pieces down for the Aphanian crowd to scramble for—"that we, Fizpopoff, Serene Mightiness, Electoral High Seignior, and Hereditary Archduke of Nexdorea, do hereby proclaim and enounce, *caeteris paribus,* and if not, why not, and how otherwise? that we, ruler by direct descent from Hollaboys the First, do, in consideration of the affiancement, spoongelt, and betroth-splice of our august sister, the serene and lovely Ninni-Asterafina, Princess of Nexdorea, with Rumtius Rex, lawful and only recognized Monarch of Aphania, claim, demand, and of right intend for to make our own, the Regency of the said kingdom of Aphania, on behalf of the said Serene Loveliness and the said recognized Sovereign. Wherefore, why, because, and on which account, we, the already-enumerated Serenity, do call upon Bungo, heir presumptive to the throne of Aphania, and at present unlawful occupant of the said throne, to vacate the same, here, now and immediately, hei presto cockalorum *ad libitum,* and in *twinkelinguio bed-postii.* In proof whereof witness our hand and seal, to counterfeit which is felony under Act of Parliament for the Better Registration of Trade Marks. And lastly, in conclusion, finally, and to sum up the matter, our aforesaid Serenity doth hereby solemnly mention that, supposing the recited Bungo do not vacate with promptitude, we, the heretofore-quoted Fizpopoff, do declare war to the last drum-stick against him, and will prosecute our righteous and just conflict with him while a parchment remains unburst. And to prove our sincerity, there lies our glove, seven and three quarters long fingers."

When Bramantip had concluded his harangue, Disamis stepped forward, and said in a loud voice,

"Oh, yes! oh, yes! oh, yes!! Does not his Serene Mightiness the Archduke of Nexdorea and Electoral High Seignior of that province very much wish he may get it? We, the august and powerful Bungo, by appointment Regent, and in presumptive right Monarch of all the Aphanias, hereby accept the Archduke's challenge, taking up his glove, and defy him to combat to the last beat of drum. Whereto witness King Bungo, his mark. Hip! hip! hurrah!"

Disamis picked up the glove which Bramantip had thrown down. Thereupon, the Archducal Herald produced a long green silk purse from the pocket of his tabard, and emptying the money it contained into the streets, exclaimed,

99

"We, the Serene Archduke, acccpt the defiance, and hereby to prove that we rely on the justice of our cause, rather than our super-eminent resources and insuperable valour, we do present our heretofore friends and henceforth enemies with a largesse to enable them to buy muniments of war. Long live Fizpopoff!"

"And now it's all over," said Disamis, at once laying aside all official hauteur, "hadn't you better come in and have a stoup of something?" For, of course, all heralds, like Freemasons, were brothers, and Disamis thought a good deal more of Bramantip, the enemy's herald, than of the first general in King Bungo's army. The crowd had by this time dispersed, finding there was nothing to be got; for the money which the herald distributed was Nexdorean currency, and as the Nexdorean currency consisted of brass and german-silver, it was of no value in Aphania. The scattering of a largesse to enable your enemy to buy muniments of war was a ceremonial peculiar to the territory, and was never neglected. King Bungo, however, was so disgusted at the Archduke's meanness in sending money which was not exchangeable against Aphanian coins, that he sewed it up in a sack, and returned it by Bramantip, with "his compliments, and he was too old to play at dumps, and these medals were of no use for any other purpose."

This terribly enraged the Archduke, as you can fancy, and he vowed that he would burst his biggest drum, but he would have his revenge for the insult.

With this intention he enrolled three hundred of the bravest drummers in all his army into one regiment, and he had the returned largesse made into buttons, which were sewn on the uniform—a pale green turned up with chocolate—which he selected for this picked corps. They were to lead the van of his invading forces, and the most powerful drums in his armouries were appropriated for their use. On the front of their shakos was the regimental motto, "Pfitskyichewdiki," which is the Nexdorean of "for the honour of our halfpence."

King Bungo called his Privy Council together, and announced that he was about to enter into a war against the Duke of Nexdorea, who wished to assume the rule of Aphania, on the grounds of his sister's engagement to Rumti. The nobles were indignant at the insolence of this petty Prince, and immediately offered their services to their King. Each

101

promised to bring all his vassals into the field, and engaged to send in within three days a muster-roll of the number of drums he could lead into the camp. It was determined to assemble the people the next day, when the King should address them. It was felt that the threatened invasion of the Archduke would enrage the people against him, and restore them to their allegiance to the King.

This was exactly the effect produced, which, as you know, was the very opposite of what Fizpopoff had calculated upon. The populace cheered King Bungo loudly when he appeared in full armour on the balcony of the palace, and hundreds volunteered active service that very day. Popular excitement was at its height for the next few weeks. The papers teemed with articles breathing a warlike spirit, and the street bards chanted war-songs and played the national air of Aphania on their barrel-organs.

BUNGO FOR EVER!   DOWN WITH FIZPOPOFF!

was chalked on the walls, and a farce entitled "The Archduke's Boots," in which the Archduke was made up like the ruler of Nexdorea, and was submitted to all sorts of indignities, was produced at the principal theatre, and received with enthusiasm. The satirical journals were very severe upon the invader, who was held up to ridicule in their columns as Squib-pop-bang, and depicted as an exploding firework.

In the meantime gigantic efforts were made to bring the army into an efficient state. The Most Honourable Body of Benchers of Justice, the very flower of the legal profession, voted seven thousand sheets of parchment and two thousand of vellum for drum-heads, and the Duke Bingi, who was the largest proprietor of timber plantations in all Aphania, gave free permission to the whole army of drummers to go into his forest and cut their sticks. A spirited and ingenious civil engineer, who invented a machine for making metal drums at the rate of four a minute, was knighted on the spot, and made Chief Inspector of Drummery.

You will have noticed, I fancy, that I have spoken of nothing but drums in describing the warlike preparations of the Aphanians. The reason is that they fought with drums, and I will tell you the how, why, and wherefore of their so doing in the next chapter.

OF THE PEACE CONGRESS AND BOOTINTER

Any one who knows his "Universal History" must know all about the "War of the Shoe-strings," which lasted for thirty years and nearly depopulated seven kingdoms, two archduchies, and a republic. It began in the reign of King Goariboo of Aphania, who was, indeed, the cause of the war. For that monarch commanded his people to adjure shoe-strings and adopt button boots, which gave serious offence to King Lobo of Carinia, a country that dealt largely in hides, and consequently had an interest in the sale of shoe-strings, which were always made of leather in these regions. The Aphanians were not slow to appreciate the benefit of buttoned boots, and the commerce of Carinia languished accordingly, for the Aphanians everywhere extolled button boots, and their example and advice had great weight with the surrounding countries. Of course Lobo could not go to war on this pretext, but his representative at the Court of Goariboo was ordered to persevere in wearing shoe-strings with long ends, although the official directions for Court dress forbade shoe-strings. The Carinian Ambassador, therefore, appeared at a *lévée* with the long shoe-strings, and was not allowed to pass. A long correspondence ensued on the subject, and the diplomatists of both nations had their hands full. The quarrel spread—other countries became entangled in the dispute; and in the end, seven kingdoms, two archduchies, and one republic found themselves squabbling about an ambassador's shoe-strings. The difficulty, however, might have been avoided, but for an unfortunate accident. At a conference held in Aphania to settle the dispute if possible by arbitration the representative of Lobo was present, and, as a matter of course, wore his long shoe-strings. King Goariboo, who was also present, had the ill-luck to tread on them and untie them, and when the Ambassador rose to go, he tripped over his own shoe-strings and had an ignominious tumble. The next day war was declared, the different Powers concerned took sides, and the contest raged for thirty years, when the combatants left off from sheer weariness.

At the end of the war the various nations concerned found themselves in a very reduced state. Not only had they spent vast sums and run heavily into debt, but their male population was sadly diminished, all the men capable of bearing arms, who could be persuaded to enlist, having entered the army and got killed. Only the wise fellows who did not see the object of risking their lives on the question of a shoe-string were left, and they turned their wisdom to account as soon as peace was declared. They began an agitation against war, which resulted in the assembling of a Peace Congress of all nations.

At that Congress it was agreed that in future war must be conducted on a principle which did not involve loss of life. Bloodshed, as was shrewdly observed by the president, was not argument; wars, therefore, were not logical, and could not be carried on logically. It was necessary to find a substitute for fighting.

At first it was proposed that duels between the kings or statesmen who quarrelled should decide the matter, but this was not quite sweeping enough as a reform. It was next suggested that disputes should be settled by tossing up a coin, and crying "obverse" and "reverse;" the side which called correctly twice out of three times to be considered the conqueror.

This was scouted as democratic. Finally it was determined that battles should be fought with drums, and that the side which drummed the loudest should be held to be victorious.

This proposal gave general satisfaction for many reasons. It did not do away with armies, the pomp and circumstance of soldiering, and the solid advantages of commanding and officering; it also retained the semblance of a contest, and would encourage skill and enterprise in the construction of drums. The members of the Congress signed a solemn undertaking that from the first of next month they would settle all national disputes by appeals to drums instead of arms, and all the contracting nations vowed that they would see the agreement carried out, and unite in punishing any nation that ventured to depart from the rules of the Congress.

The Peace Congress lasted for a week, and went off without any quarrels or fisticuffs, which was rather an unusual thing for a peace congress to do.

All the nations at once set about reorganizing their war departments. Spears and guns were sold by public auction, and were bought up by the agriculturists for hop-poles and pea-sticks. Swords were utilized as carving-knives, sausage-machine blades, and scythes. The money thus realized was expended on the purchase of drums. Mutton became so cheap, in consequence of the slaughter of sheep for the sake of their skins, that you could get prime joints at three-halfpence a pound. Lamb, on the other hand, became proportionately dear, lamb parchment being too small for military purposes, and the farmers consequently feeling reluctant to kill the animals when so young.

All the inventive skill of the various countries was turned to the manufacture of drums. The Governments offered prizes for the loudest and most portable drum, and the competition was of the liveliest character. Meantime, sword and cutlass drill, bayonet exercise, and rifle-shooting fell into disuse, and all the soldiers were set to learn the tattoo. The whole vast tract of territory resounded with "rub-a-dub-dub" from morn till night.

In Aphania, which, as has been frequently recorded in this story, was a literary country, the new mode of warfare, and the noisy drum practice consequent thereon, were anything but popular. There was a stir about it

in the Talk House, and it was finally decided that a district called
Bootinter on the sea-coast should be devoted to the training of the
soldiery and the manufacture and trial of big drums.

To the scientific traveller, Bootinter was a place of great interest, and
was invariably visited by all tourists of note who could obtain a pass
from the War Department. Most interesting trials might be witnessed
there; the great contest carried on being that of "Drums *versus* Cotton
Wool."

There had been a great change in the defensive armour of the soldier,
as a natural result of the change in the method of warfare. A pith helmet
with padded ear-flaps, quilted with cotton wool, was adopted. The
object in making these helmets was to defend the organs against the
noise of the drums, and the object in making the drums was to overcome
the deadening effects of these padded protections on the sound of the
instruments.

The contest was carried on with varying results. A very loud drum
would be invented, and a large number manufactured for the troops at a
great outlay; when, suddenly, a new medicated wadding would be
discovered, which rendered the new drum inaudible. Thereupon, a bigger
and louder drum would be made, and the medicated wadding, of which
large quantities had been ordered, would be found useless, and a new
experiment had to be tried. And so the contest went on until the drum
had become a colossal instrument, from which sound was produced by
volleys of cannon-balls, and the wadded helmets had become so huge and
heavy that they had to be supported on a light wheeled framework
something like a go-cart.

The Aphanian army was inspected twice every year, and was in the
highest possible state of efficiency; although it was hinted by some of
the journals which were opposed to King Bungo's Ministers, that the
supply of drums was defective, and that, in spite of the enormous sums
spent on the trials, the best instrument had not been chosen. It must be
admitted that there was some slight ground for these complaints, for the
biggest and noisiest drum had not yet been invented; and until it was, the
authorities were desirous not to spend too much money on articles that
would have to be condemned and thrown aside. Just at the time of the
war with Nexdorea, an ingenious person had made a discovery that was

calculated to effect an enormous saving in the expenditure. Hitherto, the cotton wool used for the helmets had been a vegetable produce, but the inventor of the new article manufactured it from the fleeces of the sheep which supplied parchment for the drums. For this economical plan he was presented with a gold medal and a hundred a year. He might have made a hundred thousand a year by his invention, had he been allowed to carry on the manufacture as a private speculation, but that, of course, was not allowed—it became the monopoly of the Government.

The archduchy of Nexdorea was, as has been said before, only a small principality, and its army was far from numerous, while its drums were still of a primitive and inferior character. But Fizpopoff turned his relationship-by-marriage with so many powerful monarchs to good account. His brothers-in-law might have declined to lend him their armies if war had been still conducted on the old plan, but by the new system there was no loss of men, and only a little wear and tear of parchment, so they made no objections; indeed, they rather profited by the arrangement, as Fizpopoff, of course, would have to pay and victual the troops.

Fizpopoff took the field with a very large force, therefore, and his troops were armed with every variety of drum, from light infantry with skirmishing tom-toms, to heavy cavalry with kettle-drums, and artillery with enormous instruments drawn by twelve horses apiece.

Although Aphania was the larger and more wealthy country, nevertheless the two armies, thanks to the Archduke's allies, were on pretty equal terms. If, as the public prints of Aphania openly avowed, the Bootinter trials had not produced a really serviceable drum that would stand the wear and tear of a campaign, the prospects of King Bungo were far from brilliant, and it must be admitted that the invasion created a considerable panic, and the Funds were in a very bad way.

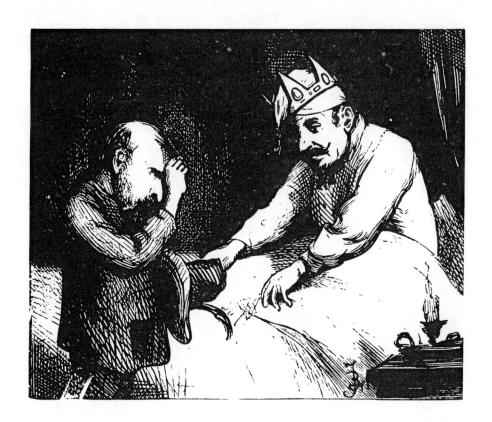

THE INVASION AND INVESTMENT

The Aphanian army was posted on the frontier, as it was expected that Fizpopoff would enter at the nearest point; but that crafty individual took a circuitous route through a friendly and neighbouring state, and entered the Aphanian territory within a few miles of the capital. The townsfolk were, of course, thrown into the utmost consternation, for the Archduke's army cut off all communication with their forces, and there seemed to be a very strong probability of the place being carried, and its inhabitants put to the drum, before the alarm of the invasion reached the defending troops on the frontier.

The news of the approach of the hostile army was brought by Remsky, who was engaged in driving the usual waggon-load of peas to the palace. On observing the approach of the enemy, he pulled up, and jumping from the shafts, concealed himself by the roadside. The vanguard of the Archduke's army, coming up almost immediately, took possession of the waggon, and in their delight at such a prize did not trouble themselves to look for its original owner. There were two things of which the Nexdoreans were passionately fond—music and vegetables; and the soldiers looked forward with rapture to a cheap but unlimited repast of pea-soup. As soon as they were out of sight, Remsky took to his heels, and avoiding the main road, ran as fast as his legs could carry him to the town. He gave the alarm, and the gates were closed, while Disamis and Dimaris hastily summoned all capable of bearing drums to the defence of the walls. There was but one regiment of regulars in the place, and that was the household troop of "Bungo's Own." Their drums were not for use but show, being headed with tissue-paper only; so that they were of no avail for the defence, which had to be entrusted to volunteers and civilians.

The alarm had already spread to the palace when Remsky reached it to report the capture of the peas. The Lord Pigeoner, true to his duties, although the whole Court was in an abject state of terror, was awaiting Remsky in the courtyard, and heard the lad's story with infinite disgust; "For," said he, "those browsing Nexdoreans are so fond of greenmeat, they won't leave a single pea in the district; they'll devour mustard and cress by the acre, and cabbages by the mile!"

King Bungo, on learning the extent of the calamity which threatened him, assembled his family and his immediate attendants, and made them a most feeling address, beseeching the latter to defend the palace to the last drum-head. He announced his determination not to relinquish the crown, even though he were deafened in its defence.

"You, my child," said he, turning to Petsetilla, "you have nothing to fear. You wear round your neck a charm which will insure your happiness and content wherever you are. But, as the value of the locket may tempt the rapacity of the invader, we will remove the posy to some less attractive keeping."

"Posy! what posy?" asked the Princess; "I shan't give up my pretty locket for any one!" And she stamped her foot.

The King was surprised at this ebullition of temper, though he had

fancied once or twice of late that his child did not display the equable temperament that had graced her younger days.

"Petsetilla, my love!" said the Queen, "do not grieve your poor papa, at a time when he has so much to harass and distress him. He is showing the greatest consideration for your welfare. In that locket is the fairy gift—the dried bunch of heart's-ease—on the retention of which depends your happiness. No one would think of stealing the withered bunch of flowers, but the locket is valuable, and might become the spoil of the enemy. You had better take out the posy, and"——

"But I never knew there was anything in it," said Petsetilla. And she at once proceeded to open the locket, which, as we know, was now empty!

At this discovery the King turned deadly pale, staggered back, and sank into a chair. The Queen fainted away, and all the attendants, as they were bound to do by Court etiquette, began to wring their hands and wipe their eyes.

"It must have been stolen!" said his Majesty, when he recovered himself.

"No," said his consort, who was examining the locket; "look here: the fastening is very defective, and I have no doubt that it opened, and the posy fell out and was lost."

"Duke Bingi," said the monarch, "take the chief executioner and seven assistants, go to the Guild of Goldsmiths and Jewellers, and bring me the heads of the eight leading craftsmen."

The Duke obeyed his monarch's orders, and, followed by the headsman and seven assistants, hastened to the Guild of Goldsmiths. But, like loyal citizens, the whole Guild had hurried off to assist in the defence of the city, so the Duke had his walk for nothing.

Every one who could in any way assist in defending the city had rushed off at the summons of the heralds. Remsky's mother, who was a laundress, had organized a corps of washerwomen, who armed themselves with tubs, upon which they drummed with no inconsiderable success.

Raggatti, who, besides being a rag-gatherer, was an honorary member of the Worshipful Company of Kettle-menders, had called together the brethren, and pointed out that they might be of immense service to the besieged town if they would set to work drumming on all the tin kettles they could lay hands on.

In fine, the inhabitants of Aphania were so energetic in their preparations, and set up such a tremendous clatter and tattoo, that the Archduke thought it prudent not to commence the assault that day, and ordered his troops to pitch their tents. His troops had had to make rapid and forced marches of great length, and it was only prudent to give them a rest.

Night closed in, and the weary soldiers of Fizpopoff sought their straw couches, while the inhabitants of Aphania retired to rest, worn out with the harass and anxiety of the day. An occasional and faint "rub-a-dub-dub" from the enemy's outposts, responded to by a dropping rattle of "tum-tum-tum" from the walls, showed that both besiegers and besieged had watchful sentries and vigilant pickets.

Within the town a solitary lamp gleamed in the casement of Raggatti's humble abode. He and his son were sitting up, contriving plans for the preservation of their native city.

"So they seemed delighted at the capture of the peas?" said the father.

"Enraptured," replied the son; "and the Lord High Pigeoner assured me that they were inveterate munchers of green food."

113

"What a pity the royal pea warehouse is not outside the walls. We could entice them all into that, and then lock them in."

"It would not hold half the army, it is so full of peas just at present."

"Very full?"

"About three-quarters. Why?"

Raggatti did not answer, but he jumped up and executed a vigorous double shuffle, which lasted for about half an hour. When he had sunk exhausted into his chair, his son questioned him as to the meaning of the demonstration.

"I've got a splendid notion!" said Raggatti.

"What is it?" asked Remsky.

His father looked cautiously round to make sure they were not observed, and then whispered something in Remsky's ear.

"Excellent!" said Remsky, his face beaming with delight.

"I'll go and lay the proposition before his Majesty," said the father.

"And I'll put the plan into execution," exclaimed the son.

They clasped hands and remained silent for some minutes.

"What's the matter *now*?" asked a royal porter, putting his night-capped head out of the window in answer to Raggatti's knocking. It was past ten, and the royal household retired early.

"I want to see his Majesty. I have an important communication to make, about the means of defending the city and defeating the invader," said Raggatti.

"Oh, bother! won't it do in the morning?" asked the Porter, gruffly.

114

"No! I must see his Majesty immediately."

With very much grumbling, the Porter went and woke the Head Porter, who, in his turn, roused the Groom of the Chambers, and he summoned the Warming-pan in Waiting, who informed the First Lord of the Bedchamber. And the First Lord of the Bedchamber tapped at the King's bed-room door.

"C-m-b-r-r-g-rum-p-h-f-r-r!" said his Majesty.

The First Lord tapped again.

"C'fnd't, wo'y wah?" growled the monarch.

"If you please, your Majesty, there's some one wants to speak to you about a plan for defending the city and routing the besiegers, and he says it's immediate!"

"Well, then," said the Sovereign, who was now fully awake, "just bring me the crown, and show him up."

So the First Lord of the Bedchamber brought the crown, which the King slipped on over his nightcap as he sat up in bed to receive his visitor.

The First Lord of the Bedchamber then communicated with the Warming-pan in Waiting, and the Warming-pan in Waiting imparted to the Groom of the Chambers, and the Groom of the Chambers intimated to the Head Porter, and the Head Porter told the Under Porter that the gentleman might walk up.

Of the details of the interview between his Majesty and Raggatti I can give you no report, for of course, under the circumstances, no reporters were present, so no record appeared in the "Gazette," and the matter was kept a secret.

But the result of the interview was that the First Lord of the Bedchamber had to step down into the library for pen, ink, and paper; and when these materials were procured, King Bungo with his own royal hand wrote out an order commanding the keepers of the royal pea-ware-house to deliver up possession of the building and its contents, together with all vans, waggons, carts, tax-carts, barrows, and trucks, and the horses, mules, and asses thereto appertaining, besides baskets, boxes, and packing-cases used on the premises, to his Majesty's faithful and well-beloved subject, Raggatti.

Armed with these credentials, and by the aid of Remsky, Raggatti removed all the peas in the royal warehouse to a range of buildings without the town. The peas were taken out under cover of night by the gates farthest removed from the beleaguering forces.

Remsky took leave of his father at the gates, and the latter returned home, while Remsky drove the last load of peas to the repository without the town, and having stored it there, drove off in the direction of the enemy's camp.

THE ASSAULT

"May your Serene Mightiness's boots never be tighter!" said Field Marshal Gagagaggum, entering the Archduke's tent with the usual salutation.

"Well, Gaggs, my boy," said the Archduke, who was of a jovial and rollicking disposition when in the field—and successful; "well, Gaggs, my boy, what is the news? Has Bungo capitulated?"

"No, your Serenity, he has not! But a young man has presented himself at the outposts, and states that he wishes to be conducted into your august presence. We have searched him, and he carries no concealed weapons, so that if your Mightiness elects to admit him, it can be done with complete safety."

"What is his object in demanding an interview?" asked Fizpopoff.

"He will not breathe a word on that subject to any one but yourself, Highness."

"What is he like?"

"Young, slightly formed, and not ill-looking."

"Is he bigger or stronger than I am?"

"Neither, your Highness."

"Then send him in."

The Field Marshal retired for a moment, and then returned leading in the son of Raggatti.

"He says he hasn't a card about him, but his name is Remsky, and he's an inhabitant of Aphania."

"That will do, Field Marshal: leave us!" said the Archduke, who had taken the precaution to cock his pistols while the Field Marshal went out to fetch Remsky.

"Now then, what is it?" asked the Archduke, sharply, turning to Remsky.

Remsky leant one hand on the back of a chair, placed the other under his coat-tails behind, cleared his throat, and alternately rising and falling on his toes as he proceeded, in accordance with the emphasis of his utterances, he began the following remarkable oration:

"Serene Mightiness, Electoral High Seignior and Hereditary Grand Archduke of Nexdorea: may it please your worshipful Highness, the humble individual who has the honour of addressing you is a frozen-out market gardener. Sire, the hearts of all market gardeners turn to your Serene Mightiness and the great and good nation over which you rule. The Aphanians are a slaughterous and beef-loving people. The Nexdorean race is gentle and vegetarian, and the market gardener yearns for annexation to your Serenity's dominions. Sire, I am a market gardener with an especial grievance. I am a copious cultivator of peas, your Mightiness, and used to be purveyor to the royal pigeonry. But of late a new Ministry has sprung up, and the most pinching economy reigns in Aphania. Will your Serenity credit it?—although the purveying of peas to the palace has been an established office for hundreds of years, my appointment has been cancelled on the shabby pretence that as there are no pigeons the peas are not wanted!

"Serene Mightiness, by this paltry economy I have thousands of waggon-loads of peas thrown on my hands. I welcome your Mightiness's arrival as an opening for disposing of my wares. I am ready to provision your whole army, on the most reasonable terms, with the requisites for that wholesome viand so beloved by the noble people of Nexdorea—pea-soup.

"Serene Mightiness! do not imagine this selfish motive is the only one that actuates me. I have reserved a more important consideration until the end. Sire, I have it in my power to give Aphania into your hands. My father, who, like myself, is disaffected, and suffers under the tyrannical rule of Bungo, is within the town, and at a given signal will fling open the gates for the admittance of your Serene Mightiness's army. By the end of four days he will have managed to carry out his operations, and your Serenity shall march into Aphania without difficulty."

"What guarantee can I have for this?" said the Archduke.

"I will not ask to be paid for my supplies of peas until after the capture of the city, and when your Mightiness orders the assault, you may tie me to the biggest drum in your arsenal, and stun me to death, if at my signal the gates are not opened as I promise."

"Just sit down, will you? and put your proposition and undertaking down in black and white."

"With pleasure, sire, if so humble an individual as a market gardener may be seated in your august presence."

"Oh, rubbish!" said the Archduke.

So Remsky sat down and drew up his offer and guarantee in a neat and legible form. The Archduke looked it over, approved of it, and he and Remsky affixed their signatures.

"And now, young fellow," said his Serenity, "as we have settled that all right, I'll trouble you to go and fetch in your peas, for I haven't tasted a spoonful of pea-soup since I quitted Nexdorea."

"At what time does your Serene Mightiness dine?" inquired Remsky.

"About two. I can't bear late dinners. Of course I have to dine late at home, because it's a matter of state; but in the field I can do as I like, so we feed at two."

"Then I regret to say that it will be impossible for me to provide the peas. My warehouses are under the drums of the garrison, and I can only remove the peas at night."

"Well, then, mind you bring me some for to-morrow. My brave fellows have not tasted peas for weeks. And, by the way, just hasten your father's operations, for the sooner we carry the city the better. News of the invasion may reach the Aphanian commanders, and if they attack us in the rear, and the garrison makes a vigorous sally in front, it would be rather ugly."

"In four days, your Mightiness, the gates shall be flung open for you. The Aphanian army, if it knew of your arrival, could only arrive by forced marches, weary and demoralized, just in time to witness your triumphal entry."

"There's something in that!" said his Serenity.

Remsky took his leave. The same night he brought his first waggon-load of peas to the Nexdorean camp, and was promptly taken prisoner by the outposts, who were, of course, unacquainted with his interview with the Archduke. Remsky begged to be taken before his Mightiness, and after some difficulty persuaded his captors to carry him to Fizpop-off's tent.

"How's this?" asked the Archduke, when he saw who the prisoner was; "what have you been doing, eh?"

"I was bringing in my first supply of peas when I was captured by your soldiers."

"Is this so?" asked the Archduke.

The captain of the guard said the prisoner was taken when endeavouring to bring a waggon-load of peas into the lines.

"Very right of you, captain," said the Archduke; "you've done your duty nobly. But this young man is in my employ on secret service."

"So he stated, your Serenity; but as he had neither pass nor safeguard, I doubted his statement."

"Ah, of course; I ought to have thought of that!" said Fizpopoff.

The upshot of the affair was that Remsky was provided with a pass which forbade any interference with his movements, and gave him right of ingress or egress at all hours and in all places. This was just what Remsky wanted. He set to work for the next three nights, and conveyed all his peas into the Nexdorean camp, where two or three large tents were given up to him for store-rooms. And for the next three days the Nexdorean forces ate pea-soup to their hearts' content.

On the fourth day Remsky waited on the Archduke, and informed him that all was ready. The army was accordingly directed to march on the city, with trumpets blowing and banners flying, but with strict orders not to discharge their drums till the Archduke gave the word of command.

His Highness led the way, mounted on his piebald charger. His staff surrounded him, and on his right a team of eight cart-horses drew along the largest drum in his arsenal. Remsky was bound to this enormous instrument. One bang of the steam hammer by which this drum was beaten would have stunned him to death. The whole Nexdorean army followed in double lines. It was an imposing sight.

As they approached the walls of Aphania, which were crowded with aged people of both sexes, Remsky gave a long shrill whistle. To the amazement and delight of the Archduke, the huge gates of the city were thrown open. He galloped up to Remsky, shook him warmly by the hand, and ordered his bonds to be at once undone.

Then he rode to the front of his army, took off his helmet, and waving it in the air, gave the word of command in a loud voice:

"GRASP STICKS! MAKE READY!! *DRUM!!!*"

Each soldier in the Nexdorean army plied his drum-sticks as if the success of the day depended on his single effort. *But not a sound came save a subdued tapping!*

The silence of the Nexdorean drums was no mystery to Remsky, who had slipped away as soon as his cords were loosed.

Remsky had made good use of the pass which the Archduke gave him, and wandered all over the camp day and night. He discovered that the drums were stacked outside the tents, to be ready for immediate use in case of a surprise. This was so much the better for the scheme he and his father had in their heads.

Armed with a small brad-awl and a large basket of peas, he spent the

121

night in stealing from tent to tent. Artfully boring a small hole in the parchment of each drum where it would be least likely to attract notice, he filled up the whole of the interior of the instrument with peas.

It was a tremendous task, and he had to work very hard to get it done, and at the same time to keep a sharp look-out, so as not to be found tampering with the arms.

His father was entrusted with the task of conveying the peas from the stores to the camp, leaving them at a place previously agreed on, whence his son could fetch them. This considerably lightened Remsky's labours. Had he been compelled to convey the peas from warehouse to camp, he would never have found time to fill the drums.

While the Archduke and his army supposed Remsky was bringing in the provisions from his distant warehouses, the artful young fellow was stealing about the camp "spiking" the drums—to borrow a term from the artillery.

THE ROUT

No wonder that Remsky was nearly worn out by his super-human exertions. When you consider the number of drums in the vast army which Fizpopoff had got together, and the enormous quantities of peas required to fill those drums, and the time consumed in the operation, the whole thing seems utterly incredible. However, if one begins to allow incredulity to interfere with one's study of Fairy History, it is time to abandon that delightful branch of one's education. I trust none of my readers are likely to doubt the Chronicles of Aphania, in which this achievement of Remsky's is duly recorded. A well-known controversial writer has taken some pains and devoted some time and a large quarto volume to proving by logic the incontrovertible nature of this historical record.

But when we remember that a lamented Archbishop proved logically that there was no such person as Napoleon Bonaparte, we, I think, shall do wisely not to rely too much on logic, which seems to be of a variable value. We shall do better to accept the unvarnished statements of the historian.

No person in his sane senses, who remembers the enormous height to which Jack's beanstalk grew in a single night, can possibly refuse to believe the story of Remsky's peas, which were, perhaps, a large and fine variety of their class, like the bean in question. The history of Jack and the Beanstalk has survived for years, defying the ravages of time and the incredulous tendencies of the age. It is to be hoped that the extraordinary narrative copied in these pages from hitherto undiscovered documents in the Record Office, will be accepted with equal faith and no less readiness. Time has given its seal of authentication to the Beanstalk and established its veracity, but there is an air of conscious truth about this younger narrative that must command the belief of all who still retain their faith in fairy tales.

When the Archduke gave the word of command, and the drums of the whole Nexdorean army hung fire, the Aphanians gave a loud shout. At the same instant the garrison made a sally. Only the aged and infirm had been left on the walls. The whole available force had been drawn up inside the gates, armed with everything that could by any ingenuity be made to do service as a drum. Necessity is the mother of invention; and as in insurrections the peasantry turn their scythes into weapons, the people of Aphania made bandboxes do service as drums.

The garrison, I repeat, sallied out, headed by the Honourable Company of Kettle-menders, mounted on the donkeys which they employed in their trade to drag their carts, and armed with tin kettles, brass saucepans, iron frying-pans, copper fish-kettles, and other resounding implements of various shapes and sizes, and of different metals. After the cavalry came a miscellaneous body of foot, armed with bandboxes, biscuit-tins, and a host of other resonant articles too numerous to mention. The rear was brought up by the corps of washerwomen, armed with washing-tubs, and headed by a grenadier company bearing large coppers from the laundries.

124

Little Miss Muffet, she sat on a tuffet
Eating of curds and whey;
There came a little Spider, and sat down beside her
And frighted Miss Muffet away

From *A New Child's Play*,
illustrated by E.V.B. (Eleanor Boyle).

From *In Elf Land*,
illustrated by Richard Doyle.

From *The Story Without End,*
illustrated by E.V.B. (Eleanor Boyle).

From *The Story Without End*,
illustrated by E.V.B. (Eleanor Boyle).

From *In Elf Land*,
illustrated by Richard Doyle.

From *The Frog Prince*,
illustrated by Walter Crane.

Such an uproar had never been heard before in the memory of the oldest inhabitant. The Nexdorean army consisted of tried veterans, but their bravery was unavailing against such an overwhelming force of noises. After a few frantic but vain efforts to get some of their drums emptied, and to elicit some sound from them, the gallant army, which had issued but a short time before full of hope and pride from the camp, broke and fled in every direction, throwing away their drums on all sides.

The Archduke made a gallant but unavailing effort to rally his troops. He tried to discharge a volley of "rub-a-dub-dubs" from the steam-drum, which he stoked with his own distinguished hand. But Remsky had artfully filled the cylinder with peas, and when the steam was turned on at full pressure the piston could not descend, though the peas were crushed into a solid conglomerate by the great horse-power employed. Seeing that further effort was useless, and fearing that the boiler would burst and injure the Archduke, Field Marshal Gagagaggum let off the steam, and turning the Archduke's charger, led him from the disastrous field. Still the Aphanian garrison rushed on, making a terrible uproar and driving all before them. The Archduke's piebald took fright and bolted.

Away dashed the terrified animal, helter-skelter, over hedges and ditches. The Archduke, finding the reins of no use, clung to the pommel of the saddle and shut his eyes. In vain did Field Marshal Gagagaggum shout "stop him!" You might as well have tried to put salt on the tail of a flash of lightning.

Away went the piebald! It knew nothing of the country over which it was going at a pace that would have turned a steeple-chaser pale. It came to a bank and rails, rose at it like a bird—but, alas! there was a terrible drop on the other side, and down it came on its nose and knees in a gravel-pit.

The Archduke was thrown and by ill luck tumbled head foremost into a large drum, which had been flung away by his retreating army. He was hurled into it with such force that he was buried up to the elbows, and as, like all the drums, it was tightly packed with peas, he could not by any means extricate himself. The horse picked himself up and hobbled away with no worse damage than a pair of broken knees, but although he was a sagacious animal, it never occurred to him to help his master out. The result was that his Serene Mightiness, when discovered some hours afterwards, had become quite black—or rather pea-green—in the face, and was, in fact, miserably smothered.

The news of his death reached the archducal palace some weeks later, and was received with universal lamentation. The Archduchess felt quite lonely now that she had no one to abuse and beat her. Even Ninni-Asterafina missed his brutality.

"Poor dear!" said the Archduchess, "how playfully he flung his top-boots at you! And to think he should be snatched away in his prime!"

"It would be something only to feel his fist between one's shoulder-blades," sobbed the sister. "It would be at least an assurance of his existence."

"He kicked one with such grace!" sighed the wife.

"He flung a plate with such accuracy of aim!" snuffled the Princess.

"He used to p-p-p-pinch one so playfully till one was black and bubbububublue!" burst out the widow breaking down utterly.

"He was so vuvuvuviolent and so googoogoogood!" echoed the weeping Ninni-Asterafina.

In alternate strophe and antistrophe these two silly women bemoaned their tyrant as the best man that ever walked probably was never mourned.

RAGGATTI A REFORMER

As soon as Remsky saw the archduchal army in full flight, he hurried off to the Archduke's tent, and hastily collecting all the valuables of the late Fizpopoff, he buried them in a heap of peas. He then hastened to get together all the spoil he could find in the officers' tents, and hiding that in the same manner, flung himself down on the top of the heap, wearied out completely. He took the precaution to write, "Don't wake me, please," on a large piece of paper, and pinned it on his breast.

As soon as the Aphanian garrison wearied of pursuing the fugitives, they returned to sack the enemy's tents, and were somewhat disappointed at not finding very much to sack. They, of course, came upon Remsky, calmly sleeping on a heap of peas, but they all knew who he was, and what was the reason of his weariness, so they respected his slumbers and left him to his repose.

Thus ended the siege of Aphania in the complete overthrow of the invading enemy and the death of his Serene Mightiness the Archduke of Nexdorea.

The defeated army bolted without reflection along the direct route to the frontier, and, as a natural consequence, fell in with the Aphanian army, which, having heard of the invasion, was falling back to protect the capital. It only needed this crowning disaster to complete the annihilation of the Nexdorean forces. The Aphanians fell on with a prodigious drumming, having had nothing to tire them, and large numbers of the fugitives were permanently deafened, or carried a hardness of hearing to their graves. Many were captured, and Nexdorea and the surrounding countries related to it by royal marriage were years before they recovered the shock.

You will have observed that little mention is made in this history of the doings of King Bungo and his Court. In truth, only the Court officials were left behind when the army marched, and they would have been as useless in the defence of the city as so many babies. As for the King, partly, perhaps, through affliction of conscience—for he had not done all he might in the matter of his brother Rumti—and partly through distress at the loss of Petsetilla's Posy, and the approaching probability of his losing the throne, and of her, consequently, marrying a beggar, he was completely unmanned. He went about the place weeping and wringing his hands in a most weak and unkingly way. He cried so dreadfully that the royal laundries, drained as they were to recruit the corps of washerwomen enrolled for the defence of the city, could not keep up the supply of clean cambric; and the Chancellor of the Exchequer protested that he should not have the audacity to quote such large sums for the royal washing in the half-yearly estimates.

Queen Belinda behaved admirably. She busied herself in preparing the palace for a state of siege. She ordered in plentiful supplies from the royal confectioner's, and by a display of courage and energy contrived to infect the courtiers with something like spirit. She locked, barred, and bolted the front door, and stopped up the keyhole with tow. Then closing all the shutters, she barricaded the windows with pillows and mattresses so effectually, that the sound of a fifty-six pounder drum could scarcely have pierced the defences.

As for Princess Petsetilla, she sat in her chamber lamenting the loss of her birthday gift. At first she was cross and silly, but when she had time for reflection, the goodness of her nature overcame the reaction which

had set in after the loss of the charm, and she began to see things in the right light. She greatly regretted that she had not been told that it was not the jewelled gold locket which would shield her from evil, but the contents—a simple bunch of withered pansies. She felt that she had taken a wrong view of life altogether, and had associated goodness and virtue with wealth, and wickedness and vice with poverty. And she was all the better for her trouble and her trial. She had been contented and happy before by instinct, as it were, because of the fairy spell; now she became

129

calm and gentle through trial and disappointment. She had lost her belief in the trinket of gold, to win a purer metal, thrice refined in the crucible of sorrow and tribulation.

So the morning after the defeat of the invading army, she got up as she had done in the early happy days, stole past her tiring-woman without waking her, and removing the feather beds with which her casement was barricaded, looked out and listened to the larks once more.

On the previous night the garrison were too tired with long vigils and vigorous drumming to make any great rejoicing over their victory; but they were astir betimes the next morning, and Petsetilla could scarcely hear the larks for the shouting and the braying of trumpets.

A sort of hasty procession was planned. The populace assembled in the market-place, and lo and behold! they found there Raggatti, basket on back and crooked stick in hand, collecting rags as quietly as if he had not been the preserver of his country.

"Long live Raggatti!" shouted they, one and all—"Long live Raggatti!"

It was not usual to shout thus for any one but the monarch of Aphania. This thought seemed to occur all at once to the whole crowd. The shout died out. Then came the second thought, "What had King Bungo done to save the city?" And then the shout, with a difference, rose again, echoing and re-echoing from end to end of Aphania. The shout, with a difference, was—"Long live King Raggatti!"

You will remember that there had been a state of discontent bordering on insurrection for a long time past in Aphania. A foreign invasion had made the populace forget their wrongs for a time in the common cause against the enemy. Now that the danger was past, the old feeling of discontent was free to arise again, not diminished by the knowledge that the King had neglected his duties during the late crisis.

At such times the tossing up of a straw is enough to move a multitude. The cry "Long live King Raggatti!" set the whole city in flames.

Before he knew where he was, Raggatti was snatched off his legs, mounted on a shutter (snatched from a baker who was opening his shop), and borne towards the palace by a shouting multitude.

In vain did the rag-collector endeavour to expostulate or to explain.

Bursting open the palace doors, they rushed up into the throne-room, and shot him rather unceremoniously into the chair of state.

King Bungo was dressing when the mob broke in; so slipping on his dressing-gown and diadem, and putting his sceptre under his arm, he hurried down. He forced his way up to the throne unnoticed; but when the people saw him on the dais, and perceived that Raggatti was vacating the chair of state, they broke out into a tempest of cries and counter-cries.

"Down with Bungo!" "Long live King Raggatti!" "Who stopped at home when the enemy came?" "Coward!" "Yah!" "Down with the tyrant!" These and a dozen other similar shouts, all raised together, made the throne-room a regular Babel for the time.

Raggatti took advantage of the uproar to explain matters to the King, who was very glad to find Raggatti was strongly disinclined towards royalty. He shook the rag-gatherer warmly by the hand, and thanked him for saving the country. The crowd observing this unexpected action, and wishing to know the meaning of it, at once became silent.

Raggatti seized the opportunity. Still holding King Bungo's hand, he sprang to the edge of the dais, and addressed the populace in a speech which I extract (by the kind permission of the author) from Kneemo's "History of the Aphanian Dynasties."

"Friends, brave friends, and patriotic fellow-countrymen (cheers) we have just achieved a great and glorious victory over a powerful enemy (loud cheers); let us endeavour to achieve a similar conquest over ourselves. You have done me the honour to connect me with the success of our arms. I very little deserve so much credit. (Cries of "No!") I repeat, you have very little to thank me for. (Loud expressions of dissent.) Gentlemen, it has been my good fortune to assist in a very small way in the preservation of our beloved country. (Loud cheers.) His Majesty King Bungo (cries of "Down with Bungo!" and great uproar) has complimented me by shaking hands with me, and I am proud to think that I have done my best to aid you in the defence of Aphania. But my son, my gallant son Remsky (cheers), has done more than I have. ("Three cheers for Remsky!") Yet neither he nor I could have done a thing—our efforts, small as they have been, would have been utterly unavailing—but for the generosity, the ardent public spirit, the influence, the ardour of one, to whom alone the glory of preserving the State belongs. (Cries of "Name!") Our poor plans must have fallen to the ground but for the solid and substantial aid which enabled us to put them into force. ("Name!") That solid and substantial aid we received from his revered Majesty King Bungo. (Sensation.) You owe your safety

132

to your King. (Great excitement. The Trimmers, seeing the popular opinion was divided, shouted "Long live the King!" which committed them to neither section.) Had not that gracious monarch confided in us, and placed at our disposal, without stint or restriction, the whole of his immense stores of peas, our plans would have been vain, and Aphania would at this moment have been the prey of the invader. You have been preserved by the King, and the King alone!"

Loud cries of "Long live King Bungo!" arose, and such was the force of Raggatti's eloquence that not a murmur of dissent was raised.

Raggatti, however, was too clever to miss the opportunity thus offered him for the redressing of the popular grievances and the restoration of the King's authority and popularity. He led King Bungo to the throne, and putting the monarch's crown straight, it having slipped over his left ear in the excitement, he laid before him a detailed account of the reforms that were necessary, and begged his Majesty to confirm them at once.

Bungo was only too pleased to make any concessions, and really felt glad of an opportunity to hear and remove the complaints of his people. He called his Ministers together at once, and consulting with them in the presence of the nation, discussed the grievances alleged to exist, and the various remedies proposed for their removal. When all had been settled to the satisfaction of the whole nation, the King turned to Raggatti, who had acted as spokesman for the people.

"And you, generous and disinterested patriot, what shall be done to reward you? Speak!"

But Raggatti's eloquence failed him now, and he could only mumble out something about having done his duty to his country.

"Shall we appoint you Assistant Under-Noodle of State in Council?" asked the King.

But Raggatti modestly said he did not think he possessed the necessary qualifications for the post.

"Well, then, name your own reward," said the monarch.

"Then, sire, my son Remsky—"

"Oh, you needn't ask for anything for him," interrupted Bungo: "he has separate claims of his own, which shall be attended to."

"Your Majesty will grant him whatever he requests?" asked Raggatti, anxiously, for he thought that of course Remsky would ask for the Princess Petsetilla's hand in marriage.

"Of a certainty I will!" said the King.

"On your royal word?"

"On my royal word. So now you make what request you choose on your own account."

Raggatti was utterly puzzled. He stood scratching his head and completely at a loss what request to prefer. His thoughts took a professional turn, not unnaturally, so at last he exclaimed,

"Well, then, since your Majesty is so kind, may I solicit the honour of the royal washing for my wife?"

"That depends greatly on the will of her Majesty the Queen. But you shall have my interest at all events. Anything else?"

"Nothing, your Majesty—except, yes!—except permission to collect all the rags about the palace."

"You shall have a free pass to every part of the basement storey, where all the rags will be found," said the King. And his Majesty gave directions to his Chief Secretary to draw up the pass and to give it to Raggatti.

So the assembly broke up. The King and his Ministers retired to luncheon, the populace betook themselves to sports and holiday-making, and Raggatti set out to the Nexdorean camp.

"Remsky has had a good long nap now, and it is time I should wake him, and tell him what the King has promised. He has only to ask for the hand of the Princess, and the King must give it. How strange! How little we expected this when the poor boy first told us of his love for her!"

RUMTI REDIVIVUS

Raggatti met Remsky not far from the town gates, driving a waggon loaded with chests and boxes, in which he had stored the spoils of the enemy.

"What have you got there, my son?" said the old man.

"Come and see!" said the lad, stopping the waggon, and opening one of the chests. It was full of precious stones and gold-dust, things which, as the readers of fairy tales are aware, are indispensable items of the baggage a General takes to war with him.

"Yours?" asked Raggatti.

135

"Mine!" answered Remsky. "I captured them from the enemy, and, as you know, they are mine by Act of Parliament."

"They are, my child!" said Raggatti, with fervour. He knew very well that an Act had been passed in the reign of Gorgius, which declared all property taken in war to belong to the actual captors. This statute was rendered necessary in consequence of a popular demonstration produced by the delays of the Government departments in the partition of prize-money. Before the reign of Gorgius, the distributions did not take place until such long periods after the capture, that the official forms were made out for convenience' sake in this style: "Pay to _____ grandson [or granddaughter] of _____."

"Remsky," said the delighted Raggatti, "this wealth comes at the right time. You ought to be rich if you marry a princess."

"What *are* you talking about?" asked Remsky, in a tone of the wildest surprise.

Thereupon Raggatti detailed the events of the morning—the popular rising and desire to place him on the throne—his speech and its effect—the King's gratitude, and his promise to grant Remsky whatever request he chose to make.

"Of course," said Raggatti in conclusion, "you will ask for the Princess's hand in marriage."

"What!" said Remsky.

"Why, the hand of Petsetilla in marriage. I know you love her, and neither your mother nor I should object to having a princess for a daughter-in-law—we love you too much for that. Our wish is to see you happy, not to consult our own humble tastes."

"Do you suppose I could entrap the King into giving his daughter to a poor low-born fellow like me, just because he was unguarded in his promises in a moment of gratitude? Besides, the Princess does not know me—has never seen me. Do you think I wish to marry a woman who does not love me?"

"Well, that did not occur to me," said the simple-minded Raggatti; "in fact, I didn't give it a moment's thought, taking it for granted that you would ask for the Princess. What *shall* you ask for?"

"Nothing—at least, nothing at present. I don't want anything. I've got a great deal more here than I know what to do with. I am going to divide it among the garrison, to whom it really belongs in justice; for, you see, I only hid it away under the peas before they returned to the camp for fear they should get quarrelling over it.''

"I think you had better keep a little of it, my boy. It's all very well to be generous, but just remember that your mother banged the bottom out of her best washing-tub yesterday in her anxiety to defeat the invaders.''

"You shan't want for anything, father; but when you've had your share, the rest must go to the others, who, I dare say, have banged the bottoms out of *their* tubs as well as my mother.''

Raggatti felt that his son's observations were sensible and just.

"Where are you going after you have seen your booty into a place of safety?''

"I shall leave it at the Bank of Aphania, and then be off to the nursery ground''——

"The garden! why, what on earth should you go there for?''

"You remember I have been away for nearly a week, and there are lots of things that will want attending to: I only fear that a good many will have gone wrong in my absence.''

"Well, I should think to-morrow would have done as well.''

"Well, I always do my duty to-day, father, as you taught me when a child.''

Raggatti, of course, had no answer to this, so father and son parted.

"Hang it, the boy's right too!'' said the old man. And then he suddenly remembered that the populace had carried him off in the midst of his work, and that he had his rag-basket on his back and his collecting-hook hanging by his side. The basket was empty, for all the rags that he had collected had been tumbled out when he was hoisted on the shutter and carried against his will to the palace.

"I'll follow the lad's example,'' said he to himself. "I've got leave to search in the basement of the palace, and I dare say I shall find a good many first-rate rags there—good quality ones, for they're uncommon wasteful in palaces, I've been told.''

So the old man presented himself at the area gate, and showed his pass. The scullery-maid admitted him, and left him to wander about where he liked.

He found that his notion of the wastefulness of palaces was somewhat erroneous. He hunted all about without finding a rag as big as the palm of your hand. At last he began to pluck up courage to explore some of the dark cellars and gloomy cupboards with which the lower part of the palace was plentifully supplied. He was a little more fortunate here, coming on a few dirty old dusters which the idle servant-maids had thrown away out of sight to save themselves the trouble of washing them out.

At length he blundered into a very dark crypt. Not a ray of light could penetrate thither, so that, though his eyes had become somewhat used to the gloom, he was totally unable to distinguish anything at all there. He groped along, stretching out his arms before him, when suddenly his shins came in contact with some obstacle, and he fell flat on his face on the pavement.

He picked himself up as well as he could, and stretching out his hands, carefully endeavoured to find out what the object was that had thrown him down. His hand encountered a cold smooth surface like marble; but before he could conjecture what it was, a sudden glow ran through it—it moved—and the next instant he felt a hand grasping his!

This was rather alarming. His teeth chattered audibly and his hair stood on end.

"O-o-o-o-o-o-o!" he exclaimed, "o-o-o! what are you?"

"Who the deuce are *you?*" was the reply in a drowsy voice; "have I been sleeping long?"

"Please, I can't say," said Raggatti, collecting his courage, for his interlocutor was evidently a human being. "Perhaps I could tell you if you'd mention who you are."

"Why, King Rumti, of course!" was the answer.

The honest hand had touched him at last!

HOW IT ALL CAME RIGHT IN THE END

I leave you to imagine the consternation of King Bungo, who was seated at dinner and had got as far as the sweets, when the door opened and King Rumti walked in.

The meeting of the brothers was not excessively cordial. Bungo was naturally not highly elated at the notion of having to abdicate, and Rumti had gathered enough from the answers Raggatti gave to his questions to make him somewhat dissatisfied with his Regent's conduct. And when you come to think that he, the lawful King, had been bundled away in a cellar with a lot of empty hampers, and that no real effort had been made to reverse the spell under which he lay, you will admit, I think, that he had some excuse for his irritation, especially as he felt certain, from the time he had been in his transformed state, that his

paper on the "Vertebral Annihilation of Space betwixt this Planet and its Satellite" was lost for ever to the "Philosophical Transactions of the Royal Aphanian Society for the Promulgation of Apparent Absurdities."

The first thing Rumti did was to take the crown off his brother's head and place it on his own brows. Unfortunately, their heads were not of the same size. Bungo had been compelled to have the crown let out slightly, owing, so the Phrenologist Royal alleged in secret, to an extra development of the bump of self-esteem. The effect of the alteration was that the diadem slipped down over Rumti's nose, an undignified proceeding on its part, but one which was promptly remedied by the insertion of a folded slip of blotting-paper inside the lining.

King Rumti next summoned the Royal Remembrancer, and called on him for a full, true, and particular account of all the events of the Regency. As my readers are aware, Bungo's reign had not been altogether undimmed by disaster, unblemished by error. As the Remembrancer proceeded with the chronicle, Rumti's brow darkened.

"An extravagant and vain-glorious christening banquet. A cruelly oppressive Poor Law, and a most injudicious discouragement of the free importation of rags. An iniquitous sumptuary law. An unconstitutional concession to popular clamour in the appointment of a new elective member of the Cabinet. General incompetence and cowardice. The desertion of the helm of State at the time of its greatest peril, and a neglect of the behests of, and a wilful abstaining from the means of restoring to his throne, your royal brother and supreme Sovereign. That, I regret to say, Bungo, is the summary of events in your Regency. I renounce you as a Vice-Regent, I disclaim you as a brother! Your estates are hereby forfeited, and devoted to the recuperation of the State losses

accruing through your mismanage-
ment. You and your family will go
into exile, and must leave this kingdom by sunset."

The news of Bungo's disgrace
spread like wildfire; and (such is the
fickleness of the mob) many who
that very morning had wanted to
dethrone him expressed their sorrow at his fall. The virtues of Rumti
had become almost forgotten, and
the calamities of one who had so
long worn the crown as Bungo,
attracted a ready sympathy.

Remsky heard with the deepest affliction of the changed fortunes of
Petsetilla and her father. He remained plunged in profound thought for
some hours; but when his mother roused him to tell him his tea was
ready, he sprang up suddenly, and telling her to keep it warm on the hob
for him, snatched up his cap and disappeared.

He immediately sought the presence of King Rumti, who held open
Court for the reception of petitions and the hearing of grievances and
complaints.

When Remsky's turn for an audience came, he sank on one knee
before the King.

"Sire," said he earnestly, "does not a righteous king keep the promises
made by his predecessor?"

"Certainly, young man," said Rumti; "but who are you?"

Remsky was about to explain, when the Royal Remembrancer
stepped forward, and gave a glowing account of the young man's bravery
and great achievement, and of the promise which the deposed Bungo had
made.

"You come to ask me to keep the ex-King's promise—is that it?"

Remsky bowed.

"Well, I will do so. Speak out and fear not!"

"I ask the reversal of the sentence of banishment passed upon Bungo
and his family."

"Consider it reversed, young man. You have behaved very generously in seeking favours for your proposed benefactor rather than for yourself. I admire your conduct, and will keep an eye on you with the view to your advancement. Mr. Home Secretary, make out a reversal of Bungo's banishment at once, and send some one to tell him he need not leave to-night."

"Am I to cancel the forfeiture of his estates, your Majesty?" asked the Home Secretary.

"Certainly not!" said the Sovereign.

"Sire," interposed Remsky, "when I asked for the reversal of the exile, I intended" ——

"Then why did you not say so?" interposed the King, sharply. "I promised to accede to your request, although not legally bound to do so, and you must not ask too much. Besides, it is a matter of national debt—the estates go to make up the deficits in the public revenue. There, now, go away, and let me hear the next applicant."

Remsky left the royal presence sadly. As he was crossing the court-yard he met Bungo, Belinda, and Petsetilla, who were about to thank Rumti for the reversal of the sentence of banishment. They all three started on beholding him.

"My brave young benefactor!" said Bungo, who had been told of Remsky's intercession.

"The gallant preserver of our country!" said Belinda, who had been informed of Remsky's gallantry.

"The handsome young gardener!" said Petsetilla, who remembered him and blushed.

Bungo shook hands warmly with Remsky, and made Belinda and Petsetilla do the same; and they both did it with great readiness.

"My Lord Bungo," said Remsky, "I have had the good fortune to prevail on his Majesty to reverse the sentence of exile pronounced against you this morning."

"Generous youth!" said Belinda.

"Nay, lady, it was Lord Bungo's generosity—you owe it to him. Had he not promised to accord me any request I chose to make, I should have been powerless. His promise, however, was honourably kept by King Rumti, and you are not compelled to leave Aphania."

"Gallant youth!" murmured Petsetilla.

"Your lordship," continued Remsky, turning to Bungo, "promised to grant **me a** request. The promise has been **kept by deputy**; but will you now in your own person accord me a favour?"

"Anything that lies in my very limited power," said Bungo.

"The favour that I ask is that you will accept as an offering of respect and faithful duty to the fairest Princess in the world, the gold, jewels, and all other spoils which I captured in the camp of the late Archduke."

"But really, sir"——expostulated Bungo.

"Nay, my lord, you promised, and I know you will not shrink from granting the favour now. It is the greatest happiness of my life to lay everything I possess at the feet of the Princess Petsetilla!"

Petsetilla blushed and sighed.

"But, my good young sir!" said Belinda, "I cannot bear to think that for our sakes you should make yourself a beggar."

"Not a beggar," said Remsky, plucking up heart, and determining to speak once for all his devotion to Petsetilla, although he did not for a moment dream that anything could possibly come of the declaration. "No! not a beggar, for I have this, which fell unnoticed from the Princess's window one day, and which I have treasured ever since!"

With that he produced the little withered bunch of heart's-ease.

"Petsetilla's Posy!" cried Bungo and Belinda, with one voice.

"My fairy gift?" said the Princess, looking at it with great curiosity, for it was the first time she had ever set eyes on it.

In a few words Bungo told the story of the posy to Remsky, who no sooner learnt the value of it than he at once restored it to its rightful owner.

"Now," said he, as he turned to go away, "now I am a beggar, indeed. While I possessed one remembrance of her I was richer than all the world. Now I *am* a beggar!"

As he uttered those words, who should appear but the good Fairy Felicia!

"Now, my worthy friend Bungo," said she, in a cheery voice, "if you must marry your daughter to a beggar, here's the very bridegroom you want."

"What an idiot I was not to think of that!" said Bungo.

"How savage old Aunt Sally will be!" laughed Belinda.

"Oh, sire," said Remsky, almost breathless at the prospect of such bliss, "if I could only think the Princess could deign"—

But Petsetilla threw herself on his breast to hide her burning cheeks, as she whispered so low that only he could hear it—

"I always thought you a darling of a boy when you used to bring the peas for the pigeons."

"Bless you, my children!" said Bungo; and the curtain falls.

THE LAST NEWS OF THE POSY

I have but few words to add. The curtain falls when the hands of the two young lovers are united, because that is the most interesting climax; and why should anybody want to know anything more about them? I can't answer the question, but I know for a fact that people do care to learn all the latest particulars, so in this case I will not disappoint them.

Remsky and Petsetilla were united, and a happier and more contented couple never breathed. People used to wonder which of them kept the posy; but I believe it was folded up in tissue-paper, and put away in the drawer to be taken care of for baby. There was a baby, of course, in due time—in fact, there were, eventually, so many babies that I think the posy would hardly have gone round the family at a stalk apiece.

On the death of King Rumti, Bungo declining to ascend the throne, Remsky and Petsetilla were crowned King and Queen of Aphania, to the great joy of their subjects, and without its in any way altering their good and kindly natures.

Rumti did not marry Ninni-Asterafina, who never reminded him of the engagement, because she felt, after that little business about the Archduke and his invasion, it would not be etiquette. The Archduchess having died of acute grief for the loss of her husband about five years after his death, the Princess Ninni-Asterafina became Archduchess Regnant and guardian of the archducal orphans, whom she ruled with a

145

rod of iron, and brought up, consequently, to be exemplary members of society.

Raggatti and his wife lived to a good old age, having been endowed with a slender pension—a pension purposely made too small to deprive the former of the necessity of working, Remsky knowing very well that there was nothing that disagreed with his father so much as idleness.

As for old Aunt Sally, she has lost all her magical power, and has become a very disreputable old woman, given to frequenting race-courses and to smoking short pipes. This last-named horrible habit so shocks even the habitual frequenters of races, that they invariably pelt her whenever they see her, so that she has not a very pleasant time of it.

About the Fairy Felicia all I have to say is that she still haunts the world, unseen. It is she who makes good children's eyes so bright, their cheeks so rosy, and their dreams so pleasant. If you want to make her acquaintance, and to win one of her posies, you must avoid petulance, impatience, grumbling, and black looks. From those she always flies. But when she sees honest, gentle eyes, and finds people, young or old, good to their fellows, kindly, affectionate, and humble-minded, she delights to come and slip a posy of her charmed flowers into the lockets they carry in their breasts—their hearts.

When you meet with any one who is generally beloved for the loving-kindness he has shown to others, who is never weary of doing good to his neighbours and assisting his poorer brethren, you may take my word for it, that he carries about with him a bunch of heart's-ease as big as PETSETILLA'S POSY.

WOODEN TONY:

AN ANYHOW STORY

BY
MRS. CLIFFORD

Lucy Lane Clifford, wife of the philosopher and mathematician, W. K. Clifford, was a novelist and dramatist who wrote three books for children. The most interesting of these is *Anyhow Stories,* which was published in two editions (1882 and 1895). "Wooden Tony"–the story of an autistic child reminiscent of the R. D. Laing case histories in *The Divided Self*–appeared only in the second edition, Mrs. Clifford having first printed it in a collection of stories for adults entitled *The Last Touches and Other Stories* (1892).

WOODEN
TONY:
AN ANYHOW STORY

Tony was the idlest boy in Switzerland. Other boys of his age chopped wood, gathered edelweiss, looked after goats and cattle; carried parcels for the strangers, guided them on short expeditions; and earned pence in many ways. But Tony did none of these things, and when his mother tried to make him useful he looked so frightened that at last she left him alone and let him do as he pleased. Gradually he grew to look quite stupid, as if his wits had gone a-wandering: and he was called the "Wooden-head"—that was the name by which all the neighbours knew him.

"Poor little Wooden-head! he's no use at all to you," they said to his mother; and at this she waxed angry, for though she often called him Wooden-head herself, she did not like to hear others do so.

"Perhaps he thinks more than he cares to say," she would answer.

"But he never tells of what he thinks; and a thinker who says nothing is like a signpost that points no way, and has nought written on it to guide him who looks up," old Gaspard said one morning.

"The signpost was made before the writing, and the talking that is worth hearing only comes after much thinking. He'll tell us enough some day," the mother answered. But though she spoke up bravely she was sad at heart. "I love thee dearly, my little son," she said. "I love thy pale face and wide open eyes, looking as though they expected to see Heaven's door creak on its hinges so that thou mightest know what the heavenly city was like; but who besides will care for thee if thou art stupid? And if thou art useless who will want thee? Even thy father gets

149

impatient." Tony turned from the faggot that was beginning to crackle and merrily lick with its long flames the black soup-pot hung over it.

"Could I be with thee and yet far off?" he asked. "I long to be far off."

"Dear mercy!" his mother exclaimed. "But why dost thou want to be far off, Tony?"

"Then would I be little and could lie in thy arms; and none would want me to do the things I cannot do and forget to do."

"But how would being far off make thee little, my son?"

"All the people are little far off," he answered. "I often watch the strangers come down the pathway from the big house. They grow bigger and bigger as they come near; they pass the door and go on by the gorge, getting smaller and smaller till they are as little as the figures in the wood that my father cuts away in the winter. When they return they grow bigger and bigger again as they come near. Yes—I want to be very little and far off."

"My son, thou art a fool," his mother said. "Is thy father ever smaller, dost thou think? It is only the distance that makes the strangers seem as thou hast said; if thou drew near them thou wouldst see that they had neither grown smaller nor larger." But Tony shook his head and would not understand.

"They are little to me," he said. "I would like to go away and be little to thee again, and then thou wouldst not be always asking me to do this thing and that, and be angry at my forgetting. There are so many things in my head that come before my eyes and make my hands useless."

"Thou are no good if thou art useless," his mother sighed. "All things have a reason for staying in the world, and the reason for the young and strong is that they are useful." But Tony answered only,—

"Some day I will go far off and be very little," and went to the sunshine and sat down on his little stool by the door. Presently he began to sing a song learnt in some strange fashion unknown to any near him, as a solitary bird might learn from its own little lonely heart.

"Ah, dear child," his mother said sadly as she listened. "He is no fool in spite of his talk, or if he be one, then his voice is sweeter than the wisest; there is not room for an evil thought anywhere within sound of it. While I listen to him I could even forgive Gaspard's wife for getting the fine linen to be washed for the English lady. It was a small thing to quarrel about."

But you do not know yet where Tony lived. In the summer his home was far up a high mountain in Switzerland. Beneath was a valley abounding in little meadows and winding pathways that had at one end a waterfall. The waterfall fell over a mountain side and was like a dream forgotten before waking-time, for though the spray went down and down, it never reached the bottom, but scattered itself in the sunshine and was lost. Tony used to watch the falling water, and try to feel as he imagined it felt—caught by the breeze and carried away in its arms. Sometimes he could almost fancy himself journeying with it—on and on, till he lost all likeness to himself, and, meeting the great winds, he became a part of them, and swept over the far-off sea. All about the valley and here and there on the mountains were the chälets or dark wooden houses of the peasants. Some were built on piles, so that when the storms and floods came the herdsmen and their beasts might still keep themselves dry; and some had heavy stones on their roofs, so that the winds might not blow them away. When Tony was very little, and before he had seen the builders at work, he thought that the piles were wooden legs on which the chälets had walked up in the darkness and stillness of the night, and that the two little windows in most of their fronts were eyes with which they had looked out to guide themselves. He often wished that he could see them staggering step by step upward along the zig-zag pathways. When he grew older it was almost a grief to know that human hands had built them on the mountain and in the valley, and that they would stay where they first rose till the winds and rains had done their worst. There was a little heap of rubbish on one side of the mountain; he had often wondered what it meant, but at last he knew, and then he stood looking at it and thought sadly of the children crouching over the fire, while the herdsman watched the sweeping storm gather to shatter their home and leave it in the past.

Just above his father's chälet was a big stone house, called the Alpine Hotel, where strangers came and stayed in the summer. The strangers talked among themselves in a language Tony did not understand, and were curious about the country round, professing to love it much, and day after day they walked over little bits of it. It seemed odd to Tony

151

that they should travel from far countries to see the things he had lived among all his life—just the hills and valleys, the snow and the edelweiss, the sunshine and the infinite stillness. Was it really for these that the strangers came? He wondered sometimes what more might be in the distances beyond his home, and in what strange forms the great world stretched itself. Yet he did not trouble often about either the strangers or the world they came from, but silent and lonely let the days and nights slip by as one that swims with but just enough movement to keep himself from drowning. So Tony seemed to swim through time, and to find each day as difficult to remember from the one that went before or came after it as he would have found it to tell one mile of sea from another. Sometimes he wondered if the strangers were people easy to break, or to kill, or to get lost, for though they never ceased praising the beauty of the mountains, yet they were afraid to go alone up the steep paths or on the snow-plains that he could have wandered over in his sleep. But it was good that they had so little courage, for they gave his father money to show them the mountain ways, to carry their food, and pull them across the little precipices and crevasses that Tony scarce noticed, to cut steps on the sheer ice to which his feet clung surely, to take care of them altogether, those foolish strangers who professed to love the mountains and yet were afraid to be alone among them. All day long while his father was away Tony stayed in the chälet watching his mother scrub and clean and wash, and make the soup ready for his father at night. Or he would sit by the doorway, listening to the falling avalanche, and letting the warm sun fall on his closely-cropped head. Happy Tony! the trees made pictures and he saw them, the wind blew and he understood: surely he belonged to the winds and the trees, and had once been a part of them? Why should he trouble to work? Vaguely his heart knew that not to work as his father and mother worked had he journeyed into the world from the mists beyond it. Had he not been very little once when he set out on that first journey? Some day, when he had done his resting on the mountain, he would go on into the distance, and be very little once more. And there were, besides, other thoughts than these that came into his heart, for he and nature were so near akin— thoughts of which those about him knew nothing; but he had few words

152

with which to talk; even the easy ones of daily life his lips found difficult to use.

When the evening came, and the soup was eaten, he stood by the doorway, listening to his father's stories of what the strangers had said and done. Sometimes when they had been niggardly or very silent or the day a disappointing one, his father would be cross and grumble at the soup, or reproach Tony for being idle; but his mother always took his part.

"Nay, nay, do not be hard on him," she would say. "Now he is as one called too soon, before his sleep has satisfied him, and his dreams overtake his waking hours. Let him get his dreaming done, and he will rouse to work as men do in the morning time."

"Ah, nonsense," the father would answer; "we can any of us dream who are too stupid to wake and too idle to work. If it were not that he could sing I would have no patience with him."

The strange thing about Tony's song was that no one knew how he had come by it. He sang a little bit of it in the days when he looked for edelweiss on the mountain. To the highest ridges he went to seek for the little white flowers that grow on the edge of the snow on the Alps, and when he brought any back they were tied in bunches and offered for sale to the strangers. That was before he had grown so silent, before the time when the great cobweb seemed to have wrapped him round, before he had wandered into a dream and shut the door on the waking world. One day he came back with his basket empty.

"But where is the edelweiss?" his mother asked.

"I did not see any," he answered, and sat down beside the smoking wood. Then he began the song he had known since he could sing at all; but this time there was something that his mother had never heard before.

"Where didst thou learn that?" she asked, but Tony would not speak.

"It is hard on thee," Gaspard's wife said, "that thy son should be a fool."

"Nay, he is no fool," the mother answered.

"But he cannot tell even where he learnt his song," the woman said.

"He learnt it in the clouds, or on the mountain side, farther up than

153

our feet can climb—what may be there—only the like of Tony can tell,"
and she waited scornfully for Gaspard's wife to go; but then she sighed
sadly enough. "Surely he will some day awaken," she thought, "or what
will be the good of him?" But from that time Tony forgot more and
more the things he was told to do, and lived among his dreams, which
grew so tangled that even he could not tell the sleeping from the waking
ones.

It was only in the summer that the days passed thus. When the storms
came and the snow descended, the hotels and all the chälets on the
mountains were closed, and the peasants and the herdsmen and their
families and their flocks went down to the valley for the winter. Tony
and his parents lived with a neighbour at the entrance to the village, all
of them huddled together in a little wooden dwelling. The floods came,
and the winds swept past, and the snow-drift piled higher and higher
against the windows till it was hardly possible for any light to enter the
close and smoky room. Tony used to watch his father cutting bits of
wood: chip by chip he seemed to take away the walls that held little
animals and men and women in prison. He never realized that his father's
sharp knife and precise eye shaped the toys, or understood that it was
just for the sake of the money they would bring that his mother placed
them away so carefully till the dealer from Geneva came to buy them, or
till it was time to put them on a tray outside the chälet door so that the
strangers might see and bargain for them.

One winter there was a dark knotty morsel of wood that fascinated
him. Every morning as he drank his milk his eyes wandered towards it. In
the evening as he crouched shiveringly by the smouldering fire beneath
the black soup-pot, he kept his eyes fixed on it and wondered what
strange thing it concealed. One day his father took it up, and, turning it
over and over, began to cut, till there came forth the figure of a little
woman who had on her face an expression of listening and waiting.
Tony's father looked at her and held her up before him when he had
taken off the last bits of wood that clung to her.

"Maybe thou are expecting some one to come and bear thee company," he said, speaking to it affectionately, as though it were a child;
"but I do not know of any thou canst have, unless Tony here will please
thee?"

154

Tony shrinking back fancied that the woman's eyes turned towards him.

"She is only wood, my lad," his mother said, "and to-morrow she will be sent to the dealer's far off—there is nothing to be afraid of, she cannot move, and in things that cannot move no danger lies. All things that live and move have power to frighten, but not this bit of wood that has been shaped by thy father's knife."

But Tony crept out of the chälet and trampled the soft snow under foot, and he was afraid of the little wooden woman lying still and wide-eyed in the smoky chälet. When he went back his mother looked up and said, just as if she had divined his thoughts, "Our neighbour Louis has gone to Geneva to look for mules for the summer; he has taken all thy father's carving with him, so thou needst not be afraid of the little woman any more."

This had happened more than a year ago, and Tony had forgotten the piece of wood and what had come from it. Now his father was carving again, and making ready for the dealer who arrived once a year to buy their winter's work from the peasants; and if the dealer would not buy, the little figures would be put away in a drawer ready for the strangers.

"If I were but like one of them," Tony used to think as he saw them wrapped in soft paper, "to be always little, to be handled tenderly and put to sleep in a drawer till the summer, and then to be warmed through and through by the sun. Why should they have legs that never ache and hands that never work?"

It was a cold morning when the dealer came—a dark, silent man, black haired, with overhanging eye-brows.

"Who is this?" he asked, looking at Tony.

"He is my son," the father said; "but little enough good is he save to sing."

"Is he the boy whose song the goatherds say was learnt in the clouds?"

"It may be."

"Ah, Tony's song is known all down the valley and over the mountain too," his mother said.

"A stranger came to Geneva once and tried to sing it," the dealer said, "but he could not remember it all."

155

"It is no good to Tony," the father said, "he is only a fool, and will not use his hands and feet." Then the mother spoke up for her son.

"Don't judge him harshly," she said. "Surely, some are made to use their hands and some their feet, and some it may be just their hearts to feel and their lips to speak. Does he not sing a song he has fetched from the clouds? Let that travel instead of his feet and work instead of his hands."

"He is called the Wooden-head," the father went on, unheeding, "and he might well be all wooden but for his song. The rest of him is no good—"

"A song has sometimes lived longer than the strongest hands that ever worked for bread, and travelled farther than the swiftest runner," said the mother.

"—And he would be like one of those," the father added, pointing to the little carved figures he had made.

"They were hidden in a block of wood, just as thy song is hidden in thee," his mother said, looking at Tony fondly.

"He would be better without his song," his father said. "He **might** dream less and work more."

The dealer considered and was silent, and when he spoke again he spoke slowly.

"Let him go to the city with me—to Geneva," he said, "and I will take the song from his lips and send it over the world."

"Tony," asked his father, "wilt thou go to Geneva? Perhaps there thou wouldst get thy wish to be far off and very little."

"Ah!" said the mother, with a heart that stood still, "but I have heard it said that a wish and its fulfillment sometimes find themselves strange company. But go if thou wilt, dear lad, there is much in the world. I would not keep thee from seeing it."

The peasants came out of their chälets and stood at their doors watching Tony as he went through the village with the dealer; but Tony did not see them. He walked as one who was dazed. The icicles hung like a fringe on the waterfall, and everywhere the sun had kissed it there rested a little golden star; but he did not look up as he passed by. He kept his eyes towards the long, straight road, and wondered if in the stems of the fir-trees beside it there dwelt strange figures like those his

156

father had set free with his knife. The dealer pulled some wire from his pocket and fashioned it carefully as he walked on, but he said no word until the village was far behind and they could no longer hear the trickle of the unfrozen water. Then he looked up and said,

"Sing."

Mechanically, as though he were a puppet, of which the string had been pulled, Tony began to sing, and the dealer twanged the wire in his hands till it almost echoed the song. But Tony did not hear it. Over his senses had stolen a great rest; he walked as though before him he saw the land of his dreams and presently would enter its gateway.

Twang, twang, went the wire.

The fir-trees swayed a very little in the breeze; more and more as the twilight deepened, as the night came on. Tony turned his face towards them; he felt as if he knew them, he wanted to go to them, to walk among them as his friends, but something held him and he could not. The trees knew him and held out their arms: they whispered a message but he did not understand it. But he was going to understand them, to learn their language and ponder their secrets.

Twang, twang, went the wire.

The trees were wrapped in darkness at last, but Tony did not stop, he went on, on and on without stopping, into the blackness till that too was behind, and towards him slowly stole the morning light. There was a range of low mountains far in the distance. They rose higher and higher as he drew near as if to greet him.

"Sing," said the dealer.

But his song was different, it seemed no longer to come from his heart but only from his lips, and as he sang he heard the notes repeated. The song was going out of him and on to the dealer's wire. He did not look towards it, he did not care; he felt nothing keenly. His legs were growing stiff and his feet were hard, yet lighter to lift than they had been. He was not tired, or warm, or cold, or glad, or sorry, but only in a dream.

The fir-trees were far, far behind now. Tony and the dealer had passed other villages than the one from which they had started yesterday. They were nearer to the mountains that had looked so low at first, and before them was a blue lake reflecting the bluer sky. Beside the lake was a long road that led to the city of Geneva—the city towards which they were

157

journeying. But there were more villages and little towns to go through first—towns with white houses on the hill-side and others low down close to the water's edge. There were carved wooden balconies to some of them, and some were built altogether of wood. Tony wondered in what strange forest the trees of which they were made had grown. He seemed to have more and more kinship with the things that belonged to Nature's firstness—with the sky and the lake and the trees, nay, even with the dead wood that had been used on human dwelling-places. But towards human beings he felt a strangeness spring up in his heart as if between him and them had begun a separation. They seemed to be made of a different texture, of different flesh and blood from himself, and they—these people—were so tall, they overshadowed him; they took long steps and carried great loads that would have crushed him. And yet they did not look bigger than his father and mother, it was only when they were beside him that he realized the difference in height. It did not surprise him, for nothing surprised him now, or stirred his pulse, or made his heart beat quicker. He went on, on.

The dealer twanged the wire, and the music of it grew more and more to resemble Tony's song. But Tony tramped in silence looking at the lake and sky, while the sun shone, and the mountains rose higher and higher. He felt as if they were his parents or had been once in a far-off time, and now they were reaching out to him trying once more to bring him back to themselves before it was for ever too late. Too late for what? He did not know, he could not answer himself. His heart was growing still and slow, his lips were growing dumb.

"Sing," said the man again.

Then Tony opened his mouth, but the words of his song had gone, he could not remember them, he could not say them, only the notes came forth, but they had no meaning that could be written down in words, and each listener heard them differently. Gradually instead of singing he listened, for his song was all around and about, but it did not come from his lips any more. It seemed as if it came from behind him, but when he tried to turn he could not. He was clasped everywhere by the wire, and in the midst of its cold tangle he walked, strange and rigid, as if in a dream. One arm hung by his side, he could not move it; one hand was in his pocket, he could not pull it out. His clothes seemed to have changed,

to have grown as stiff as he, and to be separate from him no more. Only
his feet moved just enough to carry him forward, and that was all.

But now the last miles of the road were behind, and the sounds of a
city were before him with lines of houses standing up high and white,
and many little windows like gaping mouths talking in the air or lidless
eyes looking out on the people in the streets. Lower down there were
windows, reaching to the ground, filled with all manner of things to
please those who had money to go in and buy. Tony walked by all
scarcely knowing: but he understood, for he had seen his shadow: he was
in the distance towards which he had looked so often from his mountain
home.

He was far off and very little.

He knew that he was bound and a prisoner, but it did not matter, he
did not care. It was only part of a new life in the new world that he had
entered. Suddenly with a jerk he stopped by one of the great windows; a
door opened and he entered. All about him was wooden—wooden houses
and people and animals—and everywhere a sound of ticking. Tick, tick,
tick. He was lifted by the dealer's hand on to a height. Before him was a
house, a chälet, with a flight of stairs outside leading to a balcony.

"Go up," the dealer said, and slowly stair by stair he went, his feet
growing stiffer and stiffer with every step upward. He rested on the
balcony; there were two little doors leading into the house, they opened
suddenly and disclosed a little room behind. In the room waiting—surely
waiting for him—was the strange little woman Tony had seen his father
take from the block of wood. He remembered that he used to be afraid
of her. How foolish he had been; now he was afraid of nothing. He took
his place beside her, he felt that they would never be apart again unless
great change or sorrow came: surely it was like a marriage? He saw that
the little woman was as big as he, had she grown? or had he—but he
could not think or reason. He was jerked back, the wire twanged, the
doors closed, and all was still. He was in the darkness waiting too, but for
what or how long he did not know: all time was the same to him, he
could measure it no more.

In the distance he heard other wires twanging, and presently the
melody of his song came from many directions, as though the place were
full of it. He could hear the people in the street; they hummed it as they

passed by. Once far off he heard a band playing it. But he did not listen long, for all things grew faint as they would have grown dim too had he been in the light to see and know. For Tony's life had gone into his song; only a simple little song, just as his had been a simple little life.

Life is not only in nodding heads, and work is not only for hands that move and feet that walk; it is in many other things.

After a time there were sounds of fitting and tapping over Tony's head, a loud ticking—tick, tick, tick unceasingly, and then a strange whirring, and an iron tongue struck out clang-clang up to eleven. As the last stroke fell the little doors flew open and Tony and his companion were jerked out by the wire that bound them on to the balcony at the top of the stairs by which he had mounted, and stood together while all around and above the song was played—the song that never would come from his lips again. Before them, separating the place in which their dwelling was from the street, was a great window letting in a flood of light, and on the outer side against the glass were pressed eager faces watching; but Tony and his companion did not know this; as the last note died away they were jerked back into the little room and all was darkness till another hour had passed, and then it all happened again. Hour after hour it was always the same, day after day, week after week, month after month, in light and dark, in heat and cold.

Two weary faces once were pressed against the window, those of a woman and a man, and as the doors opened and the two little figures came forth on the clock and stood while the song was played, the woman cried,

"It is Tony, it is Tony, it is his song; there beside him is the woman you made, and he is wooden too—he is wooden."

"Thou art dreaming," said the man; "Tony is gone into the world, and we will go and seek him."

"No, no," the woman cried in despair, "his song has gone into the world, but Tony is there," and she pointed to the clock; "he is wooden—he is wooden." The man looked long and silently.

"He had always a wooden head," he answered slowly; "maybe the rest of him has gone wooden too, for he did not move enough to keep quickened. But he was useless," he added, trying to comfort his wife; "didst thou not say thyself that his song would work instead of his hands, and journey instead of his feet?"

160

"Ah, that was well enough for those who did not love him," said the mother, "but it does not comfort me. It is Tony that I want, my son Tony who sat by the door and sang, or by the fire watching the wood smoulder." While she spoke the song ceased, the figures were jerked into the darkness, and the doors closed: before the man and woman lay the long road and the weary miles that led back to the village and the mountain.

THROUGH
THE
FIRE

BY

MARY DE MORGAN

ILLUSTRATED
BY
WILLIAM DE MORGAN

Mary De Morgan was the daughter of the well-known professor of mathematics Augustus De Morgan; her brother was the artist and novelist William De Morgan, famous for his "De Morgan tiles." Their friends included William Morris and D. G. Rossetti, and Mary told her stories to her nieces and nephews, as well as to an auspicious group of children including Philip and Margaret Burne-Jones, a young Rudyard Kipling and his sister Alice, and William Morris' daughters, Jenny and May.

Mary De Morgan published three beautiful collections of fairy tales: *On a Pincushion* (1877), *The Necklace of Princess Fiorimonde* (1880), and *The Windfairies* (1900). "Through the Fire," with illustrations by William De Morgan, appears in the first volume; and "The Wanderings of Arasmon," illustrated by Walter Crane, is taken from the second collection.

Mary De Morgan was the daughter of the well-known professor of mathematics, Augustus De Morgan; her brother was the artist and novelist William De Morgan, famous for his "De Morgan tiles." Their friends included William Morris and D. G. Rossetti, and Mary told her stories to her nieces and nephews, as well as to an auspicious group of children including Philip and Margaret Burne-Jones, a young Rudyard Kipling and his sister Alice, and William Morris' daughters, Jenny and May.

Mary De Morgan published three beautiful collections of fairy tales: *On a Pincushion* (1877), *The Necklace of Princess Fiorimonde* (1880), and *The Windfairies* (1900). "Through the Fire," with illustrations by William De Morgan, appears in the first volume; and "The Wanderings of Arasmon," illustrated by Walter Crane, is taken from the second collection.

THROUGH
THE
FIRE

Little Jack sat alone by the fire, watching it sadly. He was seven years old, but so small and pale, that he looked little more than five, for he was a cripple. He had no brothers or sisters, and he was nearly always alone, for his mother, who was a widow, went out all day to teach music, and often in the evening also to play dance-music at children's parties. They lived on the third floor of a small house in a dull old street in London, and Jack spent nearly all day in the little lonely sitting-room by himself, sitting by the fire. To-night he felt sadder than usual, for it was Christmas-eve, and his mother had gone to a child's party at a grand house, and she had said that there would most likely be a Christmas-tree there, with presents on it for all the little boys and girls, and Jack thought it very hard that when other children had so much more pleasure than he, they must even rob him of his own mother.

If she were at home she would sit by him on the hearth-rug and take his head in her lap and tell him long, long stories of giants and fairies. Generally he liked her to go to parties, for, wherever it was, she never forgot to bring him something from the supper-table; no matter how little a thing it might be, only a cracker or a single sweet, but he was sure to find something waiting for him on his pillow when he woke in the morning; and, indeed, sometimes there had been quite a nice little parcel of sweets and crackers and dried fruits sent to him by the mistress of the house or some of the children, when his mother had dared to ask if she might take something to her little boy at home.

167

But to-night he wanted his mother herself, and did not care for anything she would bring him in the morning.

He sat and thought till the tears rose to his eyes, and he sobbed outright.

"It's a shame," he said, "a dreadful shame. I think it's too bad." And he seized the poker, and gave the fire a great dig.

"For pity's sake, don't do that again," said a small voice from the flames; "it's enough to break one to bits."

Jack stopped crying and looked into the fire. There he saw a little figure, the strangest he had ever beheld, balancing itself skilfully on the top of a piece of burning coal. It was just like a little man, not more than three inches high, dressed from head to foot in orange-scarlet, the colour of flame, and wearing on his head a long pointed cap of the same colour.

"Who are you?" asked Jack, breathlessly.

"Don't you know that it's rude to ask questions?" said the mannikin, winking one eye. "However, if you very much want to know, I'm a fire-fairy."

"A fire-fairy!" repeated Jack, still staring and breathless.

"Yes; is that so very strange?"

"But I don't believe in fairies," said Jack, unable to remove his eyes from the weird little figure.

The little man laughed.

"That doesn't make any difference to me," he said. "Perhaps you don't believe in wind-fairies or water-fairies either. But you'd never have a fire but for us; we light them, and keep them burning. If I were to go away now, your fire would be out in an instant, and you might blow and blow it as much as you liked; it would be all no use, unless one of us were to come back and put the light into the coals."

"But how is it you don't get burnt up?" asked Jack.

"Burnt up!" said the little man, scornfully; "why, we breathe fire and live in it; we should go out at once if we weren't surrounded by it."

"Go out! What do you mean by going out? Do you mean that you'd die?"

"I don't know about dying," said the little man, "but of course, without care, one is liable to go out. But don't let's talk of unpleasant subjects."

"But do you mean that you live for ever?" asked Jack.

"With proper care there is no reason why one should go out after one is three hundred years old," said the little man, settling himself comfortably into a corner of burning coals. "Before that age we are very delicate, and the least wind is dangerous."

"But where do you live—where do you come from?" asked Jack.

"We live in the very middle of the earth, where there is always a nice comfortable fire; but when you have fires alight up here, we have to come and attend to them."

"Then do you come to lamps and candles as well?" said Jack, "for they are fire."

"We leave that to the young folks," said the little man, with a yawn; "I never come up for anything less than a coal fire."

Jack was silent for a little; then he said:

"I wonder I never saw you before."

"I have always been there; so it has been only your own stupidity," said the gnome.

"I wish I could get into the fire with you," said Jack; "I should so much like to see what it's like."

"You couldn't come without a proper dress," said the tiny man, "and even then I am afraid you'd find it warm."

"I shouldn't mind that," said Jack. "And in your own home, where you live, is it quite red and bright, like the middle of a fire?"

"It's a great deal better. Ah, that is worth seeing!" said the fairy, thrusting one arm over a burning coal, and skilfully balancing himself in a little jet of flame. "All round the palace where our King lives there's flame—flame—nothing but flame for miles, and the Princess's windows look on to burning hills. Ah, what a pity it is people are so discontented! If there is anyone who ought to be happy, it's the Princess Pyra."

"Isn't she happy?" asked Jack.

"Don't be so inquisitive. She might be, if she liked."

"Then why isn't she?"

"It all came of sending her to school," said the little man, gravely. "If she'd never left her father's palace she would never have seen him. You must know that our King and Queen have only one daughter, Princess Pyra, and of course they are very proud of her, and wished her to make a

169

good match. A Fire Prince, whose country is close to ours, proposed to her, and her father and mother settled that they would accept him; but as she was very young, and they wished her to be well educated, they sent her to school for a year in a burning mountain, thinking it would give her a chance of seeing more of the world than if she always remained at home. But, as it turned out, it was a great mistake, for one day the Water King's son, Prince Fluvius, came and looked over the top of the mountain, and saw our princess; and they fell in love with each other, and the Princess has never been happy since·"

"Why can't they be married?" asked Jack.

The little man burst into a roar of laughter.

"Why, you ought to know that it's impossible. In the first place, they can't go near each other, lest he should be dried up, or she should be put out. Besides which, our King would never hear of such a thing, as the Water King is his bitterest enemy."

"Every evening after she first saw him, the Princess used to come to the top of the mountain, and the Prince came and sat a little way off, and then they talked together. Ah! the King little thought what mischief was brewing. But when he discovered her one evening, when he came to see her, sitting talking to Prince Fluvius, he *was* in a rage. He took her home at once, and was anxious to marry her to the Fire Prince without more ado. But she grew so thin that the doctors said they feared if she were much excited she would go out altogether. It's a great pity she should be so silly."

"Is she pretty?" asked Jack.

"Pretty? Pretty's no word for her. She is lovely—beautiful! She is much the loveliest woman in Fireland, and she's wonderfully clever as well."

"Little man," said Jack, coaxingly, "take me with you, and show me your home. I would never tell anyone, and it's *so* dull here. Do let me go with you."

"I don't see how it can be done," answered the little man. "Besides, you'd be frightened."

"I wouldn't, I wouldn't, indeed," said Jack. "Only try me, and see."

"Wait a minute, then," and the little red figure disappeared into the brightest part of the fire. In a few seconds he appeared again, carrying a little red cap, and suit, and boots.

170

"Put on these," he said, throwing them into Jack's lap.

"How shall I ever get them on? Why, they're not as long as my arm." But no sooner had he touched them than he found himself growing smaller and smaller, until the clothes seemed the right size for him, and he easily slipped into them.

"Now take this," said the red man, and threw him a thin shining glass mask. Jack drew it over his face. It fitted exactly, and left no openings.

"Now," said the Fire-man, "climb over the bars, and see how you like it."

Jack scrambled over the fender, and helping himself with the fire-irons, climbed on to the first bar. The red man leant down, and gave him his hand to help him. What a hot hand it was! It burnt like flame. Jack felt inclined to drop it, but he was afraid of seeming impolite, so he bit his lips, to prevent himself screaming, and scrambled over the bars right into the midst of the fire.

On looking round, he thought he was in a new world. He stood in the middle of rich, red-glowing hills, from which sprouted jets of flame, like trees. Here and there was a black mountain, which smoked and hissed most alarmingly. But how hot it was! At first Jack felt as if he were going to faint, and could not breathe.

"Well," said the red man, who now seemed to Jack quite full-size, "how do you feel now?"

"It's warm," murmured poor Jack.

"If you can't bear this, you won't be able to stand Fireland. Better not come any farther," said the fairy.

"I'm all right," said Jack, making an effort. "I daresay I shall soon feel quite used to it. How does one get to Fireland?"

"I'll show you," said the man, taking a thin piece of stick from his pocket. This he took in both hands, and dug into the coal beneath his feet till he had made a good-sized hole. Then he took from his pocket some little marbles, and dropped them one by one into the hole, which gradually began to grow larger and larger, until it was an immense black gulf in the coal in front of him.

"Now come along," said the red man, sitting on the edge, with his legs swinging over. "Get on to my shoulders, and put your legs round my neck, and give me your hands, and I'll take you quite safely. Only don't scream or call out, or I shall drop you."

171

Jack did as he was bid, and seated himself firmly on his companion's shoulders, holding on round his neck. He could not help feeling frightened when, without a word, his guide sprang into the hole, and began to fly through the darkness so fast that he felt giddy. They went down—down—down. It was pitch dark, and poor Jack felt quite sick with the quick motion. He would have called out for them to stop, only he feared that the red man would keep his threat of letting him fall.

At last, a long way beneath them, he saw a faint red light, growing larger and brighter every moment.

"There's Fireland," said his guide, stopping for a moment, "and we shall be there in a few seconds now." And on they went again, quicker than before towards the light, which now grew so brilliant that Jack could scarcely bear to look at it.

"Here we are!" said the little man, as they passed from the darkness into the light through a kind of archway. Then he quietly shook Jack from his shoulders on to the ground, and sat down to rest beside him. When he had a little recovered from his giddiness and fright, Jack raised himself, and looked about him. It was quite as strange as the fire had seemed to him. There were great hills, and they were of every shade of red and orange, some pale, some bright, and on the hill-sides were lakes of fire. The sky was one mass of flame, and many of the hills smoked.

"Well, what do you think of it?" asked the fire-fairy.

"It's certainly very odd," said Jack, fearful of saying what he really thought, lest he might be thought rude. "But where do you live? I don't see any houses."

"The towns are farther. If you want to see them, you must get on my shoulders again," said Jack's friend, taking him again on his back as he spoke.

On they went again, passing over the ground so quickly that Jack could not see half enough of the strange country through which they passed.

At last they came in sight of a large city, with tall spires and bridges, and a little way out of it stood a palace made of red-hot iron, and glistening with precious stones.

"That's the King's palace," said the Fire-man; "and as it's the thing most worth seeing in the whole place, we'd better go there first."

"Shall I see the Princess?" asked Jack, eagerly.

"Most likely she'll be in the garden, and then you can see her as much as you like."

They stopped in front of the garden gate, and the fire-fairy, pushing it open, told Jack he could go in, but he must not make a noise. It was the queerest palace and garden. Jack now saw that what he had at first supposed to be precious stones were nothing but different-coloured fires, spouting out all over the palace. There was blue fire, and red fire, and green fire, and yellow fire, shining against the palace walls just like jewels.

At first Jack thought that the garden was full of beautiful flowers, but when he drew near to them, he saw that they were only fireworks in the forms of flowers. There was every sort of catherine-wheel turning round as fast as possible, throwing off sparks; and every now and then a brilliant rocket went up into the air, and fell in shining stars.

Jack ran from one thing to the other, examining it with delight, when his companion, seizing his arm, drew him on one side, saying, "The Princess!" and pointed to where a group of ladies were coming slowly down the path. In their midst walked the Princess, who, Jack thought, was the most beautiful lady he had ever seen.

Her long bright golden hair fell almost to her feet. Her face was very pale, and she walked very slowly and kept her eyes on the ground, with a very sad expression.

She wore a shining flame-coloured dress, with a long train, and one corsage of pale fire orchids fixed in her bosom, and another spray in her hair.

She was surrounded by beautifully dressed ladies, but none so lovely as she; only Jack wished she did not look so very sad. The ladies all talked together, but the Princess never said a word.

"Your Royal Highness should not walk too fast," said one.

"Had not your Royal Highness better sit down?" said another.

"Will your Royal Highness not return to the palace?" asked a third. But the Princess only shook her head in silence, and walked on as before.

Then Jack, seeing her so beautiful, and so unhappy, could contain himself no longer, but burst out:

"Oh, poor Princess! how sorry I am for you!"

At this the Princess raised her eyes for the first time. Such bright eyes they were, shining just like stars, Jack could not bear to look at them, but had to turn his own another way.

"Who spoke?" said the Princess, in a low, sad voice. "Which of you spoke?"

The ladies said nothing, but looked at each other in surprise.

"Someone said she was sorry for me, and I am sure you need not mind my knowing which of you it was," continued the Princess, beginning to sob, only instead of tears, sparks fell from her eyes.

Here all the ladies drew about her, and tried to soothe her.

"You know," said one, "that the doctors said that, whatever happened, your Royal Highness was not to excite yourself, or the consequences might be fatal."

"Pray be calm, your Royal Highness," said another. "You will really make yourself seriously ill if you go on in this way."

"But who spoke?" asked the Princess again. "I think it very unkind of you all not to tell me. It's the first time I have heard a kind voice since I left school."

At this Jack could keep silence no longer, and, despite the red Fire-man, who did his best to hold him back, he strode in front of the Princess, and said:

"If it pleases you, your Royal Highness, it was I."

"You! And who are you?" asked the Princess, kindly.

"I'm a little boy, and my name is Jack."

"How did you come here?"

"I came with him," said Jack, pointing to the red Fire-man. "And you must not be angry with him, for I made him bring me."

"I am not the least angry, either with him or you," said the Princess, very graciously. "But I want to know why you said you pitied me."

"Because you look so unhappy, and I think it's very sad for you to be parted from your Prince," said Jack.

Here all the ladies crowded round him, and tried to stop his speaking, but the Princess said:

"Silence! I insist upon it. It does no harm for me to hear him, and I will not allow you to stop him in this way. Thank you, little boy, for what you have said. And for you," she added, turning to Jack's first

174

friend, "I am not the least angry with you, and I particularly desire that no one shall mention this to my father"; but just as she stopped speaking, a cloud of smoke was seen rolling over the hills, and the ladies cried:

"The King! The King!"

"Go! Go!" cried the Princess to Jack, and the Fire-man without more ado seized him, and placing him on his shoulders flew through the air with him at a great pace, and was far from the palace before Jack could get breath to speak.

"A fine mess you have nearly got me into!" grumbled the little man. "It will be the last time I ever take you anywhere with me, you may be sure. What would have happened to me if the King had come up and heard you talking to the Princess of the very subject he had forbidden us all to mention?"

Jack dared not say a word, as his companion was so angry, and on they went flying through the air at a dreadful pace. At last they reached the long dark tunnel and flew up it, and when they again came towards the light, the little man took Jack from his shoulders and flung him away with all his force, and he remembered nothing more till he found himself lying on the hearth-rug in his own room. It might all have been a dream, only he was so sure it wasn't.

The fire had gone out, and the only light in the room came from the street lamps. Jack jumped up and searched everywhere for any trace of the little man, but could find none. He ran to the fireplace and called, but there was no answer, and at last he went shivering and cold to bed to dream of the Princess and the strange bright country underground, of which no one knows.

★   ★   ★

In the morning he was waked by his mother placing a little parcel in his hand as she kissed him. Jack was delighted when he opened it and found some crackers and sugar cakes and a wooden soldier off a Christmas-tree. He amused himself all the morning playing with them, but he could not forget the Fire-people and the pale pretty Princess. He dared

175

not tell his mother, lest he might make the Fire-man angry, and prevent his showing himself again. Next evening he was alone again, and sat looking anxiously between the bars, but nothing could he see of the Fire-people. Then he ran to the window and looked out, in search of the Water-Prince or the little Wind-fairy, but neither could he see, though it rained hard, and the wind blew loudly. So night after night passed, his mother went out and he was left alone, and yet he saw no trace of him, and he began to fear he should never know more of the Fire-people.

New Year's-eve came, and Jack's mother had to go out and leave him to watch the new year in alone. It was a miserable night. It rained in torrents, and the wind blew, in great melancholy gusts. Jack sat by the window, and looked out on the wet street and the driving clouds. He had given up looking in the fire for his little red friend, and to-night he was busy thinking of the new year which would begin to-morrow.

"When this next year is done," he said to himself, "I shall be eight years old. Mother says I am very small for my years. I wonder if I shall be bigger then."

"Little Jack!" called a low sighing voice from the grate.

Jack started, and ran to the fireplace. The fire was almost out. There was only a dull red glare in the coals, but kneeling in it holding on to the bars, was the Fire-Princess. She was paler than before, and looked quite transparent. Jack could see the coals plainly through her.

"Put on some more coal," she said, shivering. "There is not enough for me to burn here, and if I don't keep up a good blaze I shall go out altogether."

Jack did as he was bid, and then sat down on the hearth-rug, staring at the Princess with all his might.

Her long bright hair fell over the bars, and though her face looked very small and pale, her eyes were immense, and glittered like diamonds.

"How beautiful you are!" he said at last.

"Am I?" said the Princess with a sigh. "So my Prince said. It was with the greatest difficulty I managed to get here to-night, but I was determined to come. Ever since I saw you, I have thought of you so much."

"Have you?" said Jack, still staring.

"Yes, you were so sorry for me, and all my people are so unkind. Now I want you to do me a favour."

"What is it?" asked Jack.

"Let the Prince come here and speak to me."

"How am I to bring him?" said Jack.

"I will show you. Is it raining to-night?"

"Yes, hard."

"That is very lucky; some of his people are sure to be about. Then all you must do is to open the window and wait."

"But the rain will come into the room," said Jack.

"No, it will not, and if it does it will not do you any harm. You can't be quenched with water. Be a good boy, and do as I tell you."

So Jack threw open one of the windows. A great gust of wind blew into the room, and blew the cold wet rain into his face. The fire around the Princess broke out into a blaze, and then sank away, but she did not move, but called to Jack to stand between her and the window to keep off the draught and wet. He did as she bade him, and then she began to sing.

First she sang in a low voice, then her song grew louder and louder, and clearer and clearer. At last she stopped and said:

"Now little Jack, look on the window-sill and tell me what you see."

Jack ran to the window, and just outside, seated on the sill, in a little pool of water, was a tiny man dressed in a dull green dress. He had long wavy hair that looked heavy and wet, and his clothes were shiny with water.

He eyed Jack very crossly for a minute or two, then he said:

"Who are you, and what do you want?"

"Tell him," whispered the Princess, "that he must bring Prince Fluvius here"; and Jack repeated to the Water-fairy what she said.

"And who are you who dares to ask me to bring the Prince?" said he. "Do you think our Prince is to be taken about anywhere and everywhere, just because mortals want him?" But, on hearing this, the Princess began to sing again in the same soft voice, growing louder and louder, till the Water-fairy sprang up, promising to bring Prince Fluvius, or do anything else Jack wished, if only the song would cease, as he could not endure the heat, for it was a spell the Princess sang, and if she had gone on he would have been dried up altogether.

Then the Princess leaned back amongst the coals in silence. The

177

Water-fairy at once disappeared, and Jack stood at the window watching for what would come with great interest.

The rain fell in torrents, and suddenly the room began to grow very dark. When the Princess saw this she raised her head.

"He is coming," she said; and immediately there shot out from her, on all sides, a brilliant golden light, in the midst of which she looked even more beautiful than before. Then there floated up outside the window a white cloud, which rested on the sill. The cloud opened, and from it stepped the figure of a young man, gorgeously dressed in silver and green. He was about the size of the Princess, and next to her Jack thought he was the most beautiful little creature he had ever seen. He had long dark curls hanging down, and a sweet pale face, with eyes of a deep blue, just the colour of the sea.

At sight of Princess Pyra he started, and would have dashed right up to the bars, had she not begged him for both their sakes not to come inside the window.

"It is you, my darling," he said, leaning into the room. "And I believed I should never see you again. Oh, let me only once take you in my arms!"

"Do not think of such a thing," called the Princess. "It would be fatal to us both."

"At any rate, we should perish together," said Prince Fluvius.

"And how much better to live together!" said the Princess.

"If that were possible," said the Prince, sighing.

"And it is possible," said the Princess. "Since I last saw you I have learnt that there is only one person in the world who can help us, and that is the old man who sits on the North Pole. He knows everything, and could we but send to him and ask his advice, he would tell us what to do."

"But how are we to send to him?" said the Prince. "If you were to go, the sea would surely quench you on the way, and I should be frozen directly I got to the Ice-people, and never return to you. As for the Wind-fairies, who are constantly there, they are such silly little things, they could never remember a message."

"Little Jack," cried the Princess, turning towards him, "you will go for us, will you not?"

178

"I?" cried Jack, frightened. "How am I to go?"

"Nothing can be easier. One of the Wind-fairies will take you and bring you back—as the Prince will direct. You shall go, to-night. Now, dear Jack, you will do it for us, will you not? And we shall be so grateful."

Jack did not know what to say, but he looked first at the Prince sitting on the window-sill with the rain pouring around him, looking wistfully towards him, with his handsome mournful eyes; then he looked at the Princess kneeling on the glowing coals, entreating him with clasped hands to help them, while sparks fell from her bright eyes. And they were both so beautiful that he could not bear to refuse them, and was silent.

The Princess saw at once that he wavered, and said, smiling, "Then it is settled; you will go for us. And now, dear little Jack, listen very carefully to all the directions we give you, and be sure you do all we tell you. The old man at the North Pole is very mischievous and cunning, and always does his best to deceive anyone who comes to him for help. And there is one thing of which you must be very careful. You must not, whatever happens, ask him more than one question. The first question that he is asked he is bound to answer truthfully, but if you ask him more than one, he will at once seize you and keep you under the ice. He will do all he can to tempt you to ask more than one, but you must not mind him. And be sure to remember exactly what he says about me."

"What am I to say, then?" asked Jack.

"Say, 'I come from the Fire Princess Pyra, and she is in love with Prince Fluvius, the Water Prince, and wants to know how they are to be married.' And then shut your lips, and do not speak again, whatever he says. When you come to the Ice-country, you will find it very cold, so I shall give you a fire-ball to keep you warm. And be sure you do not stop and talk to the Ice-people, for if you do you will be frozen to death."

"How am I to go?" asked Jack again.

"Go to the window, and you will see the Wind-fairy who is to take you."

Jack did as he was told, and saw standing beside Prince Fluvius a little man dressed in light dust-coloured clothes, which hung on him loosely, seeming barely to touch him.

179

His face was very cheerful, but there was scarcely any expression in it, and whenever he moved there came a violent gust of wind.

"Are you ready?" asked the Prince, kindly.

"Yes," said Jack, feeling very frightened.

"You need not be afraid, little Jack," said Prince Fluvius; "you have nothing to do but to sit on his shoulders, and he will take you quite safely."

So saying he touched him on the head, and Jack began to feel himself growing smaller and smaller, till he was the same size as the Prince and Princess.

"Come on, then," said the Wind-fairy, in an odd gusty voice. Jack sat down on his shoulders in the same way as he had before sat upon the Fire-fairy, and they prepared to start.

"Goodbye, little Jack," called the Princess from the fire. "When your turn comes, you will find that we shall not forget to help you."

"Goodbye, little Jack," echoed the Prince. "Do not forget all we have told you, and be sure you ask no second question of the old man."

"Goodbye," called Jack, and off they went. The rain beat into Jack's face, and he felt giddy with the rate at which they flew, but he was silent, and held on tightly to the Wind-fairy's neck.

On they went in silence, going over the tops of the houses, among the chimney-pots, in a way Jack thought frightful. Then they came to the country, and flew over fields and lanes. At last the clouds cleared away, and the moon came out and Jack could see where they were going. He was getting more used to his position now, and felt less afraid to look about him. They flew over woods and rivers, and passed villages, which looked in the distance as small as if they were made of toy houses and churches. At last they came in sight of the sea, and Jack could keep silence no longer, but burst out:

"I hope we are not going over there?"

"Indeed we are," said, or rather puffed out, his companion, for his words came out like a gust of wind. "I thought you were never going to speak, and I did not like to speak first. How are you? I hope you feel pretty comfortable."

"Pretty well," answered Jack. "But I am afraid if we cross the sea I shall tumble in."

"No, you shan't," said the other. "I shall keep tight hold of you. Oh! it's splendid when one gets into the middle of the sea. It's worth blowing there."

"Won't it be very cold?" asked Jack.

"Nothing to speak of," said his companion, carelessly. "When we get among the ice and snow you may be chilly, but I've got the fire-ball the Princess gave me to blow in front of us, and that will keep you warm. I wonder what it is you want to ask the old man. Won't you tell me?"

"I think I'd better not," said Jack. "I suppose he is a very wise old man."

"Wise! He knows everything, and whatever you ask he's sure to give you, as long as it's the first question. Now we are going over the water."

Then they began to cross the sea. Jack, who had quite got over his fear, enjoyed the journey. The sea danced and sparkled beneath them. The moon threw a silver crest on the top of each tiny wave. Here and there were little ships sailing briskly along in the breeze. Soon they lost sight of land altogether, and then Jack thought it was glorious.

Nothing but the bright sparkling sea all round for miles! He laughed aloud for pleasure, and would have been quite happy, only for a thought—a naughty little thought—which would keep coming into his mind, and which grew and grew in spite of himself. He put up his hands to his head to keep it out, but there it was all the same, and there it remained. It was this—Why should he not ask the old man something for himself, instead of asking him about the Princess at all? Who would ever know? Why should he not ask him to make him straight and well? How pleased his mother would be if she came home that night to find her little boy a cripple no longer. How easy it would be to invent something to tell the Princess, and no one else would tell the truth. He knew it was naughty. He had promised, and he ought to keep his promise, and he thought of the Princess's pale face and the Prince's sad voice. And then he thought of his mother, and his own dull home, and could scarcely keep from crying.

"Listen!" said the Wind-fairy. "Don't you hear someone singing?"

Jack listened, and heard a sad sweet voice singing a song, which was more beautiful than anything he had ever heard before.

"That is a mermaid," said the Wind-fairy, "and she is singing to a ship.

She will go on singing until the ship follows the sound. Then she will gradually lead it down into a whirl-pool, and there it will be swallowed up, and the poor sailors will never return to their wives and little children. But I will go and blow the ship in another direction, whether it likes it or no, until it is out of the sound of her song, and then it will go on all right. Ah! men little think, when they complain of meeting gales of wind, that it is often for their own good, and that we are blowing them away from danger, not into it."

"A mermaid!" cried Jack. "I have never seen one. How much I should like to see her!"

"When we have gone to the ship we will go and look at her," said the Wind-fairy. Then he flew to one side, till they came to a ship full of sailors sailing quietly along, and the Wind-fairy began to blow with all his might. He blew till the sea rose in great heavy waves. The ship leaned over on one side. The captain shouted. The sailors threw up the ropes, and all trembled for fear. Much against their will the ship had to be turned about and go in another direction, and the Wind-fairy never left off blowing till she was many miles away from the sound of the mermaid's song.

"Now we will go and look at the mermaid," said he; and back they flew again to the same spot. There, beneath them, resting on the top of the waves, Jack saw a very beautiful maiden. She had sad green eyes and long green hair. When he looked closer he saw that she had a long bright tail instead of legs, but he thought her very beautiful all the same. She was still singing in a sad sleepy voice, and as he listened he began to long to jump into the sea beside her. And the longing grew so strong that he would have thrown himself into her arms at once, had not the Wind-fairy seized him and flown off with him before he had time.

How pleased the Wind-fairy was about the ship!

"I am so glad we came up," he said. "A few minutes later and the mermaid would have got it, and I could have done nothing," and he laughed for pleasure.

Then when Jack thought of the poor ship, and how nearly she had perished, and saw how glad the good little Wind-man was that he had saved her, all the naughty thoughts left his mind.

"Surely," he said to himself, "if this poor silly little Wind-fairy can be so glad when he has done a good deed, I ought to be glad to help other people and not to think of myself," and he made up his mind that whatever happened he would not desert the Princess, but would do exactly what she had told him.

On they went. Presently it began to grow very cold. In the sea beneath were great lumps of floating ice, and all sorts of strange sea monsters appeared on the surface.

"We had better stop here, and I will get out the Princess's fire-ball," said the fairy, and he placed Jack on a great lump of floating ice. On it there sat a family of seals, and much frightened they looked when he was dropped among them.

"Don't you know," said the old seal, turning sharply to him, "that it is exceedingly rude to come on to a person's block of ice without asking leave?"

"I am very sorry, I am sure," murmured Jack.

"Let him alone," said another younger seal; "I am sure he is very nice-looking. Would you like me to fetch you a little fish? I dare say you're very hungry, and I can catch you some in a moment if you like it."

Jack had not time to refuse before an older seal turned to him and said:

"I am in want of a servant, if that's what you are come for, and as you are a nice tidy-looking person, I don't mind trying you; only I am very particular about my ice being bright, and the water all round it being kept clean."

They were all crowding round him, when the Wind-fairy came up, and with one puff sent them all into the water again.

"See," he said, taking Jack up again, "I have sent on the ball before us, and it will keep you nice and warm."

Jack looked in front of him and saw a great ball of light which the Wind-fairy blew along as he went, and which sent out a soft warmth.

"How did you manage to carry it?" he asked of the fairy.

"It was quite a little thing when Princess Pyra gave it to me," he answered, "no bigger than a spark of light, and I have blown it up to its present size. I doubt if it will keep alight till after we reach the North

Pole, but it will keep you warm till then, and I shall be able to bring you back very quickly. Now we are coming to the Ice-world."

Looking about him, Jack saw that the blocks of ice were growing larger and larger as they went on, and the spaces of water less and less, until at last they disappeared altogether, and nothing could be seen but an immense plain of solid ice. The moon shone upon it brightly, and moving noiselessly over the surface were a number of almost transparent forms of men and women, with deadly white faces and cold glittering eyes. They never spoke, but moved about swiftly and silently. They fled at the sight of the fire-ball, but when they saw Jack some of them stopped and motioned to him to stop too.

"Who are they?" he asked.

"They are Ice-people," said his guide; "they live on the ice, and never speak, but always glide about as you see them now."

"Why mayn't we stop and see them?" said Jack.

His companion said nothing, but pointed down to where some dark heavy-looking figures lay motionless beneath the clear ice.

"Do you see?" he said. "These are the bodies of men and women whom the Ice-people have caught and frozen to death. If any unfortunate ship is wrecked among the ice-blocks, the Ice-people at once flock round it and seize the passengers, and carry them over here and freeze them. They are as wicked and cruel as the mermaids. If I were to leave you for only a second, you would be frozen, and nothing could save you. Now we are coming near the North Pole. Look over there."

Jack looked away across the ice, and saw a clear pink light that darted up into the sky in bars. It seemed to come from a curious dark lump in the form of a mushroom, which stood up into the air.

"That is the North Pole," said his friend, "and the light comes from the old man's lantern."

"Does he live there all alone?" asked Jack.

"All alone, and he quarrels with everyone. He used to be very good friends with the old man at the South Pole, and they often slid up and down the Pole to see each other. But one day they had a quarrel, and now they're not on speaking terms."

"What did they quarrel about?" inquired Jack.

"How should I know?" said the Wind-fairy, a little crossly. "One

184

really can't be expected to remember all these little things," for the Wind-fairies cannot bear to be reminded of their want of memory. "Now say what you have to say to him quickly, and get it done, and then I'll take you back." So saying, he put him down on the ice, and sat down himself a little way off.

Jack looked about him, and began to think he must be dreaming. It was such a strange scene. All round was the clear cold ice, and just in front of him was the great lump in the form of a mushroom, made of some thick shining stuff like ivory, and seated right in the middle of it was a little old man. He nursed his knees with his arms and hugged a huge brown lantern full of holes, from which shot up into the air on each side the long bright pink rays which Jack had seen before. The old man wore a big brown cloak, and on his head a small skull-cap, from beneath which fell his long straight white hair.

He was a very ugly old man; there was no doubt about that. His face was almost flat, and he had a large hook-nose. He seemed to be asleep, for his head hung over on one side, and his eyes were shut. Jack dared not wake him, and stood watching him. He might have remained there for ever; the old man would never have moved of himself, if the Wind-fairy had not blown a tremendous gust, which made the pink light in the lantern flicker, and the old man start up and open his eyes and see Jack.

"And who are you?" he asked, in a deep rolling voice. "Come to ask a question, I am sure. No one ever comes to see me unless they want to ask something. Come nearer and let me see you."

Jack drew near to the old man's seat, trembling much.

He tried to remember what the Princess had told him to say, but somehow or other it had gone out of his head, and he did not know how to begin.

"Now what is it?" asked the old man, with a low chuckle. "Do you want me to tell you how to grow tall and straight, or where to find a big bag of money to take home to your mother? What do you want? Speak out, and don't be afraid."

Again the naughty thoughts came back into Jack's mind. He looked across to where the Wind-fairy had fallen asleep on the ice. He gazed up at the pink light shining into the black sky. He thought of his mother,

185

then of the poor Fire Princess, and making a violent effort, and shutting his eyes that he might not see the grinning face of the old man, he said:

"I'm come from the Fire Princess, Princess Pyra, and she wants to marry the Water King's son, Prince Fluvius, and they're afraid of touching each other, lest he should be dried up, or she put out. So, please, they want to know what to do."

Here Jack stopped, and opened his eyes, and saw that the old man was shaking so with laughter that he feared he would tumble off the Pole altogether. He went on chuckling for such a time that Jack thought he would never stop. And when he had done, it was some time before he could find breath to speak, but sat panting and sighing, and every now

186

and then beginning to laugh afresh. After a time, however, he was more calm, and then he said:

"Oh, the stupidity of people! And all this time they are afraid of doing the very thing they ought to do. Of course it's impossible for them to marry till he is dried up, or she is put out. What puts out fire but water? And what dries up water but fire? Princess Pyra has been educated at a good school, I should think she might have known better. You had better go back to Prince Fluvius, and tell him to *give her a kiss*"; and then the old man began to laugh again.

Jack stood by, sorely puzzled; yet he dared not ask again. Then the old man turned to him, and said:

"And now what do you want to ask next? Let it be something for yourself this time, my little man. What shall it be? I'll tell you whatever you want to know."

A dozen questions flashed into Jack's mind at once. How he longed to ask them! But he remembered the Princess's warning, and held his tongue. He looked at the Wind-fairy, who was still asleep, and wondered how he could wake him. The ice was so slippery that he dared not walk upon it. He was just trying to move off gently, when the old man caught him by his wrist with a long skinny hand, and held him firmly back.

"Come, now," he said, coaxingly, while his eyes sparkled cunningly; "you'll never go back after asking only one question, when you have come so far. That would be very foolish. Ask something else while you *are* here."

He held Jack so tightly that he began to be frightened, and gave a violent wriggle, which knocked over the old man's lantern. It fell with an enormous crash, and woke the Wind-fairy, who was at his side in an instant.

"Well," he said, "are you ready?"

"Quite," said Jack, his teeth chattering with fear, for the old fellow had flown into a violent rage, and was stretching out his long thin arms to catch him; but the Wind-fairy blew in his face till he was forced to shut his eyes, and turn his head away. Then he took Jack on his shoulders, and flew off with him without another word.

"The fire-ball is gone out," he said to Jack, after they had gone a little way; "so I'm afraid you'll be cold. If you feel sleepy you may as well go to sleep. I won't let you fall; and I am about to go so quickly that you won't see anything we pass."

Jack did feel both sleepy and cold, and was very glad to fall into a doze, although he woke every now and then to ask if they were getting near home. At last the fairy said:

"Now we are over London, and you'll be home in a few minutes."

"I hope my mother hasn't come home yet," said Jack. "She'd be so frightened if she came back, and didn't find me."

"Come back!" laughed the fairy. "Why, it isn't twelve o'clock yet, and the New Year is not come in. Here is the street where you live."

Jack could not believe that they had not been gone more than an hour. It seemed more like twenty.

From outside the window he could see the Prince kneeling on the sill in exactly the same position as when he had left him, and he wondered if the Princess was still sitting in the fire. Yes. When the Wind-fairy placed him in the middle of the room, there she was in exactly the same place, with her golden hair falling over the bars.

"Well," cried she and the Prince together, "what did he say, little Jack? Tell us at once."

"I'm so cold," said Jack; "I'm almost frozen."

The Princess made a great blaze in the coals till the room was quite light. Then she turned to Jack again.

"Now," she said, "you must be warm. Do not keep us any longer in suspense."

Jack hesitated for a minute; then he looked at the Princess, and repeated what the old man had said. " 'What puts out fire but water? What dries up water but fire? Tell him to give her a kiss!' "

Both Prince and Princess were silent when they heard this. Then the Prince said, with a sigh:

"It is as I thought. He means **that** there is no hope for us, and that we must perish together. For my part, I am quite willing, as anything would be better than life without you, my Pyra."

"He meant no such thing," cried the Princess. "And I think now I begin to understand him. We must both be changed before we can be happy. Come, then, my Prince, I have no fear, and will willingly risk being quenched altogether, if there is a chance of our union."

188

So saying, the Princess rose up, and stepped lightly from the grate on to the floor, surrounded by a halo of shining flame.

Jack screamed aloud, afraid lest the room should take fire; but in the same moment the Prince swept down from the window, and a flood of water splashed on to the floor. Then, without another word, the two rushed into each other's arms.

A great crash—a sound like a clap of thunder; then the room was filled with smoke, through which Jack could see nothing. He felt frightened, and inclined to cry; but in a minute or two he heard the soft voice of the Princess, calling to him:

"Jack, Jack!" and he saw the smoke clearing away.

There, in the middle of the room, stood the Princess Pyra—the same, yet not the same; and beside her was Prince Fluvius, like himself in face and figure, and yet altered. His arm was about the Princess, and she leaned her head on his shoulder.

She was no longer surrounded by flames, and the weird brightness had passed from her face and dress.

Her hair looked softer and glittered less, and her eyes no longer seemed to burn, but beamed on Jack, with a soft, mild light. The fire-coloured orchids had disappeared from her bosom, and in its place was a bunch of real water-lilies. The Prince was no less changed. His eyes were bright and clear, his hair had lost its wet gloss, and was dry and curly; his clothes looked crisp and firm.

The Princess bent her head with a sob, and this time real tears fell from her eyes. The Prince stooped to kiss them away, and as he did so the clock began to strike twelve, and all the bells in the great city rang out to tell the world that the New Year was born. And as they rang, the room was filled with the strangest forms. Fairies, goblins, elves, beautiful, ugly, and strange, floated in at the open window, and pressed around the Prince and Princess, and filled every nook and corner of the room. But they all looked kindly at Jack, and smiled at him, whilst he sat and cried for joy. With every stroke of the clock, with every clash of the bells, their number increased, but at the sixth stroke, the young couple rose from the ground, and began to float slowly towards the window.

"Goodbye, little Jack; we shall never forget you," called the Princess, as she floated away, and she waved her hand and smiled sweetly.

189

"Goodbye, little Jack," echoed the Prince; "we shall come when you want us"; and as the clock struck the last hour of twelve they passed out of the window. But still the Princess looked back, and kissed her hand. Then all the strange company who had filled the room a moment before, arose and floated away around the Prince and Princess, and the room was left empty and cold, and little Jack was left alone.

★　　　　　★　　　　　★

A whole year had passed away, and Jack was turned eight years old. A whole long year, and he had heard or seen nothing of his fairy friends.

He had stirred the fire, he had watched the water, but in vain. They had gone, he feared, never to return, and he was fast beginning to think it must all have been a strange dream.

Christmas had come round again, but this was a very different Christmas to last year's, for little Jack was very ill, sick unto death, and lay in bed and could not move. His mother went out to no parties, for all day and night she sat by her little boy's bedside. How she cried! Jack could not quite understand why, for, when he was not in pain, he liked very well to lie in bed, with his mother sitting beside him to pet and amuse him.

Christmas week passed, and New Year's-eve came. His mother was so weary with watching, that she could keep awake no longer, and slept in spite of herself, in the arm-chair at the bedside.

Jack lay still, looking at the bright new moon through the window. A white crisp layer of snow covered the housetops, on which the moon's light shone silver and clear. As he lay and watched, the candle flickered down in its socket, and then went out altogether.

"This time last year I saw the Princess," said Jack to himself, "but I shan't see her again," and he sighed.

"Little Jack," called a low sweet voice that made him start and tremble.

He looked up at the window, and there, standing in a moonbeam, was the Princess, looking far more beautiful even than before, and the Prince stood close beside her.

"Did you think you would never see us again?" she asked. "But this will be for the last time, for we are going to live on the other side of the moon, and shall never come back again. Now see what we have brought you. This is a magic belt, and we have been a whole year making it. You must put it on, and it will make you quite strong, and in a few years you will no longer be a cripple."

Jack then saw that between them they bore a kind of silver hoop, which they carried to the bedside, and the Princess said:

"No one will know it is there, for directly it is upon you it will become invisible. Neither will you feel it yourself. Now sit up, and I will put it on for you."

"Thank you, dear Princess," said Jack, sitting up in bed.

Then the Prince and Princess slipped the belt over Jack's head, and fastened it round his waist, but when it was on he could neither feel nor see it.

"Then farewell, dear little Jack," said they. "This time we part for ever." And the Princess stooped and kissed Jack on the forehead. Such a kiss it was, he had never felt anything so nice in his life.

"Goodbye, dear, kind Princess," he said, huskily, stretching out his hands towards her, for he felt very sad at the thought that he should never see her again.

Then both Prince and Princess floated up the moonbeam, and the Princess looked back and kissed her hand as before, and they flew out of the window, and Jack never saw them again.

But the next day, when the doctor came, he said Jack was much better, and would soon be well, and it was all the new medicine he had given him.

And when Jack told his mother about the Princess, and the wonderful belt he wore, she only shook her head and said with a smile, "Dear boy, you have had a dream, and I am glad it was such a pleasant one."

Years afterwards, when he had grown to be a tall strong boy, he often felt for the belt, but never could find it; and when his mother rejoiced over his cure, and said it all came of his growing so much stronger after the illness he had had that winter, he smiled to himself and said:

"Nay, it all came of my going to the North Pole for the Fire Princess."

THE
WANDERINGS
OF
ARASMON

BY
MARY DE MORGAN

ILLUSTRATED
BY
WALTER CRANE

THE
WANDERINGS
OF
ARASMON

Long ago there lived a wandering musician and his wife, whose names were Arasmon and Chrysea. Arasmon played upon a lute to which Chrysea sang, and their music was so beautiful that people followed them in crowds and gave them as much money as they wanted. When Arasmon played all who heard him were silent from wonder and admiration, but when Chrysea sang they could not refrain from weeping, for her voice was more beautiful than anything they had ever heard before.

Both were young and lovely, and were as happy as the day was long, for they loved each other dearly, and liked wandering about seeing new countries and people and making sweet music. They went to all sorts of places, sometimes to big cities, sometimes to little villages, sometimes to lonely cottages by the sea-shore, and sometimes they strolled along the green lanes and fields, singing and playing so exquisitely, that the very birds flew down from the trees to listen to them.

One day they crossed a dark line of hills, and came out on a wild moorland country, where they had never been before. On the side of the hill they saw a little village, and at once turned towards it, but as they drew near Chrysea said,

"What gloomy place is this? See how dark and miserable it looks."

"Let us try to cheer it with some music," said Arasmon, and began to play upon his lute, while Chrysea sang. One by one the villagers came out of their cottages and gathered round them to listen, but Chrysea thought she had never before seen such forlorn-looking people. They were thin and bent, their faces were pale and haggard, also their clothes looked old and threadbare, and in some places were worn into holes. But they crowded about Arasmon and Chrysea, and begged them to go on playing and singing, and as they listened the women shed tears, and the men hid their faces and were silent. When they stopped, the people began to feel in their pockets as if to find some coins, but Arasmon cried,

"Nay, good friends, keep your money for yourselves. You have not too much of it, to judge by your looks. But let us stay with you for to-night, and give us food and lodging, and we shall think ourselves well paid, and will play and sing to you as much as you like."

"Stay with us as long as you can, stay with us always," begged the people; and each one entreated to be allowed to receive the strangers and give them the best they had. So Arasmon and Chrysea played and sang to them till they were tired, and at last, when the heavy rain began to fall, they turned towards the village, but as they passed through its narrow streets they thought the place itself looked even sadder than its inmates. The houses were ill-built, and seemed to be almost tumbling down. The streets were uneven and badly kept. In the gardens they saw no flowers, but dank dark weeds. They went into a cottage which the people pointed out to them, and Arasmon lay down by the fire, calling to Chrysea to rest also, as they had walked far, and she must be weary. He soon fell asleep, but Chrysea sat at the door watching the dark clouds as they drifted over the darker houses. Outside the cottage hung a blackbird in a cage, with drooping wings and scanty plumage. It was the only animal they had yet seen in the village, for of cats or dogs or singing-birds there seemed to be none.

When she saw it, Chrysea turned to the woman of the house, who stood beside her, and said,

"Why don't you let it go? It would be much happier flying about in the sunshine."

"The sun never shines here," said the woman sadly. "It could not pierce through the dark clouds which hang over the village. Besides, we do not think of happiness. It is as much as we can do to live."

"But tell me," said Chrysea, "what is it that makes you so sad and your village such a dreary place? I have been to many towns in my life, but to none which looked like this."

"Don't you know," said the woman, "that this place is spell-bound?"

198

"Spell-bound?" cried Chrysea. "What do you mean?"

The woman turned and pointed towards the moor. "Over yonder," she said, "dwells a terrible old wizard by whom we are bewitched, and he has a number of little dark elves who are his servants, and these are they who make our village what you see it. You don't know how sad it is to live here. The elves steal our eggs, and milk, and poultry, so that there is never enough for us to eat, and we are half-starved. They pull down our houses, and undo our work as fast as we do it. They steal our corn when it is standing in sheaves, so that we find nothing but empty husks"; and as she ceased speaking the woman sighed heavily.

"But if they do all this harm," said Chrysea, "why do not some of you go to the moor and drive them away?"

"It is part of the spell," said the woman, "that we can neither hear nor see them. I have heard my grandfather say that in the old time this place was no different to others, but one day this terrible old magician came and offered the villagers a great deal of money if they would let him dwell upon the moor; for before that it was covered with golden gorse and heather, and the country folk held all their merry-makings there, but they were tempted with the gold, and sold it, and from that day the elves have tormented us; and as we cannot see them, we cannot get rid of them, but must just bear them as best we may."

"That is a sad way to speak," said Chrysea. "Cannot you find out what the spell really is and break it?"

"It is a song," said the woman, "and every night they sing it afresh. It is said that if anyone could go to the moor between midnight and dawn, and could hear them singing it, and then sing through the tune just as they themselves do, the charm would be broken, and we should be free. But it must be someone who has never taken their money, so we cannot do it, for we can neither see nor hear them."

"But I have not taken their money," said Chrysea. "And there is no tune I cannot sing when I have heard it once. So I will go to the moor for you and break the spell."

"Nay, do not think of such a thing," cried the woman. "For the elves are most spiteful, and you don't know what harm they might do to you, even if you set us free."

Chrysea said no more, but all the evening she thought of what the woman had told her, and still stood looking out into the dismal street. When she went to bed she did not sleep, but lay still till the clock struck one. Then she rose softly, and wrapping herself in a cloak, opened the door and stepped out into the rain. As she passed, she looked up and saw the blackbird crouching in the bottom of its cage. She opened the cage door to let it fly, but still it did not move, so she lifted it out in her hand.

"Poor bird!" said she gently; "I wish I could give this village its liberty as easily as I can give you yours," and carrying it with her she walked on towards the moor. It was a large waste piece of land, and looked as though it had been burnt, for the ground was charred and black, and there was no grass or green plant growing on it, but there were some blackened stumps of trees, and to these Chrysea went, and hid herself behind one to wait and see what would come. She watched for a long time without seeing anyone, but at last there rose from the ground not far from her a lurid gleam, which spread and spread until it became a large circle of light, in the midst of which she saw small dark figures moving, like ugly little men. The light was now so bright that she could distinguish each one quite plainly, and never before had she seen anything so ugly, for they were black as ink, and their faces were twisted and looked cruel and wicked.

They joined hands, and, forming a ring, danced slowly round, and, as they did so, the ground opened, and there rose up in their centre a tiny village exactly like the spell-bound village, only that the houses were but a few inches high. Round this the elves danced, and then they began to sing. Chrysea listened eagerly to their singing, and no sooner had they done, than she opened her lips and sang the same tune through from beginning to end just as she had heard it.

Her voice rang out loud and clear, and at the sound the little village crumbled and fell away as though it had been made of dust.

The elves stood silent for a moment, and then with a wild cry they all rushed towards Chrysea, and at their head she saw one about three times the size of the others, who appeared to be their chief.

"Come, quickly, let us punish the woman who has dared to thwart us," he cried. "What shall we change her to?"

"A frog to croak on the ground," cried one.

"No, an owl to hoot in the night," cried another.

"Oh, for pity's sake," implored Chrysea, "don't change me to one of these loathsome creatures, so that, if Arasmon finds me, he will spurn me."

"Hear her," cried the chief, "and let her have her will. Let us change her to no bird or beast, but to a bright golden harp, and thus shall she remain, until upon her strings someone shall play our tune, which she has dared to sing."

"Agreed!" cried the others, and all began to dance round Chrysea and to sing as they had sung around the village. She shrieked and tried to run, but they stopped her on every side. She cried, "Arasmon! Arasmon!" but no one came, and when the elves' song was done, and they disappeared, all that was left was a little gold harp hanging upon the boughs of the tree, and only the blackbird who sat above knew what had come of poor Chrysea.

When morning dawned, and the villagers awoke, all felt that some great change had taken place. The heavy cloud which hung above the village had cleared away; the sun shone brightly, and the sky was blue; streams which had been dry for years, were running clear and fresh: and the people all felt strong, and able to work again; the trees were beginning to bud, and in their branches sang birds, whose voices had not been heard there for many a long year. The villagers looked from one to another and said, "Surely the spell is broken; surely the elves must have fled"; and they wept for joy.

Arasmon woke with the first beam of the sun, and finding Chrysea was not there, he rose, and went to seek her in the village, calling, "Chrysea, Chrysea! the sun is up and we must journey on our way"; but no Chrysea answered, so he walked down all the streets, calling "Chrysea! come, Chrysea!" but no Chrysea came. Then he said,

"She has gone into the fields to look for wild flowers, and will soon be back." So he waited for her patiently, but the sun rose high, the villagers went to their work, and she did not return. At this Arasmon was frightened, and asked everyone he met if they had seen her, but each one shook his head and said, "No, they had seen nothing of her."

Then he called some of the men together and told them that his wife had wandered away, and he feared lest she might lose herself and go still

201

farther, and he asked them to help him to look for her. So some went one way, and some another, to search, and Arasmon himself walked for miles the whole country round, calling "Chrysea! Chrysea!" but no answer came.

The sun was beginning to set and twilight to cover the land, when Arasmon came on to the moor where Chrysea had met her fate. That, too, was changed. Flowers and grass were already beginning to grow there, and the children of the village, who till now had never dared to venture near it, were playing about it. Arasmon could hear their voices as he came near the tree against which Chrysea had leaned, and on which now hung the golden harp. In the branches above sat the blackbird singing, and Arasmon stopped and listened to its song, and thought he had never heard a bird sing so sweetly before. For it sang the magic song by which Chrysea had broken the elves' spell, the first tune it had heard since it regained its liberty.

"Dear blackbird," said Arasmon, looking up to it, "I wish your singing could tell me where to find my wife Chrysea"; and as he looked up he saw a golden harp hanging upon the branches, and he took it down and ran his fingers over the strings. Never before did harp give forth such music. It was like a woman's voice, and was most beautiful, but so sad that when Arasmon heard it he felt inclined to cry. It seemed to be calling for help, but he could not understand what it said, though each time he touched the strings it cried, "Arasmon, Arasmon, I am here! It is I, Chrysea"; but though Arasmon listened, and wondered at its tones, yet he did not know what it said.

He examined it carefully. It was a beautiful little harp, made of pure gold, and at the top was a pair of golden hands and arms clasped together.

"I will keep it," said Arasmon, "for I never yet heard a harp with such a tone, and when Chrysea comes she shall sing to it."

But Chrysea was nowhere to be found, and at last the villagers declared she must be lost, or herself have gone away on purpose, and that it was vain to seek her farther. At this Arasmon was angry, and saying that he would seek Chrysea as long as he had life, he left the village to wander over the whole world till he should find her. He went on foot, and took with him the golden harp.

He walked for many, many miles far away from the village and the moor, and when he came to any farmhouses, or met any country people on the road he began to play, and everyone thronged round him and stared, in breathless surprise at his beautiful music. When he had done he would ask them, "Have you seen my wife Chrysea? She is dressed in white and gold, and sings more sweetly than any of the birds of heaven."

But all shook their heads and said, "No, she had not been there"; and whenever he came to a strange village, where he had not been before, he called, "Chrysea, Chrysea, are you here?" but no Chrysea answered, only the harp in his hands cried whenever he touched its strings, "It is I, Arasmon! It is I, Chrysea!" but though he thought its notes like Chrysea's voice, he never understood them.

He wandered for days and months and years through countries and villages which he had never known before. When night came and he found himself in the fields alone, he would lie down upon his cloak and sleep with his head resting upon the harp, and if by chance one of its golden threads was touched it would cry, "Arasmon, awake, I am here!" Then he would dream that Chrysea was calling him, and would wake and start up to look for her, thinking she must be close at hand.

One day, towards night, when he had walked far, and was very tired, he came to a little village on a lonely, rocky coast by the sea, and he found that a thick mist had come up, and hung over the village, so that he could barely see the path before him as he walked. But he found his way down to the beach, and there stood a number of fisherwomen, trying to look through the mist towards the sea, and speaking anxiously.

"What is wrong, and for whom are you watching, good folk?" he asked them.

"We are watching for our husbands," answered one. "They went out in their boats fishing in the early morning, when it was quite light, and then arose this dreadful fog, and they should have come back long ago, and we fear lest they may lose their way in the darkness and strike on a rock and be drowned."

"I, too, have lost my wife Chrysea," cried Arasmon. "Has she passed by here? She had long golden hair, and her gown was white and gold, and she sang with a voice like an angel's."

The women all said, "No, they had not seen her"; but still they strained their eyes towards the sea, and Arasmon also began to watch for the return of the boats.

They waited and waited, but they did not come, and every moment the darkness grew thicker and thicker, so that the women could not see each other's faces, though they stood quite near together.

Then Arasmon took his harp and began to play, and its music floated over the water for miles through the darkness, but the women were weeping so for their husbands, that they did not heed it.

"It is useless to watch," said one. "They cannot steer their boats in such a darkness. We shall never see them again."

"I will wait all night till morning," said another, "and all day next day, and next night, till I see some sign of the boats, and know if they be living or dead," but as she stopped speaking, there rose a cry of "Here they are," and two or three fishing-boats were pushed on to the sand close by where they stood, and the women threw their arms round their husbands' necks, and all shouted for joy.

The fishermen asked who it was who had played the harp; "For," they said, "it was that which saved us: We were far from land, and it was so dark that we could not tell whether to go to left or to right, and had no sign to guide us to shore; when of a sudden we heard the most beautiful music, and we followed the sound, and came in quite safely."

" 'Twas this good harper who played while we watched," said the women, and one and all turned to Arasmon, and told him with tears of their gratitude, and asked him what they could do for him, or what they could give him in token of their thankfulness; but Arasmon shook his head and said, "You can do nothing for me, unless you can tell me where to seek my wife Chrysea. It is to find her I am wandering"; and when the women shook their heads, and said again they knew nothing of her, the harp-strings as he touched them cried again,

"Arasmon! Arasmon! listen to me. It is I, Chrysea"; but again no one understood it, and though all pitied him, no one could help him.

Next morning when the mist had cleared away, and the sun was shining, a little ship set sail for foreign countries, and Arasmon begged the captain to take him in it that he might seek Chrysea still farther.

They sailed and sailed, till at last they came to the country for which they were bound; but they found the whole land in confusion, and war and fighting everywhere, and all the people were leaving their homes and hiding themselves in the towns, for fear of a terrible enemy, who was invading them. But no one hurt Arasmon as he wandered on with his harp in his hand, only no one would stop to answer him, when he asked if Chrysea had been there, for everyone was too frightened and hurried to heed him.

At last he came to the chief city where the King dwelt, and here he found all the men building walls and fortresses, and preparing to defend the town, because they knew their enemy was coming to besiege it, but all the soldiers were gloomy and low-spirited.

"It is impossible for us to conquer," they said, "for there are three of them to every one of us, and they will take our city and make our King prisoner."

That night as the watchmen looked over the walls, they saw in the distance an immense army marching towards them, and their swords and helmets glittered in the moonlight.

Then they gave the signal, and the captains gathered together their men to prepare them for fighting; but so sure were they of being beaten that it was with difficulty their officers could bring them to the walls.

"It would be better," said the soldiers, "to lay down our arms at once and let the enemy enter, for then we should not lose our lives as well as our city and our wealth."

When Arasmon heard this he sat upon the walls of the town, and began to play upon his harp, and this time its music was so loud and clear, that it could be heard far and wide, and its sound so exultant and joyous, that when the soldiers heard it they raised their heads, and their fears vanished, and they started forward, shouting and calling that they would conquer or be killed.

Then the enemy attacked the city, but the soldiers within met them with so much force that they were driven back, and had to fly, and the victorious army followed them and drove them quite out of their country, and Arasmon went with them, playing on his harp, to cheer them as they went.

When they knew the victory was theirs, all the captains wondered what had caused their sudden success, and one of the lieutenants said, "It was that strange harper who went with us, playing on his harp. When our men heard it they became as brave as lions." So the captains sent for Arasmon, but when he came they were astonished to see how worn and thin he looked, and could scarcely believe it was he who had made such wonderful music, for his face had grown thin and pale, and there were grey locks in his hair.

They asked him what he would like to have, saying they would give him whatever he would choose, for the great service he had done them.

Arasmon only shook his head and said,

"There is nothing I want that you can give me. I am seeking the whole world round to find my wife Chrysea. It is many many years since I lost her. We two were as happy as birds on the bough. We wandered over the world singing and playing in the sunshine. But now she is gone, and I care for nothing else." And the captains looked pityingly at him, for they all thought him mad, and could not understand what the harp said when he played on it again, and it cried,

"Listen, Arasmon! I too am here—I, Chrysea."

So Arasmon left that city, and started again, and wandered for days and months and years.

He came by many strange places, and met with many strange people, but he found no trace of Chrysea, and each day he looked older and sadder and thinner.

At length he came to a country where the King loved nothing on earth so much as music. So fond of it was he, that he had musicians and singers by the score, always living in his palace, and there was no way of pleasing him so well as by sending a new musician or singer. So when Arasmon came into the country, and the people heard how marvellously he played, they said at once, "Let us take him to the King. The poor man is mad. Hear how he goes on asking for his wife; but, mad or not, his playing will delight the King. Let us take him at once to the palace." So, though Arasmon would have resisted them, they dragged him away to the court, and sent a messenger to the King, to say they had found a poor mad wandering harper, who played music the like of which they had never heard before.

The King and Queen, and all the court, sat feasting when the messenger came in saying that the people were bringing a new harper to play before his majesty.

"A new harper!" quoth he. "That is good hearing. Let him be brought here to play to us at once."

So Arasmon was led into the hall, and up to the golden thrones on which sat the King and Queen. A wonderful hall it was, made of gold and silver, and crystal and ivory, and the courtiers, dressed in blue and green and gold and diamonds, were a sight to see. Behind the throne were twelve young maids dressed in pure white, who sang most sweetly, and behind them were the musicians who accompanied them on every kind of instrument. Arasmon had never in his life seen such a splendid sight.

"Come here," cried the King to him, "and let us hear you play." And the singers ceased singing, and the musicians smiled scornfully, for they could not believe Arasmon's music could equal theirs. For he looked to be in a most sorry plight. He had walked far, and the dust of the roads was on him. His clothes were worn threadbare, and stained and soiled, while his face was so thin and anxious and sad that it was pitiful to see; but his harp of pure shining gold was undulled, and untarnished. He began to play, and then all smiles ceased, and the women began to weep, and the men sat and stared at him in astonishment. When he had done the King started up, and throwing his arms about his neck, cried, "Stay with me. You shall be my chief musician. Never before have I heard playing like yours, and whatever you want I will give you." But when he heard this, Arasmon knelt on one knee and said,

"My gracious lord, I cannot stay. I have lost my wife Chrysea. I must search all over the world till I find her. Ah! how beautiful she was, and how sweetly she sang; her singing was far sweeter than even the music of my harp."

"Indeed!" cried the King. "Then I too would fain hear her. But stay with me, and I will send messengers all over the world to seek her far and near, and they will find her much sooner than you."

So Arasmon stayed at the court, but he said that if Chrysea did not come soon he must go farther to seek her himself.

The King gave orders that he should be clad in the costliest clothes and have all he could want given to him, and after this he would hear no music but Arasmon's playing, so all the other musicians were jealous, and wished he had never come to the palace. But the strangest thing was that no one but Arasmon could play upon his golden harp. All the King's

harpers tried, and the King himself tried also, but when they touched the strings there came from them a strange, melancholy wailing, and no one but Arasmon could bring out its beautiful notes.

But the courtiers and musicians grew more and more angry with Arasmon, till at last they hated him bitterly, and only wanted to do him some harm; for they said,

"Who is he, that our King should love and honour him before us? After all, it is not his playing which is so beautiful; it is chiefly the harp on which he plays, and if that were taken from him he would be no better than the rest of us"; and then they began to consult together as to how they should steal his harp.

One hot summer evening Arasmon went into the palace gardens, and sat down to rest beneath a large beech-tree, when a little way off he saw two courtiers talking together, and heard that they spoke of him, though they did not see him or know he was there.

"The poor man is mad," said one; "of that there is little doubt, but, mad or not, as long as he plays on his harp the King will not listen to anyone else."

"The only way is to take the harp from him," said the other. "But it is hard to know how to get it away, for he will never let it go out of his hands."

"We must take it from him when he is sleeping," said the first.

"Certainly," said the other; and then Arasmon heard them settle how and when they would go to his room at night to steal his harp.

He sat still till they were gone, and then he rose, and grasping it tenderly, turned from the palace and walked away through the garden gates.

"I have lost Chrysea," he said, "and now they would take from me even my harp, the only thing I have to love in all this world, but I will go away, far off where they will never find me," and when he was out of sight, he ran with all his might, and never rested till he was far away on a lonely hill, with no one near to see him.

The stars were beginning to shine though it was not yet dark. Arasmon sat on a stone and looked at the country far and near. He could hear the sheep bells tinkling around him, and far, far off in the distance he could see the city and the palace he had left.

Then he began to play on his harp, and as he played the sheep stopped browsing and drew near to listen.

The stars grew brighter and the evening darker, and he saw a woman carrying a child coming up the hill.

She looked pale and tired, but her face was very happy as she sat down not far from Arasmon and listened to his playing, whilst she looked eagerly across the hill as if she watched for someone who was coming. Presently she turned and said, "How beautifully you play; I never heard music like it before, but what makes you look so sad? Are you unhappy?"

"Yes," said Arasmon, "I am very miserable. I lost my wife Chrysea many years ago, and now I don't know where she can be."

"It is a year since I have seen my husband," said the woman. "He went to the war a year ago, but now there is peace and he is coming back, and to-night he will come over this hill. It was just here we parted, and now I am come to meet him."

"How happy you must be," said Arasmon. "I shall never see Chrysea again," and as he spoke he struck a chord on the harp, which cried, "O Arasmon, my husband! why do you not know me? It is I, Chrysea."

"Do not say that," continued the woman; "you will find her some day. Why do you sit here? Was it here you parted from her?"

Then Arasmon told her how they had gone to a strange desolate village and rested there for the night, and in the morning Chrysea was gone, and that he had wandered all over the world looking for her ever since.

"I think you are foolish," said the woman; "perhaps your wife has been waiting for you at that village all this time. I would go back to the place where I parted from her if I were you, and wait there till she returns. How could I meet my husband if I did not come to the spot where we last were together? We might both wander on for ever and never find each other; and now, see, here he is coming," and she gave a cry of joy and ran to meet a soldier who was walking up the hill.

Arasmon watched them as they met and kissed, and saw the father lift the child in his arms, then the three walked over the hill together, and when they were gone he sat down and wept bitterly. "What was it she said?" he said. "That I ought to go back to the spot where we parted.

She will not be there, but I will go and die at the place where I last saw her." So again he grasped his harp and started. He travelled many days and weeks by land and sea, till late one day he came in sight of the hill on which stood the little village. But at first he could not believe that he had come to the right place, so changed did all appear. He stopped and looked around him in astonishment. He stood in a shady lane, the arching trees met over his head. The banks were full of spring flowers, and either side of the hedge were fields full of young green corn.

"Can this be the wretched bare road down which we walked together? I would indeed it were, and that she were with me now," said he. When he looked across to the village, the change seemed greater still. There were many more cottages, and they were trim and well kept, standing in neat gardens full of flowers. He heard the cheerful voices of the peasants and the laughter of the village children. The whole place seemed to be full of life and happiness. He stopped again upon the mound where he and Chrysea had first played and sung.

"It is many, many a long year since I was here," he said. "Time has changed all things strangely; but it would be hard to say which is the more altered, this village or I, for then it was sunk in poverty and wretchedness, and now it has gained happiness and wealth, and I, who was so happy and glad, now am broken-down and worn. I have lost my only wealth, my wife Chrysea. It was just here she stood and sang, and now I shall never see her again or hear her singing."

There came past him a young girl driving some cows, and he turned and spoke to her. "Tell me, I beg," he said, "is not your village much changed of late years? I was here long ago, but I cannot now think it the same place, for this is as bright and flourishing a town as I have ever seen, and I remember it only as a dreary tumble-down village where the grass never grew."

"Oh!" said the girl, "then you were here in our bad time, but we do not now like to speak of that, for fear our troubles should return. Folks say we were spell-bound. 'Tis so long ago that I can scarcely remember it, for I was quite a little child then. But a wandering musician and his wife set us free; at least, everything began to mend after they came, and now we think they must have been angels from heaven, for next day they went, and we have never seen them since."

"It was I and my wife Chrysea," cried Arasmon. "Have you seen her? Has she been here? I have sought all over the world ever since, but I cannot find her, and now I fear lest she be dead."

The girl stared at him in surprise. "You? you poor old man. Of what are you talking? You must surely be mad to say such things. These musicians were the most beautiful people upon the earth, and they were young and dressed in shining white and gold, and you are old and gray and ragged, and surely you are very ill too, for you seem to be so weak that you can scarcely walk. Come home with me, and I will give you food and rest till you are better."

Arasmon shook his head. "I am seeking Chrysea," he said, "and I will rest no more till I have found her"; and the girl, seeing that he was determined, left him alone and went on her way driving her cows before her.

When she had gone Arasmon sat by the wayside and wept as though his heart would break. "It is too true," he said; "I am so old and worn that when I find her she will not know me," and as he again fell a-weeping his hand struck the harp-strings, and they cried, "I have watched you through all these years, my Arasmon. Take comfort, I am very near," and his tears ceased, and he was soothed by the voice of the harp, though he knew not why.

Then he rose. "I will go to the moor," he said, "and look for the tree on which I found my harp, and that will be my last resting-place, for surely my strength will carry me no farther." So he tottered slowly on, calling, as he went, in a weak voice, "Chrysea, my Chrysea! are you here? I have sought you over the world since you left me, and now that I am old and like to die, I am come to seek you where we parted."

When he came upon the moor, he wondered again at the change of all the country round. He thought of the charred, blackened waste on which he had stood before and now he looked with amazement at the golden gorse, the purple heather, so thick that he could scarcely pick his way amongst it.

"It is a beautiful place now," he said, "but I liked it better years ago, deserted and desolate though it was, for my Chrysea was here."

There were so many trees upon the common that he could not tell which was the one on which his harp had hung, but, unable to go any farther, he staggered and sank down beneath a large oak-tree, in whose branches a blackbird was singing most sweetly. The sun was setting just as of yore when he had found his harp, and most of the birds' songs were over, but this one bird still sang sweet and clear, and Arasmon, tired and weak though he was, raised his head and listened.

"I never heard bird sing like that," he said. "What is the tune it sings? I will play it on my harp before I die." And with what strength remained to him he reached forth his trembling hand, and grasping his harp struck upon it the notes of the bird's song, then he fell back exhausted, and his eyes closed.

At once the harp slid from his hand, and Chrysea stood beside him—Chrysea dressed as of old, in shining white and gold, with bright hair and eyes.

"Arasmon!" she cried, "see, it is I, Chrysea!" but Arasmon did not move. Then she raised her voice and sang more sweetly than the bird overhead, and Arasmon opened his eyes and looked at her.

"Chrysea!" cried he; "I have found my wife Chrysea!" and he laid his head on her bosom and died. And when Chrysea saw it her heart broke, and she lay beside him and died without a word.

In the morning when some of the villagers crossed the common they saw Arasmon and Chrysea lying beneath the oak-tree in each other's arms, and drew near them, thinking they were asleep, but when they saw their faces they knew they were dead.

Then an old man stooped and looked at Chrysea, and said,

"Surely it is the woman who came to us and sang long ago, when we were in our troubles; and, though he is sadly changed and worn, it is like her husband who played for her singing."

Then came the girl who had driven the cows and told them how she had met Arasmon, and all he had said to her.

"He searched everywhere for his wife, he said," said she. "I am glad he has found her. Where could she be?"

"Would that we had known it was he," said they all, "how we would have greeted him! but see, he looks quite content and as if he wished nothing more, since he has found his wife Chrysea."

WANTED— A KING

BY
MAGGIE BROWNE

ILLUSTRATED
BY
HARRY FURNISS

Maggie Browne is the pseudonym for Margaret **Andrewes** an undeservedly neglected writer of Victorian children's literature. *Wanted—A King, or How Merle Set the Nursery Rhymes to Rights,* with illustrations by Harry Furniss, was first published in 1890. Like her children's fantasy *The Book of Betty Barber* (1900), *Wanted—A King* clearly reveals the influence of the Alice books. In both of her works, Margaret Andrewes plays with and explores the nature of nonsense in order to investigate—in an amazingly "modern" manner—a realm of continually shifting identities, a reflection, perhaps, of the Victorian era's post-Darwinian ontological anxiety. As one of the characters in *Betty Barber* says: "I used to live always in the beautiful Land of Poetry. Then one day I found myself in Nonsense Land, and since then I cannot find my way back home."

WANTED—A KING

THE BEGINNING OF IT ALL

It certainly was a beautiful screen. Merle always said that she liked the pictures on it better than all her story-books put together.

It was a screen covered with brightly-coloured pictures of all the Nursery Rhymes. On one side were Jack and Jill rolling down a hill, Bo-peep and Boy Blue, to say nothing of the Man in the Moon and the Old Woman who lived in a Shoe; and on the other side were illustrations of all the Fairy Tales.

The screen always stood by the side of Merle's bed, between the bed and the door; so that when Merle was in bed she could look at the pictures and say the rhymes over to send herself to sleep.

She had needed something to send her to sleep, too, since the day she tumbled. Merle dated everything from that tumble. Two months had passed since then, but Merle was still in bed. It had been a bad fall, so bad that at first every one thought that Merle would never again be able to run about and play like other children; but after a time the doctors said that if only Merle would lie still and wait patiently, some day she would be able to romp as much as she used to do.

Merle thought it was very easy to say "lie still and wait patiently," but she knew it was very difficult to do it when her head was so hot, and her body seemed full of aches and pains.

This afternoon, too, the pain was bad, and would not let Merle get any sleep.

She was staring at the screen, and gently singing to herself—

> *"Jack and Jill went up a hill*
> *To fetch a pail of water,"*

when there was a tap at the door, and an old gentleman came into the room.

"Uncle Crossiter," said Merle—for this old gentleman was Merle's uncle—"Uncle Crossiter, I cannot get to sleep. What shall I do?"

"Well, my dear," said the old gentleman, "I should say you had better let me move the screen away; you are not likely to go to sleep staring at those silly nursery rhymes. Such nonsense! Filling children's heads with such rubbish!"

"It is not rubbish, Uncle," said Merle, indignantly. "Please don't move the screen; I love to look at it."

But Uncle Crossiter took no notice of Merle, and only continued to grumble to himself.

220

"I should like to burn all the silly nursery rhyme books," he growled.

"That would do no good, Uncle," said Merle, quietly—"the rhymes are in the children's heads, and they will never be forgotten. I wonder what hill it was that Jack went up. It always says 'a hill,' you know, Uncle."

Uncle Crossiter started up. "Oh dear! oh dear!" he said to himself, "the child is wandering. There, keep quiet, my dear," he said to Merle; "I will send your mother to you."

"I am all right, Uncle," said Merle. "I won't talk about the nursery rhymes if you don't like them; but why don't you like them, Uncle?"

"Such silly nonsense, my dear!"

"Not nonsense, Uncle—they are beautiful. I do wish I had known Boy Blue and Bo-peep. It would have been such fun playing with Bo-peep's sheep," said Merle, quite forgetting that she had promised not to mention the rhymes.

But it did not matter, for Uncle Crossiter had disappeared. He was a matter-of-fact old gentleman, with no sentiment in him, and with rather a short temper. He was very fond of his little niece, and was very sorry for her; but he did not know in the least how to show his affection, for he did not understand children at all, his one idea about them being that they ought not to read nursery rhymes.

Merle, however, did not notice that he had left the room. She kept on talking to herself, saying, "Bo-peep's sheep—Sheep's Bo-peep—Bo-sheep's peep," and so on. How long she would have gone on with this silly nonsense I do not know, if she had not been startled by a voice behind her, saying quickly,

"IF YOU WANT TO COME IN,
YOU MUST LEAVE YOUR BODY OUTSIDE."

"If you want to come in you must leave your body outside," said the voice again. "You need not be alarmed; I shall give you a ticket for it, and it will be quite right under my care."

Merle turned round astonished. The bed, bedroom, and screen had all disappeared, and she herself was no longer lying down, but standing—actually standing—in front of a turnstile.

Behind it was a little man, and he was evidently waiting for an answer to his question. Merle looked at him when she had recovered from her surprise. He was an ugly fellow—so short, really, that he only came up to Merle's shoulder, but as he wore a very tall pointed black hat he looked much bigger than Merle.

He was dressed all in black, for a long black cloak covered him from head to foot. In front of his hat were two red letters—two G's.

"G. G.," said Merle to herself; "what can that mean?"

"Children are so rude," grumbled the little man, who was still waiting for an answer, "they cannot even reply to a question. I suppose this child does not *want* to come in."

He turned round as he spoke, and was just going back into his little ticket-office, when Merle at last found her voice, and ventured to ask how she should get on without her body.

"Children ask so many questions," said the little man; "this child shall *not* come in."

This time he walked straight into his office and slammed the door.

Merle felt very much disappointed, and rather inclined to cry. She had no idea what she was going in to; but, nevertheless, it was very annoying to be shut out.

Just then she saw a big, thin, yellowish-brown thing—a thing rather like a very large stiff piece of paper being blown towards her. It was curled round, and bent at the top.

To her astonishment, the thing stopped in front of her, and bending a little more, as if making a bow, said—

"Can I do anything for you, Merle? You don't know me, of course, but I know you very well. My name is Topleaf. I am—or perhaps I ought to say I was—the leaf that was on the top of the highest branch of the

lime-tree in your garden. I have often peeped in at your window and nodded to you."

"I saw you this morning," said Merle, "and I know I said to mother that I should think you must be very lonely up there all by yourself. The other leaves have fallen long ago."

"It was lonely," said Topleaf; "but I could see a very long way, so that comforted me. At last I got my friend Mr. E. Wind to help me down, and here I am."

"But how is it you are so very big?" asked Merle. "You were not that size this morning."

"Ah, my dear! That shows how little you know. Have you never yet heard that every leaf tries as soon as ever summer is over to make its way up to Endom?"

"Endom?" said Merle, "where is Endom?"

"There," said the leaf, and he pointed over the turnstile. "I thought you were going there, perhaps, and I was glad, for a fresh child is badly wanted."

Merle did not know what Topleaf meant by the last part of his remark, so took no notice of it, but said again, "But how did you grow so tall?"

"Ah, dear!" sighed Topleaf, "I forgot all about your question, and as usual, my dear, wandered from the subject. Have you not noticed how leaves never go anywhere straight, and never keep to one purpose? They run off in a most flighty manner with the first breeze that takes any notice of them."

As the leaf was speaking the little man appeared at the gate once more.

"Hullo, Topleaf!" he said, "so you've arrived at last. I cannot say I am glad to see you. Are you coming in?"

Then he caught sight of Merle.

"That child still here?" he growled. "Disgraceful, I call it! Children are so obstinate," and without waiting to say another word to Topleaf, he shook his fist at Merle, and went back into his ticket-office.

"Who is that?" whispered Merle.

"That, my dear, is the evil spirit of Endom. He it is who has done all the harm to Mistress Crispin and her family. He it is who is the curse of all leaves," said Topleaf, and he rustled with rage. "If he could help it, we should never reach Endom. He puts every difficulty in our way. I had a brother"—here Topleaf lowered his voice—"but it is too sad a story to relate here. I only say that now he is a skeleton leaf." Topleaf was so overcome with his anger and sorrow that he curled up tightly.

Merle did not quite know what to do or say. She was anxious to hear the rest of Topleaf's story, but did not like to disturb him. At last, to her great relief, he uncurled, and once more began to speak.

"I got here in spite of him," he said. "I conquered every difficulty, and so, of course, I grew. You know, my dear, that every time a leaf conquers a difficulty he increases in size. But we are wasting precious time. Come, let us go together into Endom."

Topleaf stood in front of the turnstile and shook himself vigorously. Once more the little man appeared.

"So you've made up your mind to leave your body outside at last, have you?" he said, turning to Merle.

"Indeed I have not. I shall do nothing of the kind," said Merle quietly.

"But you *must!* you *must!*" said the little man angrily, stamping his foot. Merle noticed that the red letters on his cap grew brighter and brighter.

"All children must leave their bodies in my care. You mortals can only enter Endom in this way. Now then, if you are coming, come. Very well, I am not going to wait any longer," and he locked up his office and disappeared. Merle could not make out where he had gone to this time.

"Now what is to be done?" said she. "I did so want to go in—what a perfect little wretch he is!"

"My dear," said Topleaf, "you don't know what you have done. You have offended the mighty, the powerful

"GRUNTER GRIM!!!"

"Grunter Grim?" said Merle.

"Yes, Grunter Grim," said Topleaf. "I can't understand why he's acting as porter to-day: for no good purpose, I am quite sure."

"Well, it is done now, and cannot be helped," said Merle. "All the same, I must get in. Can't you help me?"

225

BEYOND
THE
LOOKING
GLASS

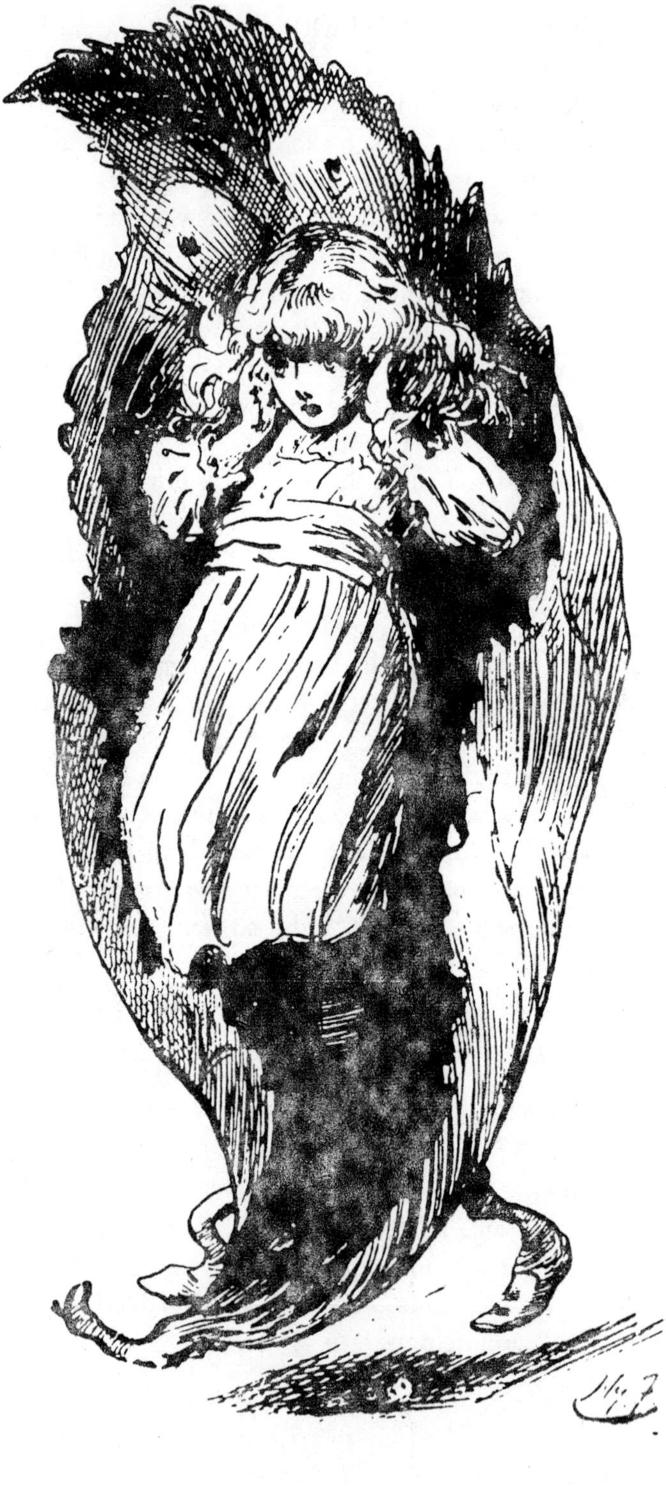

"I might, perhaps, if one of the Mr. Winds would give a helping blow. The worst of it is, you are so heavy. You don't happen to know anything about the Wind Family, I suppose?"

"I am afraid I don't," said Merle.

"Very well, then; I will do the best I can. Get inside me," said Topleaf. He carefully uncurled himself, and then getting behind Merle, slowly curled himself up again round her, so that she was completely hidden from sight.

"Now hold on tight!" shouted Topleaf. "Here comes Mr. East Wind."

Then Merle heard someone whistle loudly, and she supposed that must be Mr. Wind; next she heard Topleaf slowly chanting these words:—

"Blow, blow, blow,
Wind of the ice and snow;
Just one gentle puff
Will be quite enough,
And over the fence we'll go;"

and then she felt herself lifted from the ground, and carried into the air.

It was all over in a moment, for it was a very short journey—only over the turnstile—and Merle soon found her feet touching the ground once more. Topleaf slowly uncurled, and Merle stepped out.

She began to thank Topleaf, but he did not take any notice of her. He just waited to see that she was uninjured by the journey, and then whirled away with his friend Mr. East Wind.

WHAT MERLE FOUND IN THE BOX

For a minute or two after Topleaf had left her, Merle stood perfectly still. Although the journey through the air had been short, it had also been quick, and had quite taken Merle's breath away.

"Well," she said at last, "here I am in Endom, I suppose. I wonder what kind of a place it is, and what sort of people live here? This is a funny kind of ticket-office."

As Merle spoke she was staring about her, and yet did not notice a long box on the ground. As she was leaning forward to peep in through the office window, her foot knocked against the box, and immediately a deep groan was heard.

Merle started back frightened, expecting to see the horrid little man once more, but he was not there.

"It must have been my fancy," said Merle.

But it was not, for by accident she knocked against the box again, and again came the groan; and this time it was louder than before.

"Why, it comes from the box, I do believe," said Merle, when she had looked in the ticket-office and could see no one. "It comes from the box! I do wonder if there can be anything or anybody inside?"

"Anybody inside? Of course there is. I'm inside," said a voice. "Who ever you are, let me out, oh do let me out!" The groans grew louder than ever.

"It is all very well saying that," said Merle, "but the box is fastened, and I don't know how to open it."

"Get the key, of course. It is in the office," said the voice, impatiently.

Merle ran quickly to the little door, and tried to open it, but it was fastened. Peeping in through the window to see if she could catch sight of any keys, Merle was astonished to see rows of paper-covered books standing on shelves round the walls, and she wondered what they were. However, there were no keys, so once more she returned to the unhappy creature in the box, who by this time seemed too tired to groan, and was only sighing faintly.

"I cannot get into the office," said Merle, sorrowfully; "and if I could, I don't see any keys hanging up."

"Hanging up? Whoever heard of keys hanging up? How would you hang them up?" asked the voice, angrily. "Didn't you see them standing on the shelves?"

"I saw some books on the shelves, but——"

"And what else would you have?" interrupted the angry voice. "If you want to open this box, you must find the right book, and read the proper rhyme, of course. You don't seem to know what a key is. What is the key to your arithmetic book like?"

Merle felt there was something wrong somewhere, but she didn't quite know where. She felt, however, that arguing wouldn't release the poor creature from his sufferings, so she hastened to say—

"But the office door is fastened."

"Then there is nothing else for it—you must sit on me—I will do my best not to hurt you," said the voice; "but if I don't get out somehow, I shall certainly die."

"You won't hurt me," said Merle, "but if I sit on you I am afraid I shall hurt you. However, I will do as you wish."

She sat down on the box, and the groaning grew louder than ever. Presently, however, it altogether ceased. There was a very loud noise, as of something bursting, and then Merle felt herself shot up high into the air.

The box-lid seemed to have tossed her as if she had been sitting on the horns of a bull. It was startling, and she did not recover from her astonishment for some time. When she did, she found herself sitting on the ground. Staring at her, standing upright in the box, was a very tall boy, dressed in a very old-fashioned coat, with large round buttons. Round his neck was a big, wide, stiffly-starched frill, which Merle thought must be decidedly uncomfortable.

"Thank you very much," he said, bowing politely. *"What a good boy am I!"* he continued.

Merle looked somewhat astonished.

"My name is Jack Horner," he said, bowing again, "and I——"

"Sit in a corner," interrupted Merle, eagerly, "eating a Christmas pie; and you put in your thumb——"

The boy frowned and looked very cross, but Merle did not notice it, and went on talking——

"And pulled out a plum, and said——"

230

But the boy could bear it no longer, and began shouting at the top of
his voice, "To be a good boy I will try——"

"That's quite wrong," said Merle, indignantly. "You made a very conceited remark—you said, 'What a good boy am I!' "

"But I didn't, I didn't!" said Jack Horner. "It was Grunter Grim who told the fairy who makes the Rhymes that I said so, and now I have to keep on saying—'What a good boy am I.' "

As he said this he got very excited, waved his arms about, and sat down suddenly in the box. At once the lid closed down, and he was a prisoner again.

Merle released him as quickly as she could, but begged him not to do it any more, as she did not enjoy being shot up into the air.

"I hope you are not hurt," said Jack.

"Not a bit, thank you," said Merle—"I only feel rather giddy. Would you mind telling me why you got into that box at all? It surely isn't very comfortable?"

"What a good boy am I!" said Jack, angrily. "Comfortable!—Got in!—Do you suppose I got in? It was Grunter Grim who shut me up, and even now I can't get right out."

"Why, you are a regular Jack-in-the-box," said Merle, beginning to laugh.

"There," said Jack, indignantly, "that is another thing Grunter Grim has done. He not only puts me in the box, but he tells the fairy who makes the Toys about it, and then the children hear of my disgraceful situation. He is horrible! I suppose you thought I did nothing all day but sit in a corner and say, 'What a good boy am I?' "

"Why, do you do anything else?" asked Merle.

"Do anything else!" screamed Jack. "Why, I am the porter of Endom, and Grunter Grim shut me up to-day, so that I couldn't let you in. He is nothing less than a monster!"

"He does seem to have treated you badly," said Merle, sympathisingly. "I must say I am very glad to know that you are not really so conceited as I always thought you were."

"What a good boy am I!" said Jack, very dolefully. "Yes, I know that sounds conceited, but you understand now, don't you, that I only said, 'To be a good boy I'll try?' It is all Grunter Grim's fault."

231

"He must be dreadful!" said Merle.

"But you will save us all, I hope," said Jack. "Go up the hill and talk to mother: she will show you what to do——"

He was about to tell Merle more about his mother, when it suddenly began to grow dark, as though a black cloud were coming down from the sky to the earth.

"Run, run!" shouted Jack. "Grunter Grim is coming!" and he quickly sank down into his box.

Merle did not wait to be told twice, but ran quickly away from the office. She never stopped, and never once looked behind her until she found herself in front of a large black house.

"It is a queer house," said Merle, aloud: "a very queer house. It's such a funny shape."

Merle was quite right: it was a queer house, and a very peculiar shape. To begin with, the house was certainly not built of bricks; then it was very long and low, and what Merle called "uppy-downy." The windows were in such funny places—and as for the front door, why, there was none. The only way to get into this house seemed to be to climb up a rope ladder which hung down from the middle of it. Part of it, too, was entirely without a roof, and another part was so narrow that Merle felt quite sure she would never be able to get into it. She noticed that there was a bright shining piece of brass fastened on to the narrow part, and when she looked at this more closely, she found that it was evidently used as a door-plate, for on it was written, in very plain letters,

> MISTRESS CRISPIN.

"I suppose that is the name of the person who lives in the house?" said Merle; "but what a funny door-plate: why, it has a big hole in the middle! And what a very, very, very funny house!" Merle walked right round it twice. "It is not a house at all," she said, and she walked round it again. Then a bright idea came into her head—"Why, why, why," she cried, "it's nothing but a big shoe!"

And so it was—a great big shoe. The rope ladder was the shoe-lace, and the brass door-plate the shoe-buckle!

"Now," said Merle, in a satisfied tone, "the next thing, of course, is to find the old woman and the children.

"*There was an old woman who lived in a shoe.* Of course, this is the shoe, and I suppose the old woman's name is Mistress Crispin."

By standing on tiptoe, she managed to peep through one of the little windows that was let into the side of the shoe. She could see what looked like a very comfortable little room inside. There was a fine big fire burning brightly, and on the fire were two huge pots, which were

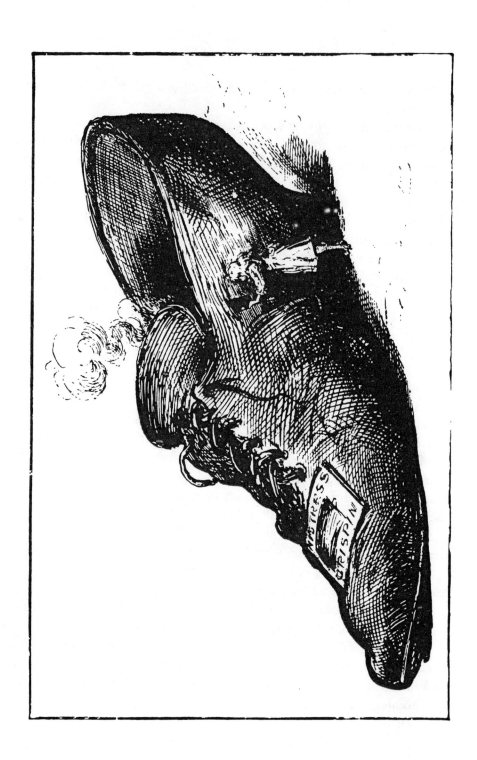

evidently bubbling and boiling with all their might and main, for the smoke was coming from them in big clouds.

There was no one in the room, but there was evidently some one in the house, for Merle heard a very great noise of beating and banging.

"Oh dear!" said Merle, greatly distressed, "she must at the *whipped them all soundly*' part, I should think, by the noise. I must go and stop her."

She ran quickly round the house to the rope ladder, and, after some little trouble, managed to climb right up it and get inside the shoe.

She found herself in a tidy little room, evidently a sleeping room, for there were a number of little beds, as many as could be got into the room, against the wall. Merle thought she heard a noise in the next room, so she hurried on.

Directly afterwards she found herself in the room she had seen from outside; but now there was some one in it.

By the side of the fire was a tiny little old lady. She was stirring something in the pot with one hand, and with the other was wildly waving a big birch-rod, nearly as big as herself. As she waved she kept knocking the chairs and tables that were within her reach, so that she made a good deal of noise.

"What I expected," said Merle; "this, of course, is Mistress Crispin."

The old lady turned as Merle pronounced her name, and said, in the very crossest of cross voices,

"So delighted to see you, my dear!"

Merle was most astonished.

"Do keep out of my way, darling," said the old lady, angrily, "or I shall be obliged to beat you."

Merle quickly got outside the door, and only popped her head in to talk to the old lady. The voice and tones were so very cross, and yet the words were so kind, what could it mean?

"Where are the children?" asked Merle, at last summoning up all her courage.

Poor Mistress Crispin looked crosser than ever, though the tears rolled down her cheeks as she said,

"Gone, my dear, gone! They simply could not stand the beating and the broth."

"Why, how wicked of you!" said Merle. "How cruel of you to drive all your children away from you!"

"Oh, my dear! you don't understand, or you would never talk like that. Come and stir this broth whilst I fetch something soft to beat, so that I shan't make such a noise, and then I will tell you all about it."

Merle ran at once, and took the spoon from the old lady's hand. Mistress Crispin turned away directly, so as not to be able to beat Merle; but although she tried her hardest, she could not help hitting her twice.

Merle looked rather angry, but before she could say anything the old lady kissed her, and ran to fetch a pillow from the bedroom.

Then when Merle was comfortably settled in a chair, and Mistress Crispin had once more taken the spoon to stir up the broth, she began her story.

"A long time ago I lived happily with my family in this comfortable roomy house, I had so many children——"

"That you did not know what to do," interrupted Merle.

"On the contrary, my dear, I always knew what to do. I never had a minute to spare, I was so busy; but I did not mind that, for I loved my children, and they loved me."

"But if you loved them so much, why did you whip them all soundly and send them to bed?" asked Merle.

"If you will wait a minute, I will come to that," said Mistress Crispin. "Well, as I was saying, we were once all very happy, but troublous times came to the country, and discontent seized the land. Grunter Grim deceived us, and by deceiving us got power over us."

"All the same, I don't see why you gave those poor children broth," said Merle. "I don't like broth myself, especially without any bread."

"Oh, my dear!" said Mistress Crispin, in the crossest of cross voices, whilst the tears rolled down her cheek, "I didn't give them broth. I cooked the dinner as usual, and a very good dinner it was—roast beef and plum pudding. Well, I cooked the dinner, and put it all on the table, and told the children to begin, while I went out just to wash my hands. When I came back—I hadn't been away more than a minute—I found all the children fighting and quarrelling——"

"Oh, how dreadful!" said Merle.

"Indeed it was. When I asked them what was the matter, they said they wanted to know why I had given them such a dreadful dinner."

"What peculiar children! How funny of them not to like beef and plum pudding!" said Merle.

"That was what made me angry; and without stopping to think," said the old woman, beginning to cry again, "I fetched out the birch-rod and began beating them."

"And they quite deserved it," said Merle, very decidedly.

"No, they didn't: it was all a mistake. Let me finish my story," said poor Mistress Crispin. "In the middle of the bother, when they were crying, and I was beating, it grew dark, and in came Grunter Grim. He laughed a horrid laugh. 'I am glad you like my broth,' he said; 'you shall always have it; and since you are so fond of beating, you shall always beat,' and then with another laugh he went away."

"What did he mean by talking about broth?" asked Merle.

"Why, don't you see," said Mistress Crispin, "it was he who had changed the beef and plum pudding into broth."

"Oh, how wicked of him!" cried Merle.

"Next day," continued the old lady, "I was still obliged to speak angrily and beat the children, and every day after, until at last they ran away and left me. And now, although I am all alone, I can do nothing but beat the children that are not there, and make this horrible broth."

"What a shame!" said Merle. "I wish I could punish Grunter Grim."

"You can," said Mistress Crispin.

Just then a girl popped her head in at the window.

"Good morning, mother," said she. "May I come in?"

"Don't, dear, don't," said the old lady, angrily. "You know I must beat you if you do. Have you found the tails?"

"No, mother, not yet," said the girl. "I dream of them every night, but in the morning I find my poor sheep still without them."

"Are you Bo-peep?" said Merle, eagerly. "I have long wanted to know you. I have heard of you so often," and she began to sing—

> "Little Bo-peep has lost her sheep,
> And doesn't know——"

But she stopped suddenly, for she saw the girl look very angry, and then run away from the window.

"There, of course, she is offended," said Mistress Crispin; "it was very

237

rude to remind her of that insulting story. But perhaps you do not know who stole the sheeps' tails. You must get her to tell you some day."

"Is she your daughter?" said Merle, hoping to change the subject.

"Of course she is my own dear daughter Bo-peep. You have much to learn yet about my family, and I want you to do it quickly, for then you will help us. Can you not see that it is Grunter Grim who is our great enemy? He has done all the harm, and worked all the mischief."

In her eagerness and excitement, the old lady had gradually spoken louder and louder, and had drawn nearer and nearer to Merle.

At last she was so close that her birch-rod actually touched Merle, and at once, though poor Mistress Crispin tried to stop herself, she began to beat Merle. Each time she apologised most humbly in the angriest tone of voice.

"I beg your pardon," she said, stamping her foot. "I am so sorry. I hope I don't in any way hurt." Thwack, thwack, went the birch-rod, and Merle began to make her way to the door. "I don't want to hurt you," continued the old lady, "but I feel one of my bad attacks coming on. Please, oh, please, do get out of the house!"

She followed Merle, beating her all the time with the birch-rod, and begging her pardon, until Merle once more reached the ladder and got out of her way.

As soon as she reached the bottom of the ladder, Merle stopped to think. The question was, what ought she to do next?

She was very anxious to find out all about the Rhymes and Grunter Grim, but she certainly could not go back to Mistress Crispin, it was too dangerous. She shut her eyes tightly. When she opened them again, to her surprise, Mistress Crispin's house and the road to the turnstile had entirely disappeared, and in front of her rose a high hill. At the foot of the hill was a sign-post, and on it was written "A—— Hill."

"That's the name, I suppose," said Merle; "but why don't they put it in full. What is the use of giving only the first letter of a name?"

"That shows you don't know anything about it," said a voice quite close to her ear. Merle turned round quickly, and was surprised to see a girl and boy, carrying an empty pail between them, walking beside her.

The boy and girl did not seem at all astonished to see her, however.

"Well, you've come at last!" said the boy, crossly. "It was time you did, though I don't suppose you'll be any better than all the others."

The girl took no notice of his remark.

"The name is put like that," she said to Merle, "so that other children shall not have to waste their time as we do, fetching and spilling water."

"Excuse me," said Merle, very politely; "but are you Jack and Jill?"

"Of course," said the boy, "and we are going up Argument Hill to fetch a pail of water."

"Oh, Jack," interrupted Jill, "you shouldn't have told her the name. Now every child will find out where the hill is, and will follow our example, and try to carry pails up it. You know what a bother it was to me to persuade the Rhyme Fairy to leave the real name out of the story-books."

"I can't help it," said Jack, "I forgot."

All this time they were gradually climbing the hill—indeed, they had almost reached the top.

"You're always forgetting," said Jill.

" 'Tis your fault," said Jack.

"It's yours," retorted Jill.

"Oh dear, please don't quarrel," said Merle, stepping between them.

But she was too late, for just then the hill seemed somehow to rise up, and in a minute Jack fell, and began rolling down the hill. As for Jill, she didn't even wait to fall, but at once lay down, and rolled after Jack.

"Just what I expected," said Merle. "I only hope Jack's crown is not quite broken."

When the two reached the bottom, they picked themselves up, and Jack immediately pulled some plaster out of his pocket, which Jill fastened on his head, and then shaking hands, they once more started to carry the pail up the hill.

They seemed to be friends again, and to be talking quite kindly to one another. Merle sat down on the ground, and determined to wait until they arrived.

"Don't quarrel again," she shouted.

Jack nodded and smiled, and Jill put her finger over her mouth to show that she was not going to talk at all.

It was no good, however, for, just as they reached Merle, Jack kicked a stone. At once Jill turned round, took her finger from her lips, and said angrily,

"Do be careful."

"It was your fault," said Jack.

The words were scarcely out of his mouth before down he tumbled, down sat Jill, and away the two went rolling to the bottom of the hill.

"This is all very well," said Merle, "but if they are going to do that for ever, of course I can't stop here."

She only waited to see that neither the brother nor sister was badly hurt, and then picking herself up, walked on over the top of the hill and down the other side.

She had not walked very far before she came to a narrow, straight lane, with a high hedge on each side. It looked dismal and lonely, and Merle was just coming to the conclusion that she would not go any further, when she caught sight of a bit of blue petticoat and a black shoe peeping out from underneath the hedge, half-way down the lane. She walked quickly to the place, and there found a girl lying fast asleep under the hedge, and she at once recognised her as the one who had come to see Mistress Crispin.

"*Little Bo-peep fell fast asleep,*" said Merle, gently, for she did not want the girl to be offended again.

As she said the words, however, Bo-peep sat up and rubbed her eyes.

"Come, my pretty lambs," she said, sleepily. "I am glad indeed to see you again."

Merle stared at her, and wondered whatever she was talking about. She was just going to ask a question, when Bo-peep suddenly stood up and burst out crying.

"They are not there," she sobbed, "and I dreamt so plainly that I heard them bleating."

"Never mind," said Merle, kindly. "I'll help you find them. Who stole your sheep, dear, was it Grunter Grim?"

"Of course it was," said Bo-peep; "but come, let us hasten," and she quickly wiped her eyes and stopped crying. "If we are sharp, we shall be in time for the meeting."

"What meeting?" asked Merle.

"The meeting of the Family," said Bo-peep. "Every night at twelve o'clock we are all free for one hour. Until one, Grunter Grim has no power over us, and we are able to leave our work. Then we meet together and discuss our plans for overcoming the tyrant."

"But can I come?" said Merle. "Won't he be angry if he knows I am there?"

"He won't know," said Bo-peep. "I will get you in, it is a secret meeting."

She took hold of Merle's hand, and at once everything became dark. Then she heard a clock begin to strike twelve, and then another, and then another, until all round her the air seemed full of the sound of striking clocks. Some had deep notes, some silvery ones, but the noise was so great that Merle put her hands over her head to keep out the sound. When she took them away again, she was no longer in the narrow lane, but in a large room.

It was a very large hall indeed, and quite unlike any hall that Merle had ever seen before. Instead of having a raised platform at one end for the speakers, and rows of chairs in front of it for the listeners, nearly the whole room was taken up by an enormous platform, and there was only one row of chairs in front of it. Even this, as Bo-peep told Merle, was not really necessary, for every one always wanted to talk, and no one to sit down and listen.

"Well," said Merle, "there will be some one to listen to-day, so I will sit on one of the chairs."

But Bo-peep would not hear of it, because she said if Merle sat by herself Grunter Grim would notice that a child was present.

There were several people already on the platform when Merle and Bo-peep took their seats. The clocks were still striking; but whenever any clock struck for the twelfth time, some new visitor arrived.

Merle soon recognised her friend Mistress Crispin sitting quietly in a chair, and not even trying to beat any one. Jack and Jill were sitting side by side, laughing and talking happily together, although Jack's head was tied up in a big red handkerchief, and Jill's arm was in a sling.

Merle soon found out, too, who all the others were, for each one wore a small ticket, on which a name was written.

There was little Boy Blue, as wide-awake as could be, and next to him the Man in the Moon. In the front row of chairs Goosey Goosey Gander and Miss Muffet, sitting side by side, were talking away to Pollie Flinders and Tom, Tom, the Piper's Son, and making a great deal of noise. Miss Muffet looked such a dashing young lady, that Merle wondered how it could have happened that she should have been frightened by a spider.

Just as the last clock finished striking, Mother Hubbard came hurrying into the hall, followed by a dog and quite a number of people, a cobbler, a baker, a tailor, and many others. Merle was just going to ask Bo-peep who these people were, when Mistress Crispin stepped forward and began to speak.

"My children," she said, "it must be fully twelve by the earthly clocks; what is the time by the nursery clock?"

Directly she asked the question, each one present produced a dandelion clock, and began solemnly and seriously to blow upon it. Mistress Crispin counted aloud "One—two"—and so on, up to twelve, and by that time the seeds were scattered in every direction, and she and the others held dandelion stalks only in their hands. At the same time, the hall, which Merle had thought very badly lighted before, became brilliantly bright. It seemed as though the stars had come down from the sky, and had fastened themselves upon the walls, but really there were no stars. Each dandelion seed had turned into a bright shining lamp.

Then once more Mistress Crispin began to speak.

"Merle," she said, "listen to our wrongs, and help us to make them rights. You **can** do it if you will. You know my story, now listen to some of the others."

She quickly sat down, without wasting more time, and at once Bo-peep, Humpty Dumpty, the Man in the Moon, and Boy Blue all rose together, and began talking very quickly.

Merle could not in the least understand what they were saying. She only heard one name, which they each used several times, and that name was Grunter Grim. After they had been speaking a minute, Mistress Crispin held up her hand, and they all stopped and sat down.

"There, Merle," she said, "you know now how wrongly and wickedly Grunter Grim has treated us all. It saves so much time if four of the children speak at once, and it does not matter if you do not hear each word, for you can judge of the tyrant by his deeds. You have seen the result of his actions, and after that, words make no difference."

"But how can I send him away?" asked Merle.

"Choose us a king," said Humpty Dumpty.

"Have faith in yourself, and defy him," said Boy Blue.

"Do anything you like, only do it quickly," said Mother Hubbard.

"Yes, indeed," said the cobbler, the baker, the tailor, and all the other people who had come with Mother Hubbard, "do it quickly."

Merle stared at them all. She did not in the least understand what they were talking about.

"A king?" she said at last; "what do you want a king for?"

"Oh **dear**! oh dear!" said Mistress Crispin, "we must go back to the beginning of all things, and explain matters to her. Well, Merle, we had a

243

king who was able to keep Grunter Grim in order. At that time Grunter Grim had no power over us, he could only growl and grumble to himself."

"Then the time came," said the Man in the Moon, taking up the story when Mistress Crispin paused to take breath—"then came the time when our king finished his reign, and because Grunter Grim deceived us, we had not chosen a new one. We could not agree which of the claimants was the right one, and so we quarrelled."

"That's the whole point," interrupted Boy Blue, "we quarrelled. You see, Merle, as long as we were all contented Grunter Grim had no power over us; but as soon as we quarrelled he just took the power into his own hands, and since then he has treated us shamefully."

"But how very silly of you to quarrel!" said Merle.

"It is easy enough to say that now," said a girl who had not spoken before.

Merle did not have to ask who she was, for she saw at once by the ticket fastened on her dress that she was "Mary, Mary, quite contrary."

"Hush, hush, Mary!" said Bo-peep, "please don't be rude to Merle."

"But why don't you stop quarrelling?" asked Merle.

"Because as long as Grunter Grim has power over us, we can't help it," said Mistress Crispin.

"If we only once got up that Hill without disagreeing," said Jack, "we shouldn't tumble down, of course, but it isn't all our fault. Grunter Grim makes us fall out, and fall down too," he added, rubbing his head.

"If this goes on much longer my arms will be too much bruised ever to get well again," said Jill, dolefully.

"It isn't all temper that makes us quarrel, Merle, don't you see that?" said Mistress Crispin.

"Besides," put in Bo-peep, "if you spent your whole day looking for sheeps' tails, I don't think you would be sweet-tempered."

"Now, Bo-peep! don't get cross," said Mistress Crispin, "that is no good. Our time is nearly up, it is a quarter to one. Cannot some one tell this child what she is to do to help us?"

"I will," said Goosey Goosey Gander, drawing herself up, and stretching out her feathers. "Merle, listen. The next time you see our common foe, you must stand up and defy him, and banish him from the

244

land. You *can* do it, if you *will*. Then, when he has gone you must choose a king for us."

"I will do my best," said Merle, "but I'm afraid I am not much good."

"I never expected you would be," said Mary, Mary, quite contrary.

"Do be quiet, Mary!" shouted Boy Blue.

"She can give her opinion if she likes," said Jill.

"Yes, of course," said Mother Hubbard.

"Of course, of course," called out the cobbler, the baker, the tailor, and the others.

"Oh, please don't begin quarrelling now," said Mistress Crispin. "It is only five minutes to one, and then——"

But the hall was beginning to grow dark, although the dandelion-seed lamps were shining as brightly as ever. Merle took hold of Bo-peep's hand, for she felt rather frightened. But Bo-peep did not take any notice, for she seemed to be gradually dropping off to sleep. Then Merle looked at Mistress Crispin, and she was no longer sitting still, but was moving her hands about, feeling for her stick.

It grew darker and darker, and somehow it seemed to Merle as if some one outside the hall were shouting. She felt sure she heard some voice in the distance—what could it mean? She was getting more and more frightened. She turned again to Bo-peep, but Bo-peep was fast asleep, and evidently dreaming, for from time to time she turned in her sleep and muttered something about her sheep. Darker and darker!

Merle at last could bear it no longer, and she started to her feet with the intention of getting down from the platform and running out of the hall. But instead of running away, she stood perfectly still, for there shining at the end of the hall were the fiery letters "G G." They came closer and closer to her, and she knew it was Grunter Grim. Then she remembered all that Goosey Goosey Gander had said to her, how she was to defy the tyrant, and banish him from Endom. She summoned up her courage and began to speak.

"I de——" but got no further, for just then the clocks outside began striking one, and as the red letters came closer and closer to her, she heard a voice saying—

"Once more in strife now ends your hour,
Once more I have you in my power."

245

All thought of finishing her sentence and banishing Grunter Grim went out of Merle's head. She was terrified.

As the fiery letters came closer to her, she screamed at the top of her voice, "Topleaf—somebody—help! help!"

She quite expected to feel Topleaf's arms round her, but instead, something seemed to come between her and the horrible letters, and she heard beautiful music, and a soft voice singing a lullaby gently and slowly.

Merle knew the tune, but somehow she could not think of the words. Gradually the lullaby grew louder and louder, and the voice appeared to come nearer and nearer. At the same time the fiery letters on Grunter Grim's cap became fainter and fainter, until at last they faded away. Then the darkness lifted, and once more it became light.

By the time that Grunter Grim's cap had disappeared, and the darkness with it, Merle's courage had returned. As soon as it was quite light again, she stood up and prepared to speak to Bo-peep; but, strange to say, Bo-peep, Mistress Crispin, Jack and Jill—all the Nursery Rhymes, in fact, and even the Hall—had entirely vanished. Merle could scarcely believe her eyes, but it was indeed the case. She herself was the only thing that had not disappeared.

All this time the lullaby was still going on, though now it was fainter—so faint that Merle scarcely noticed it, as she had so many other things to think about. She was now standing out of doors, in the middle of a road, or rather at a place where four roads met.

Not far from her stood a sign-post, with each of its four arms pointing towards one of the four roads.

Merle walked up to the post to see what was written on it. On the arm pointing to the road on her right was written—

G—– G—–.

Merle felt quite frightened when she saw the dreadful letters, and was going to hurry on to see if anything better were written on the next arm, when she heard some one speaking to her.

"Look closer before you run away, my dear," said the some one.

Merle could not in the least understand where the voice came from, but she once more looked at the sign-post, and then found that there were other letters besides the two G's. Carefully she spelt it out, and found, after some trouble, that

TO GRUMBLING GREATLY

was written there.

"That doesn't sound very inviting," said Merle.

"Of course not," said the some one again; "look at the next."

On the next Merle discovered—

written in the same way as the first, with the G's large and the other letters small. Very disappointed, she turned to the third, and on that was written, just in the same way—

TO GOSSIPING GRANDLY.

"This is too provoking," said Merle. "I shan't trouble to look at the other. That horrid Grunter Grim is everywhere. I hate the sight of those wretched letters G—— G——."

"Don't lose your temper, my dear, that never does any good," said the some one.

By this time Merle was quite angry.

"I wish you would show yourself, whoever you are," she said.

"Look up, and you will see."

Merle looked up, and to her surprise saw that it was the sign-post itself that was talking to her. It was not like an ordinary sign-post, for right at the top, some distance above the arms, there was a head. It looked as if it were only carved wood, but it was quite as able to talk as Merle herself.

"Don't apologise," said the post, "you are only making the mistake that other people have made before you. They only look at a sign-post; if they talked to it they would get much more information, for have we not stood in our places for a very long time? And do we not know a great deal more about the country than we can possibly put on our arms?"

Merle determined that she would no longer make the mistake of only looking at the post, and decided to get as much information as she could. She was rather ashamed of herself, so she said, humbly—

"Would you mind telling me why you have those horrid letters G G on your arms?"

"Do you think I wrote them?" said the sign-post, very indignantly, and he got so excited that his arms shook. "Is it likely that I should write such stuff?"

"Then I suppose Grunter Grim has power over you, as well as over every one else. Did he write them?" asked Merle, hoping to calm the excited post.

"Of course he did," said the post, sulkily.

"What do they mean, please?" said Merle; "surely there isn't really a place called 'Grumbling Greatly.' I wish you would tell me, because I must go somewhere, and I don't know which way to go, and you said I was to talk to you, because you know so much. Please help me."

The sign-post had been getting calmer and less sulky as Merle spoke, and when she reached the end of her long speech he said, quite mildly—

"Well, I will help you. Now listen. A long time ago, when we had our own king, I was a sensible sign-post, with proper directions written on my arms."

"Then you quarrelled with some one, I suppose?" said Merle, "and so Grunter Grim got power over you. It is the same story over again."

"Not quite," said the post, sadly, "I did not quarrel with any one. I suffer because of other people's wickedness. Every one *would* quarrel with me."

"That is pretty much the same thing, isn't it?" asked Merle.

"Not at all, not at all, but it had the same effect. Grunter Grim came and spoiled all my arms, and now every one goes the wrong way."

"Well, help me to go the right. What does 'To Gliding Giddily' mean?" asked Merle.

"That means really, 'To Jack and Jill's Hill.' Jack and Jill spend all their time 'gliding giddily,' you know, so instead of writing on my arms 'To A—— Hill,' Grunter Grim has put 'To Gliding Giddily.' He likes that name, partly because it misleads every one, and partly because he can use his favourite letters, G G."

"Oh, I understand now. Then, 'To Grumbling Greatly,' let me think—now, what does it mean? I know—the way to Mistress Crispin's of course, and 'To Gossiping Grandly' is the way to the Hall."

"That's right, my dear," said the post. "You really are a clever girl, though you have only two arms."

"Why, of course I've only two arms," said Merle. "However many did you expect me to have?"

"Four, of course," said the post. "How can you point each way if you haven't four? Why, you wouldn't be any good at all on a cross road."

Merle felt that this was unanswerable, and decided to turn the conversation, so she said—

"You haven't told me now which way I am to go. It's no use my following those three roads, for I know all about them."

"Try the fourth, then," said the post.

Merle remembered that she had not even looked at what was written on the fourth arm of the sign-post, so she walked round to it.

It was quite as difficult to understand as the other three, for on it was written—

B—— B——.

"That is not much help; I don't know what that means. Who is B—— B——?" said Merle.

There was no answer. Merle looked up at the sign-post, but it seemed to have lost the power of speech—it only stared at her.

"Well, this *is* stupid," said Merle.

The sign-post took no notice, but the arm pointing to B—— B—— shook slightly. It might have been the wind, it might have been fancy, but Merle certainly thought the arm shook. She at once decided that at any rate she would go along the road leading to B—— B——, and try to find out who B—— B—— was. Directly she had come to this conclusion she heard the voice singing the lullaby once more. It seemed, too, as if some one were holding her hand, and she felt as if she were floating along in the air rather than walking.

The farther she got from the four roads and the sign-post, the louder the lullaby grew and the firmer her hand was held, and at last the lullaby stopped, and a voice said—

"Merle, I am delighted to see you. Will you come in and see the claimants to the throne? for you must find a king of Endom."

251

Merle looked about her. She could not see any one, and, what was worse, she could not see anywhere to go in. But she was getting used to queer things by this time, so she simply said—

"Show me the claimants, and I will do the best I can."

At once she saw in front of her a long low building. It had not been there before, or rather, Merle had not seen it there before; but she was not at all surprised, and walked straight towards it. The door opened, and Merle found herself in a long room. It was almost entirely filled with babies' cradles.

Babies' cradles of every description! Some quite grand ones, trimmed with rows of ribbon and lace, so grand that you would never have thought of giving them such a simple name as cradle, but would have at once decided that they were "bassinettes." Some quite ordinary basket cradles, some old-fashioned wooden ones that had evidently been used for more than one generation of babies, and some not proper cradles at all. One was an old tin bath, another a big basket, and another a wooden box.

Yet they were all—the grand ones, the ordinary ones, and the funny ones—they were certainly all cradles, for each one contained a baby. There was perfect silence in the long room, although there were so many children and not a single nurse—perfect silence, absolute quiet!

Merle at first thought that all the babies must be asleep, and, fearful of waking them, stepped very quietly up to the cradle nearest to her, and peeped in.

She was most devoted to any baby; she loved the whole baby race, as every girl should do, and, in fact, as every right-minded girl does.

Well, Merle peeped into the first cradle. It happened to be one of the grandly trimmed ones. In it was lying a very small, very thin, very pale, but very clean baby. Any one who was not fond of babies would have said, "What an ugly baby!" Merle only thought, "That poor baby looks ill!" The baby, however, seemed happy enough—it was not asleep, but was lying contentedly on its back. As soon as it caught sight of Merle it gave a delighted crow, and at once from every cot of every kind came a baby's joyful crow or coo.

252

You know, if you know anything about babies, how enjoyable it is to hear one happy, comfortable baby coo. Just fancy what a glorious thing it would be to hear dozens and dozens of perfectly happy babies gently coo with delight.

Merle smiled, simply because she couldn't help it, and then she laughed, at what she did not know. Then she looked once more at the baby in the gorgeous cradle, and noticed for the first time that there was a ticket fastened to one of the curtains. On the ticket was written—Merle looked twice, she thought she must have made a mistake; but no, there it was plainly written, "The Finest Baby in the World."

She was rather astonished, for she felt sure that she had seen finer babies many a time.

In the next cradle—the tin bath one—lay a very bonnie baby, also wide-awake and perfectly happy. This was quite a different-looking baby. It had rosy cheeks and curly hair, though rather a dirty face. It really was a fine baby. Merle saw a ticket fastened to this cradle, and

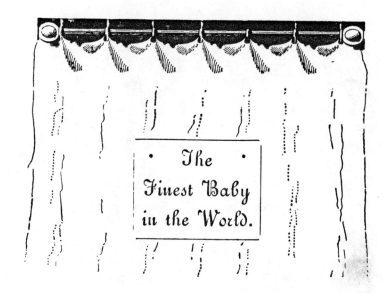

when she looked at it, she saw written on that too, "The Finest Baby in the World."

Then she looked at the next cradle, and on that was another ticket with exactly the same words on it. She looked at another, and another, and another—it was just the same all the way round—every baby, pretty or plain, clean or dirty, thin or fat, each one was labelled, "The Finest Baby in the World."

Merle stood bewildered. What could it all mean?

"It is simple nonsense!" she said aloud. "There can be only one *finest* baby in the whole world."

"That's just the point," said the voice Merle had heard when she had left the sign-post—the voice that had invited her to look at the claimants. Merle turned round, for now there was something more than a voice. Standing close beside her was a small boy who looked about three years old, but who spoke as if he were very much older.

"Just it," he repeated decidedly; "that's just what we want to find out, which is the finest?"

Merle stared at him, amazed.

"Where did you come from?" she said at last.

"I came in long ago," said the boy, "but I was weak. When Grunter

Grim told me, as he told you, I could only come in by leaving my body outside, I left it."

"But you got it back, I suppose?" said Merle.

"No, I didn't," said the boy, indignantly, "not my own body. This one doesn't belong to me. I really am a girl, and I was ten years old when I came to Endom, and when I wanted to go out again Grunter Grim said he had given my own body away, and this was the best he could do for me. That's what he does—gives back the wrong bodies, and then down in that stupid world, every one is astonished because big people are often cowards and little people brave, some girls more like boys, and some boys more like girls. It is easy enough to explain it if they only knew the reason why."

"I suppose it is Grunter Grim's doing," said Merle, thoughtfully.

"Of course it is," said the boy. "Children get to Endom, leave their bodies in charge of Grunter Grim, and enter without them. Of course they are unable to help the poor Nursery Rhymes, and when they go away disgusted Grunter Grim gives them back wrong bodies. I am not going back until I get my own property. He knows where it is."

"But how will you get it—er——" Merle stopped and hesitated. "Would you mind telling me your name? It is so much easier for me to talk to you, if I know your name."

"My name? Certainly," said the boy. "It is Thomas Muriel."

Merle stared.

"Don't you see," he continued, "Muriel is my own proper name, but Thomas is the name of this body that I am now in."

Merle looked still more amazed, but the boy was getting so indignant that she did not like to say any more about his name—so asked how he thought of getting his own body back again.

"Why, *you* will help me to do that—any one of these babies could answer that question," said the boy.

Merle did not understand how she was to get the boy's own body for him, but he seemed to know all about it and the babies too, so she thought she would probably find out in good time.

"Now then," said Thomas Muriel, when Merle stood perfectly still, without saying anything, "now then, be quick and decide."

255

"What am I to decide?" asked Merle.

"Which really *is* the finest baby in the world. You said yourself that there could only be one."

"But why do you want me to decide such a difficult question at all?"

"Because we want a king," said Thomas Muriel. "Before the last king finished his reign the Rhymes were all quite happy, but when he was forced to resign——"

"Why did they make him resign if they were all so happy? How very silly of them!" said Merle. "Oh, I am sorry! I never thought before that Nursery Rhymes could be silly."

Poor Merle was so excited that she almost began to cry.

"Wait a minute, my dear, wait a minute," said Thomas Muriel, not in the least disturbed by Merle's excitement. "You don't know what you are talking about. The last king was not forced by the Rhymes to resign, but he lost all his power. He got to be able to talk and walk."

"Talk and walk?" said Merle.

"Yes, talk and walk. What are you astonished at now? Don't tell me that you don't know about the Kings of Endom—you can't be as ignorant as all that."

"But I am," said Merle. "I don't know anything about it. Do explain."

At first, when Merle made this dreadful confession, Thomas Muriel looked horrified, and turned round as if he were going to leave her, but Merle looked so much ashamed of herself and so humble that he relented, and once more began to speak to her.

"A long time ago, Endom, which you know means Nurserydom or Nurseryland, was the very happiest land in the whole world. All the Rhymes were merry, jolly, and contented, and never even thought of quarrelling. The finest baby in the world who could not walk or talk was always made king."

"Who made him king?" asked Merle; "who chose him?"

"Who chooses your king," said Thomas Muriel—"I mean your King of England?"

"But we haven't a King. We've a Queen," said Merle; "and she isn't chosen a Queen, she's born it."

"Well, it was exactly the same with the Kings of Endom," said

Thomas Muriel, getting rather impatient, "they were born it. You can't make a baby the *finest*, it has to be born the finest."

"Well, then, I don't see what was the difficulty," said Merle. "Why is there no King of Endom now? and how is it that all these babies are labelled, 'The Finest Baby in the World?' Who gave them their labels?"

"Their mothers, of course," said Thomas Muriel. "Don't you see, when the Rhymes couldn't decide for themselves which was the finest baby in the world, they sent messengers into the world to find out what the mothers thought. And each mother thought her own baby the finest."

"They might have expected that," said Merle.

"Of course," said Thomas Muriel, "but that doesn't settle the question. It is very easy to be clever now, but then at the time Grunter Grim deceived the Rhymes——"

"How?" asked Merle.

"Twins," said Thomas Muriel. "Twins were at the bottom of it all."

"Twins!" said Merle; "twins!"

"Yes–don't you believe me? I think you are very stupid."

"I think you are very rude," said Merle.

It was beginning to grow dark–but the two children were so busy talking that they did not notice it.

"Of course I believe you; but I can't understand what twins had to do with it."

"Not real ones," said Thomas Muriel, very crossly.–It grew darker. "Imaginary ones."

"Now you are talking simple nonsense," said Merle. "Imaginary twins–that's rubbish."

By this time it was quite dark, and Merle could no longer see Thomas Muriel. All at once it flashed across her mind that darkness meant Grunter Grim. Immediately her anger vanished.

"Thomas Muriel," she began, "don't let us quarrel."

All at once the babies began to coo, and it began to grow light.

For a little time it was quite bright in the room once more–but when Merle looked round for Thomas Muriel, he had disappeared, and she was alone with the babies.

"Now, what is to be done?" said Merle. "I shall never find out quite all about the Kings of Endom. Grunter Grim is evidently doing his best to stop me. I expect he made Thomas Muriel cross. All the same, I do wonder what he meant by talking about twins. Whatever could twins have to do with the Kings of Endom?" Merle was talking aloud, standing in the middle of the big room; but as she asked the last question she walked slowly towards one of the cots.

To her surprise, the baby in the cot immediately began to talk, and not only that baby, but all the other babies. Every baby in the room was talking hard. The funny thing was that though the babies were using just the same baby language of coos and gurgles and a-goos that they generally use in the world, Merle perfectly understood what they said, and they evidently understood each other.

Merle listened with the greatest attention, for the babies were answering her question about the twins, and telling her the true story about the Kings of Endom. As you cannot understand baby-talk, I must tell you in proper language what the babies said to Merle.

Listen, then—

"The Finest Baby in the World was always made king, and before he was able to walk and talk properly, his successor was chosen. Well, it happened once that Grunter Grim was admitted to the meeting at which the future king was to be chosen. Now you must know that the king's name was always announced by the Messenger from the Leaves—for the Leaves know which is the finest baby, as they hear all that goes on in the world, and only come to Endom when they are old and need rest. When the name of the future king was given, Grunter Grim got up, and asked very quietly and innocently if the Rhymes were sure that their friends the Leaves had fixed on the finest baby, for he knew that the one named had a twin brother.

"This remark at once upset the meeting. No one ever thought of finding out if what Grunter Grim said was true. They know now that it was false. But at that time they immediately began to discuss what should be done.

"There was, of course, great disagreement. Some thought there ought to be two kings, others declared that idea absurd, but all were agreed that where there were twin-babies, one could not be very much finer than the other.

"Finally, the meeting broke up in the greatest confusion, without any king having been chosen.

"At the next meeting, Grunter Grim spoke still more strongly. As a result, there was more disagreement. At the next, it was worse. Then he suggested that the mothers of all the babies should be asked which was the finest, and, as you know, that only caused greater trouble. Time passed on, and still no king was chosen.

"Then there was not only discontent at the meetings, but before them and after them. The time was taken up in discussion and argument, and nothing was done.

"At last the king was obliged to resign, and no successor had been chosen.

"On that day the last meeting was held. Grunter Grim was present, and when the assembly broke up in confusion, he shouted, 'I will give you a king; I will be your king myself. Henceforward, obey Grunter Grim!' Then all was dark—that was the day on which Mistress Crispin's dinner was changed; that was the day on which Jack and Jill, as they went up the hill quarrelling, were thrown down; that was the day on which Bo-peep's sheeps' tails were cut off and the Man in the Moon burnt his mouth. Every misfortune, every trouble that has come to the Rhymes, dates from that day."

This is the story, as the babies told it to Merle.

When they had finished speaking, Merle waited quietly for two minutes, then nodding to them, she said—"Thank you; at last I understand all about it. Now I must set to work to find a real king for Endom, and he ought to be a king for all time, so that there may never be any more disputes and quarrels."

After she had made this little speech to the babies, she bowed, gave them each a kiss, and then walked out of the room. She felt sure that the future king of Endom was not there, and made up her mind that she ought to begin looking somewhere else for him without wasting any more time.

She passed through several rooms, filled with babies and cradles, and

259

at last came to a very small room. At first she thought that this was quite empty, for there seemed to be nothing in it; but then she noticed that though there was nothing actually in the middle of the room, round the walls there were glass cases. When she looked closely at these cases, she saw that they were filled with rows and rows of letters.

"Very curious," said Merle. "I wonder whose letters they are, and why ever they keep them here?"

Then she looked still closer, and then gave a loud cry of astonishment. It was so loud, that if any one had heard her I am sure they would have come quickly to the rescue, for they would have thought that she was in pain. However, no one did hear, so that it did not matter. After her first surprise, Merle seemed to know exactly what to do. She opened the glass case and took out one of the letters, and then she opened it.

Perhaps you may think it was very wrong of Merle to open somebody else's letter. So it would have been, but this was not some one else's; it was her own, for it was addressed to Merle.

And this was not the only one. Every letter,—and there were hundreds of them—every letter in those cases was meant for Merle to read, although they were not all actually addressed to her.

On some of the envelopes, "To any Human Child who can read" was written, and on others, "Let any child who comes to Endom read this." On a great many Merle's own name was written in very plain letters.

Well, Merle opened one letter, and this is what she found inside—

"If you would banish Grunter Grim,
Have not the slightest fear of him."

"I've heard that before," said Merle, "there's nothing new in that. What is in the next?"

She opened another letter, and found the very same words in that. Then she opened another and another, and about twenty others, and every one was exactly the same.

At last she opened one of the letters directed "to any Human Child who can read," and there she found something different, for in that the following words were written:—

> "If you'd help us, quickly bring
> Unto Endom Endom's king.
> Find his name, you'll then find him.
> Who has got it? Grunter Grim.
> Search his house, you'll find at last,
> 'Tis written down, but sealed up fast."

"Grunter Grim's house," said Merle; "why, I haven't seen that; I didn't know he had a house. I will go at once; but perhaps I had better finish reading the letter first, as there may be something more in it."

There *was* more in it, and this is what Merle read:—

> "If you ask who wrote it down—
> 'Twas one who never wore a crown.
> But the monster Grunter Grim
> Stole the secret—shame on him!
> If you'd get it back again,
> Remember this, I write it plain—
> When Grunter Grim says "Yes"—say "No";
> When he says "Come"—then quickly go;
> When he says "Fly"—be sure to stay;
> When he says "Stop"—then run away.
> Defy, Deride, Desist, Deny,
> Heed not a growl, or scowl, or sigh."

Merle read it all through twice, and put it in her pocket. At last she really understood what she was to do.

She wondered very much who had written all these letters. She was leaving the room when she remembered that she had not yet opened one

261

of the letters that had "Let any child who comes to Endom read this" written on it. She thought she had better do so, and she walked back to the glass case, took out a letter and opened it. This was a very short letter, there were only a few words written on a big sheet of paper.

> *"Beware my fate,*
> *I thought too late,*
> > *I'm Kate."*

"Whatever does that mean?" said Merle. "I had better look at another."

She found in the next—

> *"Do as the letters say—*
> *Be careful to obey,*
> *Or you will fail in the way*
> *That I did—Maggie May."*

"I wonder if these are from children who have been to Endom, and then have been unable to defy Grunter Grim? I wonder what has become of them, and what will become of me? Well, I can but do my best."

So saying, Merle shut the glass case, picked up all the opened letters, made a little heap of them, and then walked out of the room. She was determined to do her best, determined to try to follow the directions in the long letter which she had put in her pocket. As she left the babies' house she repeated aloud the last words—

> *"Defy, Deride, Desist, Deny,*
> *Heed not a growl, or scowl, or sigh,"*

and somehow she found them very comforting.

Outside the house, Merle found herself standing facing a broad pathway, with a high hedge on each side of it. She walked a little way down the path, and found that it divided, and several paths led out of it. Each road was closed in by high hedges, so high that Merle could not see over them, and could only wander aimlessly on and on.

The paths twisted and turned, wound in and out, crossed one another, curved, and sometimes suddenly came to an end.

It **was** fatiguing work, and Merle soon began to feel very tired. Her feet ached, her legs ached, and her head ached. For she was beginning to feel not only tired, but worried and frightened, for it was evident that she had lost her way. Then it began to grow dark, but she was not at all disturbed by that, for she knew that darkness only meant Grunter Grim. And when she remembered Grunter Grim, she took courage, and began to walk more quickly. She felt sure that this crooked, roundabout way must be connected with him, and she felt convinced that she would soon find herself at his house. She was quite right. The road grew narrower, the hedges higher, and, almost directly after, Merle found herself in front of a dark, dismal house.

Like everything else belonging to Grunter Grim, the house was black. It was not straight up and down. Like the way to it, it was very crooked. The walls leant on one side, they seemed as if they must surely tumble down soon. The few windows—and there were very few—were scattered about, as it seemed, anyhow. One end of the house was very high, and looked as if there might be six or seven storeys, and the other end was quite low, only one storey high. Everything about the house looked crooked, and wrong, and uncomfortable.

Merle was not at all surprised at this, however, for she did not expect to find anything pretty or straightforward in connection with Grunter Grim. She looked about a long while for the door, and at last discovered it high up, in what seemed like the top attic. You would scarcely have thought that a door could be put in such a funny place, but this evidently was a door, for there was a knocker fastened to it and a door-plate, but certainly it **was** not the least bit of use to any one inside or outside of the house.

Merle looked about to see if she could find any sign of a side-door or a

263

back-door. They were quickly found, but they were in such queer places that nobody could use them. Since there was no door for her to enter, Merle decided to try a window. She noticed one, quite close to the ground, in the one-storeyed end of the house, and quickly walking to it, she peeped in.

She could not see very much inside, as it was dark, and it was only a little window. After peering in for a few minutes, Merle gently tapped. There was no answer, and no sign of any movement inside the house.

Merle knocked much louder; still no sign. She knocked again, and this time called, "Grunter Grim, Grunter Grim, are you in?"

Still there was no answer, so Merle pushed the window to see if she could open it, but it was fastened very securely.

She did not know at all what to do, so she pulled out her letter of directions, to see if she could find out anything from that.

She opened it out, and began to read aloud from it—

"If you'd help us——"

Merle got no further, for she heard a sudden click. She quickly turned round, but she could see no one. She began reading her letter again. Just as she got to the words "Search his house," she happened to look at the window, and, to her amazement, she saw that it was actually opening, as it seemed, by itself.

For a moment Merle stood still, overcome by astonishment, and then she stepped lightly over the low window-sill, and in at the open window.

She fully expected to find Grunter Grim waiting to receive her, but when she got inside the little room she found no one there, and as soon as she was out of the way, the window quietly shut down.

Merle found herself in a very queer place. The room had no wall-paper—at least, if there was one it was quite impossible to see it, for each of the four walls, as well as the ceiling, was covered with something that looked like a kind of rough woollen material. It was a very light colour, nearly white in some places.

Merle thought it looked rather peculiar, and so went up and touched it. It felt like wool, it *was* wool, but Merle found it was all in loose pieces. She pulled one of the pieces apart from the rest.

264

"Why, it looks just like——" she began, and then she stopped. She remembered that Grunter Grim might be in the house, and might hear her remarks.

"It looks like sheeps' wool," she continued, in a whisper. "I do believe it is a sheep's tail."

She looked again. Then she very nearly shouted, "Of course, of course, these are Bo-peep's sheeps' tails. I've found them."

She was so pleased with her discovery that she determined to examine the rest of the room very carefully.

It contained a perfect mine of treasures. Evidently it was Grunter Grim's store-room, where he kept everything he had stolen from the Rhymes. In one corner Merle found Little Boy Blue's horn.

"Of course," she said, "this explains it. Little Boy Blue couldn't very well blow his horn when Grunter Grim had it here."

In another corner were some gardening tools, and these were labelled, "Johnny's Tools." Merle stood before them for a long time, wondering who "Johnny" was. Then, all at once, the rhyme came into her head—

> "See-saw, Margery Daw,
>   Johnny shall have a new master.
> He shall have but a penny a day,
>   Because he can't work any faster."

"Of course Johnny wasn't able to work quickly when Grunter Grim had his tools."

Merle was continuing her examination of the room, when suddenly she remembered her letter. She had forgotten the directions, and instead of looking for the packet in which the future king's name was written, she was amusing herself. She put Johnny's tools down, and began soberly and seriously to hunt in every nook and corner for the sealed packet.

She left the little store-room and went into the other parts of the house, but found no sign of the packet.

At last she returned to the store-room, and once more began to hunt there. She noticed something black in a very dark corner that she had not seen when she looked before. She picked the something black up, and found when she shook it out that it was a long cloak.

265

"Grunter Grim's cloak," said Merle, with a shudder.

Again she looked in the corner—there was something more in it. This time she pulled out Grunter Grim's big pointed hat. Merle looked at the front of it, wondering if the fiery letters would be there, but there was not a sign of them.

Scarcely thinking what she was doing, Merle wrapped the cloak round her and put the big hat on her head. She began to feel quite queer immediately. A change seemed to be taking place in her character.

Before, she had felt happy, peaceful, and interested, for she was always a very contented girl, even down in the world, where she had to lie in bed all the time. As soon as she put Grunter Grim's clothes on, however, she felt herself growing very miserable. Somehow she felt dissatisfied and unhappy, and yet she could give no reason for it.

If she had given way to this feeling, there is no knowing what would have happened; but she was a sensible girl, and she made an effort, and pulled herself together, shook herself, and said very earnestly—

"Now then, be sensible, Merle."

At once she began to feel stronger, very much stronger. The uncomfortable feeling had almost disappeared, and she was about to take off the cloak and hat, when she heard a very loud noise. The whole house seemed to shake—the sheeps' tails waved in the air, Boy Blue's horn stood up and made a bow, the window opened, and Merle saw a dark little man jump into the room.

It was Grunter Grim, come home at last!

HOW MERLE FOUND THE STOLEN PACKET

It was Grunter Grim, but for the first minute or two Merle did not recognise him. He looked so much smaller, so much meaner, so much less formidable without his hat and cloak, that Merle did not feel the least bit frightened of him, and was only amused.

He was evidently in a bad temper, for he was no sooner safely inside the room than he began stamping and storming and raging.

Merle was in a dark corner, and he did not notice her at first, so she silently listened to him.

"Jackanapes, Jingles, and Jaguars!" he muttered. "Was there ever in this stupid world any one so stupid, so silly as I? Shall I never learn how very risky it is to go out without my cloak and hat? Fortunately, no one has found me out this time."

Merle shrank farther into her corner.

"But I had a quick run for it. That Thomas Muriel nearly cuaght me. And if he had, by the toes of all the sardines, what would have become of me? He knows the secret only too well."

The little man was dancing with rage, up and down the room. He looked so small, yet he had such a big voice and talked so quickly. Presently he looked into the corner. He had evidently come to the conclusion that he would not be without his clothes any longer.

"Beetles, Biscuits, and Bandboxes!" he cried, "has any one been here? Can my cloak and hat be gone? No, they must be in the other room." And he bounced out of the door.

Merle came out of her corner and listened. She could hear him running and jumping all over the house, calling and shouting all the time. Presently, before she could disappear, back he came into the room. Directly he caught sight of her in his hat and cloak, he gave a furious yell, a wild leap into the air, and then began dancing up and down the room—talking and shouting the while.

In spite of the cloak and hat, which had made her feel so brave and strong, Merle began to think that she was just the least little bit frightened. You see, she knew only too well what dreadful things Grunter Grim had done to other people, and she did not know, that as long as she kept the cloak and hat on, he could do nothing to her.

The little man stormed, and little man raged, and then he began to threaten.

"I'll lock you in a dungeon!" he shouted, at the top of his voice. "I'll make you into mincemeat! I'll, I'll——"

He hesitated what to say next. Then, as he saw the colour going from Merle's face, he screamed—

"Now will you give me back my cloak and hat? Say 'Yes' at once!"

Merle lifted her hand to her head to take off the hat—but she still hesitated, and it was well she did. The little man noticed it, and repeated his last words.

"Say 'Yes,' at once!" he shouted, stamping his foot, "and give me the hat, and you shall go."

But these words reminded Merle of her rhyme—

"*When Grunter Grim says 'Yes,' say 'No,'*"

and plucking up all her courage, Merle pulled the hat down more firmly on her head, and said—

"No, I won't give you your hat and cloak, Grunter Grim!"

She fully expected to find herself blown into the middle of next week or that something dreadful would happen, and she shut her eyes tightly. When she opened them again she was still in the little room, and Grunter Grim had not gone, but he seemed somehow to be completely changed. He was standing silently in one corner. He looked no longer angry and threatening, but dreadfully, painfully miserable.

He was shivering and shaking from head to foot, and big tears were rolling down his cheeks.

Merle felt inclined to cast the cloak and hat before him, if only to cheer him up.

"What is the matter? Are you very cold, Grunter Grim?" she asked, in a gentle voice.

"Cold! I am shivering so much that I cannot keep still," said Grunter Grim, in the mildest, meekest, softest of voices. "Oh! have pity on me, and give me back my cloak. Have you never been cold yourself? Will you not have some mercy?"

269

As he spoke Merle began to think she must be a very bad girl to steal some one else's cloak, and let them shiver for want of it.

She looked at Grunter Grim as he stood before her crying and shaking, then a tear rolled down her own cheek, and giving a big sigh, she raised her hand to unfasten the cloak. As she did so she heard a much bigger sigh close beside her, and she noticed that the sheeps' tails were waving up and down, looking somehow very miserable. The room seemed filled with one big sigh, and outside the winds appeared to have caught it up, and were carrying it onwards with them. Merle stopped and looked at Grunter Grim again, then instead of taking off the cloak, she wrapped it more tightly round her, saying softly to herself—

"Defy, Deride, Desist, Deny,
Heed not a growl, or scowl, or sigh."

Grunter Grim watched her closely, but said not a word. He stopped shivering and crying, his whole appearance seemed to change, and he was again the angry, sullen, mean little man. Then he gave Merle a withering glance of hatred and scorn, and walked out of the room.

Merle did not know what to do next. She did not feel much inclined to follow Grunter Grim, and yet she knew that she could do no good until she had made him give her the sealed packet. She was just making up her mind to have one more really good search, when she noticed that the little window had opened itself again.

"That clearly means that I am to get out of this house, and I am very glad of it," said Merle, and she stepped over the window-sill and out into the garden.

She was preparing to make her way down the crooked road when she heard a low chuckle close to her elbow. It was a very wicked chuckle, and Merle turned quickly round, fully expecting to find Grunter Grim at her side.

Instead of this, however, she found a little man, or rather a boy. He was fat, and looked as if his clothes were much too small for him. He was dressed in bright green, and ugly enough he looked.

As Merle turned round and faced him, he gave a jump, as though he were frightened, and ran against Merle, but as soon as he caught sight of her face, he chuckled again.

270

"Beg pardon, Miss, I'm sure," he said, "but I thought until you turned round that you were Grunter Grim. However did you manage to get his cloak and hat?"

"Why do you want to know? Who are you?" asked Merle, for somehow she felt suspicious of the boy.

"Beg pardon," said the boy, grinning, "but I'm Johnny Green."

"Johnny Green! I seem to know that name," said Merle. "Are you one of the Rhymes?"

"Of course," said the boy, grinning again.

Merle felt very comforted when she heard that, for when she first saw him she had quite expected to find that he had something to do with Grunter Grim.

All at once the boy began laughing loudly, apparently without reason.

"You seem to be amused," said Merle, politely.

The boy laughed still louder. At last he managed to gasp out—

"It would be such fun, you know!"

Merle ventured to say she did not know what he meant.

"I want to play a trick on Grunter Grim, and you must help me," said the boy.

"I don't like Grunter Grim, and I don't like playing tricks," said Merle, "but tell me what it is. If it will help me to get what I want, and if it will be of use to the Rhymes, perhaps I might do it. Tell me what it is."

"Well, to begin with, you must give me the cloak and hat," said Johnny Green, beginning to laugh again.

"Oh, I am not likely to do that. I don't know enough about you to trust you with anything so precious," said Merle.

"Well, you know I am one of the Rhymes; didn't I tell you I was Johnny Green?"

As he spoke the boy came nearer to Merle, and took hold of the cloak.

"Johnny Green; I do remember the name, of course," said Merle. " '*Who put her in? Naughty Johnny Green.*' Why, you're the boy that put Pussy in the well, ding dong bell. I won't have anything to do with you."

Merle pulled the cloak away from Johnny. It needed a hard pull, for he had taken firm hold of it, and evidently meant to get it.

Merle indeed was only just in time; in another minute he would have had it off her shoulders.

"You're a bad boy, Johnny Green; don't touch **me**. I won't look at you," she cried.

But something was happening to Johnny Green. He had begun to alter as soon as he touched the cloak. His green clothes became much darker, and he grew thinner. When Merle shouted to him to go away and not touch her, the person who stepped back and stamped his foot was no longer Johnny Green, but Grunter Grim!

"You thought to catch me in that way, did you?" said Merle. "You pretended to be a harmless Rhyme, and hoped to make me help you in your tricks."

"My cloak and hat, give them to me," said the little man.

"I won't give them to you. Now find me the sealed packet which you stole," said Merle, defiantly, for she was not a bit afraid of him.

"I can't find the packet without my hat. Give me my hat, and I promise you I will give you the packet," begged Grunter Grim.

Merle hesitated.

"Well, give me the packet first," she said, "and then you shall have the hat."

There didn't seem to be any way of finding it without Grunter Grim's help, so she determined to sacrifice the hat.

"You promise?" said Grunter Grim.

"Yes," said Merle; but as she said it she shuddered, and then she knew that had made a mistake, but it was too late now.

"You've got the packet," said Grunter Grim, dancing, "it is in the hat, stuck right in the pointed top. Wasn't it a good place to hide it? Now give me my hat."

He tried to snatch it away from Merle before she was able to get the packet out; but this time she was too quick for him. She just managed to get a very small parcel out from the top of the pointed hat before Grunter Grim snatched it away from her, and giving one big jump, reached the door in the top attic, and disappeared inside the house.

When Grunter Grim disappeared with his hat, Merle felt almost inclined to cry. She fully realised, now that it was too late, how silly she had been. Still, she had acted as she thought for the best, for of course she had no idea that the packet she wanted was concealed in the hat.

"Well," said Merle, "at any rate I have done some good. I have the cloak, and nothing shall get that from me, and I have the packet. Perhaps if I find the king's name in that, he will be strong enough to get Grunter Grim's hat away. Now to see what is in the packet. I wish that I were in the babies' house, so that"—but Merle stopped, something very peculiar was happening.

The cloak which she had wrapped so tightly round her was spreading out. It seemed to be dividing into two at the back. Then one part wrapped itself tightly round one of Merle's arms and the other round the other, and then Merle began without thinking to move her arms out from her side and back again. Suddenly she felt herself lifted from the ground into the air.

"Why, I am just like a bird," she shouted, with great delight. "I can fly! I can fly!"

And she was very much like a bird. If you had seen her as she flew swiftly through the air, you might have mistaken her for a big black crow.

Presently she found that she was above the long, low house in which the babies were, and she decided to go down there, and open the mysterious packet which she still held in her hand. She was anxious also to find Thomas Muriel, and tell him her adventures.

She closed her wings down by her side and gently dropped to the ground. The moment her feet touched the earth the wings became a cloak once more.

She was now standing in front of the babies' house, before the very same door by which she had entered the last time, but now that door was shut, and then it had been open.

At first, however, Merle was not disturbed by this, but when she tried to turn the door handle, to her surprise, she found it would not open,

and though she pushed, and pulled, and knocked, and tapped, it was all no good—the door still remained tightly shut.

"This is the queerest thing," said Merle. "I thought with this cloak I could could get anywhere—I don't understand it at all. Never mind, perhaps the packet explains everything, and if I can't get inside why I must open it outside."

As she spoke, Merle began to look more closely at the mysterious packet which she had managed to get from Grunter Grim.

It seemed at first sight very much like a small brown paper parcel, and yet Merle could not find out how it was fastened, for there was no string tied round it, nor was it sealed. She tried to tear it open, but could not. She turned it first one way and then the other, pushed and poked, pulled and fumbled, but could find no beginning or ending to it, and above all, no opening of any kind.

She tried for a long time very patiently, but at last she began to lose her temper.

"This really is too stupid," she said, stamping her foot. "I have the packet, and now I can't get it open. This is one of Grunter Grim's tricks, of course. I wish I could get hold of him. I wish I were at——"

She got no further, for in an instant the cloak had shaped itself into wings, and she felt herself lifted from the ground. "I shall have to be careful," she said, as she rose higher and higher in the air. "It is quite evident that I have only to wish to be at a place, and the cloak will take me there. No wonder Grunter Grim was able to get about so quickly, and to be everywhere at once. Now the only question is, where shall I go?"

She hesitated, but only a second, for just then she felt something touching her nose. She let her wings drop, and began to descend to the ground, to get out of the way; but the something seemed to be following, and she had to flap her wings in front of her face to protect herself. At last, by a good deal of flapping, she managed to get above the something, and as she looked down at it—still following her—she managed to make out that it was a small bird which had been attacking her face.

As soon as she could, Merle dropped to the ground, and just as the wings joined and again became a cloak, the bird also reached the ground, and hopped up to her.

He seemed much astonished when he looked at her, and began to apologise.

"I beg your pardon for attacking you, but I thought you were Grunter Grim, and——" here he paused, and began to flutter his wings as though he were much distressed.

Merle did not know what to say, and waited for him to continue.

At last, after flying rather close to her face, he once more settled down on the ground and began to speak again.

"Would you mind putting your hand over your nose, so that I cannot see it. I am sorry to trouble you, but——"

Merle began to laugh. "What a very queer thing to ask me to do!" she said. "Whatever am I to do that for? Who are you?"

"My name is Master Richard—Master Richard Bird—and unfortunately I am forced by Grunter Grim to attack every nose that I see, and to try to pull it off."

"How curious!" said Merle. "Don't you think it is cruel of you?"

275

"It would be if I did it, but then, you see, I am only forced to *try* to pull a nose off, so of course I never do it," explained Master Richard.

Merle did not quite understand, but was afraid to ask any more questions, lest the bird should think her rude.

"Would you mind telling me if that is Grunter Grim's cloak? I suppose it must be," said Master Richard, after a minute's silence.

"Of course it is," said Merle, "and I have the packet too. I managed to get them both, but it is not much good, because I can't open the packet."

"Why not?" asked the bird. "You have the hat, I suppose, if you have the cloak. Use the hat to open the packet; it will open anything."

"But I haven't got the hat," said Merle, almost beginning to cry. "I gave the hat back to Grunter Grim."

"Well, that is a pity," said Master Richard. "Didn't you know that the cloak is of no use without the hat; for though the cloak will take you to any house, the hat only will get you inside. If you have the hat, you can open any lock, any door, any window, anything—even the parcel."

"Then I must get the hat as soon as possible," said Merle. "Won't you help me?"

"Yes, indeed, I will, if you will keep your nose out of the way, and I'll get the four-and-twenty blackbirds to help, too," said Master Richard.

Merle stared at him. "Four-and-twenty blackbirds," she said to herself. "Richard Bird and my nose! What does it all mean?"

Master Richard, however, took no notice of her, but flew as high as he could into the air, and began chirruping and whistling.

Close behind her Merle heard an answering chirrup, and in a minute a pert young blackbird perched himself on her shoulder. Then a whistle, and behold there was a bird on the other shoulder; then a bird flew on her head, and another, and another, and another, until black birds seemed flying all round her.

At last Master Richard stopped whistling, and came down to the ground. He placed himself right opposite Merle, called to the blackbirds once more, and they formed a line behind him, and then they began to sing.

Merle only listened for a while, then quite suddenly she too began to sing. She sang simply because she could not help it—she felt obliged to sing at the top of her voice:

> *"Sing a song of sixpence,*
> *A pocket full of rye,*
> *Four-and-twenty blackbirds*
> *Baked in a pie;*
> *When the pie was opened*
> *The birds began to sing,*
> *Wasn't that a dainty dish*
> *To set before a king?"*

The birds did not appear to mind at all; indeed, they seemed to enjoy it. Merle went on with the second verse, about the king being in the counting-house and the queen in the parlour, but when she sang,

> *"The maid was in the garden, hanging out the clothes;*
> *There came a little dicky-bird, and pecked off her nose,"*

she found that the birds had stopped and she was singing alone. When she finished, all the blackbirds began to shout at her, "Shame! Tear her to pieces! It isn't true! Shame!" It was evident that somehow she had offended them, and they were very angry. Merle tried to speak, but there was too much noise. Then she shouted, but it was no good. At last Master Richard stepped forward, and at once there was silence.

"Blackbirds, be quiet, it is ignorance; she means no harm," he said, and then he turned to Merle. "I am sure you would not have sung the last part of that song if you kad known how it offends us. I am Dicky Bird. I told you my name was Richard, but sometimes I am called Dicky. I am Dicky, and that day that I hurt the maid—and, by the way, I did not peck off her nose, though I'm sorry to say I tried to—I was very much upset. It was partly Grunter Grim's fault——"

"I understand," interrupted Merle, "and I am so sorry. But I will nevei sing it again, and you must help me to banish him. The first thing to do is to get the hat. Let us quarrel no longer, but all set to work."

At the word of command from Master Richard all the blackbirds formed themselves into a circle round Merle, and they were just as quiet and polite as they had been noisy and rude before. They only spoke when they were spoken to, and indeed, took little part in the discussion. Merle and Dicky did all the talking, and at last agreed upon a plan of action.

It was arranged that all the blackbirds, with Dicky at their head, were to fly to Grunter Grim's house, get in, if possible, and look for the hat; and if not, to hover about, find Grunter Grim, and try to get some information from him.

Merle, meantime, was to stay behind and keep out of sight, for fear Grunter Grim should recognise her, and try to get back his cloak.

Everything being thus settled, Dicky Bird flapped his wings and flew upwards, crying "Forward!" All the four-and-twenty blackbirds followed his example, and soon Merle was left alone to await their return.

She made herself very comfortable on the stump of a moss-grown tree. As she sat down, she heard a voice singing softly—

"Little Miss Muffet
Sat on a tuffet,
Eating curds and whey."

Merle sprang to her feet and looked round, but she could see no one. Then she looked again at the stump of the tree, and noticed that there was a small label fastened to one side of it, on which was written—

"MISS MUFFET'S TUFFET."

"This is very interesting," said Merle. "I wonder if the spider will come?"

"Of course he won't," said a voice just behind her. "Grunter Grim is the spider, and how can he come when you have the cloak? He is a prisoner!"

Once more Merle turned round, and this time a girl was standing in

279

front of her. She recognised her as the girl she had seen at the meeting, and anyhow, she would have known who it was, because the girl's name was written on the label fastened on her dress.

"So Grunter Grim was the spider," said Merle. "I thought you didn't look the kind of girl to be frightened by a real spider."

"Frightened by a spider—no indeed. Let me tell you my story," said Miss Muffet.

"I suppose it is like all the others," said Merle. "Grunter Grim is the cause of all your trouble, is he not?"

Miss Muffet was just going to answer, when Merle saw two of the blackbirds flying towards them.

"Look, look!" she cried, "they are coming back. Now we shall get some news."

"News?" said Miss Muffet; "news of what?"

But Merle did not answer her, for by this time the blackbirds had reached the two girls, and had perched themselves on Merle's shoulders.

"Tell me—what have you seen or heard?" said Merle.

"I went to the house," said Blackbird Number One.

"Just like *me*," said Number Two.

"And there I saw a window," continued Number One.

"*Just* like me," cried Number Two.

"And I looked in and saw Grunter Grim," went on Number One.

"Just *like*——" began Number Two; but Merle interrupted him.

"Do tell me a little quicker," she said. "Had he the hat on? Did you see it? Did you ask him anything? And what did he say?"

" 'No,' to the first question; 'No,' to the second; 'Yes,' to the third and fourth," shouted both blackbirds.

"I asked him where the hat was," said Number One.

"Just like me," said Number Two.

"And he said, 'Ha, ha, ha!' " said Number One.

"No, he didn't," said Two; "he said, 'The hats,' as if there were six or seven magic hats."

"HA! HA! HA!—THE HATS," said Merle, slowly; "what could he have meant?"

But the two blackbirds made no reply, they seemed to think they had done enough work for one day. They flew down from Merle's shoulder, and perching on Miss Muffet's Tuffet, tucked their heads under their wings, and went to sleep.

Merle was beginning to feel angry with them for being so stupid when she saw quite a number of their brothers flying towards her.

"Ah! here they come," she said to Miss Muffet. "Now, this time I will tell them what they saw, and try to get the news more quickly."

"I believe I begin to see what it all means," said Miss Muffet. "You have the cloak, and you are trying to get the hat."

"Hush!" said Merle, as twenty-two blackbirds flew to the ground and hopped in front of her.

As soon as they were settled, without waiting for them to speak, Merle began—

"You went to the house."

"Just like me!" shouted each blackbird.

"And there you saw a window, and you looked in and saw Grunter Grim," said Merle, very rapidly; "and he had not the hat on, and you didn't see it, and you asked him a question, and he said——"

All the blackbirds shouted at the top of their voices something, but, as they all spoke together, Merle could not understand a word.

"Say it one at a time," said Merle; but the blackbirds took no notice of her, they just hopped on to the tuffet, and went off to sleep.

"Oh dear!" said Miss Muffet, "how tiresome of them. What shall we do?"

"Never mind," said Merle, "here comes Master Richard—he will help us."

"Yes, that he will," said Miss Muffet—"only cover up your nose, my dear."

She only spoke just in time, for Master Richard flew straight at Merle's face, and would certainly have touched her nose had she not covered it up.

"I beg your pardon," he said—"but you know——"

"Never mind," said Merle, "give us the news."

"I have very little to tell, unhappily," said Master Richard. "I haven't

281

found the hat, and though I saw Grunter Grim, he wouldn't answer any questions, and whatever I said to him, he only said, 'No one else can.' What he meant by that I don't know. Have the others come back?"

"Yes, but look at them," said Merle, dolefully. "They have all seen Grunter Grim, and he has said some nonsense or a bit of a sentence to each of them; but as they all shouted together, I couldn't exactly make out what it was."

"Put all the bits together, and see if they make a proper sentence," said Miss Muffet.

"But the birds are fast asleep, they won't say it again," said Merle.

"I'll soon make them," said Master Richard. "That is a good idea, Miss Muffet."

Directly Master Richard called to them, the blackbirds woke up; when he called to them a second time, they all jumped to the ground; and at the third call they formed themselves into a line in front of him.

"Now, Blackbirds," said Master Richard, "tell me what you each heard Grunter Grim say. Speak one at a time, clearly and distinctly."

Without a murmur, or even a "Just like me," the birds began—

"To me Grunter Grim said 'HA! HA! HA!' " said Number One.

"To me he only said 'THE HATS,' " said Two.

"To me 'SAFE,' " answered Three.

"To me he only said 'AWAY,' " said Four.

"When I spoke to him he said 'RIGHT,' " said Five.

"When I asked where the hat was, he said 'WELL HIDDEN,' " said Six.

"And when I said 'Is it lost?' he said, 'FOR EVER AND A DAY,' " said Seven.

"Stop a minute," said Merle, "I see something."

"Yes, so do I," said Miss Muffet. "Put those words together, and you get a rhyme."

"Of course you do," said Master Richard; "it's just what I expected. Listen.

> *"Ha! Ha! Ha! the hat's safe away,*
> *Right well hidden for ever and a day."*

"It doesn't tell us much," said Merle.

"Wait for the rest," said Master Richard. "Now, Number Eight, what did he say to you?"

" 'DING, DONG,' " answered Eight.

"He only said 'THE' to me," said Nine.

"And only 'BELL' to me," said Ten.

"When I questioned him, he said, 'OF COURSE I KNOW,' " continued Eleven.

"And he said to me 'NO USE,' " said Twelve.

"I only caught the word 'IN' when he spoke to me," said Thirteen.

"And as far as I could make out, he said 'THAT' to me," said Fourteen.

"I heard him say 'WITHOUT THE CLOAK,' " said Fifteen.

"And he called out 'HO! HO! HO!' to me," said Sixteen.

"Two more lines of the rhyme," cried Miss Muffet, excitedly. Listen Merle.

> *"Ding, dong, the bell, of course I know,*
> *No use in that without the cloak, Ho! Ho! Ho!"*

"Go on, go on," said Merle.

"To me he said 'MERLE,' " said Seventeen.

"To me he whispered 'STOLE,' " said Eighteen.

"And to me 'THE CLOAK,' " said Nineteen.

"I heard the words 'FROM THE POOR OLD MAN,' " said Twenty.

"He only said 'SHE' to me,' " said Twenty-one.

"And to me he said 'MIGHT GET,' " said Twenty-two.

"I heard him say 'THE HAT,' " said Twenty-three.

"And to me he said 'BUT,' " said Twenty-four.

"And that's all," said Merle.

"Wait a minute," said Master Richard, "you are forgetting what I heard. He said 'NO ONE ELSE CAN' to me."

"Now say the whole rhyme slowly," said Miss Muffet, getting more and more excited.

Master Richard pointed to one bird after the other, and this is what they said—

> *"Ha! Ha! Ha! the hat's safe away,*
> *Right well hidden for ever and a day.*
> *Ding, dong, the bell, of course I know,*
> *No use in that without the cloak, Ho! Ho! Ho!*
> *Merle stole the cloak from the poor old man;*
> *She might get the hat, no one else can."*

"It isn't a little bit of good; it just tells us what we knew before," said Merle, in a very disappointed tone.

"It's a trick of Grunter Grim's," said Miss Muffet, very sadly.

Even Master Richard looked down-hearted. The Rhyme was, as Merle said, "no good at all."

Presently, however, just as the blackbirds were dropping off to sleep again, Merle called out—

"Stop! Perhaps the words would make another Rhyme if we took them in different order."

"You are clever," said Miss Muffet. "I expect you are right. Try them backwards."

But that was no good, it only made nonsense. Then they tried all kinds of ways, but could not get anything at all sensible. At last, just as Merle had made up her mind to give it up altogether, Miss Muffet had a brilliant idea.

"I expect the Rhyme begins with 'Ding, dong, bell,' " she said, "for that is Grunter Grim's favourite rhyme."

"Why didn't we think of that before?" said Master Richard.

"And perhaps, oh! perhaps," said Merle, excitedly, "the hat's hidden in the well. Do let us try to get the Rhyme once more."

They did try very hard. They made the blackbirds stand first one way, and then the other, they mixed them up, and made them shout until they were nearly hoarse, and at last they placed them side by side in this order, with Master Richard in the middle:—8, 10, 3, 13, 9, 6, 5, 4, 7, 17,

22, 23, Master Richard, 21, 18, 19, 20, 1, 24, 11, 14, 2, 12, 15, 16. Then they each said the word or words they had heard once through, and there was such a cry of delight from Merle, such a shout of joy from Miss Muffet, such a lively chirp from Master Richard, and such a twittering and chirruping from the four-and-twenty blackbirds! The secret was found out!

"Now, say your words once more," said Master Richard, and the birds shouted each in turn, and this is how the Rhyme sounded this time:—

> *"Ding, dong, bell,*
> *Safe in the well,*
> *Hidden right away*
> *For ever and a day.*
> *Merle might get the hat, no one else can;*
> *She stole the cloak from the poor old man.*
> *Ha! Ha! Ha! but of course I know*
> *That the hat's no use without the cloak, Ho! Ho! Ho!"*

Then came another cheer, and then Merle, Master Richard, and Miss Muffet set off running, flying, and jumping, to find the well and get the hat.

DOWN THE WELL

Merle found the well quite easily. With her magic cloak she moved through the air so quickly that Master Richard and Miss Muffet could not keep up with her, and they were soon left far behind. The well was surrounded by thick trees—so thick, that Merle could not help thinking, as she dropped gently to the ground, that she would never have been able to make her way through the bushes on foot, and that had she not had the cloak to help her, she would not have found the well at all.

It was very like an ordinary well—indeed, the only difference between it and most wells was that above it was fastened a very large bell, from which dangled a very long rope.

Merle knelt down on the ground and peeped into the well. To her delight, she could not see any water in it.

"Hurrah!" she cried, "it will be easy to search that well thoroughly. I was wondering how I should be able to go underneath the water."

She wrapped her cloak round her, wished, and soon felt herself falling gently down, down, down. She reached the bottom quite safely, and at once began her search.

"It is a very large well," she said, as she felt her way about, for it was much too dark to see anything, "and the walls are certainly very damp."

The walls were very damp, though perhaps that was not strange. Every one expects the bottom of a well to be damp. Every one does not usually, however, expect the walls of a well each time they are touched to send out little jets of water, but that was happening in this well.

The water, too, rose rapidly, and in a little time it reached above Merle's knees as she stood in it.

"I see what is the matter," said Merle, slowly, "Grunter Grim means to try to drown me. It is not a bit of good, I mean to find his hat before I go up."

She moved about quickly, but the well seemed to grow larger, and the water was still rising rapidly.

It reached her waist. Should she give up the search? Just then her foot knocked against something, something pointed. Could it be Grunter Grim's hat?

Forgetting all about the water, she stooped down, seized hold of the point, and pulled. The hat—for it was the hat—was pushed very tightly into a hole in the wall.

"One more tug," said Merle.

But she did not give the one more tug, for she felt something pulling her from above, and before she could cry out or object in any way, she found herself lifted out of the water, out of the well, and on to the ground.

She struggled to her feet and looked about indignantly, expecting to find Grunter Grim before her.

There was no Grunter Grim, only a very tall, very thin, very stupid-looking boy was standing staring at her. He carried a fishing-rod in one hand and a pail in the other, and he was trying to jerk the fish-hook out of Merle's dress, in which it was tightly fastened.

"Whatever did you do it for?" asked Merle, crossly.

"I thought that I had found the whale at last," said the stupid boy.

"Why, you *are* a Simple Simon," said Merle.

The boy frowned angrily.

"Whose fault is that?" he asked.

Merle looked at his pail, at his rod, and then at the ticket fastened on his coat. Sure enough, on it was written "Simple Simon."

"I beg your pardon," she said; "I didn't know."

"It was all Grunter Grim's fault," said Simon; "I was——"

But Merle interrupted him.

"Then why did you fish me out of the well, just when I was going to find his hat?" she said.

"Oh, I am sorry! I am sorry!" said Simon. "You see usually I spend all my time fishing in this pail, but somehow to day I can do what I like, and fish in other places."

"That is because I have Grunter Grim's cloak," said Merle, "and he has lost some of his power."

"Hurrah!" shouted Simon, and he threw his cap into the air.

As it came down it caught in the bell-rope, and at once the bell began ringing.

Ding, dong, bell! Ding, dong, bell!

"What a noise!" said Merle.

But it did not go on ringing very long, and when Merle looked into the

well once more, she found that it was empty again, the water had all run away. She wrapped her cloak round her, and turning to Simple Simon, said—

"Don't pull me out this time. I'm not a whale, you see."

"Then I had better be off," said Simple Simon. "I can't help fishing you out if I stay here."

Merle watched him disappear through the trees, and then went down, down, down to the bottom of the well again.

The walls seemed wetter than ever, and the water had risen to her waist before she had even found the point of the hat. It rose so rapidly that she was beginning to feel rather frightened. In spite of her fears, however, she felt very angry when once more she found herself lifted out, and dropped on to the ground.

"I told you to leave me alone," she said, impatiently. Then forgetting her anger, she began to laugh as she looked at the round smiling face of the boy standing over her.

He took off his cap, made a low bow, and said politely—

"Who pulled her out? Little Tommy Stout."

And then he bowed again.

"I wish you had left her in," said Merle. "I never shall find the hat if you and Simon keep fishing me out of the well."

"So sorry," said Tommy, still smiling; "but the fact of the matter is I thought you were Pussy. And you'll excuse me mentioning it, but you didn't seem to be thoroughly enjoying the water, though you are not as wet as you might have been under the circumstances."

"No," said Merle, "I wasn't enjoying the water, and I am afraid I shall be drowned before I can get the hat, the water rises so quickly."

"You don't mean to say," said Tommy, without even a little bit of a smile, "that you stayed in the well when the water was rising."

Merle nodded.

"Then the only thing I wonder at is that you are not drowned this minute. My dear young lady, it is quite evident to me that you are not in the habit of pulling pussies out of wells. If you went into that well seven or eight times a day, as I do, you would know better than to venture in when it was full of water."

"It was empty when I started," said Merle.

"Then of course you did not ring the bell," said Tommy, "though I thought I heard it ringing just now."

"Is that the way you manage?" asked Merle.

"Of course," said Tommy. "What is the bell put there for? I'll show you how it is done."

He jumped into one of the buckets, and seized hold of the bell-rope.

Ding, dong, bell! Ding, dong, bell!

The bell rang loudly all the time Tommy was in the well, and when he reappeared at the top once more, smiling as usual, he was perfectly dry.

"That's the way," he said, cheerfully; "but I think you are mistaken about the hat. I don't think it is there. I saw no sign of it."

But Merle was certain she was not mistaken, and taking hold of the rope and setting the bell ringing, she jumped into the bucket. In a few moments she reappeared with a smile of triumph on her face and the hat in her hand.

"What do you think of that?" she asked, as she put it on her head. "Now, Grunter Grim, you have indeed lost your power!"

Although she no longer held the bell-rope, the bell was ringing loudly, and all the birds in the wood were singing and trilling. Tommy was laughing heartily and shouting at the top of his voice "Hurrah!" and Merle trembled all over as she drew the parcel from her pocket.

She did not need even to touch the parcel with the hat, for as she drew it out she saw that it was open, and these were the mysterious words she found written inside it:—

> *"Who shall be Endom's king?*
> *A baby he*
> *Must always be;*
> *For a baby is Endom's king.*
>
> *"What baby is Endom's king?*
> *A baby that's glad*
> *When others are sad;*
> *For contented is Endom's king.*

> *"How to find Endom's King?*
>   *The cloak he must wear,*
>   *Yet be free from care;*
> *For not all can be Endom's king.*
>
> *"Who then is Endom's king?*
>   *The baby that's glad*
>   *When others are sad;*
> *And his name it is Baby——."*

Merle read it through aloud twice. She looked very puzzled, for there seemed to be something wrong with the last verse.

"I see what it is," she said at last.

"So do I," said Tommy.

"It's the same old story," said Merle.

"It's Grunter Grim," said Tommy; "he's scratched out the most important word in the whole rhyme."

"Yes, so he has," said Merle: "the word after 'baby' in the last line."

"Of course that was the name," said Tommy; "Oh dear! Oh dear!" and he seized hold of the bell-rope, and jumping into the bucket, disappeared down the well.

As soon as Tommy had disappeared Merle turned away from the well.

"It's no use staying here," she said. "It is quite certain that there are no babies in the well; perhaps I had better go back to the baby-house."

She wrapped the cloak round her, and was going to wish, when she remembered the hat, and determined to try its power.

"If I can get through anything with this hat," she said, "I should think I can get through these trees."

Pulling the hat firmly down on her head, she prepared to push her way into the very thickest part of the wood which surrounded the well; but as soon as she reached the trees they seemed to move away from her. They crowded together on each side until there was quite a clear pathway, and at last there were so few trees that at the end of the pathway Merle could see a very tall tower. As she drew nearer to it, she noticed that there was a large clock at the top of it, and above the clock face were three letters—

H. D. D.

"Well, at any rate, I may as well go up the tower," said Merle. "Perhaps I shall be able to get a good view from the top."

It was easier, however, to say she would go up the tower than to do it, for there did not seem to be any door to it, or any way of getting into it.

"It's a good thing I have the hat," said Merle. "I suppose I must make a door for myself."

She took the hat off her head, and was just going to touch the walls of the tower with it, when she heard a loud booming sound which almost deafened her. Whatever could it be? Then she remembered the clock—perhaps it was only the clock striking.

She walked round to the front of the tower, and stared up at the clock-face. Now she noticed for the first time that instead of figures on the face, there were letters.

She began spelling out the letters slowly, "S M I R G R E T—" But she stopped, for she heard a great noise of scratching and scraping, and a sound of something tumbling, then it seemed as though nearly the whole front of the tower opened, and to Merle's great surprise three kittens came rolling out of the huge door. They rolled over and over until they were at her feet, when suddenly they stood up on their hind legs and bowed solemnly.

They were pretty kittens—so pretty that Merle longed to pick them up and cuddle them.

One was perfectly black, another quite white, and the third was a very handsome tabby. Each had a ribbon tied round its neck, and on the front of each ribbon was worked a name.

Merle tried hard to see what the names were, but she could only make out the shortest—the one tied round the grey kitten's neck, and that was "Dock." She was going to ask the names of the others, when all three bowed once more.

Then the black kitten stepped forward, and said, politely—

"Allow me to introduce myself—I'm Hickory."

"Then of course you are Dickory?" said Merle, pointing to the white kitten.

"Exactly so," said all the kittens together.

"And that's the clock," said Merle, pointing to the tower. "But what do the letters mean? 'S M I R G R E T N U R G'—doesn't seem to spell anything."

Hickory looked at Dickory, and Dickory looked at Dock.

"My whiskers!" said Hickory.

"After all this time she doesn't know," said Dickory.

"Rats and mice! who'd have thought it?" said Dock.

Then they all laughed, as only three little kittens can.

Merle went very red, she thought the kittens were rather rude. She turned round, and was going to walk right away, when Hickory said—

"Excuse me, but whose cloak have you got on?"

"Grunter Grim's," said Merle.

"And to whom does the hat belong?" asked Dickory.

"To Grunter Grim," said Merle again.

"Well, now look at the clock again," said Dock.

"Of course—how stupid of me!" said Merle. "I was reading it backwards. The letters spell 'GRUNTER GRIM'S.' I might have guessed that."

293

"So you might," said Hickory.

"Exactly so," said Dickory.

"Precisely so," added Dock.

Then the three little kittens joined paws and danced in a circle round Merle.

"Well, you are certainly the most remarkable kittens," said Merle. "I'm sure you never lost your mittens, or began to cry."

The kittens stopped dancing immediately, and put their paws behind their backs.

"Oh, you did, did you?" said Merle, beginning to laugh.

"Tell her," said Hickory.

"Was it Grunter Grim?" asked Merle.

"Exactly so," said Dickory.

"And I'm forgetting all about the Rhyme and the King of Endom"; and pulling her packet out of her pocket, she read aloud the Rhyme to the kittens.

"Now," she said, "can you guess the missing word?"

"Of course, it means that the king must be a Rhyme Baby, you see that?" said Hickory.

"A Rhyme Baby?" repeated Merle.

"Exactly so," said Dickory.

"A Nursery Rhyme Baby, not a real world baby," said Dock.

"Well, I never thought of that," said Merle. "Of course it does. 'A baby who'll ne'er be a man' can't be a human baby. I never thought of that."

"And, of course, there are not many Rhyme Babies," said Hickory.

"Exactly so," remarked Dickory. "I've an idea."

"It's the first you ever had, then," said Dock, rather rudely. "You don't usually think for yourself."

"Oh, please don't quarrel," said Merle.

"Let us think," said Hickory.

The three little kittens, without any warning, stood on their heads. Merle was too much astonished to say anything, and waited patiently to see what would happen.

Presently Hickory gave a loud miaow, and immediately all three kittens again stood on their hind legs.

"I see," said Hickory, in a very mysterious ghostly voice, waving his tail in the air, "I see a cradle in a wood on a treetop, the bough is rocking, and the child is laughing.

> *"When the bough breaks, the cradle will fall,*
> *Down will go baby, and cradle, and all."*

"I hear," said Dickory, "a voice singing a lullaby to a baby. Listen to the words."

Swaying from side to side, the three kittens began singing softly—

> *"Dance a baby diddy,*
> *What shall his mother do wid'e?*
> *Sit in her lap, give him some pap,*
> *And dance a baby diddy."*

As the lullaby died away, Merle looked at Dock, and waited eagerly for him to speak.

"And I see," said Dock, excitedly, "a lonely house in a lonely wood, a lonely baby in a lonely cradle, a——"

But just then the loud booming sound was heard once more from inside the clock.

"The mouse is up the clock—away!" cried Hickory.

"Exactly so!" said Dickory.

"Precisely so!" added Dock.

And away up the tower, as fast as their legs could carry them, scampered the three little kittens.

"Now, that's a pity," said Merle, as she watched the three tips of the three tails disappear. "I wanted to ask them ever so many questions."

She wrapped the cloak round her, once more wished, and immediately felt herself floating in the air.

After flying a short distance, she saw the baby-house beneath her, and to her astonishment she found herself dropping down to the earth.

"This is curious," she said. "I wished to be at the Rhyme Babies' house, but perhaps they all live together."

Directly she reached the ground Thomas Muriel came hastening towards her, and as soon as he had heard the story of her adventures, he began to talk very fast.

"You have only one hour more," he said, "to find the king, then there will be another meeting, and you must go back to the earth. Let me help you, and let us be very quick."

"Shall I give you the cloak?" asked Merle.

"It is no good to me, I cannot wear it," said Thomas Muriel, sadly; "only a contented person can wear it."

"Then I must find a contented baby, I suppose," said Merle.

"Of course, the Rhyme says so," said Thomas Muriel; "but don't waste any more time in talking. Come this way."

Merle followed him down several passages, and at last found herself in a large room.

In one corner of it was a cradle, and in the cradle a baby was jumping up and down energetically.

Some one in the room was singing—

"Dance a baby diddy,"

but Merle had not time to see who it was.

"Put the cloak round him," said Thomas Muriel.

Merle obeyed. The baby was laughing and crowing at the top of its voice, but no sooner did the cloak touch him, than he began to cry and scream loudly.

Such a noise! Merle had never heard anything like it. She did not wait a moment, but snatching away the cloak ran out of the room as fast as ever she could.

"He seemed a very contented baby," she said, as soon as they were safely outside.

"I can't make it out," said **Thomas** Muriel. "Say the Rhyme again."

Merle repeated it slowly—

> *"A baby that's glad*
> *When others are sad."*

"That's it," said Thomas Muriel, "of course. That baby has never been glad when others were sad."

"Well, let us try another baby," said Merle. "Do you happen to know where the baby in the cradle on the tree-top is to be found?"

"I know where to find her," said Thomas Muriel, "but I am afraid she won't be any good, she hasn't been sad."

"Then don't you think a bough breaking, a cradle falling, and a baby and all tumbling down, would make you sad?" asked Merle, rather indignantly.

"Don't you see it says *when* the bough breaks," said Thomas Muriel; "and of course it never does break. It isn't likely it would. Why the baby would be killed."

"Well, I am very glad of that," said Merle. "All the same, I don't see what we are to do next."

Thomas Muriel looked puzzled.

"I wonder which baby Dock meant?" said Merle, quite suddenly. "perhaps you know a lonely baby in a lonely house."

"No, I don't," said Thomas Muriel, sadly.

Merle began repeating the last verse of the Rhyme slowly—

> *"Who then is Endom's king?*
> *The baby that's glad*
> *When others are sad;*
> *And his name it is Baby——"*

"Stop!" cried Thomas Muriel, "I see something. The baby's name must rhyme with 'king.' "

298

"Of course," said Merle. "Oh, don't you know a name that will rhyme with 'king?' "

"I don't," said Thomas Muriel, "but I know some one who does; come along quickly."

He seized hold of Merle, pulled her along, and before she had time even to look round her, pushed her in at the door of a small house, and saying—"Now, be quick, I can't stop any longer," ran away and left her.

Merle felt quite bewildered. She could not speak, because she had lost her breath, but she managed to use her eyes, and found that she was in a small shop.

Behind the counter sat a very small person with a very big head, writing busily. She was so much occupied that she did not seem to see Merle at all.

All round the room were shelves, with sheets and sheets of paper packed tightly into them. Each shelf had a number and a label.

One of these labels was quite close to Merle, and she took it up and looked at it. "Little Jack Horner" was written upon it, and as Merle peeped at the papers inside the shelf, she saw that each one was a copy of the Rhyme about Jack Horner.

She was pulling one out to see what the last line was, when she heard some one speaking to her, and turning round quickly, found herself in the presence of the Rhyme-Fairy.

She had a very small voice, so small that Merle could scarcely hear what she said.

"What do you want, little girl?" asked the Rhyme-Fairy; but before Merle could answer she went on, "There are plenty of rhymes to 'girl'—hurl, whirl, curl, furl, for instance, but the proper one on this occasion is 'Merle.' "

Merle stared at her; then she managed to screw up her courage to say gently—

"If you please, I want a rhyme to 'king.' "

"Certainly," said the Fairy. "Rhymes to Order, you know," and she pointed to the sign above her head, on which was printed in large letters, "RHYMES TO ORDER. ANY RHYME FOUND ON THE SHORTEST POSSIBLE NOTICE. THE TRADE SUPPLIED, WHOLESALE AND RETAIL, BY THE RHYME-FAIRY."

Then she reached down a big fat book, marked "K," and began to turn over the leaves, talking quickly all the time—

"K–Ki–Kin–King. There you are! Plenty of rhymes to 'king.' "

She showed Merle a long list of words, and ran her finger down it quickly.

"Is it comic poetry you are writing?" she said, "because, if so, allow me to recommend 'fling,' the noun, not the verb, you know."

Merle shook her head.

"Oh, something sarcastic! Then try 'sting.' No, something rather tender, perhaps? Then I should strongly recommend 'cling,' or even 'ring.' I find 'cling' in great demand."

Merle turned away, she did not understand what the Fairy was talking about, and her precious minutes were flying fast.

She felt very sad. She did not want to go back to the world, leaving the Rhymes unhappy. But the little Fairy was still speaking to her.

"Won't you let me look at the whole line, Miss?" she was saying. "I feel sure I have something that will suit you, and answer your purpose."

Merle pulled the packet out of her pocket, and began to read the verse.

At once the Fairy's manner completely changed. She got down from her chair, pushed away her books and papers, and listened eagerly.

When Merle finished the first verse, she shouted—

"Go on! Go on! I'll help you. Down with Grunter Grim! I'm sick of Rhymes. Give Endom a king, and I'll make no more Nursery Rhymes. I shall be free."

Merle began the fourth verse, and as soon as she finished the Fairy cried, "I see, I see—

'Who then is Endom's king?
The baby that's glad
When others are sad;
And his name it is Baby BUNTING.'

That's the word you want."

"Of course it is," said Merle; "Baby Bunting—B——B——. He's always contented, though *his father's a-hunting.*"

"*His mother's a-milking*," cried the Fairy, excitedly.

"*His sister's a-silking and his brother's gone to buy a skin*," cried Merle. "He is contented through trouble and care, that is quite certain; only let me find him—

> " '*The baby that's glad*
> *When others are sad;*
> *And his name it is Baby BUNTING.*' "

But as she said the words she heard a wild shout. It seemed as if there were numbers of people repeating the words after her. She looked up, looked down, the shop had disappeared, and she was back again on the platform in the big hall.

But how different the Hall looked! No lamps were needed, for the whole room was flooded with sunlight. In each corner shone a big sunbeam, and in each beam hundreds of fairies were dancing madly. It scarcely looked like the same place, and Merle found it very difficult to believe that she really was in the big hall.

But the clocks were striking and the Rhymes were fast assembling.

Mistress Crispin and Jack and Jill were the first to arrive, and they were so busy talking together that they did not notice Merle.

"Just fancy, Mother," said Jill: "we really carried the pail full of water right up to the top of the hill, and we did not tumble down at all. What can it mean?"

"What can it mean, indeed?" said Mistress *Crispin*. "What do you think has happened to me? The broth is no longer broth, it is once more——"

"Not roast beef and plum pudding," said Jack.

Mistress Crispin nodded her head.

"Hurrah!" shouted Jack. "We'll all come home!"

"Yes, they have come home," cried Bo-peep, as she came hurrying into the room. "What do you think I've found?"

"Not the sheep's tails?" said Jack Horner, who was just behind her.

"Yes, the sheep's tails—and on the sheep, too, my boy," said Bo-peep, triumphantly.

"Well," said Jack Horner, "to be a good boy I *will* try." Bo-peep stared at him.

"Can you say it?" she said eagerly.

"Indeed I can," said Jack; "not once this morning have I said the other thing."

Just then Mother Hubbard, the Man in the Moon, Miss Muffet, and Boy Blue came into the Hall together.

Each one looked more surprised than the other.

"What does it mean?" said the Man in the Moon. "I ate the porridge, and it didn't burn my mouth."

"What has happened?" said Boy Blue, almost in the same breath. "I've found my horn."

"Look at my tools!" shouted Johnny at the top of his voice, as he rushed into the Hall towards the platform with a hop, skip, and a jump. "I've found my tools, now I'll get more than a penny a day."

The clocks were still striking, and the platform was getting more and more crowded.

And when the last clock struck twelve every Rhyme had arrived, and every one seemed overcome with astonishment and amazement.

On all sides there were heard whispers, cries, and shouts of "What has happened? What does it all mean?" Hickory, Dickory, and Dock were thinking hard, standing on their heads, and Simple Simon was shaking his head solemnly, as much as to say, "I don't understand it a bit."

At last Merle stepped forward and held up one hand. There was a loud cheer, and then perfect silence as she began to speak.

"I have found you a king," she said. "He is contented through trouble and care, and he will banish Discontent, he will banish Grunter Grim, and you will be happy for ever."

The Rhymes began once more to cheer.

"His name——" said Merle.

But at that moment there was a wild shriek, and Grunter Grim, without hat, without cloak, looking small, and mean, and miserable, came bounding into the room.

"My hat, my cloak, my power!" he said.

The Rhymes laughed, they were not a bit afraid of him.

"All gone," said Pollie Flinders; "you'll never spoil any more of my new clothes."

"Gone!" said Tom the Piper. "Yah! who stole the pig? Why, you! And who got beat? Why, me!"

"Quite, quite gone," said Hickory.

"Precisely so," observed Dickory.

"Exactly so," said Dock.

And the three little kittens joined paws, and danced round and round the miserable little man.

"Yes, they are gone," said Merle, "but I have not got them. Behold them there!"

Grunter Grim turned, the kittens stopped dancing, and they and all the Rhymes looked in wonder.

For there, in front of the platform, stood a cradle, and by it stood Thomas Muriel.

Merle stepped forward, lifted the baby out of the cradle, and held him up in her arms. The cloak was wrapped round him, and in his small hand he held the magic hat. Yet he crowed and cooed, and seemed perfectly happy.

The Rhymes cheered and shouted—

> *"The baby that's glad*
> *When others are sad;*
> *And his name it is Baby BUNTING."*

For a few moments there was wild confusion, and then Merle looked round for Grunter Grim. He seemed even smaller than when he first came into the Hall.

"Go, Grunter Grim!" cried Merle.

"Go!" cried Mistress Crispin, "and take that with you," and she threw her birch-rod away from her.

"Yes, go!" cried Jack and Jill, Bo-peep, Humpty Dumpty, Pollie Flinders, Tommy Stout, and all the other Rhymes.

But above the cheers and shouts a clear, silvery voice was heard, and as Merle looked towards the cradle, she saw a beautiful Fairy hovering above it. Her face was the most lovely that Merle had ever seen. It was so sweet, so pure, so calm, and so peaceful.

The Rhymes were hushed. They too were gazing at the beautiful Fairy, and they too were listening to her.

"I am the Spirit of Contentment," she said in her soft silvery voice; "henceforward Endom shall be the land of contentment, the land of peace. Go, Grunter Grim! Go, live in the world, you are not fit for Endom. Go, live with the people who call Nursery Rhymes nonsense!"

There was a happy "coo" from Baby Bunting, and where Grunter Grim had stood there was only a little black heap.

The Hall was growing darker. The Rhymes seemed getting smaller. Crash! Bang! Crash!

305

Merle rubbed her eyes.

"Such nonsense, nonsense! staring at those Rhymes. No wonder the child dreams uneasily."

Was it Grunter Grim's voice? No, Grunter Grim was banished.

What was it? Merle rubbed her eyes again. The Hall, and the beautiful Fairy, the Rhymes, Baby Bunting, all had vanished. She was in her own little room, and Uncle Crossiter was standing by her bedside. She looked up at him solemnly, and then said slowly—

"I suppose you have a bit of Grunter Grim in you?"

Uncle Crossiter started.

"What is the child talking about?" he said. "I thought she was very much excited when she knocked the screen over. I will fetch her mother."

Merle watched him leave the room, and then looked at the screen lying on the floor. Had she knocked it down? Had she been asleep? and was it only a dream, after all?

She felt quite bewildered.

As her mother came into the room she said solemnly—

"I wonder if the Rhyme Fairy will alter all the Rhymes, and make them end properly now."

Her mother looked at her; she began to think that Uncle Crossiter was right, and that the child was delirious.

But Merle saw the puzzled look on her mother's face, and began to laugh.

"I'm all right, mother," she said, "only I've had a wonderful dream. Let me tell you all about it."

And Merle told her all about it.

"Only you see, mother," she said, when she had finished, "Thomas Muriel never got his right body back again, so that there must be some boy walking about in a girl's body now. I wish I knew him. I mean her—no, I mean him. Don't you?"

But her mother only smiled and kissed her.

TINYKIN'S
TRANSFORMATIONS

BY
MARK LEMON

ILLUSTRATED
BY
CHARLES GREEN

Mark Lemon, a minor playwright and actor, is best known as one of the founders and the first editor of *Punch*, which was first published in 1841. His most popular work for children, *The Enchanted Doll*, is an over-moralized tale about the disease of selfishness. *Tinykin's Transformations*, published in 1869 and almost unknown today, is, in spite of its stereotyped ending, his most inventive work in this genre, especially impressive in its presentation of the half-motherly, half-erotic Titania, as well as in the way it depicts the little hero's four possession trances. Dedicated to Lemon's six grandchildren, *Tinykin's Transformations* features the illustrations of Charles Green.

TINYKIN'S
TRANSFORMATIONS

PART ONE

HEN good King Horsa was Lord of the West Saxons, the Fairies were at the height of their power, and there was scarcely a pleasant glade or mountain side where the dark green rings, which mark their dancing-grounds, were not to be found. One of their favourite haunts was in Tilgate Forest, which had hitherto been left in its primeval solitude, undisturbed by the presence of man. Nearly in the midst of the forest there was a beautiful glade, through whose centre flowed a clear, sweet-voiced stream, that, through the summer time, made low and soothing music, that seemed a hymn of thankfulness. The fish that swam to and fro within its waters had scales of silver and gold, some of them enamelled with purple, and green, and

313

scarlet, that flashed in the sun, when, in the excess of their enjoyment, the fish sprang upwards into the air. The grass in the glade was as short, and close, as the richest velvet, and when the sweet white clover, the yellow primrose, the tufted vetch, and our Lady's mantle, the star-eyed daisy, and the flowering heath, were in full bloom, no embroidery worked by the most skilful hand could equal them in beauty. The glade was surrounded by stately beech trees of tremendous girth, covered with silver bark, and their bright green leaves glittered in the sunlight, when the wind sported with them. The roots of one of these stately trees were more gnarled and fantastic than the rest, and those who could discern fairies and fairy work—such as Sunday children*—would have seen that the moss had so grown as to form a sort of throne or royal couch, whereon Titania, the Fairy Queen, often reposed herself. And well she might prefer this glade to any other in the old forest, as the water of the stream was so sweet and agreeable, that all the song birds came there to drink, and never flew back to their homes in the trees without first singing their thanks to the rivulet. There also came the beautiful deer—the antlered hart, the meek-eyed doe, and the lithe, sportive fawn—to slake their thirst, when the noonday sun had made the air of the shade, even, hot and oppressive.

The beauty of the glade was changed when winter came, and the hoar frost powdered the green turf with diamonds, and made the great beeches seem like trees of silver; or the pure white snow spread a coverlid of down over the surface of the glade, whilst the branches of the trees assumed a thousand fantastic forms. The little stream still flowed and sung, until the black frost came and bridged it over with a covering of ice, which would not let its soothing voice be heard—although it was not silent—even if the fairies had been there to listen. But they are away, some sleeping through the winter-time in hollow trees, or in little caverns made by the mole and field-mouse. Some have taken flight

To realms more fair, and skies more bright,

until the time of year when

*Children born on a Sunday were said to have the power of seeing fairies.

bright April showers
Will bid again the fresh green leaves expand,
And May, light floating in a cloud of flowers,
*Will cause earth to rebloom with magic hand.**

That time returned in due season, and the glade was restored to Titania and her fairy court. The song birds came again to welcome her, mingling their melody with the murmuring of the rivulet.

And there were other sounds never heard before in that peaceful glade. They were heard at early morn, and throughout the day. Dull heavy sounds, followed by a loud crash and shouts of men!

Titania guessed their meaning.

The woodman's axe was at work, felling down trees still covered with verdure, and the old forest was to be at peace no more. The Fairy Queen ordered Swiftwing, her Lord Chamberlain, to learn immediately if she had conjectured rightly; and that distinguished courtier, attended by a

*Robert Millhouse.

315

detachment of light horse, proceeded instantly in the direction of the hideous sounds, and soon returned with the unwelcome tidings, that a number of woodmen, under the direction of one of the King's Verderers, were clearing divers rides through the forest: a sad intimation that it was his Majesty's intention to hunt in the forest of Tilgate.

Titania, though very lovely and good-natured at times, had the proverbial malice of the fairy race, and she resolved at once to put the invaders to all the inconvenience that she could devise.

By her magic power, therefore, she called forth vast legions of gnats, which flew about the heads of the woodmen and nearly blinded them; but a rebellious fairy, named Monkshood, sent a hundred night-hawks, and a thousand swallows, who soon put those gnats to flight that they did not devour.

When night came, the woodmen went to their huts made of boughs, and, having had their suppers, were soon sound asleep. Titania then ordered her Chief Carpenter to set his staff to work to partly saw

316

through the hafts of the axes of the men, so that, when they resumed work in the morning, the handles broke at the first stroke, and the work was delayed until fresh tools could be supplied.

When the woodmen went to work again, Titania's people caught the chips that flew in all directions, and hurled them about the ears of the Chief Verderer, who was so annoyed and perplexed, that he sought shelter in the lodge which had been built for himself and his family. Thither Titania followed him, and assuming the appearance of an old woman, pretended that she had lost her way in the forest, intending to play him some prank should he bid her into his lodge, as she could not enter without an invitation, a horse-shoe being nailed on the lintel of the door, and this potent spell against her intrusion she was compelled to obey.

The Verderer was made so cross by the treatment he had received, that he had not a good word for his wife, and, as she had a spirit of her own, she contrived to provoke him so much the more by her sharp words, that he took a strap, with which he used to couple his dogs together, intending to give his wife a good beating.

At this critical moment Titania arrived at the door of the lodge, and asked for leave to enter and rest herself.

"Aye, come in, good woman," said the Verderer's wife, "and see this coward beat the mother of his child!"

The Verderer's arm was raised, the strap was about to descend on his irritating helpmate, when Titania sent such a twinge into the fellow's elbow, that he was fain to drop his weapon and roar out with pain.

"What ails thee, master?" asked Titania, although she knew well enough the cause of his howling.

"My elbow! It's out of joint!" cried the Verderer.

"And serve thee right," said his wife, "for your evil intention toward me. Here, let's see what's the matter."

Margery, the Verderer's wife, was too used to family quarrels to bear any ill-will towards her husband, so she stripped off the man's leather jerkin and examined his elbow. After turning it about a short time, she found a long black thorn, close to the funny-bone, and this she extracted by taking hold of it with her teeth.

But the removal of the thorn did not take away the pain, and the

317

Verderer continued to moan piteously, until Titania pitied the poor fellow, and said:

"Hast thou a cobweb in the house?"

"No, woman, the lodge has not been built a week," replied Margery.

"Hast thou a piece of white wheaten bread?"

"No, woman, our flour is never bolted—we can't afford white bread," replied Margery.

"Hast thou a stock fish, or the part of one?"

"Not we, woman. We ate the last on the feast of St. Hubert."

At this moment, a little boy, between six and seven years old, ran into the cottage, but stopped suddenly at the sight of the strange woman, and on hearing the horrible howling of his father.

The child was very beautiful. His large blue eyes, now opened to their full extent, seemed like two corn-flowers embedded in a mass of apple-blossom, so exquisitely mixed were the red and white of his plump little face! His hair was like gold-coloured silk—floss silk—so soft and light that a breath would stir it.

Titania's quick nature was instantly touched; she felt that she loved the child, and that, for his sake, all her enmity was at an end.

"Give me one hair from that sweet boy's head; I will bind it round his father's arm, and the pain will cease—"

Margery hesitated to comply with this request, but Thomas the Verderer ordered her to obey, and no doubt but he would have cropped the boy as short as his own beard, to have been released from his suffering. "Come to thy mother, Tinykin!" said Margery, but the child was either too astonished or too frightened to move.

Margery therefore went to the boy, and drew one golden hair from his head. This she gave to the strange woman, who bound it round the Verderer's arm, and the pain ceased instantly.

"Many thanks, good dame," said the Verderer, "My wife hath no such skill as thou hast. Whence art thou?"

"From Fairy-land!" cried Tinykin; "I can see bright wings under her rags, and a pretty face through the wrinkled skin that covers it!"

"What's the brat mean?" asked Thomas.

"Hast forgotten?" exclaimed Margery. "I have not, if thou hast. The boy is a Sunday child, and can see the fairies."

Whilst the mother was speaking, the boy had run to the door, as Titania, finding she was discovered, had instantly taken flight.

"Yonder she goes! Yonder, over the tops of the trees," thought Tinykin. "O that I had wings as she has, and could fly as she does!"

The Verderer and his wife were both greatly frightened at the notion of having been in the presence of a fairy, the more especially as Thomas conjectured that his recent tribulations had proceeded from something he had done to displease "the good people," as the fairies were called.

Tinykin—whose real name was Uluf—dreamed nearly all night of the fairies, and in the morning, as soon as he had eaten his breakfast of broth, went out in the direction that Titania had taken in her flight. Lying amongst the grass he saw something shining, which he picked up, and—had he known of such things—would have thought, no doubt, that he had found a diamond. It was, however, but a small fragment of a shooting star, which the fairies knew how to gather before it reached the earth. Further on, he found another and another sparkler, until he had wandered some way into the forest. On looking back, he saw that the way he had come was closed up with underwood, but there was a path before him green and fresh, and free from any obstruction, unless the patches of wild flowers could be considered impediments. Tinykin, half frightened, commenced running forward, and so continued until he arrived at the beautiful glade we have mentioned at the beginning of our story.

As Titania knew the boy's gift of discerning fairies, she and all her attendants kept themselves hidden behind the clusters of flowers and ferns, and there watched Tinykin's wonder and delight at the beautiful scene around him. Titania felt she loved him more and more every moment that she gazed upon the pretty boy, who had now thrown himself upon the grass, resting his blooming face between his hands, whilst he listened to the feathered songsters.

"O bird!" he said, half aloud, "how I wish I could sing like you! How

319

I wish I could fly with your wings, and play amongst the green leaves of those great beech trees!"

Titania could conceal herself no longer; so, assuming the shape of a little girl about the same age as Tinykin, she stole gently to his side.

"What is it you are saying, Tinykin" said Titania, in a voice as sweet as the bird's; "that you would like to be a bird?"

Tinykin looked up in surprise, his large blue eyes again opening to the full. He did not detect that Titania was a fairy then, as her face was towards him, and he could not see her filmy wings, then hidden beneath her little red cloak.

"Well, I was thinking I should like to be able to sing and fly like yonder pretty black ouzel—and I should, too," replied Tinykin, rather sharply.

"If you will let me kiss your forehead, you shall have your wish," said Titania, blushing as though she had been a mortal.

"That's not much to ask for," answered Tinykin, springing up; "so kiss as often as you please, whether you perform **your** promise or not."

Titania kissed the boy's forehead, and when she removed her lips, there was left a small red spot like a rose-leaf upon it. The effect of the kiss upon Tinykin was to make his eyes full of sleep, and a delicious dreaminess to fill his brain, until he sank down upon the green turf. As he touched the grass, a fine young ouzel flew up from the spot, and made its way across the stream to the thicket.

Tinykin was a bird as he had wished to be, and, to his greater delight, the little maiden had changed also, to keep him company.

Tinykin tried his voice! It was in the finest order, and he sang such a brilliant roundelay that all the other birds became silent from envy. And then, accompanied by his bashful playfellow, he darted along the borders of the brook, flashing his strong wings in the bright sunlight, and hiding himself among the green bushes in the forest.

After a time he was hungry, and thought he would fly home and get his dinner. He tried to put his resolution into practice, and found himself, not at his father's lodge, but perched beside a newly-made nest formed of mud and dried bents of grass. Yes, that was Tinykin's home now; but there was no cupboard, no savoury mess of hare or rabbit; so Tinykin began to look very miserable!

Titania laughed—not aloud, she could not do that—but knowing the cause of her poppet's distress, flew **away** for a few minutes, and returned with two great beetles, which she dropped into the nest. Tinykin never waited to say his Grace, but instantly pounced upon the beetles, swallowing one after the other as fast as he could. Now the beetles were alive when Tinykin made of them his dinner, and his greediness was punished. Fancy how uncomfortable he must have been, when, as you might have seen by the heaving of his shining black bosom, his dinner was disagreeing with him!

As soon as the evening star appeared in the sky, Titania put a spell upon Tinykin, and having seen him tumble half asleep into his nest, took her flight back to the glade, knowing that her darling boy would come in his bird shape to drink at the stream in the morning.

But though Titania had power to change Tinykin into a bird, she could not alter the instincts which he shared with his feathered companions in the forest. So when the first streak of morning was seen, and all the birds awoke from their slumber and began to plume their wings, Tinykin woke also, and arranged his pretty black suit according to ouzel fashion. Having, as it were, dressed himself for the

day, he bethought him of breakfast, and flying to an open place in the forest, was soon lucky enough to see a fine, fat worm pop out his head from beneath a turf—to see how the day promised, no doubt—but before he could form an opinion, Tinykin darted upon him, and after some fruitless wriggling, the unfortunate lob went the way of the beetles.

Again, for a minute or two, Tinykin's sensations were not agreeable, as he opened his beak several times, and his black waistcoat seemed to be disturbed from within by the wriggling of the unfortunate lob-worm. As Titania expected, her darling directed his flight to the stream in the glade, and was proceeding at a leisurely pace for a swift-winged ouzel, when he heard behind him a rushing sound of wings, and, turning his head, discovered that he was being pursued by a villanous hawk, in search of a breakfast. Instinct suggested increased speed of flight, and when that appeared to be useless, a sudden retreat into the thicket. The hawk followed a short distance into the bushes, but Tinykin had got the start, and at last his pursuer soared into the air, continuing, however, to make circles round the spot where Tinykin was sheltered.

Tinykin was so inexperienced a bird that he did not understand the tactics of the hawk, and so, after a time, he ventured forth into the open. The hawk saw him in a moment, and the chase was renewed. Tinykin was terribly frightened, and fear increased his powers of flight, but it is doubtful whether he would have escaped a cruel death, had not his father's lodge been at hand, and into its open door he flew. The hawk followed, but before he could seize his prey, Margery, having her bucking-stick in her hand, struck him his death blow, little thinking that she had saved her son, and for whose unaccountable absence she was then grieving.

Tinykin was so grateful for his mother's timely rescue, that he allowed himself to be caught, and as Margery stroked her hand over his ruffled feathers, he put up his little beak to kiss her. She did not, however, understand the action, but grasping her captive somewhat rudely round the body, carried him away to a rough wicker-work cage, recently the prison of a very untidy magpie. Tinykin's heart beat quickly as he remembered the long captivity of the magpie, and how he had often fancied that the poor bird pressed itself against the bars of its prison as though he were longing to revisit the green woods again.

"Oh, if my dear Tinykin were but here!" cried Margery, the tears streaming from her eyes. "He would be pleased enow at having this pretty bird to tend and feed, as he used to with his magpie! Would that Thomas would come home! He has been in search of the boy since sunset yesterday."

Tinykin showed his great concern at what he heard by hopping about his cage—now on to his perch, now off again—whilst Margery walked up and down the room with her apron to her eyes, weeping bitterly.

"Oh, if he should be dead! If he has died of cold and fright in the forest, I shall never be happy again. For his sake I have borne the strap and hard words, but if my boy be taken from me, I can bear them no more!"

At this moment the Verderer came into the lodge, looking fatigued and sorrowful.

"Where's the boy, Thomas?" asked Margery, almost fearing the answer to her question.

"I know not," replied Thomas, in a husky voice; "I'm afraid harm has come to him, as I have searched far and wide and can find no trace of him."

"Then he's dead! he's dead!" cried Margery, until her tears choked her utterance.

"I trust not! I trust not!" said Thomas, drawing the back of his brown hand across his eyes; "I'd as lief be dead myself, I'm thinking."

"Oh, Thomas! dear Thomas!" and Margery threw her arms around her husband's neck, and for a minute or so the two roared in concert.

Tinykin, being an ouzel, did not know how to cry, but he hopped about quicker than ever. He had never thought that his parents loved him so dearly, especially his father, who had more than once made his back acquainted with a hazel rod. He now remembered how often he had been warned not to ramble in the forest, to which he and his parents had newly come, and justly considered that his disobedience was the cause of the family troubles.

Worn out by fatigue and anxiety, the Verderer and his wife went after a time to their straw pallets in an inner room, Margery forgetting to shut the wooden shutter which closed the opening in the wall, through which light and air came into the lodge.

The moon was at the full, and shining brightly; its rays, falling on the cage of Tinykin, kept him awake. He was very unhappy, and would have been glad enough to have forgotten his sorrow in sleep. It was about midnight, as near as he could guess, when, to his surprise, there came to the opening, or window, a most perfectly shaped creature, resembling the little girl whose kiss had changed him into a bird, only she was much smaller. She had wings, too, and carried in her hand a wand, on whose top shone a star-fragment, similar to those which had lured him into the forest.

325

"Ah! my pretty bird!" said Titania, for it was she; "you are safe at home again."

Tinykin tried to say, "Yes!" but he only made a sort of croak.

"Are you tired of being a bird?" asked Titania.

"Croak," answered Tinykin.

"If I restore you to your proper shape again, will you promise to come to the glade before the moon wanes out?"

"Croak."

Titania then unfastened the door of the cage, and Tinykin flew to the window sill.

"Follow me," said the fairy.

Tinykin obeyed her.

After a few moments' flight, they came to a small opening in the forest, and there, on a mound of turf and flowers, a form such as Tinykin remembered his own to have been, was lying in the moonlight.

Titania held out her small arm for Tinykin to perch upon, and then she kissed him as she had done before, and in an instant the ouzel disappeared.

A deep sigh came from the figure of the sleeping boy, and Titania, spreading her filmy wings, flying round him thrice, then left him.

At the dawn of day Tinykin awoke. He felt confused, as after a deep slumber; he could remember nothing that had passed; he wondered where he was, and how he had got there. The branches of the underwood seemed to be forced aside as though by a strong wind, and the boy felt himself impelled to follow the path thus opened to him. In a short time it brought him to the clearing around his father's lodge, and, with a beating heart, he ran to the door made of withies, and shook it as well as he could.

Margery, who was already awake, heard the noise, and with a mother's instinct knew it was her boy.

"He's come home, Thomas! He's come home!" she cried, giving her still snoring husband a sharp shaking, and then, opening the door received into her arms her truant son.

Some people are always cross when first awakened, and Thomas the Verderer was of the number. He no sooner satisfied himself that his son was safe, than he threatened him with the strap for causing so much anxiety, and had proceeded so far in the performance of his threat as to have taken down the correctional strap, when the pain returned into his elbow, and continued there until the instrument of punishment fell from his hand.

Titania had flown unperceived through the open window, and was then resting, in the form of a bat, on the roof-tree of the lodge.

PART TWO

THE moon began to wane, and Tinykin would never go to bed until he had seen it, much to the surprise of his mother, and noticed how much nearer she had assumed the crescent shape of which the Fairy Queen had spoken. At last the time arrived, when the boy had promised to revisit the glade in the forest. Whilst his father was away with his woodmen, and his mother busied with her household affairs, Tinykin stole out of the small enclosure of the lodge, and went to the edge of the forest where he had first seen the fragments of stars, but alas! none were now to be seen, and only brambles and undergrowth, through which it was impossible for him to force his way. He was on the point of crying with vexation, when he saw spring up close to his feet a tuft of daisies, and then another, and another, the brambles threw out a profusion of small roses, and then the undergrowth separated as before. A number of bees played about the roses, and their humming sounded like a song:—

On, little Tinykin, on to the glade,
Where the grass is the greenest, and coolest the shade;
Where the scent of sweet flowers perfumeth the air,
And the clear-flowing streamlet makes melody there.

The bees were fairies sent by Titania to guide her pretty boy safely to the glade. He would have discovered what they were, no doubt, had not his attention been directed to the springing up of the flowers at his feet, and which he rightly conjectured were to lead him to the opening in the forest.

When he arrived at the beautiful glade, he looked around, expecting to see the little girl whom he had met there before, and with whom he had had such a strange adventure. She was nowhere to be seen; the truth being, that Queen Titania and her royal lord Oberon did not lead the happiest of married lives, and were frequently at odds with each other. There had been a domestic squabble between the royal pair that very morning, and Oberon had forbidden Titania to leave the fairy palace. The Queen was forced to obey, as she was closely guarded by the Gentlemen-at-Arms, who formed the King's bodyguard, and it was not until late in the day that Titania and her Maids of Honour succeeded in eluding the vigilance of the sentinels, and making her escape to the forest.

Tinykin would have grown very tired of being alone, had it not been for the music of the birds, and the song of the rivulet. He sat down on the margin of the stream, and continued to watch the bright waters flow past him, until, his eyes ceasing to be dazzled by their brightness, he could see clearly the pebbles and water-plants at the bottom of the stream. After a time the fishes, becoming accustomed to his presence, resumed their usual gambols, darting here and there as though chasing each other, and then, in the fulness of their mirth, springing up into the air, their silver scales and tinted fins flashing in the sunlight. Tinykin had never noticed these inhabitants of the waters before, and now he was enchanted with them.

"Pretty creatures!" he thought, "what a happy life is yours! Swimming about in this beautiful clear streamlet, playing all day out of the heat of the sun, and then, if it should rain, no doubt you would enjoy yourselves the more, and not run into the lodge as I do, to be scolded and sent to bed, and be made to swallow one of mother's nasty possets if I get wet, in case I should catch cold. O pretty fishes! how I envy you! How I wish I could be a fish."

Titania, who had arrived at the glade unnoticed, and had been feasting her eyes on the beauty of her foundling, assumed the shape in which she had formerly appeared to Tinykin, and said:

330

"You want to be a fish, pretty Tinykin, do you?"

The boy started at her voice, and, looking up, saw the same beautiful face smiling upon him as he had seen on his last visit to the glade, and which he had never forgotten, having dreamed of it again and again. As soon as he could speak he said:

"Can you make me a fish, little girl?"

"Yes, for a time, I can," replied Titania, "if you wish for such a change. But remember, when you were a bird, how nearly you were killed by the cruel hawk."

"When I was a bird?" asked Tinykin, he having lost all recollection, as we have said, of his former transformation. Titania had forgotten, for the moment, that her power over mortals was only, as it were, the creation of a dream, when no real change took place, and that all which happened during the operation of her spells only left a confused recollection of events, as our ordinary dreams will do.

"A foolish question of mine," replied Titania, smiling sweetly. "If you would be a fish, dear Tinykin, repeat your wish as I kiss your forehead."

"As you did once before?" asked the boy, adding, "I remember that."

Titania stooped down her head, and the boy repeated the words of his wish, as the Fairy Queen pressed her lips upon his forehead.

In a moment a dreamy unconsciousness came over the boy, and falling apparently into a quiet sleep, he stretched himself upon the grass. At the same moment a silver-scaled fish sprang up from the grass, and fell into the water.

All the delightful sensations that Tinykin had imagined the fish experienced, were fully realised. He darted through the bright waters, which yielded, yet sustained him; now he rose to the surface to inhale the fresh air, leaving a transparent bubble on the top, which for a moment reflected all the varied colours of the prism, and then was seen no more; now he hid himself under the shelter of an overhanging root, or beneath a piece of rock, thence to dart out and scare some of his fellows, floating past him at their ease, and who in their turn pursued him.

Good as this sport was, Tinykin found, after a time, that "all play" was not to be, even for fishes, as he felt hungry, and did not know where to look for a dinner. He had not learned how to eat—if he had how to drink—like a fish, and he would have fared badly, had not he been

331

attracted by a shadow on the water, caused by a large dragon-fly circling round and round. Floating on his side to discover what was the occasion of the shadow, he saw with the eye which was undermost, a perfect banquet of food for fishes, and which no doubt had been cast into the water by the dragon-fly above. It was really so, as Titania, not daring to enter the stream from fear of the Water-horses,*—had watched her darling from the banks of the stream, flitting, in the form of a dragon-fly, from branch to branch of the overhanging bushes, and, guessing the cause of Tinykin's uneasy motion, supplied the means for his dinner.

Exercise had increased Tinykin's usually good appetite, and he feasted himself to repletion until he was hardly able to swim about to find a comfortable lodging. He did so at last under the friendly shelter of a lump of rock, and then he fell into that state which fishes consider as sleep.

With the early dawn he was astir, and watching how other fishes proceeded, he contrived to pick up a satisfactory breakfast. His new state continued to delight him, and onward he swam with the stream, never considering whither it led, or how he should get back to the fairy glade when he should be desirous of becoming himself again.

The streamlet, after many meanderings, flowed into a vast lake (long since drained of its waters), which communicated also with a large river emptying itself into the sea. It was in this lake that a great Baron among fishes had his principal castle, and all the inhabitants of the streams which communicated with the lake and the great river came, at stated priods, to do homage and to pay tribute. This Baron was notorious for his cruelty as well as power. Thousands of his subjects were devoured every year, and though his unhappy victims knew the fate which awaited them, they were compelled, by the necromantic influence of the Baron, to come to the castle and offer themselves as willing sacrifices. When Tinykin entered the lake, he was surprised to see shoals of fishes

*Or Kelpies, as these malignant sprites are called in Scotland.

swimming in the same direction, whilst ever and anon he heard a sound resembling thunder, coming as it were from the centre of the lake. Had he been really a fish, he would have known that the noise proceeded from the Baron's trumpeters, blowing through huge shells, which some of his dependants had brought from the sea, whither they were compelled to go at certain seasons, and that all who heard those sounds were constrained to present themselves outside the walls of the Baron's castle.

A very unsightly place was this under-water fortress, being formed of boles of trees that had been buried in the mud until they were as black as coal, and heavy and hard as iron. These made the walls, and around them was an embankment of mud and clay, coated with green slime. As yet, no adventurous mortal had seen that great lake, or he would never have thought that the bright water-mirror on which he looked covered such a hideous place as the Fish-Baron's castle, or gave shelter to such a monster as the wicked Baron himself.

Tinykin's natural curiosity was aroused, and he followed in the wake of a shoal of fishes, formed and clothed like himself. Had he known his danger, he would have tacked about and steered himself back to the little stream where he had been so happy.

When Tinykin drew near to the castle, he saw it was surrounded by thousands of fishes of different shapes, their trembling scales shewing the bodily fear they were suffering. Tinykin himself began to feel very uneasy, as he observed that the Baron's guards were hemming them round, and rendering retreat dangerous, if not impossible.

These guards were terrible creatures to look upon. They were of gigantic size, cased in black armour, like lobsters, having claws like them, and also great projecting eyes; they had fins like dragons, and their tails appeared to be tipped with steel. With them were the trumpeters, who were equally ugly, if not so destructive in appearance. They appeared to have blown themselves into a round shape, like the tunny-fish, and their eyes were round and distended, so that the appearance was quite hideous enough to frighten any timid fish out of its wits. As these terrible creatures continued to swim round and round the collected multitude, numbers were compelled to enter an opening in the castle walls, and which led to the Baron's great Stew, or, to give it a better name, the Pond of Despair: as the fish which entered there never got out, except (figuratively speaking) into the frying-pan in the Baron's kitchen.

Tinykin was unlucky enough to be one of the doomed party, but happily for him he was ignorant of the probable fate which awaited him.

The Baron's wife was quite of a different nature to her brutal husband. She had been taken captive in the neighbouring river, and, being singularly beautiful, the Baron preferred marrying her to eating her. Her form was very graceful, and was well set off by a close-fitting robe of silver scales. Fortunately, she was the mother of an only daughter, who inherited all her gentleness and beauty, which would, no doubt, have been displeasing to the Baron, had he not had a son as brutal as himself by a former marriage.

The princess was named after her mother, and called Salmonida. Her race had been singularly favoured, and had been so endowed that they could exist in the sweet waters of the river or the salt waters of the sea. Shortly after the birth of the Baroness, and on her first visit to the ocean, there chanced to be a shipwreck on the coast where she was staying, and amongst the passengers in the vessel was the great magician, Merlin. Powerful as he was when surrounded by his charms and philters, in the great sea he was as helpless as less favoured mortals. He was a bad swimmer, and would no doubt have shared the fate of some of his comrades, had not the elder Salmonida swam before him and piloted him to land. For this service Merlin showed his gratitude by confiding to her certain cabalistic words, which would greatly increase her happiness whenever she could utter them in the ear of a mortal. This mighty charm she could impart to her children. But as a fish never was known to converse with man, woman, nor child, the efficacy of the spell had never been tested.

Tinykin was terribly frightened when he saw two hideous creatures covered with moving scales, and whose great fins were like scoops full of holes, like a sieve or a colander. These were the Baron's purveyors, who had come to gather from the Stew fishes for their lord's dinner.

The poor victims seemed stupified with terror, and allowed themselves to be gathered by the purveyors, without an effort to escape. Not so Tinykin: he swam about, now diving to the bottom, now rising to the surface, until he had sprung nearly six feet out of the water, and fell back with a loud splash close to where the Baroness and her daughter were taking their mid-day repast of delicate water-plants, which had been collected for them by their attendants.

There was something so assuring in the expression of the two ladies Salmonia, that Tinykin lost half his fears, and remaining stationary, showed by the quivering of his fins that he sought to pay them homage, and to ask their protection.

The noble ladies evidently understood their suppliant, and by a

335

graceful inclination of their heads, told to Tinykin that his suit was granted, and they themselves were affected by a singular feeling, which made them regard the stranger fish with an uncommon interest, amounting almost to respect. This feeling, no doubt, arose from the fact that Tinykin was human, and though transformed for a time, he had not lost his claim to supremacy over the creatures made for the use of man. So powerful is the influence of man's superiority, that the brutal Baron, whilst revelling with his ferocious sons, felt an undefined dread of evil; and though eating to excess produces a similar effect on fishes as drinking to excess does with earth-born creatures, the Baron was not at ease in his mind until he became oblivious from repletion.

Meanwhile the Baroness and her lovely daughter, having finished their vegetable repast, took each of them a beautiful shell, and blowing through an aperture at one end, produced such delicious harmony that Tinykin was enchanted by it. Again his fins quivered, but more gently than before, and the Royal instrumentalists were plainly gratified by his admiration.

The music lesson over, the Baroness proceeded to teach her daughter certain graceful gyrations and movements in the water, which far excelled any polka, waltz, or quadrille, of our time, and threw Tinykin into an ecstasy of delight.

The dancing lesson at an end, the two noble ladies remained almost motionless, and began to murmur sounds of which Tinykin did not understand the meaning at first; but, after a time, he discovered that the Baroness was imparting wise counsels to her daughter.

"And now, my darling," said the Baroness, "I will repeat to you, as is my daily custom, the strange words the Wizard Merlin confided to me, although I fear me they will benefit us little owing to the condition attached to them."

"You mean, mamma, that they must be heard by mortal ears?" replied Salmonia.

"Yes, my dear!"

The heart of Tinykin beat quickly, for he knew that he was human, and young as he was the wondrous power of the Great Merlin was known to him.

The Baroness then uttered some strange words—the exact formula has been long lost—and instantly the clear waters became turgid and troubled exceedingly. The Baron and his brutal fellows were roused from their heavy sleep, and, in their terror, fought furiously with each other, not knowing who were their assailants, owing to the obscuration of the water. A single current like liquid amethyst showed to Tinykin and his noble friends a way of escape. At their utmost speed they glided through the water until they came to the entrance of the little rivulet which Tinykin had traversed, and which flowed through the Fairy glade.

The fugitives knew then they were in safety, and therefore proposed to rest themselves.

The Baroness and her daughter were profuse in their thanks to Tinykin, who had been the means of their escape from the Baron's castle; but Tinykin endeavoured to prove that he was the obliged fish, as, had he remained in captivity, his turn to be cooked or eaten would certainly have arrived.

It was twilight when the three fugitives had reached the rivulet; and it was nearly an hour before the rays of the full moon fell upon the waters, and penetrated to the bottom where the Ladies Salmonia were dozing. As soon as the influence of the Ruler of the Tides was felt by the noble pair, the Baroness involuntarily repeated the charm of Merlin. Sensations similar to those which had been experienced by Tinykin when Titania kissed his forehead, possessed the Baroness and her daughter, and in a few moments they were changed into two Undines, or water nymphs of exceeding beauty.

The condition of Merlin's charm was now revealed. He had not the power—potent as he was—to raise Salmonia from the condition in which she was created, but he brought her as nearly as possible to the perfection of humanity, by making her an Undine.

A great boulder rose out of the stream near the place where this transformation had taken place. As the two beautiful creatures seated themselves upon this rock, their long hair and filmy garments glittering in the moonlight, Tinykin thought he had never seen anything half so lovely, and was somewhat mortified to find that he was compelled to admire at a distance, as whenever he attempted to get upon the boulder, he fell back into the stream in an attitude far from graceful or becoming.

Titania was greatly concerned for her pretty boy, when she discovered

327

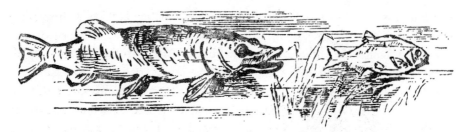

that he had passed out of the boundaries of the stream. She had long known how cruel was the Baron of the Lake, and her supernatural, or rather her protective power, only extended to the land. She had therefore placed fairy sentinels on the border of the lake, near to the efflux of the streamlet, with orders to bring her intelligence the moment Tinykin returned. Her trusty people, therefore, no sooner saw the boy and his companions re-enter the stream, than they flew off to their royal mistress to apprise her of the circumstance.

The Fairy Queen was soon at the border of the stream where Tinykin was resting; and so became a witness of all that occurred.

When Titania saw how beautiful the Undines were, and how anxious Tinykin appeared to join their society, she grew dreadfully jealous. Jealousy was one of the great defects of fairy natures, and most of the quarrels which occurred between King Oberon and his Queen arose from that miserable feeling. Titania was jealous; but as she had no power under the water, she waited until the dawn of day, when the Undines were compelled, by their natural laws, to hide themselves from the sunlight. Having taken the form of a beautiful kingfisher, she flew up and down the stream, creating the utmost alarm among the smaller fishes, until Tinykin, who had scarcely recovered from his recent fright, was seized also with panic, and darted about like his companions, whose instinct warned them to avoid the kingfisher, one of their natural enemies.

Titania was malicious enough to enjoy the terror of her favourite, who now continued to swim up stream as fast as he could, and no doubt but his fairy tormentor would have continued her sport, had not a real danger beset her darling. The happiness of the dwellers in the little rivulet would have been perfect, but for the presence at intervals of a

great Pike or Jack, who invariably carried off one or more of the inhabitants, to devour them. This formidable ruffian was now on a visit to the stream; and Tinykin, in his hurry to escape from the danger above, nearly swam into the jaws of the danger below. He dashed past the pike before he was aware of his presence, and the ferocious fellow instantly gave chase. Tinykin's career as a fish would have certainly ended fatally, had not Titania perceived the danger of her darling, and in a moment struck the surface of the stream with her wings, which so alarmed the pursuing monster, that he turned swiftly round, and hid himself at the bottom of a deep hole, which he was in the habit of frequenting.

This incident occurred where the stream passed through the beautiful glade; and so frightened was Tinykin, that he sprang out of the water, and, Titania receiving him upon her back, carried him to land, where he lay gasping and almost dead.

The figure of a boy was lying upon the grass; the cheeks were pale as lilies, and the lips were also colourless. When Titania saw the change which had taken place in the form of Tinykin, she became alarmed, fearing that her spell had continued too long, and that her pretty boy was dying. She instantly kissed his forehead. Again, as no colour came into the cheeks.

The fish upon the grass gasped feebly, but at last rolled slowly into the stream as Tinykin gave signs of returning consciousness, and after a time opened his round blue eyes, and endeavoured to raise himself, but in vain. What was to be done? The boy was faint with hunger. There were no fruits growing on the trees, nothing that could restore his failing strength. At last Titania bethought her of what she should do. She flew

away to the lodge, and, imitating the voice of Tinykin, called aloud,—

"Mother!"

Poor Margery had fallen asleep, having passed the preceding night in the forest; as Thomas the Verderer had declared that the undutiful boy might have his fill of wandering, and get back as he could. But Margery was a doating mother; and whilst her husband slept, had gone into the forest calling her boy by every endearing name she could remember. She had returned in time to get her husband's breakfast, as she knew he would be more incensed against his son, if his mess of hot broth was not ready for him, before he went to marshal his woodmen. She returned in time to do this, though not to prevent Thomas from going forth, grumbling and promising Tinykin a good thrashing when he returned to the lodge.

Poor Margery said nothing, but resolved to expose her own shoulders to the terrible strap rather than that her boy should suffer.

Judge, then, with what pleasure she heard the call of "Mother," though it seemed to be spoken in a dream.

Perhaps, she was dreaming, as she heard it again and again, and followed it through the brambles and the underwood, which opened a way for her to pass through, until she came to the beautiful glade.

Ah! what was that lying on the grass? Her Tinykin, her darling boy,—almost swooning at the sight of her!

She guessed instantly that he was faint for want of food. What good fortune! She had in her pocket a piece of oaten cake, which she had hidden away at breakfast-time, so that Thomas her husband should not see that she could not eat, on account of the hard words he spoke, and her anxiety for her boy. She carried Tinykin in her arms to the stream. She moistened the oaten bread in the clear water, and then her boy ate of it; and after a while the look of death passed out of his face, and the apple-blossom came back again.

How she contrived to carry him to the lodge, she could not remember; but when Thomas the Verderer came home to dinner, the boy was sleeping so peacefully on his couch of dried heather, and looking so like an innocent angel, that Thomas rubbed his own rough beard with his rough hand, and said nothing more about the strap.

PART THREE

MONTH had passed, and Tinykin still lay upon his bed of dried heather; his pillow, according to the custom of the times, being a hard log of wood, which his mother had now tried to make more comfortable by folding up her best red lindsey kirtle, and placing it beneath the head of the invalid. The pallid face of the boy contrasted strongly with the tint of the petticoat, and no doubt made poor Margery's heart sadder than it would have been. The long time that Tinykin's natural body had been without sustenance had so impaired his strength, that only for his mother's careful nursing, and the constant supply of nutritious food, it is more than probable that he would have died.

Tinykin bore his confinement and suffering so patiently, that Thomas the Verderer was often moved almost to tears, but his manly will drove them back into his heart which they tended to soften. He had been wont to use hard words to poor Margery, and to threaten more blows than he gave; but now his voice was gentler in its tone, and his words were kinder, whilst the terrible strap was taken from the peg on which it usually hung in the Verderer's lodge, and found a more appropriate place in the kennel where two of the king's hounds were kept at walk.

And so it is, that our own sorrows and the observance of the sorrows of others, correct our selfishness and make us more kind and forbearing. One can hardly understand a proper "love to our neighbour" if we ourselves have no experience of griefs and disappointments.

After a time, when Tinykin could sit up by the aid of supports, Thomas would place his stool beside the bed and amuse his son by showing him how to make lines for taking fish, and springes to catch birds, and snares for hares and rabbits. He also fashioned him a cross-bow and bird-bolts, and promised that he should learn how to handle both when he should be strong enough. Then when the boy could leave his bed, he made a kind of arbour near the door of the lodge, so that Tinykin could sit in the sun or in the shade, as it pleased him.

Poor Margery had never been so happy—now that she saw her darling growing stronger every day—never since she left King Kitchen to become the wife of King Verderer Thomas à Clout. One day, when she helped Tinykin to walk to his little bower, she was surprised to see that the osier twigs of which it was composed had thrown out clusters of roses and honeysuckle! Tinykin instantly guessed who had been at work for him, but he said nothing, fearing that his mother would do something to offend the fairies, to whom she rightly attributed the troubles of her son. As they drew nearer, a cloud of bees rose from the flowers, and having hummed a chorus of welcome, flew away over the tops of the surrounding trees into the forest. Tinykin saw that they were fairies, but he said nothing, hoping that if no accident occurred, the pretty maiden he had seen in the glade, might come and play with him when his mother and father were absent.

On entering his little bower, Tinykin saw lying on the seat a bunch of pale blue flowers. They were not violets, nor forget-me-nots, nor like any other flowers he had seen before; they gave out a scent so aromatic and delicious, that Tinykin was nearly overpowered by the excess of sweetness. When his mother looked at him she was surprised to see that the cheeks of her darling boy were no longer flaccid and pale, but had recovered their former roundness, and healthful display of mingled red and white. His hands, which had become almost transparent and white as death, now grew under her very eyes, brown and plump, as they used to be.

The flowers! the wonderful flowers, had produced this sudden healing, and Margery, like a good Catholic, ascribed the miracle to the beneficence of her husband's patron saint, the holy St. Hubert.

Tinykin, for his own reasons, did not seek to undeceive his mother; but he had given all the credit of his sudden recovery to a being far more interesting to him than the grim St. Hubert, whose effigy, rudely carved in wood, hung over his father's bed.

Before Thomas returned in the evening, the roses and honeysuckles had all disappeared; but the beautiful aromatic flowers continued to bloom, and yield their perfume as freshly and as freely as when first discovered in the bower.

Thomas, the Verderer, had all the superstition of the times in which he lived, and quite agreed with Margery, that the good St. Hubert had restored their darling to health. He vowed that the first hart of grease which he should shoot, albeit it were in troth the property of the king, his master, should go to the buttery of the neighbouring monastery, there to be paid for in Aves to his patron saint, who had so befriended him.

As time went on, Tinykin was often tired of being idle, although Margery employed him to do odd matters about the lodge, and the little garden attached to it, where they grew the few vegetables then known to the peasantry. They were not many: small, dry, stringy turnips, parsnips, carrots, and leeks, and perhaps a little wild colewort, the ancestor of the great family of the cabbages. These were all they had for the pot, and a little barley and rye for bread, and wormwood for beer.

They had also two or three hives of bees, from whose honey Margery made her mead, to be drunk only on great feast days, and merry-makings.

Thomas had been as good as his word, and now and then took Tinykin with him a-birding, and the boy soon became an expert marksman with the cross-bow. He learned readily how to make lures, and springes, and could soon set a snare almost as well as his father. Still there were times when Tinykin became sad and sullen, his thoughts always turning to the beautiful glade and his fairy friends.

Titania, however, had been so much alarmed at the narrow escape the pretty boy had had from death, that she determined to overcome her own desire to have him near her, and never again to allow him to run any risk of danger through her agency. She therefore closed up all access to the fairy glade, and after Tinykin's restoration to health, withdrew herself and her court to a distant part of the kingdom. But fairies, like mortals, were not the controllers of their own destinies at all times.

The woodmen, who served under the Verderer, had made many rides through the forest, the lodge being the point from which they started, as it was intended to enlarge that building before the king came there to hunt, and to add others for the use of the hunters, horses, and hounds. To the great delight of Tinykin, orders were given to make an opening through the forest in the direction of the glade, which had hitherto only been visited by him and his mother. Indeed, Margery had noticed none of the beauties of the spot, as all her attention was directed to the condition of her prostrate son, so that she had never given another thought to the place where she had found him.

A hundred woodmen soon cleared away the grand old trees and the surrounding brushwood, and once more Tinykin was able to visit at his pleasure the glade, where he only remembered to have seen and talked with the beautiful fairy.

But she came not, though the flowers were fading fast, and the mast began to fall from the beech trees, and the lovely green of their leaves

345

was changing every day to a tender brown. The nightingales were silent, and the notes of other song birds were less sweet and constant. Still the deer came to drink at the streamlet, and the waters flowed on ever murmuring in song.

One night Tinykin awoke. The moon shone into the lodge through the open window—it was rarely closed except in bad weather, or winter time—and Tinykin could see the ruler of the night moving along in all her glory. He could not compose himself to sleep, but obeying an impulse which he could not control, he arose, and putting on his clothes, stole noiselessly to the door, which was only fastened by a latch. He listened for a moment or two to learn if his parents still slept, before he raised the slender fastening, and their loud snoring satisfied him that he had not disturbed them. Stealing softly out, he closed the door after him, and then ran swiftly down the ride leading to the glade.

What was his rapture when he arrived there, to see the fairies dancing in a ring around their beloved Queen, who for a moment or two was so pleased by the homage of her subjects, that she did not detect the presence of a mortal. When her quick instinct discovered that an intruder was a witness to their revels, she uttered a cry peculiar to the fairies, and which was like the sound of a trumpet giving the alarm to a surprised camp of soldiers.

In an instant, Tinykin was surrounded by myriads of small gnats, that almost blinded him, and he cried out in terror; but Titania instantly recognised the voice of her pretty boy, and rescued him from his tormentors. All her former love for him returned, all her resolutions to avoid him vanished, so that when Tinykin could see again, he beheld his beautiful playmate smiling upon him as before.

"Oh, how good of you to save me from those cruel gnats!" said Tinykin. "They would have stung me to death had you not driven them away."

"How do you know I did so?" asked Titania, smiling more prettily than ever.

"No one else had the power. You are the Fairy Queen, are you not?" replied Tinykin.

"I am, and you must be a Sunday child to know me. Why have you come here to-night?"

"Because I could not sleep, and when I came out of our lodge into the bright moonlight, I could not resist the desire to visit this glade, hoping to see you once again."

Titania understood why he had felt this strong desire to visit the glade, as she had thought of him the moment she had arrived there, and had uttered involuntarily a wish that he were there also.

As Titania remained silent, Tinykin said,—

"Let me see your fairies dance again; but do not you join them, as I would rather have you sit beside me on this knoll. I feel so happy now you are near me."

Titania was delighted to hear her pretty boy say this, and then bidding her fairies resume their dance, she sat down beside Tiny-

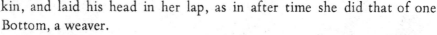

kin, and laid his head in her lap, as in after time she did that of one Bottom, a weaver.

The moon had nearly ended her night's journey, and in the east the first streak of day appeared. In a short time, a fine dappled deer came to the stream to drink, and Tinykin felt a similar strange inclination as had possessed him formerly, to change his condition, having had, as we have said, no remembrance of anything which had befallen him.

"Oh, what a beautiful creature!" cried Tinykin; "how I wish I could be a deer, if only for a day."

Titania started at these words. For a moment she resolved not to gratify the wish of her pretty boy; but thinking, that, if she refused him, he would never come again, and that by granting it she should keep him near her for some hours longer, she took his pretty face between her hands, and kissed him on the forehead, as before. Instantly, a milk-white doe was seen in the glade, and at her side a dappled fawn—Titania and Tinykin; as the Fairy Queen had resolved to keep by the side of her favourite, believing that, by so doing, she should be able to preserve him from all danger, and restore him to his human shape before injury could

arise from the want of sustenance, or from exposure to the dews of night, or the baneful moonlight.

The white doe and the dappled fawn paced several times round the glade, scattering the dew-drops in tiny showers with their small feet, until, as with one consent, they bounded over the rivulet and disappeared in the forest. The white doe then led the way along certain winding tracks, which the fawn would not have discovered, until they came to an open space almost as beautiful as the glade they had just left. Here the doe stopped to graze, and the fawn following the example of its seeming dam, made an excellent breakfast off the most delicious pasturage, short crisp grass mixed with sweet herbs for which no names had as yet been found. When satisfied with eating, the fawn drew nearer to the doe, which, having ceased grazing, now, with its rough black tongue caressed her dappled darling with the fondness of a mother. Withdrawing into the shade of the forest, they came to a mossy knoll overshadowed by the branches of an oak, whose gnarled trunk declared how many score of years had passed since it had been an acorn. On this knoll the white doe and the fawn laid down to rest, and soon fell into a repose which was not sleep, but which was a state of rumination only accorded to a part of the creatures made for the use of man.

After a time they arose again, and wandered along winding paths, until they came to a large open space hitherto untrodden by a human foot-step.

Hundreds of deer were there grazing or reposing, and on the appearance of the white doe and the fawn, the entire number stood erect, the harts throwing back their great antlers as though ready to do battle, whilst the hinds stretched to their utmost their long necks, and opened their round dark eyes to the full. In an instant the new comers were surrounded. The doe and fawn understood by the gestures of the others they were prisoners, and required to obey their guards, who led the way to a bosky-looking corner of the wood, where the Lord of the Forest of Tilgate kept his state.

A noble fellow was he! Nearly ten feet in height, with wide-spreading antlers of polished steel. On his broad forehead was a plate of gold, and his breast was covered with bosses of the same precious metal. He was standing on his throne, a mound of the greenest grass, with tufts of flowers which seemed like gems. Erect around him were his body-guard, composed of warriors whose broken antlers told of many a hard-fought fray with the neighbouring chiefs of Brantridge and St. Leonards. Sometimes they had been the aggressors, penetrating nearly to the stronghold of the lords of those vast forests, returning often victorious, bringing with them the loveliest hinds and fawns of their enemies. At other times they were the attacked, and never but upon one occasion were the warriors of Tilgate made to mourn a serious reverse.

The beauty of the white doe and her dappled fawn, struck the Lord of Tilgate and all his court with admiration; and the anxiety of the captives was instantly removed by the kind actions of the chieftain, and the ready services of his followers. A portion of the great plain was given to the white doe, and there she could graze at peace with her young charge, sure of the protection of every antlered warrior.

This introduction was scarcely over, when a loud noise was heard in the distant forest, and though its cause was unknown to Tinykin, and even to Titania, it was instantly recognised by the more experienced deer as the "belling"* of an approaching stranger.

The body-guard instantly closed round their lord, and the hinds and their fawns hurried behind a double line of harts drawn up in order of battle.

After a short delay, a noble deer presented itself at the furthest confine of the plain, bearing in his mouth a small green branch, as a token that he was a noble herald, and claimed free passage to come and go according to the usages of sylvan chivalry.

The Lord of Tilgate instantly despatched his own chief herald, to assure the stranger messenger of safe conduct and honourable treatment; and then the two advanced to the foot of the mound on which the Lord of Tilgate stood erect and alone.

The herald's message was short, and quickly delivered. "He had come," he said, "from the great Lord of Brantridge, as the bearer of mortal defiance to the Lord of Tilgate, in order that by the defeat of one or the other, the two forests should own but one ruler, and that henceforth the villains or serfs of both houses, should live in peace and security."

The Lord of Tilgate did not wait to consult his warriors, and hardly allowed the Brantridge herald time to complete the delivery of his hostile message, before he declared his readiness to accept the challenge, and ordered the herald to make his utmost speed back to his insolent lord, as the warriors of Tilgate should not sleep until they saw their lord lord also of Brantridge.

The white doe and the fawn were completely appalled at the horrible discord produced by the loud belling of the warriors in approval of their lord's accession, and in a very few minutes the whole herd were in motion, following the track of the challenger.

As many of the hinds determined to accompany their harts to witness the combat, the doe and the fawn could not resist their curiosity to be present also, and joining the ruck, therefore, found themselves about mid-noon at the entrance to a valley, which formed a kind of neutral ground between the two domains.

*The noise made by deer is so called.

The Lord of Brantridge was waiting to receive his noble enemy. He was in all respects a worthy match for his valiant foe, and was equipped at all points in the same manner, excepting that his antlers were of polished brass.

The heralds of the two combatants met in the centre of the valley, and arranged the order of battle, and signed on behalf of their respective lords the conditions of surrender of territory to the victor.

The belling of the heralds announced the completion of these preliminaries; and when they had returned to their respective hosts, the two noble chieftains advanced to meet each other in the centre of the valley, where the ground was level, and the turf firm and short.

With heads erect they regarded each other for a few moments. Lowering their antlers until their heads nearly touched the turf, they rushed furiously at each other. Such was the force of the onset that the ring of their antlers might have been heard far beyond the limits of the valley, and each warrior recoiled on to his haunches. Again and again they charged, tearing up the turf with their hard hoofs. Now their antlers becoming entangled, they struggled fiercely for the mastery, their partizans belling in turn as their chiefs appeared to have the advantage. Now their antlers are free again! Again they dash their heads together, again they are locked and struggling! Again free. The Lord of Brantridge staggered for a moment as the last tine of his antlers was disengaged. In a moment his skilful rival saw his advantage, and making a sidelong blow at his adversary, produced a fearful wound.

The noble fellow knew his death was certain, but he scorned to turn his front, or fly for safety. Again he rushed upon his foe, but every moment his strength was failing, flowing away through the wound in his side. His aim became uncertain, and then his victorious opponent drove his antlers once more into the wound. The battle was over, and the victory was won.

Long before the end of the fight, however, the white doe and the fawn had returned into the forest, shocked at what they had seen, and which was so unlike the peacefulness always associated with the dwellers in the greenwood. They would have stolen away to the quiet glade where the mortal part of Tinykin was lying; but they found the Lord of Tilgate had placed a cordon of guards round his domains, to prevent any surprise from his old enemy of St. Leonards.

The transformed were, therefore, compelled to pass the night in the forest, and they made their couch on some bracken, which completely sheltered them from dews, and wind, and moonlight.

Long before sunset the victorious lord and his followers had returned and were soon at rest, none dreaming of the new danger which threatened them, and for years to come, the denizens of the forest.

The belling of an out-lying sentinel early on the following morning aroused the sleepers. The trusty guard, almost breathless with speed, rushed to his lord with the astounding news, that King Horsa and his nobles were preparing to hunt in Tilgate Forest, and the rides which had been lately constructed were to assist the hounds and horsemen in the pursuit of their prey.

The Lord of Tilgate was alone undismayed at this news. He rose up and cast aside his frontlet and breastplate of gold, and prepared himself to become the chase; ordering all his vassals to seek the shelter of the forest, and to continue to retreat if by chance the hounds should hit upon their track.

In a short time the whole herd were astir, and retreating slowly into the depths of the forest, from the approach of their natural and most powerful enemies.

But the white doe and the dappled fawn were not of the herd, and Titania feared to follow them, lest ill should again overtake her darling Tinykin, and her spell she knew would have fatal consequences unless removed within a certain time. Oh! how she blamed her selfishness which had made her accede to the wish of her pretty boy, knowing that he might be exposed to some such danger as now beset him!

These remorseful thoughts were interrupted by the distant sounds of horns and the shouts of the prickers seeking to rouse the chase. Titania, greatly alarmed, withdrew with the fawn into some thick underwood,

unluckily crossing one of the newly-made rides as they did so. They had just concealed themselves, when the noble Lord of Tilgate came slowly down the ride, as though to face his enemies. He knew the danger which beset his race, and he resolved to direct its course away from his own particular herd. Suddenly he paused, and stood at gaze as King Horsa and his courtiers, his huntsmen and his prickers, came into the entrance of the ride at some half mile distance.

The royal party soon viewed their noble quarry; and the hounds, released from the slips which held them, and cheered on by the horsemen, were soon in full cry; their deep-mouthed baying scaring the birds in the trees.

It caused no pulse of fear in the bold heart of the noble Lord of Tilgate Forest, who proceeded for a time at a sharp trot, and then went away at his best speed; as it would have been no proof of valour not to have availed himself of every chance of escape, even while offering himself as the object of pursuit. The sound of his hard hoofs upon the firm turf, was heard distinctly by the white doe and the fawn in their retreat, until the baying of the hounds, and the shouts of the hunters overpowered it.

Titania in her fear for the safety of Tinykin, had forgotten to close up their track through the underwood, and two of the hindermost hounds hitting on their scent turned from the ride into the forest, baying fiercely. In a moment the white doe dashed away with the fawn beside her; but to her horror discovered that they were about to enter an open space in the forest, and the hounds would surely outstrip the fawn in speed. Their only chance of safety was to intertwine the brambles and brushwood behind them, but the powerful hounds broke through this defence, although it lessened their speed and enabled the chase to cross the open space and gain the thicket. The strength of the fawn began to fail, and Titania's alarm increased; but as good fortune would have it, they had taken the direction of the Verderer's lodge.

"Courage, dear Tinykin," said the white doe, "a little more exertion, and we shall soon be in safety. See, yonder is your father's lodge, and the door is open."

Thus encouraged, the weary fawn gathered fresh strength, and in a few minutes was once more at home.

It was fortunate that the transformed Tinykin had not been guided to the fairy glade, or probably he would have been too late to have saved his pretty human form from death.

It had chanced, however, that when Margery again missed her truant boy, she guessed he had gone to the glade of which he had often spoken to her, as being so very beautiful. Thither went Margery, and discovered, to her great alarm, that her Tinykin had fallen into a trance, and must have continued in that state throughout the day. She at once carried him to the lodge, and then strove in vain to restore him to consciousness. Thomas the Verderer was away making arrangements for the King's hunting on the morrow, and she feared to leave the boy to seek for help at the neighbouring convent. As the night came on, she lighted a candle made of thin slips of fir soaked in grease and bound together with flax, but the lurid flame made the face of the boy more death-like, and she could feel that the beating of his heart grew fainter and fainter. She knew not what to do; she could only pray.

As soon as it was dawn, she went to the boy's little bower, and sought

355

about it to find some of the healing flowers which had restored him before; but not one! not one could she see!

Presently her husband returned with other verderers and hunters to collect the hounds about the lodge. To make them more eager for the chase, the hounds had been kept without food since the preceding mid-day, and now they clamoured loudly, seeing their feeders. As Thomas and his men had enough to do, to fasten on the straps and collars which coupled them together, Margery knew her husband would take no heed then to anything but the hounds, and so she re-entered the lodge, crying bitterly.

It was high noon when the white doe and the dappled fawn rushed into the lodge, frightening Margery almost out of her wits. She soon recovered herself, and when she saw the two beautiful creatures which had sought shelter or protection, her kindly nature was touched, and she showed by her manner that she would do what she could for their safety. She then proceeded to fasten the wattled door, and the latch being somewhat out of order from want of use, she was thus occupied two or three minutes. During this short space of time, Titania had discovered to her delight, that her pretty boy was lying on his couch, but so pale and so quiet that she knew not a moment was to be lost. She instantly disenchanted the fawn, and Tinykin, heaving a deep sigh, opened his large blue eyes, now so dim as to be almost sightless.

When Margery had finished making fast the door, she turned round, and to her dismay, saw the dappled fawn lying dead upon the clay floor of the lodge, whilst the white doe seemed to be caressing it. Margery was readily moved to tears, and she now wept again as she thought that her own Tinykin might be taken from her. Hastening to the boy, her delight was indeed great, when she saw that consciousness had returned, and heard him call her "Mother!"

Margery knelt down by the couch of the boy, and hugged him tenderly, and so continued until Tinykin said in the feeblest voice, "Drink, mother; drink!"

Margery went to the wooden vessel in which she kept water, but it was empty. Regardless of danger to the white doe, she threw open the door, and hastened to the spring whence she drew her supplies.

On her return she noticed, in spite of her anxiety to relieve the thirst of Tinykin, that the white doe and the dead fawn had left the lodge. When the boy had drunk sufficiently, Margery looked again for her late visitors, but they were gone. On the spot where the dead fawn had lain, Margery saw springing up through the clay floor of the lodge, and taking the outline of the animal, similar pretty blue flowers to those which had restored her boy to health. In a few moments an aromatic odour filled the little hut, and as Tinykin inhaled it, the rosy colour came back into his cheeks, and his large blue eyes were as bright and beautiful as they had ever been.

Margery was alarmed, and yet delighted at this sudden change, and would have feared that witch-craft had been at work, only she remembered the horse-shoe which Thomas had nailed over the door—a sure safeguard against the entrance of witch or wizard.

PART FOUR

T was late in the evening when Thomas the Verderer came home. He was very cross, and two or three circumstances had occurred to make him so.

In the first place, the Lord of Tilgate had outstripped his pursuers, and had found refuge in his newly acquired domain of Brantridge. The King had been very angry at the escape of the chase, and had rated Thomas and his fellows because they had not made the rides in the forest of greater length. Kings in those days could not bear disappointment, and were not at all times reasonable in their anger. Again, two of the hounds had gone astray, and could not be recovered. They were those which had followed the scent of the white doe and the fawn, and whom Titania had contrived so to entangle in the brambles and brushwood, that they could neither advance nor retreat. Another cause, and the least excusable for the ill-humour of Thomas, was this. He had drunk more than was good for him of the strong mead and beer which the attendants of the King had brought with them from the royal buttery.

Tipsy men are generally cross, and Thomas was not of an amiable temper at any time. Strong drink make him both cross and cruel, and poor Margery had a sharp box on the ear because she asked him to go to his bed, and not drink any more mead. At last he went to sleep on the settle, and then rolled on to the floor, among the aromatic flowers which had sprung up there. They had no other effect upon Thomas than to make him snore louder; and when he awoke in the morning the flowers were all gone, but Tinykin was restored to health.

Margery told her husband all that occurred, thinking to put him into a good humour; but the toper's head was aching, and he was glad to find some one on whom to vent his spleen. He at once declared that Tinykin had been the cause of all the preceding day's misadventures, and that the stray hounds had followed the white doe through the contrivance of Tinykin's friends the fairies. He would have beaten the boy there and then, had not Margery's spirit been roused by the love of her child; and for once in her life she resisted the will of her husband, and gave him a sound drubbing into the bargain.

The poor woman was sorry for this afterwards, as she thought it was sinful not to obey her husband—all good wives should think the same; but Thomas was very careful, for some time afterwards, not to risk another application to his shoulders of his wife's bucking-stick.

As Tinykin grew older he became a fine, handsome lad, that any father ought to have been proud of. Thomas, however, called him womanish, and never took kindly to the lad, no doubt remembering the humiliation he had undergone on his account.

He would often scold the poor lad for no fault at all, and if Tinykin really was to blame, he never failed to beat him if they were away together in the forest. Tinykin never told his mother of this ill-usage, as he knew she loved him so much, that it would grieve her sadly; but he would sometimes cry out in his sleep, and if Margery heard him it was not easy to escape answering her questions without telling an untruth. Margery guessed that Thomas was not a kind father to her boy, and again she prayed to good St. Hubert to befriend her darling.

But Tinykin was to be released from his father's unkindness for awhile, in a way of which he little dreamed.

The King and the King's daughter were hunting one afternoon in Tilgate Forest, and the chase was a long one. The Princess and a single attendant had separated themselves from the rest of the hunt, and when the horns sounded the *mort,* or death of the stag, the King's daughter did not appear. Search was made throughout the forest, but without success; until the attendant was found lying senseless at the foot of a tree. He could give no account of his royal mistress further than this: as they were riding forward a flame of fire burst out of the ground, and so frightened the horse on which the attendant was riding, that it plunged furiously into the thicket, whilst a bough of a tree struck the rider on the forehead, at once stunning and unhorsing him.

The King was devotedly attached to his daughter, and when three days

had passed without any tidings of the Princess, he became sick with grief, and it was feared that he would die. Before this sickness came on, the King had given way to strong bursts of passion, and had been unjust enough to declare, that the loss of his daughter was owing to the careless way in which Thomas the Verderer had managed the forests, saying, "The knave has permitted freebooters to harbour there, or the rides in the forest had been so improperly contrived, that the Princess had been misled, and had fallen into one of the pitfalls which were likely to abound there."

Thomas knew not what to say, and would certainly have been hung up in the forest if the Queen had not pleaded for his life, and obtained permission to have him shut up in a dungeon of the King's castle, on a cooling diet of black bread and spring water.

Poor Margery was in great sorrow at this trouble of her husband, for in spite of his ill-usage she really loved him in her rude way. She would have been hardly put to it to have gained her daily bread, had not the good Queen taken compassion upon her and her handsome boy, and ordered them to be supplied with food from the royal buttery.

Three months had passed since the disappearance of the Princess, and no word of her had been heard, although the King promised to ennoble whomsoever should discover her, and at last went so far as to declare that her deliverer should become her husband, unless the Princess made an objection. But all was of no use. No tidings came of the lost lady.

Amongst those who had made constant search for the Princess was Tinykin. He was not incited so much by the reward, of which he scarcely understood the value, as he was to procure the liberation of his father for his mother's sake, who continued to grieve for her dear Thomas, notwithstanding the comfort in which she lived by the Queen's bounty, and the remembrance she must have had of hard words and harder blows.

Towards the close of a long day's search Tinykin unexpectedly found himself in the "grovy lawn" where he had met the fairies. He was slightly alarmed at first, as he had been so often threatened with a beating by his father, should he ever again seek an interview with the good people; but he remembered presently that the stick would not beat him without his father, and that he was closely clapped up in a dungeon.

Tinykin had had no remembrance of anything which had occurred during his transformation, or perhaps he would not have sought a second adventure after the experience of the first. All he remembered was the presence of the pretty fairy, who smiled upon him so kindly, and kissed his forehead, by which he had had such a pleasant dreaminess come over him, although followed by such bodily weariness.

Now it chanced that Titania had had one of her domestic brawls with her royal husband, and in a huff had fled from him without regarding the direction taken by her couriers. They, recollecting the pleasure their royal mistress had always experienced in the glade of Tilgate Forest, directed their flight thitherwards, and reached the place not half an hour after Tinykin had thrown himself once more upon the grass to listen to the song of the birds and the music of the streamlet. Titania had avoided this once favourite haunt, fearing to lead her pretty boy into more danger; but being somewhat selfish in her nature, she was pleased at the accident which had again brought them together.

She stole unperceived to where Tinykin was lying, and could scarcely recognise in the stalwart lad the pretty boy she had loved years ago.

Tinykin was speaking aloud, and so Titania knew of what he was thinking.

"Sweet birds," he said, "you have undergone no change. You sing as sweetly as when I first heard your songs. You fly wheresoever you please, with no cruel father to chide or beat you. And you, bright stream, you still flow on, making the same low music with the rocks and the roots of the great trees. How much happier than I am, who, though I seek to free my father from his prison, yet dread that he should come home to beat and scold my dear mother and myself. Yet he shall be set free if I can free him!"

Titania heard these lamentations, and in a moment resolved what she would do. Stamping her little foot three times upon the ground, there came forth, close to Tinykin, a pretty pink mole, and quite unlike anything which Tinykin had ever seen.

The little creature played about as though anxious to be admired, and at last approached so near to Tinykin that he could stroke it with his hand.

"Who has sent you to change my sad thoughts," said Tinykin. "Only one could be so kind, and I shall never see her again, I fear."

"You are mistaken," replied a sweet voice near him; and on looking in the direction whence the sound came, he saw the pretty maiden of former years. She appeared to be much smaller than she had been of old, but there was the same sweet smile, the same beautiful form.

"Well, Tinykin," said Titania, "you are still wishing for change, I hear, and are desirous at this moment to change forms with this pretty pink mole."

"That was indeed my thought," replied Tinykin; "I remember wishing to be a bird, a fish, a deer, and though some change came over me, I do not remember anything which may possibly have happened to me."

"Because the time has not yet come when you can profit by your

experience. Your race can only acquire wisdom by degrees, and you learn many things when you least think you are doing so." She paused a moment, and then said, "And so you wish to be that pretty pink mole?"

"I do," replied Tinykin, firmly.

"Have then your wish!" said Titania, and again pressing her lips upon the lad's forehead, he fell back upon the grass, as though overcome by slumber, whilst the mole disappeared under the turf. Mole though he now was, it was some time before Tinykin could discover his whereabout. He found at last that he was in a long narrow tunnel, which seemed to have no end. He must have travelled many, many miles before he came to the entrance of a spacious cavern, where more than a thousand little creatures, clothed in grey jackets and pointed caps, and not bigger than himself, were beating flakes of gold upon anvils of adamant, until the metal became almost a film.

Tinykin watched these busy workers for some minutes, being under the impression that he himself was unnoticed. In this he was mistaken, as the gnomes have the singular power of seeing through the earth, and the approach of the pink mole had been observed by some of the numerous sentinels around the royal mint of the King of the Gnomes. Presently, Tinykin found himself impelled forward by certain sharp points, which he afterwards discovered to be spears of the underground sentinels, and at last he was forced into the cavern, where he was instantly surrounded by the police, who secured his little hands with fetters of gold, his captors maintaining perfect silence.

Tinykin could only keep a brave heart, and be prepared to make the best of the fate which awaited him.

The gnome police were clothed in cloth of gold, with breast plates and helmets of gold also; their weapons were also of the same precious metal, and their lanthorns were each a single diamond, which was strongly luminous.

The faces of the gnomes were very ugly, but neither cruel nor savage

in their expression. Tinykin and his captors were unnoticed as they passed through the cavern, so busy were the workers with their hammers and anvils. At last they came to what appeared to be the entrance to a great castle, or palace, more properly speaking, as the pillars were of crystal and gold, whilst the gates were studded over with large rubies, almost as large as hen's eggs. The sentinels on duty having received the countersign from the police, gave a signal to those within the castle, and then a wicket in one of the larger gates was opened, and the captors and captive admitted.

Tinykin was astonished at the size of the cavern into which he had been taken, and at the beautiful and wonderful decorations of the vast walls and roof.

The groundwork appeared to be of black glistening jet, overlaid with gems and precious stones, cut into thousands of facets, which reflected back the light of the glowing fire burning in the centre of the cavern. The fire itself was a beautiful object to look upon, as round the cauldron-like opening in the jet, the boiling lava kept surging, continually changing its colour, now blue, now red, now yellow.

Tinykin had guessed that this was the palace of some great potentate, and was therefore not surprised when he was led through files of richly dressed guards, to find himself in the presence of the Gnome King.

His majesty could not be mistaken, his noble bearing at once proclaimed his dignity. He was much taller than any of his subjects, being nearly eight inches in height. He was not the lineal possessor of the crown, but having lived for some years under the furnace of a great magician, he had learned many secrets of the black art, and by a wise

exercise of them, had obtained an influence over the less instructed gnomes, who on the death of their old king (he being childless), with one accord elected Zuberghal the First, King of the World Underground.

The gnomes and their inferior brethren, the trolls, possessed the power of assuming the human shape, but only for a very short time; but King Zuberghal could retain it for days together, and it was often his royal will and pleasure to occupy the carcass of some knight, squire, or vassal, as the whim suited him.

The sight of the pink mole made the King laugh, as he had never seen one before, nor indeed any mole in the custody of the police. He ordered the manacles to be removed from Tinykin's little hands, making a motion at the same time that the captive should approach the royal footstool. The mole would have knelt, but his formation was not adapted to that attitude of homage, so he contented himself by crawling upon all fours.

The King spoke a few gracious words to Tinykin, and then bidding

him assume the perpendicular, desired him to account for his presence in the dominions of the gnomes, from which moles, lobworms, and fieldmice, had been excluded for centuries.

Tinykin found, to his surprise, that he could understand the language of the Gnome King, and that he was able to speak a *lingua* that his majesty could also interpret. It would not be convenient to transcribe the conversation which then ensued, in the original dialect used on the occasion, and we must therefore be content with a summary of what was said.

As Tinykin had but a vague recollection of his human experiences, he merely told the King of the strange abduction of the Princess, and the imprisonment of Thomas the Verderer in consequence thereof, omitting entirely King Horsa's promise of reward.

Zuberghal seemed to be more interested in the pink mole's narrative than was due to the simple facts, plainly stated. His deep interest in Tinykin's story was soon to be explained.

The lord chamberlain of Zuberghal's court, now approached, attended by a numerous train, bearing a large sheet of filmy gold.

The King and the chamberlain conferred together for a short time, and then the whole court and the bearers of the sheet of golden film, proceeded to an opening in one side of the cavern, before which hung curtains of crystal threads, woven into figures resembling the fantastic forms made by the frost upon modern glass windows. It required the combined strength of more than five hundred gnomes to draw aside these curtains. When this act was done, Tinykin saw lying on a couch of pure white asbestos, sprinkled over with emeralds, rubies, diamonds, and amethysts, the sleeping form of a young and beautiful girl. She was clothed in a long green kirtle, hemmed with gold, whilst her bodice was of amber-coloured velvet, lined with royal ermine. Her rich brown hair fell in clusters about her neck and shoulders, having escaped from the net of seed pearls which had confined it, whilst her red rosy lips contrasted strongly with the lily whiteness of her cheek. Her long white fingers were decked with rings of gold, and the hunting rod, which one hand grasped, had a jewelled handle.

Tinykin recognised in a moment the daughter of his King, and knowing that she was enchanted, wrung his little hands in the agony of his grief. Zuberghal had been watching for the effect to be produced upon his captive by a sight of the Princess, doubting in his own mind whether Tinykin was of the humble origin he had professed to be, and that his only interest in the recovery of the Princess, arose from the hope of obtaining his father's release from prison.

It would have fared badly with Tinykin had he expressed his grief in a more refined manner, and so excited the jealousy of Zuberghal, who had fallen deeply in love with the beautiful Princess, when hunting in the forest, and had by his magic art conveyed her away to the World Underground. As it was, the Gnome King was satisfied that the pink mole was only devoted to the Princess as became a true thrall and vassal.

The bearers of the sheet of golden film had reached the couch on which the entranced Princess was lying, and Tinykin then comprehended why the gnomes he had first seen had been so busily employed. Zuberghal fearing that the Princess might suffer from cold during her trance, had ordered this coverlid of beaten gold to be prepared, in order that it

might be placed over her motionless body. Why this trance continued must now be explained.

Zuberghal had a powerful enemy in a witch named Sycorax. This hideous enchantress haunted forests and caves in all parts of the world, and not unfrequently those in the Isles of Albion. She had the power of transforming herself into what seemed rocks and trees, and lords and serfs were alike terrified when journeying through forests and lonely places, being scared by the sight of her hideous form, which after a time proved to be only a gnarled oak or a projection of limestone.

It was her custom to hide away during the broad daylight in some hollow tree, from whose remaining boughs she drank the sap, until they withered also, and it was easy for those who had the power of finding witches, to trace the resting places of the baneful Sycorax.

She had been thus concealed on the day that the Gnome King had frightened the horse of the Princess's attendant, and in the few moments which passed before Zuberghal could return to clasp the lovely lady in his arms, Sycorax had thrown her into a trance, which all the power of the Gnome King could not remove.

Zuberghal knew who had deprived his lovely captive of consciousness, and though the Princess would not die, she would never charm him with

370

her melodious voice, or look upon him with her beautiful eyes, for the space of one hundred years. Zuberghal had sought the chief priestess of the Ruler of the Spirits, in the hope to obtain the removal of the spell which bound the Princess in slumber, but had only received from her a scroll, on which was written three seemingly impossible conditions, by which Sycorax could be made to disenchant the sleeper:—

Search about until you find
That which sees yet seemeth blind;
On the earth it may be found,
But the oftener under ground.
When this creature you have sought
And hold, the spell may be unwrought;
If it can excel in flight
The Bat which comes forth every night
From the witch's knotted hair,
Where it hides from noontide glare.

When this flight is fairly won,
One-third of the Spell is done;
Then this creature without fin
Or scales, a second race must win
'Gainst the fish, the potent witch
Keeps alive in seething pitch.
If this fish be beaten ever
In your underflowing river,
The witch's spell will then retain
But one charm for you to gain.

When the moon is bright and round,
Seek a space on upper ground
Where poor four-foot cannot see!
Where he creepeth awkwardly;
There against the fleetest horse
He must run and win a course!
Be this well and featly done,
And the Lady's freedom's won!

Zuberghal had these hard conditions placed at the head of the couch on which the Princess was sleeping, and had vowed to reward with the

Viceroyship of the Ruby Mines of Golconda, whoever among his subjects could find the means of fulfilling them.

Tinykin understood these doggerel rhymes by instinct as it were, and felt, he knew not why, that he was destined to be the happy means of restoring the lovely Princess to life again. Yet, he thought, what will that avail her if she be compelled to live in this cavern, away from her royal kindred and noble friends? Better that she continue to sleep, and know not the misfortune which has befallen her. At last, he thought he might make some conditions with the Gnome King which would be to his own benefit as well as to the happiness of the Princess.

Tinykin, therefore, made bold to say,—

"Most mighty Monarch of the World Underground, I recognise in that lovely sleeper, my good King's daughter, and for whose loss he mourns night and day. His sorrow makes him unjust, and he keeps my innocent father in a noisome dungeon, with only rats and lizards for his companions."

"Well," replied the Gnome King, "all that you say is nothing to me. I have no sympathy with human suffering, although I am moved by human beauty."

"Most mighty monarch," said Tinykin, "I would say more, if permitted."

The Gnome King nodded his head, graciously, and Tinykin proceeded:—

"I am convinced, O mighty monarch, that I am the creature destined to fulfil the hard conditions of the oracle, and I am prepared to make the venture."

"You!" exclaimed the King, laughing heartily. "Why, you are round as a dumpling, and have neither wings to fly, nor a tail to steer, if you had them."

"If, O mighty monarch," said Tinykin, glad to see the King in such good humour, "if you will place at my service fifty of your best workmen, I will teach them how to make me a pair of wings; and then, when it is your royal pleasure to witness the experiment, I will fly round this vast cavern, I doubt not!"

The King laughed again, although he ordered that fifty or a hundred of the most skilful artisans should place themselves at the disposal of Tinykin.

As the curiosity of the gnomes was aroused, they went to work with a good will, and in an hour or two had hammered out a thousand flakes of gold into a film much finer than that which covered the sleeping Princess. These flakes of film, they then welded together as Tinykin directed, and formed two bat-like wings that a breath could inflate, but so tough that they would resist the strongest pressure.

When these were completed, Tinykin ordered his workmen to make several bands of gold to go round his body, and to these he had the wings attached with still stronger bracelets, for his powerful wrists and ankles.

Being thus equipped, he desired the gnomes to carry him to a projecting rock, and then to cast him off. He was obeyed, and instantly, to the surprise and admiration of the lookers-on, he flew through the air with all the strength and darting motion of the black ousel, whose form he had once assumed in the forest of Tilgate.

"And now, O mighty King," replied Tinykin, firmly, "I will undertake the release of the Princess from the power of her enchantment, if you will give me one promise?"

"What is it?"

"That should I restore the Princess to a state of consciousness, you will at once release her from your power, should she refuse to share your throne?"

"Willingly! Zuberghal would not have a queen that did not covet her position."

"And for this I have your royal word, O mighty monarch!" said Tinykin.

"You have, and more," replied Zuberghal, his little eyes glowing like stars. "I promise you also, that if you fail in this adventure, you shall, as I am a king, be thrown into yonder burning crater."

"Agreed, sire!" said Tinykin, made bold, he knew not why; although the fate which awaited him in case of failure would have been very dreadful.

PART FIVE

LTHOUGH Tinykin knew it not, it was the instinct of the ousel which had made him think that he could fly, and rendered him bold enough to trust himself to his wings.

When the King of the Gnomes saw Tinykin's performance, he went into such ecstasies of delight, that he made himself perfectly ridiculous. He pelted his nobles with diamonds, rubies, and emeralds, and other precious stones; threw his lord chancellor's wig into the crater burning in the centre of the cavern (as he had promised to throw Tinykin); and made the chancellor himself turn flipflaps like a clown in a pantomime.

When he became rational again, he called his first minister of state, and ordered him to despatch a messenger to Sycorax with a challenge to match his flying mole against her celebrated black bat, and to hear was to obey in the court of King Zuberghal.

Sycorax was in one of her worst humours, when the gnome messenger arrived, as a certain dainty spirit, named Ariel, had that day been set free from bondage by one Prospero, much against the will of the old witch. This message, however, of Zuberghal's pleased her so much (as she felt sure of an easy victory), that she made a horrible jibbering noise, which she called laughing. Then pulling her hideous elf-locks about, she roused the black bat from his sleep, and ordered him to prepare for the contest.

This black bat was quite unlike the pretty, harmless creatures which fly about on summer evenings, catching their light supper of gnats and other winged insects. The black bat was coated with bristles, and its round yellow eyes glowed like burning brimstone. The tips of the ribs of his wings were like crab's claws, and kept opening and shutting, as though to declare the spiteful nature of the bat, and how he was longing to be nipping something.

When he heard of Zuberghal's challenge, he spread out his wings to their full, and flew round the cavern, which was then the abode of the witch, making the damp streaming on the roof and the walls glisten by the light of its terrible eyes.

"Tell Zuberghal, the fool," said Sycorax, in a screeching voice, "that I accept his challenge, and will be at his palace by midnight. If I am the winner, another fifty years of trance will be added to the sleep of the Princess. Away!"

The gnome messenger did not care to wait for a second bidding to go; for though he was far from beautiful himself, the ugliness of Sycorax made him ill to look upon her.

The fairy bells—they are called fox gloves now—were ringing out midnight as Sycorax, like a black cloud, swept through the air, until she came to the upper entrance to Zuberghal's palace underground, closely followed by her unsightly attendant, the bat.

King Zuberghal received her in full state, but the rude old witch only smiled scornfully, as though to say, "What do I care for all this fuss and show? I know I am ugly, and I am proud of it. All this is done to make me and my pretty black bat appear to disadvantage—but we like being frightful and disagreeable." The cavern was, as we have said, very spacious, and it was agreed that the course should be thrice round it, the King and Sycorax being the judges of the race.

If Sycorax had laughed when she heard the challenge of Zuberghal, she might now be said to have been in convulsions of merriment when a hundred gnomes bore the round little mole to the edge of the rock which was to be the starting place. But her laughter was of short duration when she saw with what skill and power Tinykin used his

375

artificial wings, now allowing the black bat to approach quite close to him, and then darting away, just as the ousel flies from bush to bush.

The black bat began to suspect that he had found his master, and resolved that if he could once get near enough to his antagonist, that he would with the claws, seize his opponent's wings, and rend them into holes.

Tinykin at last gave him the opportunity of putting this unfair jockeying into practice, but the hard gold of which the mole's wings were fashioned, resisted the black bat's nippers, and actually strained the ribs of his wings, rendering his defeat more easy. Tinykin now had the race all to himself, and not only kept ahead of his antagonist, but made several graceful motions in the air, that is, graceful for such a round, roley-poley figure as he was.

Sycorax was so mortified at her defeat, that she took her departure in great dudgeon, not waiting even to give her beaten favourite time to recover his breath, or to rest his overstrained wings.

Zuberghal was greatly delighted at the result of the race, but his pleasure was of short duration, as he remembered that only one of the

three conditions for the disenchantment of the Princess had been accomplished.

Tinykin guessed from the expression of the King's face the subject of his thoughts, and said, therefore,—

"O mighty monarch, do not grieve that the third of the spell only is broken, by which my royal lady is kept unconscious of the presence of your majesty; but send another herald to Sycorax, and challenge her demon fish to swim against me in the dark river which flows through this spacious cavern."

Zuberghal, despite his despondency, laughed aloud at this proposal of the pink mole.

"You talk folly now!" replied the King, when he could restrain his laughter sufficiently to speak. "You are too much elated by your victory, and have become boastful."

"Not so, O mighty King!" replied Tinykin; "you hardly trusted me when I asked to have wings, but you have seen I was able to outstrip in flight the black bat of Sycorax. I will also defeat her ugly fish, if your workmen are again commanded to obey my orders."

"Be it so!" said the Gnome King, and instantly, two hundred skilful workers listened to Tinykin's orders.

"Make me," he said, "a covering of filmy gold, so perfectly hammered out, that no water can enter into it, nor air escape from it. It must be fastened to my hands and my feet, to which must be added scoops, whereby I can force myself through the water. Let two thin flakes of diamond or ruby be inserted for me to see through, and then, when I am encased, let me be placed on the edge of the stream."

The clever, industrious gnomes were instantly at work, and by the time the king's herald had delivered his challenge to Sycorax, Tinykin's swimming dress was completed.

377

The old witch was only too glad to have an opportunity of revenging her defeat, by obtaining what she thought would be an easy victory over any competitor which the hated Gnome King could bring against her demon fish. The black bat was almost too hideous to look at, but the horrible fish which Sycorax now brought to contend against Tinykin made the blood run cold in his veins. He soon recovered his self-possession, and instinctively seemed to decide upon the course he should pursue.

"When the signal to start is given," he whispered to the gnomes in attendance upon him, "roll me into the river without a second's delay, as much of my success depends upon my obtaining the most trifling start of my opponent."

All promised to obey him.

Sycorax and her hideous fish were declared to be ready for the contest, and the Gnome King upraised his glittering sceptre as the signal for the competitors to be in readiness. When he should cast it down, they were to start; the course they were to swim being a quarter of a mile in length.

The sceptre fell from the King's hand, and before it quite touched the ground, Tinykin had been rolled into the river. He used his scoops rapidly, and contrived to maintain the very slight advantage he had obtained at starting. It was well for him that he could do so, as the demon fish had the power (like the cuttle fish) to discharge with every motion of its fins a black liquid, which not only darkened the waters, but made them almost unbearable from its pestiferous odour.

Tinykin, by some means unaccountable to himself, knew of this peculiarity of the demon fish, and was conscious therefore that if he did not maintain the lead, he should lose the race by not being able to discern the course.

Once again Tinykin was victorious, and as soon as he had passed the goal, he threw himself from the waters on to the strand. A number of gnomes instantly set to work to cut holes through the water-tight covering of the victor, and so admit a rush of fresh air, which was very welcome to the little mole.

The sound of trumpets, the shrill yelling of the assembled gnomes, proclaimed the triumph of Tinykin; and Zuberghal's joy was again made manifest by the most extravagant laughter and gesticulations, which so enraged the defeated Sycorax, that she seized her demon fish, and cast it into the crater burning in the centre of the cavern. Instantly, a dense black smoke, smelling like the rankest pitch, rose out of the crater, nearly filling the cavern, and all were alarmed in case the noisome atmosphere it created might prove fatal to the sleeping Princess. But the King's officers who had charge of the ventilation of the palace were of great ability, and knew their business. In a moment a hundred outlets to the upper air were opened, the fire in the crater was made to burn with a bright lambent flame, and in a very short time all trace of Sycorax and the pother she had made had disappeared.

As two out of the three conditions of the spell which bound the beautiful Princess in sleep had been satisfied, Zuberghal commanded a great festival to be held, and that all labour should cease for twenty-four hours. In a very short space of time, banqueting tables were erected in all parts of the spacious cavern, and soon covered with drinking cups and flagons of gold and silver, and a profusion of all the good things most acceptable to the gnomes and trolls. The King's tables were similarly furnished, but all the drinking vessels and dishes were made from precious stones and the purest gold.

Strains of peculiar music were heard succeeding each other, and numbers of accomplished dancers displayed their fantastic antics at appointed places.

Ever since the pink mole had been an inmate of the Gnome King's palace, he had been plentifully supplied with the daintiest insects adapted to his transformed condition, but upon this occasion, many varieties which were entirely new to him, had been collected by special command of the King. Tinykin would have been perfectly happy at the honours paid to him, had he not retained so much of his human nature as to be most anxious for the fate of the beautiful Princess; and his fear that, even should the last condition of the spell be broken, Zuberghal would not keep to his promise.

When the banquet was at its height, the great chamberlain of the palace was informed that a messenger from Sycorax demanded an audience.

The powerful witch had resolved to be the challenger, believing that she possessed an elfin horse that could outmatch in speed any four footed creature that existed on the earth or under ground. She had therefore challenged Zuberghal to contest the last condition of her spell.

The bright face of the Gnome King instantly grew dim (it was thus he became pale,) when he heard the message of the old witch, and as soon as he could speak, he commanded the pink mole into his presence.

The little heart of Tinykin beat quickly when he heard that the last condition of the spell was to be contested, but some strange instinct made him assured that he should be able once more to gain the victory.

380

"Fear nothing, O mighty King," he said, boldly; "accept the odious creature's challenge, but add these conditions: The course must be in the shape of a horse-shoe, and not less than a thousand paces in length; it must be round a centre of rugged rocks at least a hundred paces in height, and the one which first reaches the goal shall be declared the winner. Can such a course be found, O mighty King?"

"A million of trolls can make one in a night," replied Zuberghal, excited.

"Then, sire, accept the challenge of the witch, and leave the rest to me," answered the mole, boldly.

Sycorax accepted the proposal of the Gnome King, sneering as she did so; and then having supped heartily of witches' broth, she went to her lair, made of all kinds of unsightly things, and slept.

In the meantime, Tinykin, having obtained the King's permission to do whatever he pleased, ordered the same skilful workers as had equipped him before, to make four slender stilts of gold, each having a hollow hoof as it were, and then he went to sleep until the work was done. He was awakened as he had desired, and the four stilts were fastened, with bands of gold, firmly to his little hands and feet. When this had been done he trotted across the cavern and announced to the Gnome King that he was ready to depart for the singular race-course he had suggested should be prepared.

The Gnome King and his court soon passed through the earth, followed by a long train of attendants, some of them bearing the little pink mole and his golden stilts.

The million of trolls had done their work famously, and Sycorax had already arrived at the starting-point with the elfin horse.

Leaving the starting of the competitors in the race to some of the King's officers and trustworthy familiars of the witch, Zuberghal and Sycorax made their way at once to the goal.

The elfin horse was the most beautiful creature of its kind ever seen, and had been stolen by the powerful witch and kept for three years in a sort of cage, every bar having been made under a spell, which defied all the efforts of the elves to break. Sycorax had promised the elfin horse its liberty if it should prove the winner of the race; and thus stimulated she thought there could be no doubt of the result.

In due time the word to "go" was given, and though the pace of both the racers was good, the elfin horse soon outstripped the mole. When the sound of the mole's golden hoofs ceased to reach the ears of the horse, the little fellow slackened his pace, and as he saw nothing of his rival, he pulled up, and tempted by the sweet herbage growing at the foot of the rocks, he could not resist taking a mouthful or two, as a long time had passed since he had tasted such food. He then cantered on quietly again, and once more looking round he was surprised not to see his antagonist, who was possibly hidden by the curve of the course. A spring cast its bright waters down the rocks, and the elfin horse could not pass it by without drinking of the cold delicious stream; for three years he had only known the pitchy water flowing through the cave of Sycorax!

He did not pause more than a minute, and then went on at a smart canter. The next bend of the course brought him in sight of the goal, and then, to his utmost dismay, he saw the pink mole within a hundred strides of the winning-post. Like an arrow from a bow the elfin horse dashed forward! But the effort was made too late—the pink mole was at the goal before him!

Terrified at the probable consequence of his defeat, the poor little horse turned sharply round, and galloped at his utmost speed out of the sight of Sycorax. But she was too exasperated at her own defeat—her loss of power over the entranced Princess—the triumph of her enemy the Gnome King—to regard the elfin horse; and mounting into the air, muttering fearful and wicked words as she went, Sycorax returned to her

horrible home, where she continued for a short time longer to work nothing but wickedness.

Had Tinykin never been a dappled fawn, he would not have known that some of his race had the power of climbing the steepest rocks, their hollow hoofs giving them secure foothold. His golden hoofs had been so formed, and by their aid he was enabled to cross the rugged rock in the centre of the course, and by that artifice reach the goal before the fairy horse.

The Gnome King and his court hastened back to the royal cavern underground, and the first thought of all was the beautiful Princess.

The scroll over her head was rent, and the characters which had been upon it were completely obliterated.

The Princess herself was sitting up on her couch, seemingly lost in wonder, but at the sight of the Gnome King, then transformed into his human shape, she uttered a loud scream, and hid her beautiful face on the pillow.

Zuberghal understood at once that all his hopes of gaining the affection of the beautiful Princess were at end; that she remembered him as he appeared to her in the forest before Sycorax had enchanted her, and that his presence was alarming to her.

383

His nature not being human, his disappointment, therefore, did not give him much concern, and in a few minutes he cared nothing for one on whose account he had taken so much trouble.

Zuberghal did not desire, however, to have the pink mole any longer at his court, to remind him of his rejection by the Princess; so having repeated his promise to restore the Princess to her father, he dismissed the little pink mole, who suddenly found himself once more in the fairy glade, close by the sleeping form of Tinykin, the son of Thomas the Verderer, and Margaret his wife.

The sun had risen and set but twice since the pink mole started on its travels, although to the transformed weeks had seemingly passed.

Titania had been very anxious for the return of her pretty lad, fearing that ill would come to his unconscious form; but she had strewn over and around it the health-restoring flowers which had been of such benefit on former occasions, so that he awoke, as it were, from a refreshing sleep. As he sat up, leaning on one hand, he seemed to recall a strange dream, in which he had been a principal actor. He remembered that he had been engaged in some contests which had had reference to the discovery of the beautiful Princess, who had disappeared so strangely, and for a minute or two his heart beat quickly with the hope that it was to be his good fortune to restore her to the King, and so effect the liberation of his father. But he soon remembered it was only a dream, and he sighed deeply to think it was so.

He had been occupied with his thoughts so completely, as not to notice the pretty fairy standing at his side, smiling upon him more sweetly than ever. Tinykin started when he observed her, and his face showed how delighted he was to see her.

"I am glad you are pleased to look upon me once again, dear Tinykin, and you shall not regret that you have known me," said Titania, in a small, sweet voice. "You have been dreaming, you fancy; but it was not all a dream. The beautiful Princess shall be restored to her friends, and by your means. But there is no time to lose, as the captive lady is subject to hunger and thirst, and if she remain much longer in her present prison, she will suffer from both."

"Yes, in her prison underground," replied Tinykin, thoughtfully. "The ugly creature I saw has not kept his promise, then?"

384

"Yes, he has; the Princess is now in Tilgate Forest. Arise, follow me, and I will show you her prison."

Tinykin arose, and as he did so, he became aware of a great change in his appearance. His jerkin of tanned deerskin was now of thick velvet, with strappings of gold. His hose, hitherto of coarse linen, bound about his legs with leathern thongs, were of broadcloth, fastened to his jerkin with points tipped with gold also; and for his wooden clouts he had velvet shoes, such as only the nobles and gentry wore. His cap, which Margery had made out of the skin of a wild cat, was now of the softest felt with a hawk's feather fastened on one side by a small brooch of agate. His baldrick was of gold chain work, his bugle of gold, and his woodman's knife was changed into a short hunting-sword.

385

So wonder-struck was he at this marvellous change in his outward appearance, that he began to think he was still dreaming, until Titania spoke again:

"When you have ended admiring yourself, my dear Tinykin, follow me, and complete your adventure." Then with a bound she leaped over the stream which separated them from the forest, and Tinykin did not hesitate a moment to follow her.

As if by magic, they were soon in the centre of the forest, and Tinykin's heart beat quickly at the sight of the horrid shapes which the trees and rocks assumed for a moment, and then returned to their natural forms again. This was the work of Sycorax, but her power to do further ill to the Princess or to Tinykin, was impotent against the protective influence of the Fairy Queen. At last they came to a huge, knotted oak, which might have sprung from the soil left by the Great Flood.

"That is the prison of the Princess," said Titania. "Knock, and you will hear her voice."

With the hilt of his hunting-sword Tinykin struck three hard blows and then, to his great joy, he heard the voice of the Princess say from within:

"Whoever you are, hasten to release me from this terrible place! I am Udiga, the daughter of the King of the West Saxons, and I will reward you!"

"Fear nothing, royal lady," said Tinykin; "I am Uluf, the son of Thomas, the King's Verderer. Be patient for awhile, until I can gather our woodmen to make an opening into the tree."

Tinykin then sounded the golden bugle hanging at his side, blowing

the notes his father was used to sound on his cow's horn to call his verderers to him.

The woodmen at work in different parts of the forest heard and recognised the well-remembered sounds. Following the direction whence they came, they soon surrounded Tinykin, whom they at first did not know, owing to the splendour of his attire, until they heard his familiar voice, ordering them to cut at once through the bark of the great oak. For a time the gnarled mass resisted the axes, turning the edges of some, and causing others to fly from their stocks. But Titania (who was unseen by all but Tinykin) stamped her little foot upon the ground, and then there rose at the feet of Uluf an axe made of such tempered steel, that at the first blow he gave, the armour of the oak was cleft deeply.

Another and another blow widened the rent, and then some of the most stalwart of the woodmen plied their axes with a will, until an opening had been made large enough to allow the Princess to walk forth without stooping.

Whilst the work had been in progress, Tinykin had been thoughtful enough to dispatch a messenger to the King (who had had a royal lodge built on the borders of the forest) to announce to him the discovery of the Princess; and when that beautiful and beloved one stepped forth from her prison, it was to see her doating father and mother, with many nobles of their court, hastening towards her.

Her filial love made her for a time forgetful of her deliverer, but when she had satisfied her affection by kissing her parents a thousand times, she said, in a voice as sweet as the sweetest music:

"But where is he to whom I owe my deliverance?"

"Stand forth!" exclaimed the King; "and receive our royal thanks and royal bounty."

With modest step Uluf advanced towards the King. His graceful figure well became the elegant dress he wore, and none who saw him suspected his humble origin.

The beautiful Princess looked on him for a minute, and then her lovely face became red with blushes, and the lids of her eyes, fringed with long lashes, closed together. The King and Queen were also much struck by the appearance of the graceful youth who had rendered them such a great service.

"You are welcome, noble gentleman," said the King. "Your reward awaits you at the hands of our treasurer; and if our daughter can decide in your favour, the other conditional promise for her rescue shall not be denied you."

"I am too humble, most generous King," replied Uluf, gracefully, "to put our gracious Princess to the question. To have rescued her would have been happiness and reward enough, but I am too poor to refuse in part the great reward proclaimed as guerdon for the discovery of the noble lady: and if I might be bold enough to ask a boon of your majesty, I would entreat the pardon of my poor father, Thomas the Verderer."

"Poor Thomas!" said the King. "My grief made me unjust; let him be liberated instantly. We will ennoble him, and give him the fair forest of Tilgate as a recompense for his wrongs suffered at our hands."

All the court gave three lusty shouts in approval of the King's magnanimity. Uluf drew nearer to the King, and was about to kneel as though to embrace his feet.

"Not so, my noble Uluf! Stand up, and put my daughter to the question. You have won the right to do so."

But Udiga hid her beautiful face in her mother's bosom; the blushes

which covered her fair round neck and beautiful shoulders showing how her heart was beating.

The Queen was a noble lady, and valued a man for his own gallant deeds rather than for his inheritance of the fame of his ancestors, and in a few earnest words she urged her daughter to accept the newly ennobled Uluf.

The beautiful Princess gently raised her head, and having looked at Uluf with her eyes filled with love, she held forth her hand to him, saying, almost in a whisper:

"My husband!"

This was the last of Tinykin's transformations, as he never forgot that to be truly noble he must act nobly; and it was not until the great redistribution of the kingdoms of England took place, that his descendants ceased to reign over the West Saxons.

The fairies held high festival that night in the fairy glade in Tilgate Forest, which was lighted up by a myriad of glow-worms. The fairy bells of the foxglove rang joyously throughout the night; the little stream sang more melodiously than ever; and all the nightingales within hearing of it, strained their tuneful throats to outrival it.

The fairies are said to have left us for good and aye; but there are some pretty creatures as beautiful as the fairies could possibly have been, often to be seen haunting the margin of Katrine Lake in Tilgate Forest, and playing under the green oaks of Brantridge Park.

THE
GOLDEN KEY

BY
GEORGE MACDONALD

ILLUSTRATED
BY
ARTHUR HUGHES

George MacDonald is considered, along with Lewis Carroll, the greatest writer for children of the Victorian period. He has directly influenced J. R. R. Tolkien, Charles Williams, and C. S. Lewis, among others. About him, Lewis wrote: "What he does best is fantasy that hovers between the allegorical **and** mythopoeic. And this, in my opinion, he does better than any man." W. H. Auden called him "one of the most remarkable writers of the nineteenth century."

A one-time minister, MacDonald wrote scores of novels and poems, as well as two famous "adult" fantasy works: *Phantastes* and *Lilith*. But his greatest writing was for children. Deeply influenced by Novalis (who wrote: "Inwards leads the mysterious way. Within us, or nowhere, is eternity with all its worlds, the past and the future. The external world is the world of shadows, it casts its shadows into the realm of light."), MacDonald is without doubt one of the most important mystical writers in English literature.

"The Golden Key" was published in 1867. "The Day Boy and The Night Girl," the author's last story for children (originally entitled "Photogen and Nycteris"), was written in 1879 and published three years later.

The Golden Wedding, 1901: George MacDonald and his wife

THE
GOLDEN KEY

There was a boy who used to sit in the twilight and listen to his great-aunt's stories.

She told him that if he could reach the place where the end of the rainbow stands he would find there a golden key.

"And what is the key for?" the boy would ask. "What is it the key of? What will it open?"

"That nobody knows," his aunt would reply. "He has to find that out."

"I suppose, being gold," the boy once said, thoughtfully, "that I could get a good deal of money for it if I sold it."

"Better never find it than sell it," returned his aunt.

And then the boy went to bed and dreamed about the golden key.

Now all that his great-aunt told the boy about the golden key would have been nonsense, had it not been that their little house stood on the borders of Fairyland. For it is perfectly well known that out of Fairyland nobody ever can find where the rainbow stands. The creature takes such good care of its golden key, always flitting from place to place, lest any one should find it! But in Fairyland it is quite different. Things that look real in this country look very thin indeed in Fairyland, while some of the things that here cannot stand still for a moment, will not move there. So it was not in the least absurd of the old lady to tell her nephew such things about the golden key.

"Did you ever know anybody who found it?" he asked, one evening.

"Yes. Your father, I believe, found it."

"And what did he do with it, can you tell me?"

"He never told me."

"What was it like?"

"He never showed it to me."

"How does a new key come there always?"

"I don't know. There it is."

"Perhaps it is the rainbow's egg."

"Perhaps it is. You will be a happy boy if you find the nest."

"Perhaps it comes tumbling down the rainbow from the sky."

"Perhaps it does."

One evening, in summer, he went into his own room, and stood at the lattice-window, and gazed into the forest which fringed the outskirts of Fairyland. It came close up to his great-aunt's garden, and, indeed, sent some straggling trees into it. The forest lay to the east, and the sun, which was setting behind the cottage, looked straight into the dark wood with his level red eye. The trees were all old, and had few branches below, so that the sun could see a great way into the forest; and the boy, being keen-sighted, could see almost as far as the sun. The trunks stood like rows of red columns in the shine of the red sun, and he could see down aisle after aisle in the vanishing distance. And as he gazed into the forest he began to feel as if the trees were all waiting for him, and had something they could not go on with till he came to them. But he was hungry and wanted his supper. So he lingered.

Suddenly, far among the trees, as far as the sun could shine, he saw a glorious thing. It was the end of a rainbow, large and brilliant. He could count all seven colours, and could see shade after shade beyond the violet; while before the red stood a colour more gorgeous and mysterious still. It was a colour he had never seen before. Only the spring of the rainbow-arch was visible. He could see nothing of it above the trees.

"The golden key!" he said to himself, and darted out of the house, and into the wood.

He had not gone far before the sun set. But the rainbow only glowed the brighter. For the rainbow of Fairyland is not dependent upon the sun as ours is. The trees welcomed him. The bushes made way for him. The rainbow grew larger and brighter; and at length he found himself within two trees of it.

It was a grand sight, burning away there in silence, with its gorgeous, its lovely, its delicate colours, each distinct, all combining. He could now see a great deal more of it. It rose high into the blue heavens, but bent so little that he could not tell how high the crown of the arch must reach. It was still only a small portion of a huge bow.

He stood gazing at it till he forgot himself with delight—even forgot the key which he had come to seek. And as he stood it grew more wonderful still. For in each of the colours, which was as large as the column of a church, he could faintly see beautiful forms slowly ascending as if by the steps of a winding stair. The forms appeared irregularly— now one, now many, now several, now none—men and women and children—all different, all beautiful.

He drew nearer to the rainbow. It vanished. He started back a step in dismay. It was there again, as beautiful as ever. So he contented himself with standing as near it as he might, and watching the forms that ascended the glorious colours towards the unknown height of the arch, which did not end abruptly but faded away in the blue air, so gradually that he could not say where it ceased.

When the thought of the golden key returned, the boy very wisely proceeded to mark out in his mind the space covered by the foundation of the rainbow, in order that he might know where to search, should the rainbow disappear. It was based chiefly upon a bed of moss.

Meantime it had grown quite dark in the wood. The rainbow alone was visible by its own light. But the moment the moon rose the rainbow vanished, nor could any change of place restore the vision to the boy's eyes. So he threw himself down upon the mossy bed, to wait till the sunlight would give him a chance of finding the key. There he fell fast asleep.

When he woke in the morning the sun was looking straight into his eyes. He turned away from it, and the same moment saw a brilliant little thing lying on the moss within a foot of his face. It was the golden key. The pipe of it was of plain gold, as bright as gold could be. The handle was curiously wrought and set with sapphires. In a terror of delight he put out his hand and took it, and had it.

He lay for a while, turning it over and over, and feeding his eyes upon its beauty. Then he jumped to his feet, remembering that the pretty thing was of no use to him yet. Where was the lock to which the key belonged? It must be somewhere, for how could anybody be so silly as make a key for which there was no lock. Where should he go to look for it? He gazed about him, up into the air, down to the earth, but saw no keyhole in the clouds, in the grass, or in the trees.

Just as he began to grow disconsolate, however, he saw something glimmering in the wood. It was a mere glimmer that he saw, but he took it for a glimmer of rainbow, and went towards it.—And now I will go back to the borders of the forest.

Not far from the house where the boy had lived, there was another house, the owner of which was a merchant, who was much away from home. He had lost his wife some years before, and had only one child, a little girl, whom he left to the charge of two servants, who were very idle and careless. So she was neglected and left untidy, and was sometimes ill-used besides.

Now it is well known that the little creatures commonly called fairies, though there are many different kinds of fairies in Fairyland, have an exceeding dislike to untidiness. Indeed, they are quite spiteful to slovenly people. Being used to all the lovely ways of the trees and flowers, and to the neatness of the birds and all woodland creatures, it makes them feel miserable, even in their deep woods and on their grassy carpets, to think that within the same moonlight lies a dirty, uncomfortable, slovenly house. And this makes them angry with the people that live in it, and they would gladly drive them out of the world if they could. They want the whole earth nice and clean. So they pinch the maids black and blue, and play them all manner of uncomfortable tricks.

But this house was quite a shame, and the fairies in the forest could not endure it. They tried everything on the maids without effect, and at last resolved upon making a clean riddance, beginning with the child. They ought to have known that it was not her fault, but they have little principle and much mischief in them, and they thought that if they got rid of her the maids would be sure to be turned away.

So one evening, the poor little girl having been put to bed early, before the sun was down, the servants went off to the village, locking the door behind them. The child did not know she was alone, and lay contentedly looking out of her window towards the forest, of which, however, she could not see much, because of the ivy and other creeping plants which had straggled across her window. All at once she saw an ape making faces at her out of the mirror, and the heads carved upon a great old wardrobe grinning fearfully. Then two old spider-legged chairs came forward into the middle of the room, and began to dance a queer, old-fashioned dance. This set her laughing, and she forgot the ape and the grinning heads. So the fairies saw they had made a mistake, and sent the chairs back to their places. But they knew that she had been reading the story of Silverhair all day. So the next moment she heard the voices of the three bears upon the stair, big voice, middle voice, and little voice, and she heard their soft, heavy tread, as if they had had stockings over their boots, coming nearer and nearer to the door of her room, till she could bear it no longer. She did just as Silverhair did, and as the fairies wanted her to do: she darted to the window, pulled it open, got upon the ivy, and so scrambled to the ground. She then fled to the forest as fast as she could run.

Now, although she did not know it, this was the very best way she could have gone; for nothing is ever so mischievous in its own place as it is out of it; and, besides, these mischievous creatures were only the children of Fairyland, as it were, and there are many other beings there as well; and if a wanderer gets in among them, the good ones will always help him more than the evil ones will be able to hurt him.

The sun was now set, and the darkness coming on, but the child thought of no danger but the bears behind her. If she had looked round, however, she would have seen that she was followed by a very different creature from a bear. It was a curious creature, made like a fish, but covered, instead of scales, with feathers of all colours, sparkling like those of a humming bird. It had fins, not wings, and swam through the air as a fish does through the water. Its head was like the head of a small owl.

After running a long way, and as the last of the light was disappearing, she passed under a tree with drooping branches. It dropped its branches to the ground all about her, and caught her as in a trap. She struggled to get out, but the branches pressed her closer and closer to the trunk. She was in great terror and distress, when the air-fish, swimming into the thicket of branches, began tearing them with its beak. They loosened their hold at once, and the creature went on attacking them, till at length they let the child go. Then the air-fish came from behind her, and swam on in front, glittering and sparkling all lovely colours; and she followed.

It led her gently along till all at once it swam in at a cottage-door. The child followed still. There was a bright fire in the middle of the floor, upon which stood a pot without a lid, full of water that boiled and bubbled furiously. The air-fish swam straight to the pot and into the boiling water, where it lay quiet. A beautiful woman rose from the opposite side of the fire and came to meet the girl. She took her up in her arms, and said,—

"Ah, you are come at last! I have been looking for you a long time."

She sat down with her on her lap, and there the girl sat staring at her. She had never seen anything so beautiful. She was tall and strong, with white arms and neck, and a delicate flush on her face. The child could not tell what was the colour of her hair, but could not help thinking it had a tinge of dark green. She had not one ornament upon her, but she looked as if she had just put off quantities of diamonds and emeralds. Yet here she was in the simplest, poorest little cottage, where she was evidently at home. She was dressed in shining green.

The girl looked at the lady, and the lady looked at the girl.

"What is your name?" asked the lady.

"The servants always called me Tangle."

"Ah, that was because your hair was so untidy. But that was their fault, the naughty women! Still it is a pretty name, and I will call you Tangle too. You must not mind my asking you questions, for you may ask me the same questions, every one of them, and any others that you like. How old are you?"

"Ten," answered Tangle.

"You don't look like it," said the lady.

"How old are you, please?" returned Tangle,

"Thousands of years old," answered the lady.

"You don't look like it," said Tangle.

"Don't I? I think I do. Don't you see how beautiful I am!"

And her great blue eyes looked down on little Tangle, as if all the stars in the sky were melted in them to make their brightness.

"Ah! but," said Tangle, "when people live long they grow old. At least I always thought so."

"I have not time to grow old," said the lady. "I am too busy for that. It is very idle to grow old.—But I cannot have my little girl so untidy. Do you know I can't find a clean spot on your face to kiss!"

"Perhaps," suggested Tangle, feeling ashamed, but not too much so to say a word for herself—"perhaps that is because the tree made me cry so."

"My poor darling!" said the lady, looking now as if the moon were melted in her eyes, and kissing her little face, dirty as it was, "the naughty tree must suffer for making a girl cry."

"And what is your name, please?" asked Tangle.

"Grandmother," answered the lady.

"Is it really?"

"Yes, indeed. I never tell stories, even in fun."

"How good of you!"

"I couldn't if I tried. It would come true if I said it, and then I should be punished enough."

And she smiled like the sun through a summer-shower.

"But now," she went on, "I must get you washed and dressed, and then we shall have some supper."

"Oh! I had supper long ago," said Tangle.

"Yes, indeed you had," answered the lady—"three years ago. You don't know that it is three years since you ran away from the bears. You are thirteen and more now."

Tangle could only stare. She felt quite sure it was true.

"You will not be afraid of anything I do with you—will you?" said the lady.

"I will try very hard not to be; but I can't be certain, you know," replied Tangle.

"I like your saying so, and I shall be quite satisfied," answered the lady.

She took off the girl's night-gown, rose with her in her arms, and going to the wall of the cottage, opened a door. Then Tangle saw a deep tank, the sides of which were filled with green plants, which had flowers of all colours. There was a roof over it like the roof of the cottage. It was filled

401

with beautiful clear water, in which swam a multitude of such fishes as the one that had led her to the cottage. It was the light their colours gave that showed the place in which they were.

The lady spoke some words Tangle could not understand, and threw her into the tank.

The fishes came crowding about her. Two or three of them got under her head and kept it up. The rest of them rubbed themselves all over her, and with their wet feathers washed her quite clean. Then the lady, who had been looking on all the time, spoke again; whereupon some thirty or forty of the fishes rose out of the water underneath Tangle, and so bore her up to the arms the lady held out to take her. She carried her back to the fire, and, having dried her well, opened a chest, and taking out the finest linen garments, smelling of grass and lavender, put them upon her, and over all a green dress, just like her own, shining like hers, and soft like hers, and going into just such lovely folds from the waist, where it was tied with a brown cord, to her bare feet.

"Won't you give me a pair of shoes too, grandmother?" said Tangle.

"No, my dear; no shoes. Look here. I wear no shoes."

So saying she lifted her dress a little, and there were the loveliest white feet, but no shoes. Then Tangle was content to go without shoes too. And the lady sat down with her again, and combed her hair, and brushed it, and then left it to dry while she got the supper.

First she got bread out of one hole in the wall; then milk out of another; then several kinds of fruit out of a third; and then she went to the pot on the fire, and took out the fish, now nicely cooked, and, as soon as she had pulled off its feathered skin, ready to be eaten.

"But," exclaimed Tangle. And she stared at the fish, and could say no more.

"I know what you mean," returned the lady. "You do not like to eat the messenger that brought you home. But it is the kindest return you can make. The creature was afraid to go until it saw me put the pot on, and heard me promise it should be boiled the moment it returned with you. Then it darted out of the door at once. You saw it go into the pot of itself the moment it entered, did you not?"

"I did," answered Tangle, "and I thought it very strange; but then I saw you, and forgot all about the fish."

402

"In Fairyland," resumed the lady, as they sat down to the table, "the ambition of the animals is to be eaten by the people; for that is their highest end in that condition. But they are not therefore destroyed. Out of that pot comes something more than the dead fish, you will see."

Tangle now remarked that the lid was on the pot. But the lady took no further notice of it till they had eaten the fish, which Tangle found nicer than any fish she had ever tasted before. It was as white as snow, and as delicate as cream. And the moment she had swallowed a mouthful of it, a change she could not describe began to take place in her. She heard a murmuring all about her, which became more and more articulate, and at length, as she went on eating, grew intelligible. By the time she had finished her share, the sounds of all the animals in the forest came crowding through the door to her ears; for the door still stood wide open, though it was pitch-dark outside; and they were no longer sounds only; they were speech, and speech that she could understand. She could tell what the insects in the cottage were saying to each other too. She had even a suspicion that the trees and flowers all about the cottage were holding midnight communications with each other; but what they said she could not hear.

As soon as the fish was eaten, the lady went to the fire and took the lid off the pot. A lovely little creature in human shape, with large white wings, rose out of it, and flew round and round the roof of the cottage; then dropped, fluttering, and nestled in the lap of the lady. She spoke to it some strange words, carried it to the door, and threw it out into the darkness. Tangle heard the flapping of its wings die away in the distance.

"Now have we done the fish any harm?" she said, returning.

"No," answered Tangle, "I do not think we have. I should not mind eating one every day."

"They must wait their time, like you and me too, my little Tangle."

And she smiled a smile which the sadness in it made more lovely.

"But," she continued, "I think we may have one for supper to-morrow."

So saying she went to the door of the tank, and spoke; and now Tangle understood her perfectly.

"I want one of you," she said,—"the wisest."

Thereupon the fishes got together in the middle of the tank, with their

403

heads forming a circle above the water, and their tails a larger circle beneath it. They were holding a council, in which their relative wisdom should be determined. At length one of them flew up into the lady's hand, looking lively and ready.

"You know where the rainbow stands?" she asked.

"Yes, mother, quite well," answered the fish.

"Bring home a young man you will find there, who does not know where to go."

The fish was out of the door in a moment. Then the lady told Tangle it was time to go to bed; and, opening another door in the side of the cottage, showed her a little arbour, cool and green, with a bed of purple heath growing in it, upon which she threw a large wrapper made of the feathered skins of the wise fishes, shining gorgeous in the firelight. Tangle was soon lost in the strangest, loveliest dreams. And the beautiful lady was in every one of her dreams.

In the morning she woke to the rustling of leaves over her head, and the sound of running water. But, to her surprise, she could find no door—nothing but the moss-grown wall of the cottage. So she crept through an opening in the arbour, and stood in the forest. Then she bathed in a stream that ran merrily through the trees, and felt happier; for having once been in her grandmother's pond, she must be clean and tidy ever after; and, having put on her green dress, felt like a lady.

She spent that day in the wood, listening to the birds and beasts and creeping things. She understood all that they said, though she could not repeat a word of it; and every kind had a different language, while there was a common though more limited understanding between all the inhabitants of the forest. She saw nothing of the beautiful lady, but she felt that she was near her all the time; and she took care not to go out of sight of the cottage. It was round, like a snow-hut or a wigwam; and she could see neither door nor window in it. The fact was, it had no windows; and though it was full of doors, they all opened from the inside, and could not even be seen from the outside.

She was standing at the foot of a tree in the twilight, listening to a quarrel between a mole and a squirrel, in which the mole told the squirrel that the tail was the best of him, and the squirrel called the mole Spade-fists, when, the darkness having deepened around her, she became aware of something shining in her face, and looking round, saw that the door of the cottage was open, and the red light of the fire flowing from it like a river through the darkness. She left Mole and Squirrel to settle matters as they might, and darted off to the cottage. Entering, she found the pot boiling on the fire, and the grand, lovely lady sitting on the other side of it.

"I've been watching you all day," said the lady. "You shall have something to eat by-and-by, but we must wait till our supper comes home."

She took Tangle on her knee, and began to sing to her—such songs as made her wish she could listen to them for ever. But at length in rushed the shining fish, and snuggled down in the pot. It was followed by a youth who had outgrown his worn garments. His face was ruddy with health, and in his hand he carried a little jewel, which sparkled in the firelight.

The first words the lady said were,—

"What is that in your hand, Mossy?"

Now Mossy was the name his companions had given him, because he had a favourite stone covered with moss, on which he used to sit whole days reading; and they said the moss had begun to grow upon him too.

Mossy held out his hand. The moment the lady saw that it was the golden key, she rose from her chair, kissed Mossy on the forehead, made him sit down on her seat, and stood before him like a servant. Mossy could not bear this, and rose at once. But the lady begged him, with tears in her beautiful eyes, to sit, and let her wait on him.

"But you are a great, splendid, beautiful lady," said Mossy.

"Yes, I am. But I work all day long—that is my pleasure; and you will have to leave me so soon!"

"How do you know that, if you please, madam?" asked Mossy.

"Because you have got the golden key."

"But I don't know what it is for. I can't find the key-hole. Will you tell me what to do?"

"You must look for the key-hole. That is your work. I cannot help you. I can only tell you that if you look for it you will find it."

"What kind of box will it open? What is there inside?"

"I do not know. I dream about it, but I know nothing."

"Must I go at once?"

"You may stop here to-night, and have some of my supper. But you must go in the morning. All I can do for you is to give you clothes. Here is a girl called Tangle, whom you must take with you."

"That *will* be nice," said Mossy.

"No, no!" said Tangle. "I don't want to leave you, please, grandmother."

"You must go with him, Tangle. I am sorry to lose you, but it will the best thing for you. Even the fishes, you see, have to go into the pot, and then out into the dark. If you fall in with the Old Man of the Sea, mind you ask him whether he has not got some more fishes ready for me. My tank is getting thin."

So saying, she took the fish from the pot, and put the lid on as before. They sat down and ate the fish, and then the winged creature rose from the pot, circled the roof, and settled on the lady's lap. She talked to it, carried it to the door, and threw it out into the dark. They heard the flap of its wings die away in the distance.

The lady then showed Mossy into just such another chamber as that of Tangle; and in the morning he found a suit of clothes laid beside him. He looked very handsome in them. But the wearer of Grandmother's clothes never thinks about how he or she looks, but thinks always how handsome other people are.

Tangle was very unwilling to go.

"Why should I leave you? I don't know the young man," she said to the lady.

"I am never allowed to keep my children long. You need not go with him except you please, but you must go some day; and I should like you to go with him, for he has the golden key. No girl need be afraid to go with a youth that has the golden key. You will take care of her, Mossy, will you not?"

"That I will," said Mossy.

And Tangle cast a glance at him, and thought she should like to go with him.

"And," said the lady, "if you should lose each other as you go through the—the—I never can remember the name of that country,—do not be afraid, but go on and on."

406

She kissed Tangle on the mouth and Mossy on the forehead, led them to the door, and waved her hand eastward. Mossy and Tangle took each other's hand and walked away into the depth of the forest. In his right hand Mossy held the golden key.

They wandered thus a long way, with endless amusement from the talk of the animals. They soon learned enough of their language to ask them necessary questions. The squirrels were always friendly, and gave them nuts out of their own hoards; but the bees were selfish and rude, justifying themselves on the ground that Tangle and Mossy were not subjects of their queen, and charity must begin at home, though indeed they had not one drone in their poorhouse at the time. Even the blinking moles would fetch them an earth-nut or a truffle now and then, talking as if their mouths, as well as their eyes and ears, were full of cotton wool, or their own velvety fur. By the time they got out of the forest they were very fond of each other, and Tangle was not in the least sorry that her grandmother had sent her away with Mossy.

At length the trees grew smaller, and stood farther apart, and the ground began to rise, and it got more and more steep, till the trees were all left behind, and the two were climbing a narrow path with rocks on each side. Suddenly they came upon a rude doorway, by which they entered a narrow gallery cut in the rock. It grew darker and darker, till it was pitch-dark, and they had to feel their way. At length the light began to return, and at last they came out upon a narrow path on the face of a lofty precipice. This path went winding down the rock to a wide plain, circular in shape, and surrounded on all sides by mountains. Those opposite to them were a great way off, and towered to an awful height, shooting up sharp, blue, ice-enamelled pinnacles. An utter silence reigned where they stood. Not even the sound of water reached them.

Looking down, they could not tell whether the valley below was a grassy plain or a great still lake. They had never seen any place look like it. The way to it was difficult and dangerous, but down the narrow path they went, and reached the bottom in safety. They found it composed of smooth, light-coloured sandstone, undulating in parts, but mostly level. It was no wonder to them now that they had not been able to tell what it was, for this surface was everywhere crowded with shadows. It was a sea of shadows. The mass was chiefly made up of the shadows of leaves

407

innumerable, of all lovely and imaginative forms, waving to and fro, floating and quivering in the breath of a breeze whose motion was unfelt, whose sound was unheard. No forests clothed the mountain-sides, no trees were anywhere to be seen, and yet the shadows of the leaves, branches, and stems of all various trees covered the valley as far as their eyes could reach. They soon spied the shadows of flowers mingled with those of the leaves, and now and then the shadow of a bird with open beak, and throat distended with song. At times would appear the forms of strange, graceful creatures, running up and down the shadow-boles and along the branches, to disappear in the wind-tossed foliage. As they walked they waded knee-deep in the lovely lake. For the shadows were not merely lying on the surface of the ground, but heaped up above it like substantial forms of darkness, as if they had been cast upon a thousand different planes of the air. Tangle and Mossy often lifted their heads and gazed upwards to descry whence the shadows came; but they could see nothing more than a bright mist spread above them, higher than the tops of the mountains, which stood clear against it. No forests, no leaves, no birds were visible.

After a while, they reached more open spaces, where the shadows were thinner; and came even to portions over which shadows only flitted, leaving them clear for such as might follow. Now a wonderful form, half bird-like half human, would float across on outspread sailing pinions. Anon an exquisite shadow group of gambolling children would be followed by the loveliest female form, and that again by the grand stride of a Titanic shape, each disappearing in the surrounding press of shadowy foliage. Sometimes a profile of unspeakable beauty or grandeur would appear for a moment and vanish. Sometimes they seemed lovers that passed linked arm in arm, sometimes father and son, sometimes brothers in loving contest, sometimes sisters entwined in gracefullest community of complex form. Sometimes wild horses would tear across, free, or bestrode by noble shadows of ruling men. But some of the things which pleased them most they never knew how to describe.

About the middle of the plain they sat down to rest in the heart of a heap of shadows. After sitting for a while, each, looking up, saw the other in tears: they were each longing after the country whence the shadows fell.

"We *must* find the country from which the shadows come," said Mossy.

"We must, dear Mossy," responded Tangle. "What if your golden key should be the key to *it*?"

"Ah! that would be grand," returned Mossy.—"But we must rest here for a little, and then we shall be able to cross the plain before night."

So he lay down on the ground, and about him on every side, and over his head, was the constant play of the wonderful shadows. He could look through them, and see the one behind the other, till they mixed in a mass of darkness. Tangle, too, lay admiring, and wondering, and longing after the country whence the shadows came. When they were rested they rose and pursued their journey.

How long they were in crossing this plain I cannot tell; but before night Mossy's hair was streaked with grey, and Tangle had got wrinkles on her forehead.

As evening drew on, the shadows fell deeper and rose higher. At length they reached a place where they rose above their heads, and made all dark around them. Then they took hold of each other's hand, and walked on in silence and in some dismay. They felt the gathering darkness, and something strangely solemn besides, and the beauty of the shadows ceased to delight them. All at once Tangle found that she had not a hold of Mossy's hand, though when she lost it she could not tell.

"Mossy, Mossy!" she cried aloud in terror.

But no Mossy replied.

A moment after, the shadows sank to her feet, and down under her feet, and the mountains rose before her. She turned towards the gloomy region she had left, and called once more upon Mossy. There the gloom lay tossing and heaving, a dark stormy, foamless sea of shadows, but no Mossy rose out of it, or came climbing up the hill on which she stood. She threw herself down and wept in despair.

Suddenly she remembered that the beautiful lady had told them, if they lost each other in a country of which she could not remember the name, they were not to be afraid, but to go straight on.

"And besides," she said to herself, "Mossy has the golden key, and so no harm will come to him, I do believe."

She rose from the ground, and went on.

409

Before long she arrived at a precipice, in the face of which a stair was cut. When she had ascended half-way, the stair ceased, and the path led straight into the mountain. She was afraid to enter, and turning again towards the stair, grew giddy at sight of the depth beneath her, and was forced to throw herself down in the mouth of the cave.

When she opened her eyes, she saw a beautiful little creature with wings standing beside her, waiting.

"I know you," said Tangle. "You are my fish."

"Yes. But I am a fish no longer. I am an aëranth now."

"What is that?" asked Tangle.

"What you see I am," answered the shape. "And I am come to lead you through the mountain."

"Oh! thank you, dear fish—aëranth, I mean," returned Tangle, rising.

Thereupon the aëranth took to his wings, and flew on through the long, narrow passage, reminding Tangle very much of the way he had swum on before her when he was a fish. And the moment his white wings moved, they began to throw off a continuous shower of sparks of all colours, which lighted up the passage before them.—All at once he vanished, and Tangle heard a low, sweet sound, quite different from the rush and crackle of his wings. Before her was an open arch, and through it came light, mixed with the sound of sea-waves.

She hurried out, and fell, tired and happy, upon the yellow sand of the shore. There she lay, half asleep with weariness and rest, listening to the low plash and retreat of the tiny waves, which seemed ever enticing the land to leave off being land, and become sea. And as she lay, her eyes were fixed upon the foot of a great rainbow standing far away against the sky on the other side of the sea. At length she fell fast asleep.

When she awoke, she saw an old man with long white hair down to his shoulders, leaning upon a stick covered with green buds, and so bending over her.

"What do you want here, beautiful woman?" he said.

"Am I beautiful? I am so glad!" answered Tangle, rising. "My grand-mother is beautiful."

"Yes. But what do you want?" he repeated, kindly.

"I think I want you. Are not you the Old Man of the Sea?"

"I am."

"Then grandmother says, have you any more fishes ready for her?"

"We will go and see, my dear," answered the old man, speaking yet more kindly than before. "And I can do something for you, can I not?"

"Yes—show me the way up to the country from which the shadows fall," said Tangle.

For there she hoped to find Mossy again.

"Ah! indeed, that would be worth doing," said the old man. "But I cannot, for I do not know the way myself. But I will send you to the Old Man of the Earth. Perhaps he can tell you. He is much older than I am."

Leaning on his staff, he conducted her along the shore to a steep rock, that looked like a petrified ship turned upside down. The door of it was the rudder of a great vessel, ages ago at the bottom of the sea. Immediately within the door was a stair in the rock, down which the old man went, and Tangle followed. At the bottom the old man had his house, and there he lived.

As soon as she entered it, Tangle heard a strange noise, unlike anything she had ever heard before. She soon found that it was the fishes talking. She tried to understand what they said; but their speech was so old-fashioned, and rude, and undefined, that she could not make much of it.

"I will go and see about those fishes for my daughter," said the Old Man of the Sea.

And moving a slide in the wall of his house, he first looked out, and then tapped upon a thick piece of crystal that filled the round opening. Tangle came up behind him, and peeping through the window into the heart of the great deep green ocean, saw the most curious creatures, some very ugly, all very odd, and with especially queer mouths, swimming about everywhere, above and below, but all coming towards the window in answer to the tap of the Old Man of the Sea. Only a few could get their mouths against the glass; but those who were floating miles away yet turned their heads towards it. The Old Man looked through the whole flock carefully for some minutes, and then turning to Tangle, said,—

"I am sorry I have not got one ready yet. I want more time than she does. But I will send some as soon as I can."

411

He then shut the slide.

Presently a great noise arose in the sea. The old man opened the slide again, and tapped on the glass, whereupon the fishes were all as still as sleep.

"They were only talking about you," he said. "And they do speak such nonsense!—To-morrow," he continued, "I must show you the way to the Old Man of the Earth. He lives a long way from here." "Do let me go at once," said Tangle.

"No. That is not possible. You must come this way first."

He led her to a hole in the wall, which she had not observed before. It was covered with the green leaves and white blossoms of a creeping plant.

"Only white-blossoming plants can grow under the sea," said the old man. "In there you will find a bath, in which you must lie till I call you."

Tangle went in, and found a smaller room or cave, in the further corner of which was a great basin hollowed out of a rock, and half full of the clearest sea-water. Little streams were constantly running into it from cracks in the wall of the cavern. It was polished quite smooth inside, and had a carpet of yellow sand in the bottom of it. Large green leaves and white flowers of various plants crowded up and over it, draping and covering it almost entirely.

No sooner was she undressed and lying in the bath, than she began to feel as if the water were sinking into her, and she was receiving all the good of sleep without undergoing its forgetfulness. She felt the good coming all the time. And she grew happier and more hopeful than she had been since she lost Mossy. But she could not help thinking how very sad it was for a poor old man to live there all alone, and have to take care of a whole seaful of stupid and riotous fishes.

After about an hour, as she thought, she heard his voice calling her, and rose out of the bath. All the fatigue and aching of her long journey had vanished. She was as whole, and strong, and well as if she had slept for seven days.

Returning to the opening that led into the other part of the house, she started back with amazement, for through it she saw the form of a grand man, with a majestic and beautiful face, waiting for her.

"Come," he said; "I see you are ready."

She entered with reverence.

"Where is the Old Man of the Sea?" she asked, humbly.

"There is no one here but me," he answered, smiling. "Some people call me the Old Man of the Sea. Others have another name for me, and are terribly frightened when they meet me taking a walk by the shore. Therefore I avoid being seen by them, for they are so afraid, that they never see what I really am. You see me now.—But I must show you the way to the Old Man of the Earth."

He led her into the cave where the bath was, and there she saw, in the opposite corner, a second opening in the rock.

"Go down that stair, and it will bring you to him," said the Old Man of the Sea.

With humble thanks Tangle took her leave. She went down the winding-stair, till she began to fear there was no end to it. Still down and down it went, rough and broken, with springs of water bursting out of the rocks and running down the steps beside her. It was quite dark about her, and yet she could see. For after being in that bath, people's eyes always give out a light they can see by. There were no creeping things in the way. All was safe and pleasant though so dark and damp and deep.

At last there was not one step more, and she found herself in a glimmering cave. On a stone in the middle of it sat a figure with its back towards her—the figure of an old man bent double with age. From behind she could see his white beard spread out on the rocky floor in front of him. He did not move as she entered, so she passed round that she might stand before him and speak to him. The moment she looked in his face, she saw that he was a youth of marvellous beauty. He sat entranced with the delight of what he beheld in a mirror of something like silver, which lay on the floor at his feet, and which from behind she had taken for his white beard. He sat on, heedless of her presence, pale with the joy of his vision. She stood and watched him. At length, all trembling, she spoke. But her voice made no sound. Yet the youth lifted up his head. He showed no surprise, however, at seeing her—only smiled a welcome.

"Are you the Old Man of the Earth?" Tangle had said.

And the youth answered, and Tangle heard him, though not with her ears:—

"I am. What can I do for you?"

"Tell me the way to the country whence the shadows fall."

"Ah! that I do not know. I only dream about it myself. I see its shadows sometimes in my mirror: the way to it I do not know. But I think the Old Man of the Fire must know. He is much older than I am. He is the oldest man of all."

"Where does he live?"

"I will show you the way to his place. I never saw him myself."

So saying, the young man rose, and then stood for a while gazing at Tangle.

"I wish I could see that country too," he said. "But I must mind my work."

He led her to the side of the cave, and told her to lay her ear against the wall.

"What do you hear?" he asked.

"I hear," answered Tangle, "the sound of a great water running inside the rock."

"That river runs down to the dwelling of the oldest man of all—the Old Man of the Fire. I wish I could go to see him. But I must mind my work. That river is the only way to him."

Then the Old Man of the Earth stooped over the floor of the cave, raised a huge stone from it, and left it leaning. It disclosed a great hole that went plumb-down.

"That is the way," he said.

"But there are no stairs."

"You must throw yourself in. There is no other way."

She turned and looked him full in the face—stood so for a whole minute, as she thought: it was a whole year—then threw herself headlong into the hole.

When she came to herself, she found herself gliding down fast and deep. Her head was under water, but that did not signify, for, when she thought about it, she could not remember that she had breathed once since her bath in the cave of the Old Man of the Sea. When she lifted up her head a sudden and fierce heat struck her, and she sank it again instantly, and went sweeping on.

Gradually the stream grew shallower. At length she could hardly keep

414

her head under. Then the water could carry her no farther. She rose from the channel, and went step for step down the burning descent. The water ceased altogether. The heat was terrible. She felt scorched to the bone, but it did not touch her strength. It grew hotter and hotter. She said, "I can bear it no longer." Yet she went on.

At the long last, the stair ended at a rude archway in an all but glowing rock. Through this archway Tangle fell exhausted into a cool mossy cave. The floor and walls were covered with moss—green, soft, and damp. A little stream spouted from a rent in the rock and fell into a basin of moss. She plunged her face into it and drank. Then she lifted her head and looked around. Then she rose and looked again. She saw no one in the cave. But the moment she stood upright she had a marvellous sense that she was in the secret of the earth and all its ways. Everything she had seen, or learned from books; all that her grandmother had said or sung to her; all the talk of the beasts, birds, and fishes; all that had happened to her on her journey with Mossy, and since then in the heart of the earth with the Old man and the Older man—all was plain: she understood it all, and saw that everything meant the same thing, though she could not have put it into words again.

The next moment she descried, in a corner of the cave, a little naked child, sitting on the moss. He was playing with balls of various colours and sizes, which he disposed in strange figures upon the floor beside him. And now Tangle felt that there was something in her knowledge which was not in her understanding. For she knew there must be an infinite meaning in the change and sequence and individual forms of the figures into which the child arranged the balls, as well as in the varied harmonies of their colours, but what it all meant she could not tell. He went on busily, tirelessly, playing his solitary game, without looking up, or seeming to know that there was a stranger in his deep-withdrawn cell. Diligently as a lace-maker shifts her bobbins, he shifted and arranged his balls. Flashes of meaning would now pass from them to Tangle, and now again all would be not merely obscure, but utterly dark. She stood looking for a long time, for there was fascination in the sight; and the longer she looked the more an indescribable vague intelligence went on rousing itself in her mind. For seven years she had stood there watching the naked child with his coloured balls, and it seemed to her like seven

415

hours, when all at once the shape the balls took, she knew not why, reminded her of the Valley of Shadows, and she spoke:—

"Where is the Old Man of the Fire?" she said.

"Here I am," answered the child, rising and leaving his balls on the moss. "What can I do for you?"

There was such an awfulness of absolute repose on the face of the child that Tangle stood dumb before him. He had no smile, but the love in his large grey eyes was deep as the centre. And with the repose there lay on his face a shimmer as of moonlight, which seemed as if any moment it might break into such a ravishing smile as would cause the beholder to weep himself to death. But the smile never came, and the moonlight lay there unbroken. For the heart of the child was too deep for any smile to reach from it to his face.

"Are you the oldest man of all?" Tangle at length, although filled with awe, ventured to ask.

"Yes, I am. I am very, very old. I am able to help you, I know. I can help everybody."

And the child drew near and looked up in her face so that she burst into tears.

"Can you tell me the way to the country the shadows fall from?" she sobbed.

"Yes. I know the way quite well. I go there myself sometimes. But you could not go my way; you are not old enough. I will show you how you can go."

"Do not sent me out into the great heat again," prayed Tangle.

"I will not," answered the child.

And he reached up, and put his little cool hand on her heart.

"Now," he said, "you can go. The fire will not burn you. Come."

He led her from the cave, and following him through another archway, she found herself in vast desert of sand and rock. The sky of it was of rock, lowering over them like solid thunderclouds; and the whole place was so hot that she saw, in bright rivulets, the yellow gold and white silver and red copper trickling molten from the rocks. But the heat never came near her.

When they had gone some distance, the child turned up a great stone, and took something like an egg from under it. He next drew a long curved line in the sand with his finger, and laid the egg in it. He then spoke

416

something Tangle could not understand. The egg broke, a small snake came out, and, lying in the line in the sand, grew and grew till he filled it. The moment he was thus full-grown, he began to glide away, undulating like a sea-wave.

"Follow that serpent," said the child. "He will lead you the right way."

Tangle followed the serpent. But she could not go far without looking back at the marvellous Child. He stood alone in the midst of the glowing desert, beside a fountain of red flame that had burst forth at his feet, his naked whiteness glimmering a pale rosy red in the torrid fire. There he stood, looking after her, till, from the lengthening distance, she could see him no more. The serpent went straight on, turning neither to the right nor left.

Meantime Mossy had got out of the lake of shadows, and, following his mournful, lonely way, had reached the sea-shore. It was a dark, stormy evening. The sun had set. The wind was blowing from the sea. The waves had surrounded the rock within which lay the Old Man's house. A deep water rolled between it and the shore, upon which a majestic figure was walking alone.

Mossy went up to him and said,—

"Will you tell me where to find the Old Man of the Sea?"

"I am the Old Man of the Sea," the figure answered.

"I see a strong kingly man of middle age," returned Mossy.

Then the Old Man looked at him more intently, and said,—

"Your sight, young man, is better than that of most who take this way. The night is stormy: come to my house and tell me what I can do for you."

Mossy followed him. The waves flew from before the footsteps of the Old Man of the Sea, and Mossy followed upon dry sand.

When they had reached the cave, they sat down and gazed at each other.

Now Mossy was an old man by this time. He looked much older than the Old Man of the Sea, and his feet were very weary.

After looking at him for a moment, the Old Man took him by the hand and led him into his inner cave. There he helped him undress, and laid him in the bath. And he saw that one of his hands Mossy did not open.

417

"What have you in that hand?" he asked.

Mossy opened his hand, and there lay the golden key.

"Ah!" said the Old Man, "that accounts for your knowing me. And I know the way you have to go."

"I want to find the country whence the shadows fall," said Mossy.

"I dare say you do. So do I. But meantime, one thing is certain.—What is that key for, do you think?"

"For a keyhole somewhere. But I don't know why I keep it. I never could find the keyhole. And I have lived a good while, I believe," said Mossy, sadly. "I'm not sure that I'm not old. I know my feet ache."

"Do they?" said the Old Man, as if he really meant to ask the question; and Mossy, who was still lying in the bath, watched his feet for a moment before he replied,

"No, they do not," he answered. "Perhaps I am not old either."

"Get up and look at yourself in the water."

He rose and looked at himself in the water, and there was not a grey hair on his head or a wrinkle on his skin.

"You have tasted of death now," said the Old Man. "Is it good?"

"It is good," said Mossy. "It is better than life."

"No," said the Old Man: "it is only more life.—Your feet will make no holes in the water now."

"What do you mean?"

"I will show you that presently."

They returned to the outer cave, and sat and talked together for a long time. At length the Old Man of the Sea rose, and said to Mossy,—

"Follow me."

He led him up the stair again, and opened another door. They stood on the level of the raging sea, looking towards the east. Across the waste of waters, against the bosom of a fierce black cloud, stood the foot of a rainbow, glowing in the dark.

"This indeed is my way," said Mossy, as soon as he saw the rainbow, and stepped out upon the sea. His feet made no holes in the water. He fought the wind, and clomb the waves, and went on towards the rainbow.

The storm died away. A lovely day and a lovelier night followed. A cool wind blew over the wide plain of the quiet ocean. And still Mossy journeyed eastward. But the rainbow had vanished with the storm.

Day after day he held on, and he thought he had no guide. He did not see how a shining fish under the waters directed his steps. He crossed the sea, and came to a great precipice of rock, up which he could discover but one path. Nor did this lead him farther than half-way up the rock, where it ended on a platform. Here he stood and pondered.—It could not be that the way stopped here, else what was the path for? It was a rough path, not very plain, yet certainly a path.—He examined the face of the rock. It was smooth as glass. But as his eyes kept roving hopelessly over it, something glittered, and he caught sight of a row of small sapphires. They bordered a little hole in the rock.

"The keyhole!" he cried.

He tried the key. It fitted. It turned. A great clang and clash, as of iron bolts on huge brazen caldrons, echoed thunderously within. He drew out the key. The rock in front of him began to fall. He retreated from it as far as the breadth of the platform would allow. A great slab fell at his feet. In front was still the solid rock, with this one slab fallen forward out of it. But the moment he stepped upon it, a second fell, just short of the edge of the first, making the next step of a stair, which thus kept dropping itself before him as he ascended into the heart of the precipice. It led him into a hall fit for such an approach—irregular and rude in formation, but floor, sides, pillars, and vaulted roof, all one mass of shining stones of every colour that light can show. In the centre stood seven columns, ranged from red to violet. And on the pedestal of one of them sat a woman, motionless, with her face bowed upon her knees. Seven years had she sat there waiting. She lifted her head as Mossy drew near. It was Tangle. Her hair had grown to her feet, and was rippled like the windless sea on broad sands. Her face was beautiful, like her grandmother's, and as still and peaceful as that of the Old Man of the Fire. Her form was tall and noble. Yet Mossy knew her at once.

"How beautiful you are, Tangle!" he said, in delight and astonishment.

"Am I?" she returned. "Oh, I have waited for you so long! But you, you are the Old Man of the Sea. No. You are like the Old Man of the Earth. No, no. You are like the oldest man of all. You are like them all. And yet you are my own old Mossy! How did you come here? What did you do after I lost you? Did you find the keyhole? Have you got the key still?"

She had a hundred questions to ask him, and he a hundred more to ask her. They told each other all their adventures, and were as happy as man and woman could be. For they were younger and better, and stronger and wiser, than they had ever been before.

It began to grow dark. And they wanted more than ever to reach the country whence the shadows fall. So they looked about them for a way out of the cave. The door by which Mossy entered had closed again, and there was half a mile of rock between them and the sea. Neither could Tangle find the opening in the floor by which the serpent had led her thither. They searched till it grew so dark that they could see nothing, and gave it up.

After a while, however, the cave began to glimmer again. The light came from the moon, but it did not look like moonlight, for it gleamed through those seven pillars in the middle, and filled the place with all colours. And now Mossy saw that there was a pillar beside the red one, which he had not observed before. And it was of the same new colour that he had seen in the rainbow when he saw it first in the fairy forest. And on it he saw a sparkle of blue. It was the sapphires round the keyhole.

He took his key. It turned in the lock to the sounds of Æolian music. A door opened upon slow hinges, and disclosed a winding stair within. The key vanished from his fingers. Tangle went up. Mossy followed. The door closed behind them. They climbed out of the earth; and, still climbing, rose above it. They were in the rainbow. Far abroad, over ocean and land, they could see through its transparent walls the earth beneath their feet. Stairs beside stairs wound up together, and beautiful beings of all ages climbed along with them.

They knew that they were going up to the country whence the shadows fall.

And by this time I think they must have got there.

THE
DAY BOY
AND
THE NIGHT GIRL

BY
GEORGE MACDONALD

ILLUSTRATED
BY
ARTHUR HUGHES

George MacDonald, 1884.

THE
DAY BOY
AND
THE NIGHT GIRL

WATHO

There was once a witch who desired to know everything. But the wiser a witch is, the harder she knocks her head against the wall when she comes to it. Her name was Watho, and she had a wolf in her mind. She cared for nothing in itself—only for knowing it. She was not naturally cruel, but the wolf had made her cruel.

She was tall and graceful, with a white skin, red hair, and black eyes, which had a red fire in them. She was straight and strong, but now and then would fall bent together, shudder, and sit for a moment with her head turned over her shoulder, as if the wolf had got out of her mind on to her back.

AURORA

This witch got two ladies to visit her. One of them belonged to the court, and her husband had been sent on a far and difficult embassy. The other was a young widow whose husband had lately died, and who had since lost her sight. Watho lodged them in different parts of her castle, and they did not know of each other's existence.

The castle stood on the side of a hill sloping gently down into a narrow valley, in which was a river, with a pebbly channel and a

425

continual song. The garden went down to the bank of the river, enclosed by high walls, which crossed the river and there stopped. Each wall had a double row of battlements, and between the rows was a narrow walk.

In the topmost story of the castle the Lady Aurora occupied a spacious apartment of several large rooms looking southward. The windows projected oriel-wise over the garden below, and there was a splendid view from them both up and down and across the river. The opposite side of the valley was steep, but not very high. Far away snowpeaks were visible. These rooms Aurora seldom left, but their airy spaces, the brilliant landscape and sky, the plentiful sunlight, the musical instruments, books, pictures, curiosities, with the company of Watho, who made herself charming, precluded all dulness. She had venison and feathered game to eat, milk and pale sunny sparkling wine to drink.

She had hair of the yellow gold, waved and rippled; her skin was fair, not white like Watho's, and her eyes were of the blue of the heavens when bluest; her features were delicate but strong, her mouth large and finely curved, and haunted with smiles.

VESPER

Behind the castle the hill rose abruptly; the northeastern tower, indeed, was in contact with the rock and communicated with the interior of it. For in the rock was a series of chambers, known only to Watho and the one servant whom she trusted, called Falca. Some former owner had constructed these chambers after the tomb of an Egyptian king, and probably with the same design, for in the centre of one of them stood what could only be a sarcophagus, but that and others were walled off. The sides and roofs of them were carved in low relief, and curiously painted. Here the witch lodged the blind lady, whose name was Vesper. Her eyes were black, with long black lashes; her skin had a look of darkened silver, but was of purest tint and grain; her hair was black and fine and straight-flowing; her features were exquisitely formed, and if less beautiful yet more lovely from sadness; she always looked as if she wanted to lie down and not rise again. She did not know she was lodged in a tomb, though now and then she wondered she never touched a window. There were many couches, covered with richest silk, and soft as her own cheek, for her to lie upon; and the carpets were so thick, she might have cast herself down anywhere—as befitted a tomb. The place was dry and warm, and cunningly pierced for air, so that it was always fresh, and lacked only sunlight. There the witch fed her upon milk, and wine dark as a carbuncle, and pomegranates, and purple grapes, and birds that dwell in marshy places; and she played to her mournful tunes, and caused wailful violins to attend her, and told her sad tales, thus holding her ever in an atmosphere of sweet sorrow.

PHOTOGEN

Watho at length had her desire, for witches often get what they want: a splendid boy was born to the fair Aurora. Just as the sun rose, he opened his eyes. Watho carried him immediately to a distant part of the castle, and persuaded the mother that he never cried but once, dying the moment he was born. Overcome with grief, Aurora left the castle as soon as she was able, and Watho never invited her again.

And now the witch's care was, that the child should not know darkness. Persistently she trained him until at last he never slept during the day, and never woke during the night. She never let him see anything black, and even kept all dull colours out of his way. Never, if she could help it, would she let a shadow fall upon him, watching against shadows as if they had been live things that would hurt him. All day he basked in the full splendour of the sun, in the same large rooms his mother had occupied. Watho used him to the sun, until he could bear more of it than any dark-blooded African. In the hottest of every day, she stript him and laid him in it, that he might ripen like a peach; and the boy rejoiced in it, and would resist being dressed again. She brought all her knowledge to bear on making his muscles strong and elastic and swiftly responsive— that his soul, she said laughingly, might sit in every fibre, be all in every part, and awake the moment of call. His hair was of the red gold, but his eyes grew darker as he grew, until they were as black as Vesper's. He was

427

the merriest of creatures, always laughing, always loving, for a moment raging, then laughing afresh. Watho called him Photogen.

NYCTERIS

Five or six months after the birth of Photogen, the dark lady also gave birth to a baby: in the windowless tomb of a blind mother, in the dead of night, under the feeble rays of a lamp in an alabaster globe, a girl came into the darkness with a wail. And just as she was born for the first time, Vesper was born for the second, and passed into a world as unknown to her as this was to her child—who would have to be born yet again before she could see her mother.

Watho called her Nycteris, and she grew as like Vesper as possible—in all but one particular. She had the same dark skin, dark eyelashes and brows, dark hair, and gentle sad look; but she had just the eyes of Aurora, the mother of Photogen, and if they grew darker as she grew older, it was only a darker blue. Watho, with the help of Falca, took the greatest possible care of her—in every way consistent with her plans, that is,—the main point in which was that she should never see any light but what came from the lamp. Hence her optic nerves, and indeed her whole apparatus for seeing, grew both larger and more sensitive; her eyes, indeed, stopped short only of being too large. Under her dark hair and forehead and eyebrows, they looked like two breaks in a cloudy night-sky, through which peeped the heaven where the stars and no clouds live. She was a sadly dainty little creature. No one in the world except those two was aware of the being of the little bat. Watho trained her to sleep during the day, and wake during the night. She taught her music, in which she was herself a proficient, and taught her scarcely anything else.

HOW PHOTOGEN GREW

The hollow in which the castle of Watho lay, was a cleft in a plain rather than a valley among hills, for at the top of its steep sides, both north and south, was a table-land, large and wide. It was covered with rich grass and flowers, with here and there a wood, the outlying colony of a great forest. These grassy plains were the finest hunting grounds in the world. Great herds of small, but fierce cattle, with humps and shaggy manes, roved about them, also antelopes and gnus, and the tiny roedeer, while the woods were swarming with wild creatures. The tables of the castle were mainly supplied from them. The chief of Watho's huntsmen was a fine fellow, and when Photogen began to outgrow the training she could give him, she handed him over to Fargu. He with a will set about teaching him all he knew. He got him pony after pony, larger and larger as he grew, every one less manageable than that which had preceded it, and advanced him from pony to horse, and from horse to horse, until he was equal to anything in that kind which the country produced. In similar fashion he trained him to the use of bow and arrow, substituting every three months a stronger bow and longer arrows; and soon he became, even on horseback, a wonderful archer. He was but fourteen when he killed his first bull, causing jubilation among the huntsmen, and indeed, through all the castle, for there too he was the favourite. Every day, almost as soon as the sun was up, he went out hunting, and would in general be out nearly the whole of the day. But Watho had laid upon Fargu just one commandment, namely, that Photogen should on no account, whatever the plea, be out until sundown, or so near it as to wake in him the desire of seeing what was going to happen; and this commandment Fargu was anxiously careful not to break; for although he would not have trembled had a whole herd of bulls come down upon him, charging at full speed across the level, and not an arrow left in his quiver, he was more than afraid of his mistress. When she looked at him in a certain way, he felt, he said, as if his heart turned to ashes in his breast, and what ran in his veins was no longer blood, but milk and water. So that, ere long, as Photogen grew older, Fargu began to tremble, for he found it steadily growing harder to restrain him. So full of life was he, as Fargu said to his mistress, much to her content, that he was more like a live thunderbolt than a human being. He did not know what fear was, and that not because he did not know danger; for he had had a severe laceration from the razor-like tusk of a boar—whose spine, however, he had severed with one blow of his hunting-knife, before Fargu could reach him with defence. When he would spur his horse into the

429

midst of a herd of bulls, carrying only his bow and his short sword, or shoot an arrow into a herd, and go after it as if to reclaim it for a runaway shaft, arriving in time to follow it with a spear-thrust before the wounded animal knew which way to charge, Fargu thought with terror how it would be when he came to know the temptation of the huddle-spot leopards, and the knife-clawed lynxes, with which the forest was haunted. For the boy had been so steeped in the sun, from childhood so saturated with his influence, that he looked upon every danger from a sovereign height of courage. When, therefore, he was approaching his sixteenth year, Fargu ventured to beg Watho that she would lay her commands upon the youth himself, and release him from responsibility for him. One might as soon hold a tawny-maned lion as Photogen, he said. Watho called the youth, and in the presence of Fargu laid her command upon him never to be out when the rim of the sun should touch the horizon, accompanying the prohibition with hints of consequences, none the less awful than they were obscure. Photogen listened respectfully, but, knowing neither the taste of fear nor the temptation of the night, her words were but sounds to him.

HOW NYCTERIS GREW

The little education she intended Nycteris to have, Watho gave her by word of mouth. Not meaning she should have light enough to read by, to leave other reasons unmentioned, she never put a book in her hands. Nycteris, however, saw so much better than Watho imagined, that the light she gave her was quite sufficient, and she managed to coax Falca into teaching her the letters, after which she taught herself to read, and Falca now and then brought her a child's book. But her chief pleasure was in her instrument. Her very fingers loved it, and would wander about its keys like feeding sheep. She was not unhappy. She knew nothing of the world except the tomb in which she dwelt, and had some pleasure in everything she did. But she desired, nevertheless, something more or different. She did not know what it was, and the nearest she could come to expressing it to herself was—that she wanted more room. Watho and

Falca would go from her beyond the shine of the lamp, and come again; therefore surely there must be more room somewhere. As often as she was left alone, she would fall to poring over the coloured bas-reliefs on the walls. These were intended to represent various of the powers of Nature under allegorical similitudes, and as nothing can be made that does not belong to the general scheme, she could not fail at least to imagine a flicker of relationship between some of them, and thus a shadow of the reality of things found its way to her.

There was one thing, however, which moved and taught her more than all the rest—the lamp, namely, that hung from the ceiling, which she always saw alight, though she never saw the flame, only the slight condensation towards the centre of the alabaster globe. And besides the operation of the light itself after its kind, the indefiniteness of the globe, and the softness of the light, giving her the feeling as if her eyes could go in and into its whiteness, were somehow also associated with the idea of space and room. She would sit for an hour together gazing up at the lamp, and her heart would swell as she gazed. She would wonder what had hurt her, when she found her face wet with tears, and then would wonder how she could have been hurt without knowing it. She never looked thus at the lamp except when she was alone.

THE LAMP

Watho having given orders, took it for granted they were obeyed, and that Falca was all night long with Nycteris, whose day it was. But Falca could not get into the habit of sleeping through the day, and would often leave her alone half the night. Then it seemed to Nycteris that the white lamp was watching over her. As it was never permitted to go out—while she was awake at least—Nycteris, except by shutting her eyes, knew less about darkness than she did about light. Also, the lamp being fixed high overhead, and in the centre of everything, she did not know much about shadows either. The few there were fell almost entirely on the floor, or kept like mice about the foot of the walls.

Once, when she was thus alone, there came the noise of a far-off

431

rumbling: she had never before heard a sound of which she did not know the origin, and here therefore was a new sign of something beyond these chambers. Then came a trembling, then a shaking; the lamp dropped from the ceiling to the floor with a great crash, and she felt as if both her eyes were hard shut and both her hands over them. She concluded that it was the darkness that had made the rumbling and the shaking, and rushing into the room, had thrown down the lamp. She sat trembling. The noise and the shaking ceased, but the light did not return. The darkness had eaten it up!

Her lamp gone, the desire at once awoke to get out of her prison. She scarcely knew what *out* meant; out of one room into another, where there was not even a dividing door, only an open arch, was all she knew of the world. But suddenly she remembered that she had heard Falca speak of the lamp *going out*: this must be what she had meant? And if the lamp had gone out, where had it gone? Surely where Falca went, and like her it would come again. But she could not wait. The desire to go out grew irresistible. She must follow her beautiful lamp! She must find it! She must see what it was about!

Now there was a curtain covering a recess in the wall, where some of her toys and gymnastic things were kept; and from behind that curtain Watho and Falca always appeared, and behind it they vanished. How they came out of solid wall, she had not an idea, all up to the wall was open space, and all beyond it seemed wall; but clearly the first and only thing she could do, was to feel her way behind the curtain. It was so dark that a cat could not have caught the largest of mice. Nycteris could see better than any cat, but now her great eyes were not of the smallest use to her. As she went she trod upon a piece of the broken lamp. She had never worn shoes or stockings, and the fragment, though, being of soft alabaster, it did not cut, yet hurt her foot. She did not know what it was, but as it had not been there before the darkness came, she suspected that it had to do with the lamp. She kneeled therefore, and searched with her hands, and bringing two large pieces together, recognized the shape of the lamp. Therefore it flashed upon her that the lamp was dead, that this brokenness was the death of which she had read without understanding, that the darkness had killed the lamp. What then could Falca have meant when she spoke of the lamp *going out*? There was the lamp—dead indeed, and so changed that she would never have taken it for a lamp but for the shape! No, it was not the lamp any more now it was dead, for all that made it a lamp was gone, namely, the bright shining of it. Then it must be the shine, the light, that had gone out! That must be what Falca meant—and it must be somewhere in the other place in the wall. She started afresh after it, and groped her way to the curtain.

Now she had never in her life tried to get out, and did not know how; but instinctively she began to move her hands about over one of the walls behind the curtain, half expecting them to go into it, as she supposed Watho and Falco did. But the wall repelled her with inexorable hardness, and she turned to the one opposite. In so doing, she set her foot upon an ivory die, and as it met sharply the same spot the broken alabaster had already hurt, she fell forward with her outstretched hands against the wall. Something gave way, and she tumbled out of the cavern.

OUT

But alas! *out* was very much like *in,* for the same enemy, the darkness, was here also. The next moment, however, came a great gladness—a firefly, which had wandered in from the garden. She saw the tiny spark in the distance. With slow pulsing ebb and throb of light, it came pushing itself through the air, drawing nearer and nearer, with that motion which more resembles swimming than flying, and the light seemed the source of its own motion.

"My lamp! my lamp!" cried Nycteris. "It is the shiningness of my lamp, which the cruel darkness drove out. My good lamp has been waiting for me here all the time! It knew I would come after it, and waited to take me with it."

She followed the firefly, which, like herself, was seeking the way out. If it did not know the way, it was yet light; and, because all light is one, any light may serve to guide to more light. If she was mistaken in thinking it the spirit of her lamp, it was of the same spirit as her lamp—and had wings. The gold-green jet-boat, driven by light, went throbbing before her through a long narrow passage. Suddenly it rose

433

higher, and the same moment Nycteris fell upon an ascending stair. She had never seen a stair before, and found going-up a curious sensation. Just as she reached what seemed the top, the firefly ceased to shine, and so disappeared. She was in utter darkness once more. But when we are following the light, even its extinction is a guide. If the firefly had gone on shining, Nycteris would have seen the stair turn, and would have gone up to Watho's bedroom; whereas now, feeling straight before her, she came to a latched door, which after a good deal of trying she managed to open—and stood in a maze of wondering perplexity, awe, and delight. What was it? Was it outside of her, or something taking place in her head? Before her was a very long and very narrow passage, broken up she could not tell how, and spreading out above and on all sides to an infinite height and breadth and distance—as if space itself were growing out of a trough. It was brighter than her rooms had ever been—brighter than if six alabaster lamps had been burning in them. There was a quantity of strange streaking and mottling about it, very different from the shapes on her walls. She was in a dream of pleasant perplexity, of delightful bewilderment. She could not tell whether she was upon her feet or drifting about like the firefly, driven by the pulses of an inward bliss. But she knew little as yet of her inheritance. Unconsciously, she took one step forward from the threshold, and the girl who had been from her very birth a troglodyte, stood in the ravishing glory of a southern night, lit by a perfect moon—not the moon of our northern clime, but the moon like silver glowing in a furnace—a moon one could see to be a globe—not far off, a mere flat disc on the face of the blue, but hanging down halfway, and looking as if one could see all round it by a mere bending of the neck.

"It is my lamp," she said, and stood dumb with parted lips. She looked and felt as if she had been standing there in silent ecstasy from the beginning.

"No, it is not my lamp," she said after a while; "it is the mother of all the lamps."

And with that she fell on her knees, and spread out her hands to the moon. She could not in the least have told what was in her mind, but the action was in reality just a begging of the moon to be what she was—that precise incredible splendour hung in the far-off roof, that very glory

434

essential to the being of poor girls born and bred in caverns. It was a resurrection—nay, a birth itself, to Nycteris. What the vast blue sky, studded with tiny sparks like the heads of diamond nails could be; what the moon, looking so absolutely content with light—why, she knew less about them than you and I! but the greatest of astronomers might envy the rapture of such a first impression at the age of sixteen. Immeasurably imperfect it was, but false the impression could not be, for she saw with the eyes made for seeing, and saw indeed what many men are too wise to see.

As she knelt, something softly flapped her, embraced her, stroked her, fondled her. She rose to her feet, but saw nothing, did not know what it was. It was likest a woman's breath. For she knew nothing of the air even, had never breathed the still newborn freshness of the world. Her breath had come to her only through long passages and spirals in the rock. Still less did she know of the air alive with motion—of that thrice blessed thing, the wind of a summer night. It was like a spiritual wine, filling her whole being with an intoxication of purest joy. To breathe was a perfect existence. It seemed to her the light itself she drew into her lungs. Possessed by the power of the gorgeous night, she seemed at one and the same moment annihilated and glorified.

She was in the open passage or gallery that ran round the top of the garden walls, between the cleft battlements, but she did not once look down to see what lay beneath. Her soul was drawn to the vault above her with its lamp and its endless room. At last she burst into tears, and her heart was relieved, as the night itself is relieved by its lightning and rain.

And now she grew thoughtful. She must hoard this splendour! What a little ignorance her gaolers had made of her! Life was a mighty bliss, and they had scraped hers to the bare bone! They must not know that she knew. She must hide her knowledge—hide it even from her own eyes, keeping it close in her bosom, content to know that she had it, even when she could not brood on its presence, feasting her eyes with its glory. She turned from the vision, therefore, with a sigh of utter bliss, and with soft quiet steps and groping hands, stole back into the darkness of the rock. What was darkness or the laziness of Time's feet to one who had seen what she had that night seen? She was lifted above all weariness—above all wrong.

When Falca entered, she uttered a cry of terror. But Nycteris called to her not to be afraid, and told her how there had come a rumbling and a shaking, and the lamp had fallen. Then Falca went and told her mistress, and within an hour a new globe hung in the place of the old one. Nycteris thought it did not look so bright and clear as the former, but she made no lamentation over the change; she was far too rich to heed it. For now, prisoner as she knew herself, her heart was full of glory and gladness; at times she had to hold herself from jumping up, and going dancing and singing about the room. When she slept, instead of dull dreams, she had splendid visions. There were times, it is true, when she became restless, and impatient to look upon her riches, but then she would reason with herself, saying "What does it matter if I sit here for ages with my poor pale lamp, when out there a lamp is burning at which ten thousand little lamps are glowing with wonder?"

She never doubted she had looked upon the day and the sun, of which she had read; and always when she read of the day and the sun, she had the night and the moon in her mind; and when she read of the night and the moon, she thought only of the cave and the lamp that hung there.

THE GREAT LAMP

It was some time before she had a second opportunity of going out, for Falca since the fall of the lamp had been a little more careful, and seldom left her for long. But one night, having a little headache, Nycteris lay down upon her bed, and was lying with her eyes closed, when she heard Falca come to her, and felt she was bending over her. Disinclined to talk, she did not open her eyes, and lay quite still. Satisfied that she was asleep, Falca left her, moving so softly that her very caution made Nycteris open her eyes and look after her—just in time to see her vanish—through a picture, as it seemed, that hung on the wall a long way from the usual place of issue. She jumped up, her headache forgotten, and ran in the opposite direction; got out, groped her way to the stair, climbed, and reached the top of the wall.—Alas! the great room was not so light as the little one she had left! Why?—Sorrow of sorrows! the great lamp was gone! Had its globe fallen and its lovely light gone out upon great wings, a resplendent firefly, oaring itself through a yet grander and lovelier room? She looked down to see if it lay anywhere broken to pieces on the carpet below; but she could not even see the carpet. But surely nothing very dreadful could have happened—no rumbling or shaking; for there were all the little lamps shining brighter than before, not one of them looking as if any unusual matter had befallen. What if each of those little lamps was growing into a big lamp, and after being a big lamp for a while, had to go out and grow a bigger lamp still—out there, beyond this *out*?—Ah! here was the living thing that could not be seen, come to her again—bigger tonight with such loving kisses, and such liquid strokings of her cheeks and forehead, gently tossing her hair, and delicately toying with it! But it ceased, and all was still. Had it gone out? What would happen next? Perhaps the little lamps had not to grow great lamps, but to fall one by one and go out first?—With that, came from below a sweet scent, then another, and another. Ah, how delicious! Perhaps they were all coming to her only on their way out after the great lamp!—Then came the music of the river, which she had been too absorbed in the sky to note the first time. What was it? Alas! alas! another sweet living thing on its way out. They were all marching slowly out in long lovely file, one after the other, each taking its leave of her as it passed! It must be so; here were more and more sweet sounds, following and fading! The whole of the *Out* was going out again; it was all going after the great lovely lamp! She would be left the only creature in the solitary day! Was there nobody to hang up a new lamp for the old one, and keep the creatures from going?—She crept back to her rock very sad. She tried to comfort herself by saying that anyhow there would be room out there; but as she said it she shuddered at the thought of *empty* room.

When next she succeeded in getting out, a half-moon hung in the east: a new lamp had come, she thought, and all would be well.

It would be endless to describe the phases of feeling through which Nycteris passed, more numerous and delicate than those of a thousand changing moons. A fresh bliss bloomed in her soul with every varying aspect of infinite nature. Ere long she began to suspect that the new moon was the old moon, gone out and come in again like herself; also

437

that, unlike herself, it wasted and grew again; that it was indeed a live thing, subject like herself to caverns, and keepers and solitudes, escaping and shining when it could. Was it a prison like hers it was shut in and did it grow dark when the lamp left it? Where could be the way into it?—With that first she began to look below, as well as above and around her; and then first noted the tops of the trees between her and the floor. There were palms with their red-fingered hands full of fruit; eucalyptus trees crowded with little boxes of powder-puffs; oleanders with their half-caste roses; and orange trees with their clouds of young silver stars, and their aged balls of gold. Her eyes could see colours invisible to ours in the moonlight, and all these she could distinguish well, though at first she took them for the shapes and colours of the carpet of the great room. She longed to get down among them, now she saw they were real creatures, but she did not know how. She went along the whole length of the wall to the end that crossed the river, but found no way of going down. Above the river she stopped to gaze with awe upon the rushing water. She knew nothing of water but from what she drank and what she bathed in; and, as the moon shone on the dark, swift stream, singing lustily as it flowed, she did not doubt the river was alive, a swift rushing serpent of life, going—out?—whither? And then she wondered if what was brought into her rooms had been killed that she might drink it, and have her bath in it.

Once when she stepped out upon the wall, it was into the midst of a fierce wind. The trees were all roaring. Great clouds were rushing along the skies, and tumbling over the little lamps: the great lamp had not come yet. All was in tumult. The wind seized her garments and hair, and shook them as if it would tear them from her. What could she have done to make the gentle creature so angry? Or was this another creature altogether—of the same kind, but hugely bigger, and of a very different temper and behaviour? But the whole place was angry! Or was it that the creatures dwelling in it, the wind, and the trees, and the clouds, and the river, had all quarrelled, each with all the rest? Would the whole come to confusion and disorder? But, as she gazed wondering and disquieted, the moon, larger than ever she had seen her, came lifting herself above the horizon to look, broad and red, as if she, too, were swollen with anger that she had been roused from her rest by their noise, and compelled to

438

hurry up to see what her children were about, thus rioting in her absence, lest they should rack the whole frame of things. And as she rose, the loud wind grew quieter and scolded less fiercely, the trees grew stiller and moaned with a lower complaint, and the clouds hunted and hurled themselves less wildly across the sky. And as if she were pleased that her children obeyed her very presence, the moon grew smaller as she ascended the heavenly stair; her puffed cheeks sank, her complexion grew clearer, and a sweet smile spread over her countenance, as peacefully she rose and rose. But there was treason and rebellion in her court; for, ere she reached the top of her great stairs, the clouds had assembled, forgetting their late wars, and very still they were as they laid their heads together and conspired. Then combining, and lying silently in wait until she came near, they threw themselves upon her, and swallowed her up. Down from the roof came spots of wet, faster and faster, and they wetted the cheeks of Nycteris; and what could they be but the tears of the moon, crying because her children were smothering her? Nycteris wept too, and not knowing what to think, stole back in dismay to her room.

The next time, she came out in fear and trembling. There was the moon still! away in the west—poor, indeed, and old, and looking dreadfully worn, as if all the wild beasts in the sky had been gnawing at her—but there she was, alive still, and able to shine!

THE SUNSET

Knowing nothing of darkness, or stars, or moon, Photogen spent his days in hunting. On a great white horse he swept over the grassy plains, glorying in the sun, fighting the wind, and killing the buffaloes.

One morning, when he happened to be on the ground a little earlier than usual, and before his attendants, he caught sight of an animal unknown to him, stealing from a hollow into which the sunrays had not yet reached. Like a swift shadow it sped over the grass, slinking southward to the forest. He gave chase, noted the body of a buffalo it had half eaten, and pursued it the harder. But with great leaps and bounds the creature shot farther and farther ahead of him, and vanished. Turning therefore defeated, he met Fargu, who had been following him as fast as his horse could carry him.

"What animal was that, Fargu?" he asked. "How he did run!"

Fargu answered he might be a leopard, but he rather thought from his pace and look that he was a young lion.

"What a coward he must be!" said Photogen.

"Don't be too sure of that," rejoined Fargu. "He is one of the creatures the sun makes uncomfortable. As soon as the sun is down, he will be brave enough."

He had scarecely said it, when he repented; nor did he regret it the less when he found that Photogen made no reply. But alas! said was said.

"Then," said Photogen to himself, "that contemptible beast is one of the terrors of sundown, of which Madame Watho spoke!"

He hunted all day, but not with his usual spirit. He did not ride so hard, and did not kill one buffalo. Fargu to his dismay observed also that he took every pretext for moving farther south, nearer to the forest. But all at once, the sun now sinking in the west, he seemed to change his mind, for he turned his horse's head, and rode home so fast that the rest could not keep him in sight. When they arrived, they found his horse in the stable, and concluded that he had gone into the castle. But he had in truth set out again by the back of it. Crossing the river a good way up the valley, he reascended to the ground they had left, and just before sunset reached the skirts of the forest.

The level orb shone straight in between the bare stems, and saying to himself he could not fail to find the beast, he rushed into the wood. But even as he entered, he turned, and looked to the west. The rim of the red was touching the horizon, all jagged with broken hills. "Now," said Photogen, "we shall see"; but he said it in the face of a darkness he had not proved. The moment the sun began to sink among the spikes and saw-edges, with a kind of sudden flap at his heart a fear inexplicable laid hold of the youth; and as he had never felt anything of the kind before, the very fear itself terrified him. As the sun sank, it rose like the shadow of the world, and grew deeper and darker. He could not even think what it might be, so utterly did it enfeeble him. When the last flaming scimitar-edge of the sun went out like a lamp, his horror seemed to

440

blossom into very madness. Like the closing lids of an eye—for there was no twilight, and this night no moon—the terror and the darkness rushed together, and he knew them for one. He was no longer the man he had known, or rather thought himself. The courage he had had was in no sense his own—he had only had courage, not been courageous; it had left him, and he could scarcely stand—certainly not stand straight, for not one of his joints could he make stiff or keep from trembling. He was but a spark of the sun, in himself nothing.

The beast was behind him—stealing upon him! He turned. All was dark in the wood, but to his fancy the darkness here and there broke into pairs of green eyes, and he had not the power even to raise his bow-hand from his side. In the strength of despair he strove to rouse courage enough—not to fight—that he did not even desire—but to run. Courage to flee home was all he could ever imagine, and it would not come. But what he had not, was ignominiously given him. A cry in the wood, half a screech, half a growl, sent him running like a boar-wounded cur. It was not even himself that ran, it was the fear that had come alive in his legs; he did not know that they moved. But as he ran he grew able to run—gained courage at least to be a coward. The stars gave a little light. Over the grass he sped, and nothing followed him. "How fallen, how changed," from the youth who had climbed the hill as the sun went down! A mere contempt to himself, the self that contemned was a coward with the self it contemned! There lay the shapeless black of a buffalo, humped upon the grass: He made a wide circuit, and swept on like a shadow driven in the wind. For the wind had arisen, and added to his terror: it blew from behind him. He reached the brow of the valley, and shot down the steep descent like a falling star. Instantly the whole upper country behind him arose and pursued him! The wind came howling after him, filled with screams, shrieks, yells, roars, laughter, and chattering, as if all the animals of the forest were careering with it. In his ears was a trampling rush, the thunder of the hoofs of the cattle, in career from every quarter of the wide plains to the brow of the hill above him. He fled straight for the castle, scarcely with breath enough to pant.

As he reached the bottom of the valley, the moon peered up over its edge. He had never seen the moon before—except in the daytime, when he had taken her for a thin bright cloud. She was a fresh terror to

441

him—so ghostly! so ghastly! so gruesome!—so knowing as she looked over the top of her garden wall upon the world outside! That was the night itself! the darkness alive—and after him! the horror of horrors coming down the sky to curdle his blood, and turn his brain to a cinder! He gave a sob, and made straight for the river, where it ran between the two walls, at the bottom of the garden. He plunged in, struggled through, clambered up the bank, and fell senseless on the grass.

THE GARDEN

Although Nycteris took care not to stay out long at a time, and used every precaution, she could hardly have escaped discovery so long, had it not been that the strange attacks to which Watho was subject had been more frequent of late, and had at last settled into an illness which kept her to her bed. But whether from an access of caution or from suspicion, Falca, having now to be much with her mistress both day and night, took it at length into her head to fasten the door as often as she went by her usual place of exit, so that one night, when Nycteris pushed, she found, to her surprise and dismay, that the wall pushed her again, and would not let her through; nor with all her searching could she discover wherein lay the cause of the change. Then first she felt the pressure of her prison-walls, and turning, half in despair, groped her way to the picture where she had once seen Falca disappear. There she soon found the spot by pressing upon which the wall yielded. It let her through into a sort of cellar, where was a glimmer of light from a sky whose blue was paled by the moon. From the cellar she got into a long passage, into which the moon was shining, and came to a door. She managed to open it, and, to her great joy found herself in *the other place,* not on the top of the wall, however, but in the garden she had longed to enter. Noiseless as a fluffy moth she flitted away into the covert of the trees and shrubs, her bare feet welcomed by the softest of carpets, which, by the very touch, her feet knew to be alive, whence it came that it was so sweet and friendly to them. A soft little wind was out among the trees, running now here, now there, like a child that had got its will. She went dancing over the grass,

442

looking behind her at her shadow as she went. At first she had taken it for a little black creature that made game of her, but when she perceived that it was only where she kept the moon away, and that every tree, however great and grand a creature, had also one of these strange attendants, she soon learned not to mind it, and by and by it became the source of as much amusement to her, as to any kitten its tail. It was long before she was quite at home with the trees, however. At one time they seemed to disapprove of her; at another not even to know she was there, and to be altogether taken up with their own business. Suddenly, as she went from one to another of them, looking up with awe at the murmuring mystery of their branches and leaves, she spied one a little way off, which was very different from all the rest. It was white, and dark, and sparkling, and spread like a palm—a small slender palm, without much head; and it grew very fast, and sang as it grew. But it never grew any bigger, for just as fast as she could see it growing, it kept falling to pieces. When she got close to it, she discovered that it was a water-tree—made of just such water as she washed with—only it was alive of course, like the river—a different sort of water from that, doubtless, seeing the one crept swiftly along the floor, and the other shot straight up, and fell, and swallowed itself, and rose again. She put her feet into the marble basin, which was the flower-pot in which it grew. It was full of real water, living and cool—so nice, for the night was hot!

But the flowers! ah, the flowers! she was friends with them from the very first. What wonderful creatures they were!—and so kind and beautiful—always sending out such colours and such scents—red scent, and white scent, and yellow scent—for the other creatures! The one that was invisible and everywhere, took such a quantity of their scents, and carried it away! yet they did not seem to mind. It was their talk, to show they were alive, and not painted like those on the walls of her rooms, and on the carpets.

She wandered along down the garden, until she reached the river. Unable then to get any further—for she was a little afraid, and justly, of the swift watery serpent—she dropped on the grassy bank, dipped her feet in the water, and felt it running and pushing against them. For a long time she sat thus, and her bliss seemed complete, as she gazed at the river, and watched the broken picture of the great lamp overhead, moving up one side of the roof, to go down the other.

443

A beautiful moth brushed across the great blue eyes of Nycteris. She sprang to her feet to follow it—not in the spirit of the hunter, but of the lover. Her heart—like every heart, if only its fallen sides were cleared away—was an inexhaustible fountain of love: she loved everything she saw. But as she followed the moth, she caught sight of something lying on the bank of the river, and not yet having learned to be afraid of anything, ran straight to see what it was. Reaching it, she stood amazed. Another girl like herself! But what a strange-looking girl!—so curiously dressed too!—and not able to move! Was she dead? Filled suddenly with pity, she sat down, lifted Photogen's head, laid it on her lap and began stroking his face. Her warm hands brought him to himself. He opened his black eyes, out of which had gone all the fire, and looked up with a strange sound of fear, half moan, half gasp. But when he saw her face, he drew a deep breath, and lay motionless—gazing at her: those blue marvels above him, like a better sky, seemed to side with courage and assuage his terror. At length, in a trembling, awed voice, and a half whisper, he said, "Who are you?"

"I am Nycteris," she answered.

"You are a creature of the darkness, and love the night," he said, his fear beginning to move again.

"I may be a creature of the darkness," she replied. "I hardly know what you mean. But I do not love the night. I love the day—with all my heart; and I sleep all the night long."

"How can that be?" said Photogen, rising on his elbow, but dropping his head on her lap again the moment he saw the moon; "—how can it be," he repeated, "when I see your eyes there—wide awake?"

She only smiled and stroked him, for she did not understand him, and thought he did not know what he was saying.

"Was it a dream then?" resumed Photogen, rubbing his eyes. But with that his memory came clear, and he shuddered, and cried, "Oh, horrible! horrible! to be turned all at once into a coward! a shameful, contemptible, disgraceful coward! I am ashamed—ashamed—and *so* frightened! It is all so frightful!"

"What is so frightful?" asked Nycteris, with a smile like that of a mother to her child waked from a bad dream.

444

"All, all," he answered; "all this darkness and the roaring."

"My dear," said Nycteris, "there is no roaring. How sensitive you must be! What you hear is only the walking of the water, and the running about of the sweetest of all the creatures. She is invisible, and I call her Everywhere, for she goes through all the other creatures, and comforts them. Now she is amusing herself, and them too, with shaking them and kissing them, and blowing in their faces. Listen: do you call that roaring? You should hear her when she is rather angry though! I don't know why, but she is sometimes, and then she does roar a little."

"It is so horribly dark!" said Photogen, who, listening while she spoke, had satisfied himself that there was no roaring.

"Dark!" she echoed. "You should be in my room when an earthquake has killed my lamp. I do not understand. How *can* you call this dark? Let me see: yes, you have eyes, and big ones, bigger than Madame Watho's or Falca's—not so big as mine, I fancy—only I never saw mine. But then— oh, yes!—I know now what is the matter! You can't see with them, because they are so black. Darkness can't see, of course. Never mind: I will be your eyes, and teach you to see. Look here—at these lovely white things in the grass, with red sharp points all folded together into one. Oh, I love them so! I could sit looking at them all day, the darlings!"

Photogen looked close at the flowers, and thought he had seen something like them before, but could not make them out. As Nycteris had never seen an open daisy, so had he never seen a closed one.

Thus instinctively Nycteris tried to turn him away from his fear: and the beautiful creature's strange lovely talk helped not a little to make him forget it.

"You call it dark!" she said again, as if she could not get rid of the absurdity of the idea; "why, I could count every blade of the green hair—I suppose it is what the books call grass—within two yards of me! And just look at the great lamp! It is brighter than usual to-day, and I can't think why you should be frightened, or call it dark!"

As she spoke, she went on stroking his cheeks and hair, and trying to comfort him. But oh how miserable he was! and how plainly he looked it! He was on the point of saying that her great lamp was dreadful to him, looking like a witch, walking in the sleep of death; but he was not so ignorant as Nycteris, and knew even in the moonlight that she was a woman, though he had never seen one so young or so lovely before; and

445

while she comforted his fear, her presence made him the more ashamed of it. Besides, not knowing her nature, he might annoy her, and make her leave him to his misery. He lay still therefore, hardly daring to move: all the little life he had seemed to come from her, and if he were to move, she might move: and if she were to leave him, he must weep like a child.

"How did you come here?" asked Nycteris, taking his face between her hands.

"Down the hill," he answered.

"Where do you sleep?" he asked.

He signed in the direction of the house. She gave a little laugh of delight.

"When you have learned not to be frightened, you will always be wanting to come out with me," she said.

She thought with herself she would ask her presently, when she had come to herself a little, how she had made her escape, for she must, of course, like herself, have got out of a cave, in which Watho and Falca had been keeping her.

"Look at the lovely colours," she went on, pointing to a rose-bush, on which Photogen could not see a single flower. "They are far more beautiful—are they not?—than any of the colours upon your walls. And then they are alive, and smell so sweet!"

He wished she would not make him keep opening his eyes to look at things he could not see; and every other moment would start and grasp tight hold of her, as some fresh pang of terror shot into him.

"Come, come, dear!" said Nycteris, "you must not go on this way. You must be a brave girl, and——"

"A girl!" shouted Photogen, and started to his feet in wrath. "If you were a man, I should kill you."

"A man?" repeated Nycteris, "what is that? How could I be that? We are both girls—are we not?"

"No, I am not a girl," he answered; "—although," he added, changing his tone, and casting himself on the ground at her feet, "I have given you too good reason to call me one."

"Oh, I see!" returned Nycteris. "No, of course!—you can't be a girl: girls are not afraid—without reason. I understand now: it is because you are not a girl that you are so frightened."

446

Photogen twisted and writhed upon the grass.

"No, it is not," he said sulkily; "it is this horrible darkness that creeps into me, goes all through me, into the very marrow of my bones—that is what makes me behave like a girl. If only the sun would rise!"

"The sun! what is it?" cried Nycteris, now in her turn conceiving a vague fear.

Then Photogen broke into a rhapsody, in which he vainly sought to forget his.

"It is the soul, the life, the heart, the glory of the universe," he said. "The worlds dance like motes in his beams. The heart of man is strong and brave in his light, and when it departs his courage grows from him—goes with the sun, and he becomes such as you see me now."

"Then that is not the sun?" said Nycteris, thoughtfully, pointing up to the moon.

"That!" cried Photogen, with utter scorn; "I know nothing about *that,* except that it is ugly and horrible. At best it can be only the ghost of a dead sun. Yes, that is it! That is what makes it look so frightful."

"No," said Nycteris, after a long, thoughtful pause; you must be wrong there. I think the sun is the ghost of a dead moon, and that is how he is so much more splendid as you say.—Is there, then, another big room, where the sun lives in the roof?"

"I do not know what you mean," replied Photogen. "But you mean to be kind, I know, though you should not call a poor fellow in the dark a girl. If you will let me lie here, with my head in your lap, I should like to sleep. Will you watch me, and take care of me?"

"Yes, that I will," answered Nycteris, forgetting all her own danger.

So Photogen fell asleep.

THE SUN

There Nycteris sat, and there the youth lay all night long, in the heart of the great cone-shadow of the earth, like two Pharaohs in one Pyramid. Photogen slept, and slept; and Nycteris sat motionless lest she should wake him, and so betray him to his fear.

The moon rode high in the blue eternity; it was a very triumph of glorious night; the river ran babble-murmuring in deep soft syllables; the fountain kept rushing moon-ward, and blossoming momently to a great silvery flower, whose petals were for ever falling like snow, but with a continuous musical clash, into the bed of its exhaustion beneath; the wind woke, took a run among the trees, went to sleep, and woke again; the daisies slept on their feet at hers, but she did not know they slept; the roses might well seem awake, for their scent filled the air, but in truth they slept also, and the odour was that of their dreams; the oranges hung like gold lamps in the trees, and their silvery flowers were the souls of their yet unembodied children; the scent of the acacia blooms filled the air like the very odour of the moon herself.

At last, unused to the living air, and weary with sitting so still and so long, Nycteris grew drowsy. The air began to grow cool. It was getting near the time when she too was accustomed to sleep. She closed her eyes just a moment, and nodded—opened them suddenly wide, for she had promised to watch.

In that moment a change had come. The moon had got round, and was fronting her from the west, and she saw that her face was altered, that she had grown pale, as if she too were wan with fear, and from her lofty place espied a coming terror. The light seemed to be dissolving out of her; she was dying—she was going out! And yet everything around looked strangely clear—clearer than ever she had seen anything before; how could the lamp be shedding more light when she herself had less? Ah, that was just it! See how faint she looked! It was because the light was forsaking her, and spreading itself over the room, that she grew so thin and pale! She was giving up everything! She was melting away from the roof like a bit of sugar in water.

Nycteris was fast growing afraid, and sought refuge with the face upon her lap. How beautiful the creature was!—what to call it she could not think, for it had been angry when she called it what Watho called her. And, wonder upon wonders! now, even in the cold change that was passing upon the great room, the colour as of a red rose was rising in the wan cheek. What beautiful yellow hair it was that spread over her lap! What great huge breaths the creature took! And what were those curious things it carried? She had seen them on her walls, she was sure.

448

Thus she talked to herself while the lamp grew paler and paler, and everything kept growing yet clearer. What could it mean? The lamp was dying—going out into the other place of which the creature in her lap had spoken, to be a sun! But why were the things growing clearer before it was yet a sun? That was the point. Was it her growing into a sun that did it? Yes! yes! it was coming death! She knew it, for it was coming upon her also! She felt it coming! What was she about to grow into? Something beautiful, like the creature in her lap? It might be! Anyhow, it must be death; for all her strength was going out of her, while all around her was growing so light she could not bear it! She must be blind soon! Would she be blind or dead first?

For the sun was rushing up behind her. Photogen woke, lifted his head from her lap, and sprang to his feet. His face was one radiant smile. His heart was full of daring—that of the hunter who will creep into the tiger's den. Nycteris gave a cry, covered her face with her hands, and pressed her eyelids close. Then blindly she stretched out her arms to Photogen, crying, "Oh, I am *so* frightened! What is this? It must be death! I don't wish to die yet. I love this room and the old lamp. I do not want the other place. This is terrible. I want to hide. I want to get into the sweet, soft, dark hands of all the other creatures. Ah me! ah me!"

"What is the matter with you, girl?" said Photogen, with the arrogance of all male creatures until they have been taught by the other kind. He stood looking down upon her over his bow, of which he was examining the string. "There is no fear of anything now, child! It is day. The sun is all but up. Look! he will be above the brow of yon hill in one moment more! Good-bye. Thank you for my night's lodging. I'm off. Don't be a goose. If ever I can do anything for you—and all that, you know!"

"Don't leave me; oh, don't leave me!" cried Nycteris. "I am dying! I am dying! I can't move. The light sucks all the strength out of me. And oh, I am *so* frightened!"

But already Photogen had splashed through the river, holding high his bow that it might not get wet. He rushed across the level, and strained up the opposing hill. Hearing no answer, Nycteris removed her hands. Photogen had reached the top, and the same moment the sunrays alighted upon him; the glory of the king of day crowded blazing upon the golden-haired youth. Radiant as Apollo, he stood in mighty strength,

449

a flashing shape in the midst of flame. He fitted a glowing arrow to a gleaming bow. The arrow parted with a keen musical twang of the bowstring, and Photogen darting after it, vanished with a shout. Up shot Apollo himself, and from his quiver scattered astonishment and exultation. But the brain of poor Nycteris was pierced through and through. She fell down in utter darkness. All around her was a flaming furnace. In despair and feebleness and agony, she crept back, feeling her way with doubt and difficulty and enforced persistence to her cell. When at last the friendly darkness of her chamber folded her about with its cooling and consoling arms, she threw herself on her bed and fell fast asleep. And there she slept on, one alive in a tomb, while Photogen, above in the sun-glory, pursued the buffaloes on the lofty plain, thinking not once of her where she lay dark and forsaken, whose presence had been his refuge, her eyes and her hands his guardians through the night. He was in his glory and his pride; and the darkness and its disgrace had vanished for a time.

THE COWARD HERO

But no sooner had the sun reached the noonstead, than Photogen began to remember the past night in the shadow of that which was at hand, and to remember it with shame. He had proved himself—and not to himself only, but to a girl as well—a coward!—one bold in the daylight, while there was nothing to fear, but trembling like any slave when the night arrived. There was, there must be, something unfair in it! A spell had been cast upon him! He had eaten, he had drunk something that did not agree with courage! In any case he had been taken unprepared! How was he to know what the going down of the sun would be like? It was no wonder, he should have been surprised into terror, seeing it was what it was—in its very nature so terrible! Also, one could not see where danger might be coming from! You might be torn in pieces, carried off, or swallowed up, without even seeing where to strike a blow! Every possible excuse he caught at, eager as a self-lover to lighten his self-contempt. That day he astonished the huntsmen—terrified them with his reckless daring—all to prove to himself he was no coward. But nothing eased his shame. One thing only had hope in it—the resolve to encounter the dark in solemn earnest, now that he knew something of what it was. It was nobler to meet a recognized danger than to rush contemptuously into what seemed nothing—nobler still to encounter a nameless horror. He could conquer fear and wipe out disgrace together. For a marksman and swordsman like him, he said, one with his strength and courage, there was but danger. Defeat there was not. He knew the darkness now, and when it came he would meet it as fearless and cool as now he felt himself. And again he said, "We shall see!"

He stood under the boughs of a great beech as the sun was going down, far away over the jagged hills: before it was half down, he was trembling like one of the leaves behind him in the first sigh of the night-wind. The moment the last of the glowing disc vanished, he bounded away in terror to gain the valley, and his fear grew as he ran. Down the side of the hill, an abject creature, he went bounding and rolling and running; fell rather than plunged into the river, and came to himself, as before, lying on the grassy bank in the garden.

But when he opened his eyes, there were no girl-eyes looking down into his; there were only the stars in the waste of the sunless Night—the awful all-enemy he had again dared, but could not encounter. Perhaps the girl was not yet come out of the water! He would try to sleep, for he dared not move, and perhaps when he woke he would find his head on her lap, and the beautiful dark face, with its deep blue eyes, bending over him. But when he woke he found his head on the grass, and although he sprang up with all his courage, such as it was, restored, he did not set out for the chase with such an *élan* as the day before; and, despite the sun-glory in his heart and veins, his hunting was this day less eager; he ate little, and from the first was thoughtful even to sadness. A second time he was defeated and disgraced! Was his courage nothing more than the play of the sunlight on his brain? Was he a mere ball tossed between the light and the dark? Then what a poor contemptible creature he was! But a third chance lay before him. If he failed the third time, he dared not foreshadow what he must then think of himself! It was bad enough now—but then!

Alas! it went no better. The moment the sun was down, he fled as if from a legion of devils.

451

Seven times in all, he tried to face the coming night in the strength of the past day, and seven times he failed—failed with such increase of failure, with such a growing sense of ignominy, overwhelming at length all the sunny hours and joining night to night, that, what with misery, self-accusation, and loss of confidence, his daylight courage too began to fade, and at length, from exhaustion, from getting wet, and then lying out of doors all night, and night after night,—worst of all, from the consuming of the deathly fear, and the shame of shame, his sleep forsook him, and on the seventh morning, instead of going to the hunt, he crawled into the castle, and went to bed. The grand health, over which the witch had taken such pains, had yielded, and in an hour or two he was moaning and crying out in delirium.

AN EVIL NURSE

Watho was herself ill, as I have said, and was the worse tempered; and besides, it is a peculiarity of witches, that what works in others to sympathy, works in them to repulsion. Also, Watho had a poor, helpless, rudimentary spleen of a conscience left, just enough to make her uncomfortable, and therefore more wicked. So, when she heard that Photogen was ill, she was angry. Ill, indeed! after all she had done to saturate him with the life of the system, with the solar might itself! He was a wretched failure, the boy! And because he was *her* failure, she was annoyed with him, began to dislike him, grew to hate him. She looked on him as a painter might upon a picture, or a poet upon a poem, which he had only succeeded in getting into an irrecoverable mess. In the hearts of witches, love and hate lie close together, and often tumble over each other. And whether it was that her failure with Photogen foiled also her plans in regard to Nycteris, or that her illness made her yet more of a devil's wife, certainly Watho now got sick of the girl too, and hated to know her about the castle.

She was not too ill, however, to go to poor Photogen's room and torment him. She told him she hated him like a serpent, and hissed like one as she said it, looking very sharp in the nose and chin, and flat in the forehead. Photogen thought she meant to kill him, and hardly ventured to take anything brought him. She ordered every ray of light to be shut out of his room; but by means of this he got a little used to the darkness. She would take one of his arrows, and now tickle him with the feather end of it, now prick him with the point till the blood ran down. What she meant finally I cannot tell, but she brought Photogen speedily to the determination of making his escape from the castle: what he should do then he would think afterwards. Who could tell but he might find his mother somewhere beyond the forest! If it were not for the broad patches of darkness that divided day from day, he would fear nothing!

But now, as he lay helpless in the dark, ever and anon would come dawning through it the face of the lovely creature who on that first awful night nursed him so sweetly: was he never to see her again? If she was as he had concluded, the nymph of the river, why had she not reappeared? She might have taught him not to fear the night, for plainly she had no fear of it herself! But then, when the day came, she did seem frightened:—why was that, seeing there was nothing to be afraid of then? Perhaps one so much at home in the darkness, was correspondingly afraid of the light! Then his selfish joy at the rising of the sun, blinding him to her condition, had made him behave to her, in ill return for her kindness, as cruelly as Watho behaved to him! How sweet and dear and lovely she was! If there were wild beasts that came out only at night, and were afraid of the light, why should there not be girls too, made the same way—who could not endure the light, as he could not bear the darkness? If only he could find her again! Ah, how differently he would behave to her! But alas! perhaps the sun had killed her—melted her— burned her up!—dried her up—that was it, if she was the nymph of the river!

WATHO'S WOLF

From that dreadful morning Nycteris had never got to be herself again. The sudden light had been almost death to her: and now she lay in the dark with the memory of a terrific sharpness—a something she dared

453

scarcely recall, lest the very thought of it should sting her beyond endurance. But this was as nothing to the pain which the recollection of the rudeness of the shining creature whom she had nursed through his fear caused her; for, the moment his suffering passed over to her, and he was free, the first use he made of his returning strength had been to scorn her! She wondered and wondered; it was all beyond her comprehension.

Before long, Watho was plotting evil against her. The witch was like a sick child weary of his toy: she would pull her to pieces, and see how she liked it. She would set her in the sun, and see her die, like a jelly from the salt ocean cast out on a hot rock. It would be a sight to soothe her wolf-pain. One day, therefore, a little before noon, while Nycteris was in her deepest sleep, she had a darkened litter brought to the door, and in that she made two of her men carry her to the plain above. There they took her out, laid her on the grass, and left her.

Watho watched it all from the top of her high tower, through her telescope; and scarcely was Nycteris left, when she saw her sit up, and the same moment cast herself down again with her face to the ground.

"She'll have a sunstroke," said Watho, "and that'll be the end of her."

Presently, tormented by a fly, a huge-humped buffalo, with great shaggy mane, came galloping along, straight for where she lay. At sight of the thing on the grass, he started, swerved yards aside, stopped dead, and then came slowly up, looking malicious. Nycteris lay quite still, and never even saw the animal.

"Now she'll be trodden to death!" said Watho. "That's the way those creatures do."

When the buffalo reached her, he sniffed at her all over, and went away; then came back, and sniffed again: then all at once went off as if a demon had him by the tail.

Next came a gnu, a more dangerous animal still, and did much the same; then a gaunt wild boar. But no creature hurt her, and Watho was angry with the whole creation.

At length, in the shade of her hair, the blue eyes of Nycteris began to come to themselves a little, and the first thing they saw was a comfort. I have told already how she knew the night-daisies, each a sharp-pointed little cone with a red tip; and once she had parted the rays of one of them, with trembling fingers, for she was afraid she was dreadfully rude, and perhaps was hurting it; but she did want, she said to herself, to see what secret it carried so carefully hidden; and she found its golden heart. But now, right under her eyes, inside the veil of her hair, in the sweet twilight of whose blackness she could see it perfectly, stood a daisy with its red tip opened wide into a carmine ring, displaying its heart of gold on a platter of silver. She did not at first recognize it as one of those cones come awake, but a moment's notice revealed what it was. Who then could have been so cruel to the lovely little creature, as to force it open like that, and spread it heart-bare to the terrible death-lamp? Whoever it was, it must be the same that had thrown her out there to be burned to death in its fire! But she had her hair, and could hang her head, and make a small sweet night of her own about her! She tried to bend the daisy down and away from the sun, and to make its petals hang about it like her hair, but she could not. Alas! it was burned and dead already! She did not know that it could not yield to her gentle force because it was drinking life, with all the eagerness of life, from what she called the death-lamp. Oh, how the lamp burned her!

But she went on thinking—she did not know how; and by and by began to reflect that, as there was no roof to the room except that in which the great fire went rolling about, the little Red-tip must have seen the lamp a thousand times, and must know it quite well! and it had not killed it! Nay, thinking about farther, she began to ask the question whether this, in which she now saw it, might not be its more perfect condition. For not only now did the whole seem perfect, as indeed it did before, but every part showed its own individual perfection as well, which perfection made it capable of combining with the rest into the higher perfection of a whole. The flower was a lamp itself! The golden heart was the light, and the silver border was the alabaster globe, skilfully broken, and spread wide to let out the glory. Yes: the radiant shape was plainly its perfection! If, then, it was the lamp which had opened it into that shape, the lamp could not be unfriendly to it, but must be of its own kind, seeing it made it perfect! And again, when she thought of it, there was clearly no little resemblance between them. What if the flower then was the little great-grandchild of the lamp and he was loving it all the time? And what if the lamp did not mean to hurt her, only could not

455

help it? The red tips looked as if the flower had some time or other been hurt: what if the lamp was making the best it could of her—opening her out somehow like the flower? She would bear it patiently, and see. But how coarse the colour of the grass was! Perhaps, however, her eyes not being made for the bright lamp, she did not see them as they were! Then she remembered how different were the eyes of the creature that was not a girl and was afraid of the darkness! Ah, if the darkness would only come again, all arms, friendly and soft everywhere about her! She would wait and wait, and bear, and be patient.

She lay so still that Watho did not doubt she had fainted. She was pretty sure she would be dead before the night came to revive her.

REFUGE

Fixing her telescope on the motionless form, that she might see it at once when the morning came, Watho went down from the tower to Photogen's room. He was much better by this time, and before she left him, he had resolved to leave the castle that very night. The darkness was terrible indeed, but Watho was worse than even the darkness, and he could not escape in the day. As soon, therefore, as the house seemed still, he tightened his belt, hung to it his hunting-knife, put a flask of wine and some bread in his pocket, and took his bow and arrows. He got from the house, and made his way at once up to the plain. But what with his illness, the terrors of the night, and his dread of the wild beasts, when he got to the level he could not walk a step further, and sat down, thinking it better to die than to live. In spite of his fears, however, sleep contrived to overcome him, and he fell at full length on the soft grass.

He had not slept long when he woke with such a strange sense of comfort and security, that he thought the dawn at least must have arrived. But it was dark night about him. And the sky—no, it was not the sky, but the blue eyes of his naiad looking down upon him! Once more he lay with his head in her lap, and all was well, for plainly the girl feared the darkness as little as he the day.

"Thank you," he said. "You are like live armour to my heart; you keep the fear off me. I have been very ill since then. Did you come up out of the river when you saw me cross?"

"I don't live in the water," she answered. "I live under the pale lamp, and I die under the bright one."

"Ah, yes! I understand now," he returned. "I would not have behaved as I did last time if I had understood; but I thought you were mocking me; and I am so made that I cannot help being frightened at the darkness. I beg your pardon for leaving you as I did, for, as I say, I did not understand. Now I believe you were really frightened. Were you not?"

"I was, indeed," answered Nycteris, "and shall be again. But why you should be, I cannot in the least understand. You must know how gentle and sweet the darkness is, how kind and friendly, how soft and velvety! It holds you to its bosom and loves you. A little while ago, I lay faint and dying under your hot lamp.—What is it you call it?"

"The sun," murmured Photogen: "how I wish he would make haste!"

"Ah! do not wish that. Do not, for my sake, hurry him. I can take care of you from the darkness, but I have no one to take care of me from the light.—As I was telling you, I lay dying in the sun. All at once I drew a deep breath. A cool wind came and ran over my face. I looked up. The torture was gone, for the death-lamp itself was gone. I hope he does not die and grow brighter yet. My terrible headache was all gone, and my sight was come back. I felt as if I were new made. But I did not get up at once, for I was tired still. The grass grew cool about me, and turned soft in colour. Something wet came upon it, and it was now so pleasant to my feet, that I rose and ran about. And when I had been running about a long time, all at once I found you lying, just as I had been lying a little while before. So I sat down beside you to take care of you, till your life—and my death—should come again."

"How good you are, you beautiful creature!—Why, you forgave me before ever I asked you!" cried Photogen.

Thus they fell a talking, and he told her what he knew of his history, and she told him what she knew of hers, and they agreed they must get away from Watho as far as ever they could.

"And we must set out at once," said Nycteris.

"The moment the morning comes," returned Photogen.

457

"We must not wait for the morning," said Nycteris, "for then I shall not be able to move, and what would you do the next night? Besides Watho sees best in the daytime. Indeed, you must come now, Photogen.—You must."

"I can not; I dare not," said Photogen. "I cannot move. If I but lift my head from your lap, the very sickness of terror seizes me."

"I shall be with you," said Nycteris, soothingly. "I will take care of you till your dreadful sun comes, and then you may leave me, and go away as fast as you can. Only please put me in a dark place first, if there is one to be found."

"I will never leave you again Nycteris," cried Photogen. "Only wait till the sun comes, and brings me back my strength, and we will go away together, and never, never part any more."

"No, no," persisted Nycteris; "we must go now. And you must learn to be strong in the dark as well as in the day, else you will always be only half brave. I have begun already—not to fight your sun, but to try to get at peace with him, and understand what he really is, and what he means with me—whether to hurt me or to make the best of me. You must do the same with my darkness."

"But you don't know what mad animals there are away there towards the south," said Photogen. "They have huge green eyes, and they would eat you up like a bit of celery, you beautiful creature!"

"Come, come! you must," said Nycteris, "or I shall have to pretend to leave you, to make you come. I have seen the green eyes you speak of, and I will take care of you from them."

"You! How can you do that? If it were day now, I could take care of you from the worst of them. But as it is, I can't even see them for this abominable darkness. I could not see your lovely eyes but for the light that is in them; that lets me see straight into heaven through them. They are windows into the very heaven beyond the sky. I believe they are the very place where the stars are made."

"You come then, or I shall shut them," said Nycteris, "and you shan't see them any more till you are good. Come. If you can't see the wild beasts, I can."

"You can! and you ask me to come!" cried Photogen.

"Yes," answered Nycteris. "And more than that, I see them long before they can see me, so that I am able to take care of you."

458

"But how?" persisted Photogen. "You can't shoot with bow and arrow, or stab with a hunting knife."

"No, but I can keep out of the way of them all. Why, just when I found you, I was having a game with two or three of them at once, I see, and scent them too, long before they are near me—long before they can see or scent me."

"You don't see or scent any now, do you?" said Photogen, uneasily, rising on his elbow.

"No—none at present. I will look," replied Nycteris, and sprang to her feet.

"Oh, oh! do not leave me—not for a moment," cried Photogen, straining his eyes to keep her face in sight through the darkness.

"Be quiet, or they will hear you," she returned. "The wind is from the south, and they cannot scent us. I have found out all about that. Ever since the dear dark came, I have been amusing myself with them, getting every now and then just into the edge of the wind, and letting one have a sniff of me."

"Oh, horrible!" cried Photogen. "I hope you will not insist on doing so any more. What was the consequence?"

"Always, the very instant, he turned with flashing eyes, and bounded towards me—only he could not see me, you must remember. But my eyes being so much better than his, I could see him perfectly well, and would run away round him until I scented him, and then I knew he could not find me anyhow. If the wind were to turn, and run the other way now, there might be a whole army of them down upon us, leaving no room to keep out of their way. You had better come."

She took him by the hand. He yielded and rose, and she led him away. But his steps were feeble, and as the night went on, he seemed more and more ready to sink.

"Oh dear! I am so tired! and so frightened!" he would say.

"Lean on me," Nycteris would return, putting her arm round him, or patting his cheek. "Take a few steps more. Every step away from the castle is clear gain. Lean harder on me. I am quite strong and well now."

So they went on. The piercing night-eyes of Nycteris descried not a few pairs of green ones gleaming like holes in the darkness, and many a round she made to keep far out of their way; but she never said to Photogen she saw them. Carefully she kept him off the uneven places,

459

and on the softest and smoothest of the grass, talking to him gently all the way as they went—of the lovely flowers and the stars—how comfortable the flowers looked, down in their green beds, and how happy the stars up in their blue beds!

When the morning began to come, he began to grow better, but was dreadfully tired with walking instead of sleeping, especially after being so long ill. Nycteris too, what with supporting him, what with growing fear of the light which was beginning to ooze out of the east, was very tired. At length, both equally exhausted, neither was able to help the other. As if by consent they stopped. Embracing each the other, they stood in the midst of the wide grassy land, neither of them able to move a step, each supported only by the leaning weakness of the other, each ready to fall if the other should move. But while the one grew weaker still, the other had begun to grow stronger. When the tide of the night began to ebb, the tide of the day began to flow; and now the sun was rushing to the horizon, borne upon its foaming billows. And ever as he came, Photogen revived. At last the sun shot up into the air, like a bird from the hand of the Father of Lights. Nycteris gave a cry of pain, and hid her face in her hands.

"Oh me!" she sighed; "I am *so* frightened! The terrible light stings so!"

But the same instant, through her blindness, she heard Photogen give a low exultant laugh, and the next felt herself caught up: she who all night long had tended and protected him like a child, was now in his arms, borne along like a baby, with her head lying on his shoulder. But she was the greater, for suffering more, she feared nothing.

THE WEREWOLF

At the very moment when Photogen caught up Nycteris, the telescope of Watho was angrily sweeping the table-land. She swung it from her in rage, and running to her room, shut herself up. There she anointed herself from top to toe with a certain ointment; shook down her long red hair, and tied it round her waist; then began to dance, whirling round and round and round faster and faster, growing angrier and angrier, until she was foaming at the mouth with fury. When Falca went looking for her, she could not find her anywhere.

As the sun rose, the wind slowly changed and went round, until it blew straight from the north. Photogen and Nycteris were drawing near the edge of the forest, Photogen still carrying Nycteris, when she moved a little on his shoulder uneasily, and murmured in his ear.

"I smell a wild beast—that way, the way the wind is coming."

Photogen turned, looked back towards the castle, and saw a dark speck on the plain. As he looked, it grew larger: it was coming across the grass with the speed of the wind. It came nearer and nearer. It looked long and low, but that might be because it was running at a great stretch. He set Nycteris down under a tree, in the black shadow of its bole, strung his bow, and picked out his heaviest, longest, sharpest arrow. Just as he set the notch on the string, he saw that the creature was a tremendous wolf, rushing straight at him. He loosened his knife in its sheath, drew another arrow half-way from the quiver, lest the first should fail, and took his aim—at a good distance, to leave time for a second chance. He shot. The arrow rose, flew straight, descended, struck the beast, and started again into the air, doubled like a letter V. Quickly Photogen snatched the other, shot, cast his bow from him, and drew his knife. But the arrow was in the brute's chest, up to the feather; it tumbled heels over head with a great thud of its back on the earth, gave a groan, made a struggle or two, and lay stretched out motionless.

"I've killed it, Nycteris," cried Photogen. "It is a great red wolf."

"Oh, thank you!" answered Nycteris feebly from behind the tree. "I was sure you would. I was not a bit afraid."

Photogen went up to the wolf. It *was* a monster! But he was vexed that his first arrow had behaved so badly, and was the less willing to lose the one that had done him such good service: with a long and a strong pull, he drew it from the brute's chest. Could he believe his eyes? There lay—no wolf, but Watho, with her hair tied round her waist! The foolish witch had made herself invulnerable, as she supposed, but had forgotten that, to torment Photogen therewith, she had handled one of his arrows. He ran back to Nycteris and told her.

She shuddered and wept, and would not look.

461

There was now no occasion to fly a step farther. Neither of them feared any one but Watho. They left her there, and went back. A great cloud came over the sun, and rain began to fall heavily, and Nycteris was much refreshed, grew able to see a little, and with Photogen's help walked gently over the cool wet grass.

They had not gone far before they met Fargu and the other huntsmen. Photogen told them he had killed a great red wolf, and it was Madam Watho. The huntsmen looked grave but gladness shone through.

"Then," said Fargu, "I will go and bury my mistress."

But when they reached the place, they found she was already buried— in the maws of sundry birds and beasts which had made their breakfast of her.

Then Fargu, overtaking them, would, very wisely, have Photogen go to the king, and tell him the whole story. But Photogen, yet wiser than Fargu, would not set out until he had married Nycteris; "for then," he said, "the king himself can't part us; and if ever two people couldn't do the one without the other, those two are Nycteris and I. She has got to teach me to be a brave man in the dark, and I have got to look after her until she can bear the heat of the sun, and he helps her to see, instead of blinding her."

They were married that very day. And the next day they went together to the king, and told him the whole story. But whom should they find at the court but the father and mother of Photogen, both in high favour with the king and queen. Aurora nearly died for joy, and told them all how Watho had lied, and made her believe her child was dead.

No one knew anything of the father or mother of Nycteris; but when Aurora saw in the lovely girl her own azure eyes shining through night and its clouds, it made her think strange things, and wonder how even the wicked themselves may be a link to join together the good. Through Watho, the mothers, who had never seen each other, had changed eyes in their children.

The king gave them the castle and lands of Watho, and there they lived and taught each other for many years that were not long. But hardly had one of them passed, before Nycteris had come to love the day best, because it was the clothing and crown of Photogen, and she saw that the day was greater than the night, and the sun more lordly than the moon; and Photogen had come to love the night best, because it was the mother and home of Nycteris.

"But who knows," Nycteris would say to Photogen, "that when we go out, we shall not go into a day as much greater than your day as your day is greater than my night?"

GOBLIN MARKET

BY
CHRISTINA ROSSETTI

ILLUSTRATED
BY
LAURENCE HOUSMAN

Christina Rossetti, along with her brothers D. G. and W. M. Rossetti, was associated with the Pre-Raphaelite Brotherhood. She wrote three works for children: *Speaking Likenesses*; *Sing Song: A Nursery Rhyme Book,* and *Goblin Market*. Written in 1862, this last work is probably the most extreme and most beautifully elaborated example of repressed eroticism in children's literature. Although *Goblin Market* was quickly adopted as a part of the children's library, it is hard to imagine that the poem was intended specifically for children.

W. M. Rossetti has written that his sister had first entitled the poem: "A Peep at the Goblins—to M. F. R.," the initials referring to Christina's sister, Maria Francesca Rossetti. Lona M. Packer suggests that in symbol and reality the "Laura" of the poem is Christina and "Lizzie," Maria—further speculating that the poem reflects Maria's aid in ameliorating the troubled emotions attendant on Christina's unhappy love for William Bell Scott, who, at the time the poem was written, had fallen in love with another woman.

The honey-flavored fruit, to which Lizzie becomes addicted in the *Goblin Market* is obviously reminiscent of the biblical forbidden fruit, but it is also interesting to note the comments of Claude Levi-Strauss concerning the analogy between "honey" and "menstrual blood," operative in the myths of "primitive" people:

> Both are transformed substances resulting from a sort of *infra-
> cuisine,* vegetal in the one case . . . animal in the other. . . . We
> have seen that, in native thought, the search for honey represents a
> sort of return to Nature, in the guise of erotic attraction trans-
> posed from the sexual register to that of the sense of taste which
> undermines the very foundations of Culture if it is indulged in for
> too long.

The 1890 edition of *Goblin Market,* reproduced here, features the astonishing illustrations of the artist and writer, Laurence Housman, brother of the poet A. E. Housman.

GOBLIN MARKET

BY
CHRISTINA ROSSETTI
illustrated by
LAURENCE HOUSMAN

1893
MACMILLAN & Co LONDON

GOBLIN MARKET

Morning and evening
Maids heard the goblins cry
"Come buy our orchard fruits,
Come buy, come buy :

GOBLIN MARKET

Apples and quinces,
Lemons and oranges,
Plump unpecked cherries,
Melons and raspberries,
Bloom-down-cheeked peaches,
Swart-headed mulberries,
Wild free-born cranberries,
Crab-apples, dewberries,
Pine-apples, blackberries,
Apricots, strawberries ;—
·All ripe together
In summer weather,—
Morns that pass by,
Fair eves that fly ;
Come buy, come buy :
Our grapes fresh from the vine,
Pomegranates full and fine,
Dates and sharp bullaces,
Rare pears and greengages,
Damsons and bilberries,
Taste them and try :

471

GOBLIN MARKET

Currants and gooseberries,
Bright-fire-like barberries,
Figs to fill your mouth,
Citrons from the South,
Sweet to tongue and sound to eye;
Come buy, come buy."

Evening by evening
Among the brookside
rushes,
Laura bowed her head to hear,
Lizzie veiled her blushes:
Crouching close together
In the cooling weather,
With clasping arms and cautioning lips,
With tingling cheeks and finger tips.

GOBLIN MARKET

"Lie close," Laura said,
Pricking up her golden head :
"We must not look at goblin men,
We must not buy their fruits :
Who knows upon what soil they fed
Their hungry thirsty roots ? "
"Come buy," call the goblins
Hobbling down the glen.
"Oh," cried Lizzie, " Laura, Laura,
You should not peep at goblin men."
Lizzie covered up her eyes,
Covered close lest they should look ;
Laura reared her glossy head,
And whispered like the restless brook :
"Look, Lizzie, look, Lizzie,
Down the glen tramp little men.
One hauls a basket,
One bears a plate,
One lugs a golden dish
Of many pounds weight.
How fair the vine must grow

GOBLIN MARKET

Whose grapes are so luscious ;
How warm the wind must blow
Through those fruit bushes."
" No," said Lizzie : " No, no, no ;
Their offers should not charm us,
Their evil gifts would harm us."
She thrust a dimpled finger
In each ear, shut eyes and ran :
Curious Laura chose to linger
Wondering at each merchant man.
One had a cat's face,
One whisked a tail,
One tramped at a rat's pace,
One crawled like a snail,
One like a wombat prowled obtuse and
    furry,
One like a ratel tumbled hurry skurry.
She heard a voice like voice of doves
Cooing all together :
They sounded kind and full of loves
In the pleasant weather.

GOBLIN MARKET

Laura stretched her
gleaming neck
Like a rush-imbedded swan,
Like a lily from the beck,
Like a moonlit poplar branch.
Like a vessel at the launch
When its last restraint is gone.

Backwards up the mossy glen
Turned and trooped the goblin men,
With their shrill repeated cry,
" Come buy, come buy."

479

GOBLIN MARKET

When they reached where Laura was
They stood stock still upon the moss,
Leering at each other,
Brother with queer brother;
Signalling each other,
Brother with sly brother.
One set his basket down,
One reared his plate;
One began to weave a crown
Of tendrils, leaves, and rough nuts brown
(Men sell not such in any town);
One heaved the golden weight
Of dish and fruit to offer her:
"Come buy, come buy," was still their cry.
Laura stared but did not stir,
Longed but had no money:
The whisk-tailed merchant bade her taste
In tones as smooth as honey,
The cat-faced purr'd,
The rat-paced spoke a word

GOBLIN MARKET

Of welcome, and the snail-paced even
    was heard;
One parrot-voiced and jolly
Cried "Pretty Goblin" still
    for "Pretty Polly;"—
One whistled like a
    bird.

But sweet-tooth Laura spoke in haste:
"Good Folk, I have no coin;
To take were to purloin:
I have no copper in my purse,
I have no silver either,
And all my gold is on the furze
That shakes in windy weather
Above the rusty heather."

482

"You have much gold upon your head,"
They answered all together:
"Buy from us with a golden curl."
She clipped a precious golden lock,
She dropped a tear more rare than pearl,
Then sucked their fruit globes fair or red:
Sweeter than honey from the rock,
Stronger than man-rejoicing wine,
Clearer than water flowed that juice;
She never tasted such before,
How should it cloy with length of use?
She sucked and sucked and sucked the more
Fruits which that unknown orchard bore;
She sucked until her lips were sore;
Then flung the emptied rinds away
But gathered up one kernel-stone,
And knew not was it night or day
As she turned home alone.

GOBLIN MARKET

Lizzie met her at the gate
Full of wise upbraidings :
" Dear, you should not stay so late,
Twilight is not good for maidens ;
Should not loiter in the glen
In the haunts of goblin men.
Do you not remember Jeanie,
How she met them in the moonlight,
Took their gifts both choice and many,
Ate their fruits and wore their flowers
Plucked from bowers
Where summer ripens at all hours ?
But ever in the noonlight
She pined and pined away ;
Sought them by night and day,
Found them no more, but dwindled and
     grew grey ;
Then fell with the first snow,

GOBLIN MARKET

While to this day no grass will grow
Where she lies low :
I planted daisies there a year ago
That never blow.
You should not loiter so."
"Nay, hush," said Laura :
"Nay, hush, my sister :
I ate and ate my fill,
Yet my mouth waters still ;
To-morrow night I will
Buy more ;" and kissed her :
"Have done with sorrow ;
I'll bring you plums to-morrow
Fresh on their mother twigs,
Cherries worth getting ;
You cannot think what figs
My teeth have met in,
What melons icy-cold
Piled on a dish of gold
Too huge for me to hold,
What peaches with a velvet nap,

GOBLIN MARKET

Pellucid grapes without one seed :
Odorous indeed must be the mead
Whereon they grow, and pure the wave
  they drink
With lilies at the brink,
And sugar-sweet their sap."

 Golden head by golden head,
Like two pigeons in one nest
Folded in each other's wings,
They lay down in their curtained bed :

GOBLIN MARKET

Like two blossoms on one stem,
Like two flakes of new-fall'n snow,
Like two wands of ivory
Tipped with gold for awful kings.
Moon and stars gazed in at them,
Wind sang to them lullaby,
Lumbering owls forbore to fly,
Not a bat flapped to and fro
Round their rest :
Cheek to cheek and breast to breast
Locked together in one nest.

Early in the morning
When the first cock crowed his warning,
Neat like bees, as sweet and busy,
Laura rose with Lizzie :

Fetched in honey, milked the cows,

Aired and set to rights the house,

Kneaded cakes of whitest wheat,

Cakes for dainty mouths to eat,

Next churned butter, whipped up cream,

Fed their poultry, sat and sewed;

Talked as modest maidens should:

Lizzie with an open heart,

Laura in an absent dream,

One content, one sick in part;

One warbling for the mere bright day's
delight,

One longing for the night.

At length slow evening came:

They went with pitchers to the reedy brook;

Lizzie most placid in her look,
Laura most like a leaping flame.
They drew the gurgling water from its deep;
Lizzie plucked purple and rich golden flags,
Then turning homeward said: "The sunset
    flushes
Those furthest loftiest crags;
Come, Laura, not another maiden lags,
No wilful squirrel wags,
The beasts and birds are fast asleep."
But Laura loitered still among the rushes
And said the bank was steep.

And said the hour was early still,
The dew not fall'n, the wind not chill;
Listening ever, but not catching
The customary cry,
"Come buy, come buy,"
With its iterated jingle
Of sugar-baited words:

GOBLIN MARKET

Not for all her watching
Once discerning even one goblin
Racing, whisking, tumbling, hobbling ;
Let alone the herds
That used to tramp along the glen,
In groups or single,
Of brisk fruit-merchant men.

Till Lizzie urged, " O Laura, come ;
I hear the fruit-call, but I dare not look :
You should not loiter longer at this brook :
Come with me home.
The stars rise, the moon bends her arc,

GOBLIN MARKET

Each glowworm winks her spark,
Let us get home before the night grows dark :
For clouds may gather
Though this is summer weather,
Put out the lights and drench us through ;
Then if we lost our way what should we do ? "

Laura turned cold as stone
To find her sister heard that cry alone,
That goblin cry,
" Come buy our fruits, come buy."
Must she then buy no more such **dainty** fruit ?
Must she no more such succous pasture find,
Gone deaf and blind ?

GOBLIN MARKET

Her tree of life drooped from the root :
She said not one word in her heart's
    sore ache ;
But peering thro' the dimness, nought
    discerning,
Trudged home, her pitcher dripping all
    the way ;
So crept to bed, and lay
Silent till Lizzie slept ;
Then sat up in a passionate yearning,
And gnashed her teeth for baulked desire,
    and wept
As if her heart would break.

   Day after day, night after night,
Laura kept watch in vain
In sullen silence of exceeding pain.
She never caught again the goblin cry :

494

GOBLIN MARKET

"Come buy, come buy;"—
She never spied the goblin men
Hawking their fruits along the glen:
But when the noon waxed bright
Her hair grew thin and grey;
She dwindled, as the fair full moon doth turn
To swift decay and burn
Her fire away.

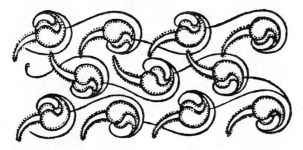

One day remembering her kernel-stone
She set it by a wall that faced the south;
Dewed it with tears, hoped for a root.
Watched for a waxing shoot,
But there came none;
It never saw the sun,
It never felt the trickling moisture run:
While with sunk eyes and faded mouth

GOBLIN MARKET

She dreamed of melons, as a traveller sees
False waves in desert drouth
With shade of leaf-crowned trees,
And burns the thirstier in the sandful breeze.

She no more swept the house,
Tended the fowls or cows,
Fetched honey, kneaded cakes of wheat,
Brought water from the brook :
But sat down listless in the chimney-nook
And would not eat.

GOBLIN MARKET

Tender Lizzie could
not bear
To watch her sister's
cankerous care
Yet not to share.
She night and morning
Caught the goblins' cry:
"Come buy our orchard fruits,
Come buy, come buy:"—
Beside the brook, along the glen,
She heard the tramp of goblin men,
The voice and stir
Poor Laura could not hear;
Longed to buy fruit to comfort her,
But feared to pay too dear.
She thought of Jeanie in her grave,
Who should have been a bride;

But who for joys brides hope to have
Fell sick and died
In her gay prime,
In earliest Winter time,
With the first glazing rime,
With the first snow-fall of crisp Winter time.

Till Laura dwindling
Seemed knocking at Death's door :
Then Lizzie weighed no more
Better and worse ;
But put a silver penny in her purse,
Kissed Laura, crossed the heath with
    clumps of furze

GOBLIN MARKET

At twilight, halted by the brook :
And for the first time in her life
Began to listen and look.

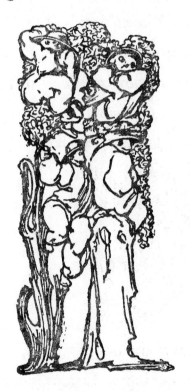

Laughed every goblin
When they spied her peeping :
Came towards her hobbling,
Flying, running, leaping,
Puffing and blowing,

GOBLIN MARKET

Chuckling, clapping, crowing,
Clucking and gobbling,
Mopping and mowing,
Full of airs and graces,
Pulling wry faces,
Demure grimaces,
Cat-like and rat-like,
Ratel- and wombat-like,
Snail-paced in a hurry,
Parrot-voiced and whistler,
Helter skelter, hurry skurry,
Chattering like magpies,
Fluttering like pigeons,
Gliding like fishes,—
Hugged her and kissed her :
Squeezed and caressed her :
Stretched up their dishes,
Panniers, and plates :
" Look at our apples
Russet and dun,
Bob at our cherries,

GOBLIN MARKET

Bite at our peaches,
Citrons and dates,
Grapes for the asking,
Pears red with basking
Out in the sun,
Plums on their twigs ;
Pluck them and suck them,
Pomegranates, figs."—

"Good folk," said Lizzie,
Mindful of Jeanie :
"Give me much and many : "—

GOBLIN MARKET

Held out her apron,
Tossed them her penny.
"Nay, take a seat with us,
Honour and eat with us,"
They answered grinning :
"Our feast is but beginning,
Night yet is early,
Warm and dew pearly,
Wakeful and starry :
Such fruits as these
No man can carry ;
Half their bloom would fly,
Half their dew would dry,
Half their flavour would pass by.
Sit down and feast with us,
Be welcome guest with us,

503

Cheer you and rest with us."—

" Thank you," said Lizzie : " But one waits

At home alone for me :

So without further parleying,

If you will not sell me any

Of your fruits though much and many,

Give me back my silver penny

I tossed you for a fee."—

They began to scratch their pates,

No longer wagging, purring,

But visibly demurring,

Grunting and snarling.

One called her proud,

Cross-grained, uncivil ;

Their tones waxed loud,

Their looks were evil.

Lashing their tails

They trod and hustled her,

Elbowed and jostled her,

Clawed with their nails,

Barking, mewing, hissing, mocking,

Tore her gown and soiled her stocking,

Twitched her hair out by the roots,

Stamped upon her tender feet,

Held her hands and squeezed their fruits

Against her mouth to make her eat.

White and golden Lizzie stood,

Like a lily in a flood,—

Like a rock of blue-veined stone

Lashed by tides obstreperously,—

Like a beacon left alone

In a hoary roaring sea,

Sending up a golden fire,—

GOBLIN MARKET

Like a fruit-crowned orange-tree
White with blossoms honey-sweet
Sore beset by wasp and bee,—
Like a royal virgin town
Topped with gilded dome and spire
Close beleaguered by a fleet
Mad to tug her standard down.

One may lead a horse to water,
Twenty cannot make him drink.

GOBLIN MARKET

Though the goblins cuffed and caught
    her,
Coaxed and fought her,
Bullied and besought her,
Scratched her, pinched her black as ink,
Kicked and knocked her,
Mauled and mocked her,
Lizzie uttered not a word ;
Would not open lip from lip
Lest they should cram a mouthful in :
But laughed in heart to feel the drip
Of juice that syrupped all her face,
And lodged in dimples of her chin,
And streaked her neck which quaked
    like curd.
At last the evil people,
Worn out by her resistance,
Flung back her penny, kicked their fruit
Along whichever road they took,
Not leaving root or stone or shoot ;
Some writhed into the ground,

510

GOBLIN MARKET

Some dived into the brook
With ring and ripple,
Some scudded on the gale without a sound,
Some vanished in the distance.

In a smart, ache, tingle,
Lizzie went her way ;
Knew not was it night or day ;
Sprang up the bank, tore thro' the furze,
Threaded copse and dingle,
And heard her penny jingle.
Bouncing in her purse,—
Its bounce was music to her ear.

GOBLIN MARKET

She ran and ran
As if she feared some goblin man
Dogged her with gibe or curse
Or something worse :
But not one goblin skurried after,
Nor was she pricked by fear ;
The kind heart made her windy-paced
That urged her home quite out of breath
    with haste
And inward laughter.

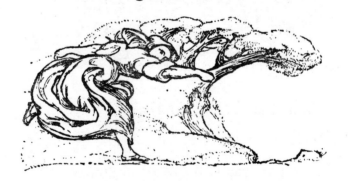

    She cried, "Laura," up the garden,
"Did you miss me ?
Come and kiss me.
Never mind my bruises,
Hug me, kiss me, suck my juices

GOBLIN MARKET

Squeezed from goblin fruits for you,
Goblin pulp and goblin dew.
Eat me, drink me, love me ;
Laura, make much of me ;
For your sake I have braved the glen
And had to do with goblin merchant men."

Laura started from her chair,
Flung her arms up in the air,
Clutched her hair :
" Lizzie, Lizzie, have you tasted
For my sake the fruit forbidden ?
Must your light like mine be hidden,
Your young life like mine be wasted,
Undone in mine undoing,
And ruined in my ruin,
Thirsty, cankered, goblin-ridden ? "—

GOBLIN MARKET

She clung about her sister,
Kissed and kissed and kissed her :
Tears once again
Refreshed her shrunken eyes,
Dropping like rain
After long sultry drouth ;
Shaking with aguish fear, and pain,
She kissed and kissed her with a hungry
mouth.

Her lips began to scorch,
That juice was wormwood to her tongue,
She loathed the feast :
Writhing as one possessed she leaped and
sung,

GOBLIN MARKET

Rent all her robe, and wrung
Her hands in lamentable haste,
And beat her breast.
Her locks streamed like the torch
Borne by a racer at full speed,
Or like the mane of horses in their flight,
Or like an eagle when she stems the light
Straight toward the sun,
Or like a caged thing freed,
Or like a flying flag when armies run.

Swift fire spread through her veins,
knocked at her heart,
Met the fire smouldering there
And overbore its lesser flame ;
She gorged on bitterness without a name :

GOBLIN MARKET

Ah ! fool, to choose such part
Of soul-consuming care !
Sense failed in the mortal strife :
Like the watch-tower of a town
Which an earthquake shatters down,
Like a lightning-stricken mast,
Like a wind-uprooted tree
Spun about,
Like a foam-topped waterspout
Cast down headlong in the sea,
She fell at last ;
Pleasure past and anguish past,
Is it death or is it life ?

    Life out of death.
That night long Lizzie watched by her,
Counted her pulse's flagging stir,
Felt for her breath,
Held water to her lips, and cooled her face
With tears and fanning leaves :

But when the first birds chirped about their
    eaves,
And early reapers plodded to the place
Of golden sheaves,
And dew-wet grass
Bowed in the morning winds so brisk to
    pass,
And new buds with new day
Opened of cup-like lilies on the stream,
Laura awoke as from a dream,
Laughed in the innocent old way,
Hugged Lizzie but not twice or thrice;
Her gleaming locks showed not one thread
    of grey
Her breath was sweet as May
And light danced in her eyes.

GOBLIN MARKET

Days, weeks, months, years
Afterwards, when both were wives
With children of their own ;
Their mother-hearts beset with fears,
Their lives bound up in tender lives ;
Laura would call the little ones
And tell them of her early prime,
Those pleasant days long gone
Of not-returning time :
Would talk about the haunted glen,
The wicked, quaint fruit-merchant men,
Their fruits like honey to the throat
But poison in the blood ;
(Men sell not such in any town) :
Would tell them how her sister stood
In deadly peril to do her good,
And win the fiery antidote :

GOBLIN MARKET

Then joining hands to little hands
Would bid them cling together,
" For there is no friend like a sister
In calm or stormy weather ;
To cheer one on the tedious way,
To fetch one if one goes astray,
To lift one if one totters down,
To strengthen whilst one stands."